The Fields of May

S0-AED-944

Lori Zehr

The Fields of May

ISBN: 978-0-9792739-6-4
Printed in the United States of America
©2008 by Lori Zehr
All rights reserved

Cover and interior design by Isaac Publishing, Inc.

Isaac Publishing, Inc.
P.O. 342
Three Rivers, MI 49093
www.isaacpublishing.com

Please direct your inquiries to admin@isaacpublishing.com

Dedication

To Rhiannon and Jeremiah, my two children, who obediently accepted some restrictive standards in their lives as they grew up in the "glass house" of a pastor's family.

To Kori, my daughter-in-law, whose willingness to step into these standards speaks of her Proverbs 31 worth.

To Clint, my wonderful husband, who encouraged me and sacrificed many hours of family time while I typed this manuscript.

To Emma Rose, my granddaughter. May your life be a link in an unbroken chain that influences future generations-for righteousness.

To My Wonderful Savior and Lord, Jesus, whose love is beyond the love of earth. You were patient with me for more than ten years as I allowed this manuscript to lay dormant in a desk drawer. May you be glorified, Lord.

Author's Preface

A love story is often just a simple tale that gains deep beauty in the telling. Sometimes such a story takes years to unfold. The Fields of May is a work of fiction. It is the story of two people who grew in friendship as the days of their lives wove in and out like threads in a tapestry.

I wish to warn the reader that this is not a romance in the usual sense of the word. It is rather a love story set in the context of a Christian courtship where the counsel of God and parents are held in high esteem.

Over the years as we home schooled our own children, my husband and I were privileged to observe the lives of Christian families that dared to stand against the popular culture in many areas, including what is currently termed "courtship." This story is a fictional account of how such a relationship might unfold.

It is intended that the readers of The Fields of May will be challenged to look to God and His holy word and be led by His Spirit as their source for everything; including a future mate if they are unmarried. Should a seasoned reader of fiction of the sort that the world is currently offering chance to pick up this book, he or she may be sorely disappointed or pleasantly surprised depending on what their heart is searching for. The characters may be thought to be "better than life," when considered from a modern standpoint, yet you will see that they are portrayed as real people that face struggles and experience difficulties that challenge them from day to day. Since the church is never to measure itself against the standards of the world in order to form convictions or opinions, I believe that it is possible for Christian young people to live in a pure, God-honoring manner much like the characters in the book.

The Lord would have His people to evangelize the world and not hide our heads in the sand. Therefore in writing this book I do not desire to make all the readers into the image of the main characters in the details of their lives, rather only to set forth an example of how lives can be directed by God. I understand that not all Christians hold exactly the same convictions concerning lifestyles where the word of God leaves room for individual preference and discernment. However, when Christians live a godly life, their families, churches and communities will change for the better. Hopefully this book will encourage faithful, consistent, Christian living.

Blessings,

Lori Zehr

Table of Contents

Table of Contents *cont'd*

Gentle Changes

On a Thursday afternoon in early December, Carrie Brooks ascended the stairs to her pretty, comfortable bedroom. Her mother had wisely suggested she take an afternoon nap before all the activity of the next few days was thrust upon her. Sleep was elusive, Carrie discovered, for with the anticipation of upcoming events she found it difficult to quiet her mind.

She lay back on the bed and pulled an afghan around her shoulders as she gazed around the room. Only a few more days and she'd be leaving this comfortable, familiar place. She would have a new home. Memories were everywhere. As she considered the different objects in the room, several items evoked sentimental thoughts. Her sewing machine, now silent after humming along for days of near constant use, the boxes piled in the corner packed with more belongings still to be moved, even her desk with objects from her school years all held wonderful memories. As she looked around the room her eyes fell upon the paperweight that lay on her desk. She smiled remembering the day when she had found the unusual rock. She had been on a scavenger hunt with her best friend, Eileen Henderson. It had been several years ago now, but looking back, Carrie realized that the time had really sped by very fast. In some ways it seemed like only yesterday; the memories were still so vivid, but truly they were both much younger then...

One morning in early May, Carrie Brooks woke with a start to the ringing of her alarm clock. "Six fifteen a.m.," she said sleepily as she reached over to shut the alarm off. She remembered her mother's advice to rise early since this particular Thursday held so much activity that everyone needed to get an early start on the day's chores.

Carried decided to close her eyes and enjoy the cozy morning for just a few more minutes. But as she lay there, she remembered the verse from Proverbs 31 about the virtuous woman, "She rises while it is yet night," Carried quoted aloud, "and gives meat to her household and a portion to her maidens." At this she decidedly threw back the covers.

Carrie knew her mother had been this virtuous example for years and now she felt privileged to give Mom a well-deserved break. Carrie decided to rise early and get some work underway for the day.

As she went about dressing and getting ready for the day ahead, Carrie thought about the Proverbs verses, rolling them over and over in her mind. As she sat at her old, antique dressing table and brushed her long, honey-brown hair, braiding and twisting it into a convenient style for a day that would include school and work around the house, she quietly hoped that she would someday be like the virtuous woman Proverbs described. With these thoughts she breathed a simple prayer for grace. As she worked with her hair, she whispered the rest of the verses.

Suddenly another verse from the chapter seemed to stand out vividly, "the heart of her husband doth safely trust in her." Carrie's hands stopped in mid-air. She stared at herself in the mirror for a moment, and then reached up to smooth the last strands of hair into place. Somehow the thought from the verse surprised her. It seemed almost foreign. Carrie had read these verses before thinking only about trying to develop the homemaking skills of this virtuous woman. She hadn't really thought much about actually being someone's wife. Laying the hairbrush down, she looked seriously at the face in the mirror. She knew her parents were committed to allowing God to lead all their family's decisions and had encouraged her not to dwell on thoughts of boys and dating relationships. They had taught her to search God's word in the matter of relationships and to be led by His Holy Spirit when seeking His will for her life, taking no thought for dating or pursuing boys as some girls seemed to do. They were convinced that God would lead them concerning a husband for Carrie when the time came.

She had never really thought much about it before, this possibility of being a wife, yet this morning it all suddenly seemed very real and not so far away. After all, she was fifteen, almost sixteen, and she knew plenty of couples that were married around twenty. Twenty years old! That wasn't even five years away!

As she slowly placed the pins in her hair, she began considering the time span of four or five years and it suddenly seemed very short! Events of five years ago when she was turning eleven paraded vividly through her mind. She found she could recall them as if they had happened only yesterday! Back then Dad hadn't yet become pastor of their church, Maplewood Christian Fellowship. Pastor Stanford was still the pastor and Dad's only job was managing the hardware in Blue Creek. The Brooks family had just started home schooling. Her brother Luke was only nine and Addy hadn't even been born yet! A lot had changed in five years!

"Is five years that short of a time? Where did those years go?" she asked herself aloud. The seriousness of growing up suddenly impacted her as never before.

As she pinned a final lock of hair into place, she realized that she was looking at the same girl she had seen in the mirror yesterday morning, but somehow today this girl seemed different. With the realization that life could speed by this fast, and the memory of being ten or eleven years old could seem like only yesterday, Carrie realized she had no time to lose in prayer for her own future. There at her dressing table in the early morning light, she began her prayer by asking God to direct her life, especially in the next few years. Then she asked Him to cause these strange, anxious feelings to subside. And finally she added, "Dear Lord, please help me with this busy day and all that needs to be accomplished."

In the early morning light as Carrie worked in the kitchen preparing the family's breakfast, she continued to ponder all the changes her family had gone through in the last few years. The decision to home school Carrie and her younger brother Luke had caused great changes in the daily routine around the Brooks' household. But Carrie remembered that her parents had been sure that God would bless them in the new endeavor. Being a full-time homemaker, a large portion of the day-to-day responsibilities of the children's education fell to her mother, Chris. And that same year her father had felt the call of God to become a pastor, again causing a major shift in the family's lifestyle.

Maplewood Christian Fellowship was the church the Brooks family had attended for years. It was one of the country churches in the area and was located about halfway between Maplecrest and Homewood. The friendly fellowship of dedicated believers was home to about forty families, a few of which drove from as far away as Minton and Red Dale—twenty miles in opposite directions.

The elders and Pastor Stanford had recognized the call on her father's life and began to ask him to carry more responsibilities in the church. Dad's job as manager of one of the Martinson Hardware stores was easily adjusted to accommodate the growing duties of the ministry. Soon he was filling the pulpit on a part-time basis to relieve the aging Pastor Stanford. Within a short time, Pastor Stanford was ready to pass the responsibilities on to a younger and more energetic man and the church decided to ordain Dad upon the older man's official retirement.

Faced with the duties of a pastor's wife and the daily challenges of home schooling, Mom would daily seek the Lord's direction and lean on His word for strength. It didn't take long for the little family to settle into a comfortable pattern of life as the Lord blessed their choices in school and ministry. Now with the birth of the new baby, Adeline Rose, Mom welcomed her oldest daughter's help even more.

This Thursday was a hectic one for the Brooks family as the school week drew to a close. Carrie had volunteered to cook breakfast for the family today to give her mother a few extra minutes to sleep in. Wisely, she had prepared a French toast casserole the night before and refrigerated it. Now it just needed to be baked.

Adeline Rose, or Addy, as everyone called the new baby, was as sweet as could be and a pleasant addition to the household, especially for Carrie, who delighted in holding and caring for her. But coupled with the tasks of home schooling, having a new baby around the house kept Mom busier than usual. Mom was glad to have Carrie's help, especially today for all the week's schoolwork needed to be finished so that the family could attend the annual picnic and fellowship time on Friday that their home school group had planned to celebrate the end of another school year.

"Smells good, princess!" Dad grinned as he came in the back door, pulling his jacket off and hanging it up in the adjoining coatroom. It was his custom to pray as he took an early morning walk along the quiet streets of Maplecrest. Carrie admired his dedication and felt privileged to know that she could trust and lean on this steady man she called "Dad."

"My little girl is really turning out to be a fine cook," he said with admiration. "I'll wake the others," was his promise. As he passed into the hall and up the stairs, Carrie piled two more plates onto the tray she was carrying in to the dining room and hurried to get the orange juice made. The sounds of the others rising was heard a minute or so later as Carrie put the finishing touches on the nicely set table.

Addy was making her morning noises, a combination of cooing mixed with an occasional restless cry alerting her care-givers that they needed to be faster or gentler or more attentive. She had been teething for the last few weeks and was not as agreeable as usual. The baby had kept Mom up for a night or two, making Carrie's help around the house a real blessing.

At the breakfast table, everyone commented on how good the casserole tasted and Carrie felt very appreciated. As Dad finished the last of his orange juice, he looked to the others and stated, "This morning for devotions I want to read a Proverb. It is found in chapter 18, verse 22. It says, "He who finds a wife finds a good thing, and obtains favor from the Lord." Your mother is a wonderful wife to me and I wanted to let you children hear me say it. And she's a wonderful mother to you three. We don't often tell her how we feel, but since this scripture was in my daily reading, I thought I'd share it with you and take the opportunity to show you that the Bible is true and very applicable to our lives. So I say a hearty, Amen, to this!" he said with a smile, as he reached over and squeezed his wife's hand. "And I want to remind you to cooperate well and do as Mom asks at all times, but especially today. She needs your cooperation and help if we're going to get this week's work done early."

"Oh, by the way," Dad winked, "it looks like Carrie will make someone a fine wife someday too if this breakfast is any indication of her cooking abilities," he praised.

"Here, here!" cried Luke, lifting his juice glass and making a great demonstration of it, more to tease Carrie than compliment her. Carrie's shyness prompted her to stare at her brother with a hint of sibling annoyance, and then she noticed the gentle reproving look both she and Luke were getting from Mom.

Dad led the family in prayer and dismissed the children to start their day. Luke cleared the table and did the dishes while Carrie got started gathering up her books for the day's school work. As soon as the breakfast was cleared away, she spread her books out on the dining room table. Dad passed through the hall and wished her a good day as he left for the hardware.

Dad's job as manager of the Blue Creek Martinson Hardware, one of several in the area, had proven to be adjustable to the growing duties of the ministry. Being a deeply committed Christian family, the Martinsons understood Pastor Brooks' need to be available if ministry obligations called him away. The Martinson family attended First Christian Church in Maplecrest and home schooled their children as well. Their oldest boy, Homer, named after Grandpa Martinson, was Carrie's age. Homer was a talented musician and singer and First Christian Church was the perfect place to nurture such talent. The beautiful old building glistened with stained glass and was crowned by a stately, old pipe organ in the balcony. First Church, as people commonly called it, was renowned for its choir and holiday cantatas and dramas. Many of Carrie's dearest friends attended First Church and she had visited there often for special services. She always enjoyed herself, though the atmosphere was a bit of a contrast to the simple country church her family attended.

After Dad left and Luke finished the dishes, he joined Carrie in the dining room, settling into the day's schoolwork. Mom cared for Addy and busied herself with other tasks around the house, occasionally checking on Carrie and Luke's progress. Most of the schoolwork today would not require Mom's teaching, as it was just an "end of the week" wrap-up.

All day as Carrie studied, the verse that Dad had read kept circling her mind. She found it hard to concentrate on her studies with her thoughts running ahead in time to the possibilities of her future. Had it been only coincidence that she had begun to meditate on marriage and her future just this morning, only to have her thoughts challenged by her father's comments and scripture reading? Carrie finally had to take a few moments to close her eyes and pray, asking God's help in quieting her mind. She needed discipline to concentrate on the business at hand and today that was the business of English literature. By one o'clock Carrie had finished all of her studies and was glad to hear her mother pronounce her finished for the week. Luke remained at the table to labor over a history test for another half hour while Carrie was dismissed to begin some preparations for tomorrow's picnic. Mom had suggested that Carrie prepare the food for their family's basket.

Carrie's first endeavor was to mix up a batch of dough for chocolate chip cookies. While they baked, she mixed up some macaroni salad, putting in a pinch of this and a dash of that until she finally gave up, resigning herself to the fact that it would never taste right until it had flavored through for a while. Next she shaped some hamburger into patties to be grilled at the picnic.

Soon Luke was finished with his schoolwork as well. Satisfied with his ninety-eight percent test score, he was only too glad to escape to the freedom of the yard where his next assignment, lawn mowing, was actually a pleasure when weighed against history tests. The sweet smell of new-mown grass was welcome to a young man who was glad school was drawing to a close. It confirmed to him that summer vacation was only days away. The weather had really taken a warm turn lately and spring seemed to be swiftly maturing into summer. All the first summer flowers were beginning to bud and the earth seemed greener everyday. The breezes were balmy and filled with the fragrances of bursting life.

As Luke plodded steadily behind the mower over the generous lawn, his mind was pleasantly occupied with thoughts and plans of swimming, baseball games, fishing, and all the pleasures of being young. He wasn't sure why, but he had a real sense of expectancy that this summer would bring some very special excitement.

Carrie looked out from the kitchen window and smiled to herself as she watched her "little" brother who wasn't so little anymore. For a moment she longed for the days when she and Luke played together, spending hours together on the swings or playing on the kitchen floor with their toy horses and Wild West corrals. She knew if he was in the kitchen though he'd be sneaking some of the fresh cookies now emerging from the oven. With that thought, she slid a few of the warm, sweet treats to the side, saving them especially for him.

Soon all Carrie's kitchen work was complete and she and her

mother worked together to finish a few other tasks before stopping their chores for the day. As she folded some of the laundry, she thought about what she wanted to wear for tomorrow and nothing seemed right. This seemed to be happening more often lately, this indecisiveness about her clothes. An increasing consciousness of her appearance found Carrie considering style as well as comfort. Finally settling on a pair of long culottes Mom had made for her and a favorite blouse, she convinced herself that this outfit was best for outdoor activities. After all, there would be a lot of games and sports and even hiking to be considered. "Yes, this outfit is the best and most sensible choice," she thought. She tried to push to the back of her mind the fact that it was one of her favorites. The blouse was a sailor style, yellow plaid with dark blue stripes, and always drew several compliments when she wore it. "It's really nothing special," she told herself. "People just like the color." She tried diligently to be modest and was determined not to become vain and overly concerned about looks and clothes like some girls were. Still she wanted to look neat and attractive.

Carrie thought of Darla Harris who loved to use every conceivable occasion as a fashion show. Carrie was more quiet and subdued, even in her choice of clothing. She was determined not to copy Darla's ways though they had been long-time friends and Carrie truly did admire the way Darla looked in many of her beautiful outfits.

Friday finally arrived after what seemed to Carrie like the longest Thursday on record. Mom gave instructions to Luke and Carrie while she got Addy prepared for the trip, packing the endless items necessary for a baby. Dad had bid them all goodbye as he left for an early breakfast meeting with First Christian's pastor, Gerald Keene. Carrie wished Dad could go along but she knew only too well that a pastor's schedule became heavier as Sunday approached and he needed to be at the hardware office for a while today as well.

With everyone finally in the car, Mom headed the family toward Red Dale. The picnic was to be held at the Peterson's large farm about a forty-five minute drive from Maplecrest. Their land bordered the beautiful Birch Lake and there were several patches of woods to explore as well as a perfect area for the picnic. The trip was not particularly scenic until one got closer to Red Dale, with just flat farmlands and familiar houses most of the way. The Peterson family had been in the home school group for years and even though their children were all graduated and out on their own now, Mr. and Mrs. Peterson still enjoyed hosting the annual event.

Carrie was anxious to arrive on time lest she miss out on any of the activities. A committee of students from the Fellowship of Christian Home Schools group was responsible for planning the day's events. If it was anything at all compared to last year's picnic, a whole day of fun was in store.

The Fellowship of Christian Home Schools was a support group the Brooks had joined the year they began home schooling. About fifty area families were involved in "FCH" as most families called it, and the group was growing every year. Many activities were provided for area home school students including sports teams and special classes on Fridays at a local church.

When the Brooks' arrived at Birch Lake Farm, several others were already there. Mr. Peterson was waving the families in car-by-car and directing them to park in the large pasture. The activities committee had volleyball nets set up and various committee members were lugging sporting equipment in preparation for a number of other games.

The Brooks' unloaded their car, emptying the picnic supplies on a table near the edge of the wooded area. Many other tables were grouped there as well and all together formed a somewhat disjointed circle around some grills next to a pavilion Mr. Peterson had built on the east side of the clearing.

The Harris family joined the Brooks' table and nearby were the Hendersons and a new FCH family, the Taylors. It worked out perfectly for the Hendersons to sit with the new family and welcome them as the Henderson family had been part of FCH since its founding. The Hendersons had lived in the area for generations and owned one of the largest farms around, Blooming Hills Orchards. Mr. Henderson's ancestors had been founding members of Maplewood Christian Fellowship and John Henderson served alongside Carrie's father as an elder in the church.

John and Esther Henderson managed the huge orchard operation as a family business including each of their five children in one way or another. Katie, the oldest daughter and her husband Joe were living in the tenant house and both worked full time on the farm. Next in age was Alice, who had already graduated. She was beginning to develop and manage a bakery and store connected with the orchard. It featured homegrown products from the farm and promised to be a success as the adept Alice was a born businesswoman.

John Mark was the next Henderson. He was five months older than Carrie Brooks. John Mark was quiet and serious and known by everyone as pleasant and level-headed. He was a hard worker who joined his father and brother-in-law in the farm work. Although he was usually quiet, the other kids in the home school fellowship counted on the serious John Mark to help with tough decisions and to offer wise suggestions concerning their activities and plans. John Mark was steady and soft-spoken but in his eyes there was a twinkle of fun. He had a distinct little sideways grin and a thick shock of unruly hair that hung over his forehead.

John Mark's younger sister Eileen was Carrie's dearest friend. Eileen was only fourteen months younger than John Mark and she and Carrie were great pals, loving the same subjects in school and enjoying similar hobbies. Eileen's bubbly, outgoing personality was a contrast to Carrie's reserved shyness. As best friends, the two girls seemed to compliment each other well.

The youngest Henderson was Tommy. With all the help from his older brother and sister, he was rapidly progressing through his school studies. He helped out with the farm work at every chance, enjoying every minute of it.

Across from the Hendersons and the Taylors, Carrie could see Mrs. Martinson and the younger children. Homer stood nearby among a gathering of the teens. He seemed to be immensely enjoying his role as entertainer of this admiring little group. You couldn't help liking Homer Martinson. If his contagious smile and freckles didn't win you, his talent surely would. Homer was an accomplished musician. Tall and husky, the red-haired boy really did not fit the typical stereotype of a musician. Carrie often chuckled to herself, thinking what a contradiction Homer seemed to be. He actually looked more like a farmer than what she imagined a concert violinist should look like! She mused that he would seem quite appropriate dressed in a pair of overalls and holding a pitchfork in his hand!

Carrie smiled as she saw Homer talking. She watched his

exuberance spill over to the others as he made flourishing gestures and took a comical bow. Homer was always the life of the party and he could make anyone feel welcome. All the onlookers were laughing and seemed to be very amused by whatever he was saying. Homer soon spotted Carrie across the clearing and with much enthusiasm he motioned for her to come join the gathering. She felt somewhat embarrassed as the others all turned to see to whom he was waving. When the girls saw Carrie they motioned for her to come as well.

"Mom", Carrie said, turning to put the last of the picnic plates out, "A whole group of my friends is over there and they're motioning for me. Do you need any more help here or may I go over there until the picnic really starts?"

"Sure, Carrie. Just come back as soon as someone gives the announcement that we're ready to eat," Chris answered.

Carrie turned and walked toward the group with a refined poise that she was lately acquiring. At this time last year, she probably would have run to see her friends without regard to her demeanor. Mom noticed this and smiled as she reflected on the change in her daughter.

As Carrie neared the gathering, Darla Harris shrieked out, "Carrie! Wait till you hear the latest news! Homer is going to work this summer as a field hand at Blooming Hills!" She blurted the news out with much more drama than the simplicity of the facts called for, but that was Darla's manner. Carrie smiled and looked to Homer whose wide grin seemed to cover his entire face.

"Yes, that's right, my lady," he crowed with a contrived English accent. "I shall be a servant in the employ of one Mr. John Mark Henderson, with whom you may already be acquainted." He bowed again with great dignity to a shyly smiling John Mark.

The whole group laughed heartily as Homer continued. "At your service, Sir!" he said to the slightly embarrassed John Mark. John Mark had the look of one who was a frequent and willing participant of his friend's good-natured teasing.

"Oh, cut it out, Homer," John Mark said with his sideways grin, "You know I'll be doing the same work you will and Joe will be boss to both of us."

"True, true," Homer conceded, still with an accent.

Inside Carrie was laughingly pondering the thought of Homer

on the farm and it seemed to her that he'd finally hit upon his true calling. That picture of Homer in overalls and holding a pitchfork flashed through her mind and she could barely stifle a giggle because of it. She listened as Homer went on to give the details with a more serious air.

"The Hendersons needed a couple of extra farmhands this season and they've agreed to give me one of the jobs." Then joking once again, he added, "Hope they're not sorry!" and rolled his eyes roguishly. All the girls giggled again. "I plan to work the rest of my high school summers so I can raise money for college. I'm hoping I can get accepted into the music department at Collier Christian."

"That's nice," was all Carrie could reply, still inwardly amused at the thought of Homer on the farm. She soon regained her composure and commented to Homer and the others that she had heard so many good things about Collier and that Homer and John Mark would have a great time together this summer.

About that time Luke sauntered up to the gathering, the youngest one in the group, yet already tall and mature-looking for his age.

"What's so funny?" he asked directly at Homer, the obvious perpetrator of the mirth.

"Oh, nothing really," Homer smiled. "I was just telling everyone how John Mark took mercy on me in my time of need and begged his father to give me a summer job at the orchard." A ripple of laughter circulated again as John Mark rolled his eyes in response to Homer's resumed performance.

"Mr. Henderson probably wants you to go out and sing to keep the birds and bugs and other pests away from the fruit! Is that it?" Luke countered with a grin. This time a roar of laughter consumed the teens as Luke had bested Homer's joke.

John Mark leaned against a tree and spoke more seriously, "Actually, Dad and Joe need extra help this year since this will be the first time we're opening the north fields for strawberries. Plus we've got a lot of trees we set in last year. We have to keep them watered if it's going to be anywhere near as dry as last season. Add Farmer's Market to that and last year we barely had any time to take a breath."

It was widely known that the Henderson farm was expanding and since Katie had married Joe Schultz two years ago, John

Henderson was able to increase the farm by including his new son-in-law in the business.

"Last I knew, Dad was still needing at least one more guy, only part time, but maybe you'd be interested in applying?" John Mark queried, looking directly at Luke.

"I might at that," Luke replied, squaring up his shoulders and suddenly seeming very tall and capable indeed. Luke had a reputation for being a good worker and an honest, dependable young man. Carrie felt proud to have him for a brother.

"What are the requirements?" Luke asked in a very business-like fashion.

John Mark paused, and then thoughtfully responded, "First, I know Dad wants to hire a Christian. Then you need to be willing to put in a fair share of work for your pay. That's all that I know of."

"I can fit that bill," Luke said with confidence.

"Then why don't you talk to my dad as soon as possible. I could even tell him you might be interested," John Mark offered.

"Ok, thanks! But of course, I'd have to clear it with Mom and Dad first," Luke remembered to add.

"Sure," John Mark said, just as someone called for everyone to be quiet. One of the senior boys stepped to the microphone in the pavilion and after giving a welcome and a few announcements, asked a blessing on the food.

Luke and Carrie hurried back to their table as soon as they heard, "Amen." Luke was so anxious to tell his mother of his job prospect that for a moment he forgot how hungry he was. He excitedly told her about the job and pleaded for her permission to talk to John Henderson.

"We'll have to talk to Dad about it first, Luke. But it does sound like a great opportunity. You'd be getting some valuable work experience and the Hendersons would be excellent employers," Mom added.

The idea of summer employment consumed Luke's thoughts for the rest of the day. He found that the picnic, the ball games, the fun—all were second to the exciting thought of possibly getting his first real job.

Luke joined in all the activities although he was actually anticipating four o'clock when it would be time to leave. He was anxious to get home to tell Dad the news of his possible summer job. Carrie, however, was having a great time with her friends and wishing the day could go on and on. She teamed up with Eileen for the three-legged race finishing second only to John Mark and Homer, the winners "by a nose."

After the games were over, the activities committee organized a scavenger hunt for the older students along the trails Mr. Petersen had made in the wooded areas years ago. Still deterred by the excitement of a job prospect, science-loving Luke was not going to go along until he realized that there was a twenty-dollar prize being awarded to the first team to successfully return with all the requested items. He had thought he could help his mother pack everything up in an attempt to hurry home until he realized that the prize would be well worth the time spent.

Luke teamed up with Tom Harris, Darla's younger brother. Carrie and Eileen registered as a team and John Mark and Homer were another team. Ten other teams registered and at two-thirty the signal was given to start the hunt.

All the participants were quickly scanning the list of items and whispering in scattered huddles. Some of the boys were the first to head off.

The rules included a forty-five minute time limit and the contestants could bring only one item back to fit each category. Brown paper sacks were given to the teams to hold the items they collected. The hunt proved to be a science lesson as well as an en-joyable activity.

Carrie and Eileen were doing well with several items, but were having quite a time deciding on others. As they stood pondering a pair of evergreens, trying to determine if either one might be a variety of which they could obtain a cone, they heard footsteps on the path behind them.

"Quick!" Eileen whispered turning her back to the evergreens and motioning for Carrie to follow suit. "Don't act like we've found anything here. Ok?" Out of the shadows came Homer and John Mark with their sack obviously full of items. Homer smiled as they passed.

"How are we doing, ladies?" he said as he patted the bulging sack with a satisfied air. The boys walked on in the direction of the pavilion area. Feeling a little discouraged Carrie and Eileen watched them walk away with their treasures. John Mark looked back and directed a pleasant, encouraging smile at Carrie that seemed to say, "It's ok, you'll do fine."

Eileen looked at Carrie and stated decidedly, "Exasperating boys! Brothers are such know-it-alls! Come on Carrie, we've still got ten minutes. Let's beat those two at their own game. Knowing Homer, probably all they had in that bag was rocks and they're just trying to bluff and discourage everybody else!"

Carrie was a little surprised at her friend's interpretation of the little scene. "After all," she thought, "Homer was just being the ever-jovial Homer and John Mark never said a word so Eileen shouldn't even blame him. And his smile was so sweet." It was strange how Eileen saw it so differently. "I guess if it had been Luke and Tom instead of John Mark and Homer I might have felt a little sisterly disgust myself," Carrie thought, dismissing Eileen's reaction. Just as Eileen decided that the pinecones they were considering were acceptable; Carrie spotted a most unusual rock beneath the trees. "Look at this beautiful rock, Eileen!" Carrie declared as she stooped to pick up an interesting and colorful specimen. "It's really pretty. Look at all the colors! I think I'll take that home for a paperweight on my desk. Do you think that's ok?" she asked.

"I suppose so, why not?" Eileen said, examining the handsome stone and dropping it in their bag. "When we get back, we'll ask Mr. Peterson if he cares. Let's get going."

On the way back to the pavilion area, the girls saw Luke and Tom heading swiftly toward the judge's table with a triumphant air. They resigned themselves to the fact that those boys probably would claim first prize.

By the time Carrie and Eileen reached the table there were others already lined up in front of the judges. Darla met them, feeling duty bound to inform them that no one had gotten all twenty items yet. Carrie glanced at the finishers and Homer and John Mark were indeed amongst that lot.

Mr. Peterson seemed to be enjoying the game as well as anyone. He was helping judge the items in each team's sack while his wife visited with the other moms who had stayed behind with the younger children. When it was time for Carrie and Eileen's items to be judged they dumped the contents of their sack on the table and the rock Carrie had found tumbled out with all the other items. Mustering all the courage she had, Carrie shyly said to Mr. Peterson, "Sir, I found this pretty rock while we were walking the trails and I wondered if I could take it home to use for a paperweight?"

"Sure, Carrie!" he replied. "On one condition--you think of Mrs. Peterson and I and remember all the fun of this day each time you look at it, ok?"

"Ok, I will. Thank you," she replied sweetly.

As Darla chattered on, asking all about what the girls had collected and exclaiming about the colorful rock, Carrie noticed that Luke and Tom's sack was being judged. There seemed to be mounting excitement as each item was checked off. Soon a loud, boyish whoop split the air as Luke and Tom congratulated each other upon being declared the first finishers to produce all the required items.

After all the teams were judged, Luke and Tom were still the only team to have gotten all the items. Several other teams lacked only one. Item number ten on the list seemed to be the difficult one that most others were missing. The judges had asked for an insect of the order, "Lepidoptera." Most of the students couldn't remember what sort of creatures belonged in this class. Luke, the science student had remembered it was the moth and butterfly family. He had spotted a cocoon on a twig that qualified for the category. Luke and Tom took great joy in discussing what they would each do with their prize money as they counted out the bills. For a while Luke had seemed to forget all about getting home to tell his father about the job offer.

The last half hour was spent cleaning up the area, repacking cars, and visiting. A few final announcements were made and the FCH Student Advisory Committee president, Jennie Cox, thanked the Petersons for their hospitality, wished all the families a safe and enjoyable summer and encouraged them all to meet in late August at the first planning meeting for the next year.

As Mom and Luke packed the last few items, Carrie held baby Addy, trying to occupy her and give Mom a break from the busy, squirming little one. Carrie was finding it difficult to keep her still and happy as she had missed her nap, was fighting sleep, and seemed to be on the verge of some serious crying.

Homer came to the rescue at just the right time and even sleepy

Addy couldn't resist his soothing voice. He held her in his strong arms and as he walked, he bounced her gently, softly singing a hymn to her. Addy was soon sleepy-eyed and quite calm. While Homer walked all around the pavilion with Addy, John Mark came over to talk to the much-relieved Carrie.

"Guess Homer just has a way with babies," John Mark said with his shy smile.

"I'm glad," Carrie conceded, "for anyone who could get her to sleep right now. She's been fussy lately since she's cutting teeth." John Mark looked at Carrie, still smiling, and hesitated as if he had something important to say but couldn't find the right words. This was John Mark's way; always slow to speak, thoughtful and carefully choosing each word.

"Uh, I was wondering," he started, "if you'd ever be interested in a summer job too?" he paused, but in an inexplicable way Carrie knew that it wasn't time to answer yet because John Mark had more to say. Having known him a long time, she was used to his definite, calculated manner and let him continue. As he spoke, he looked down at his feet, then glanced off in the distance. Carrie noticed it seemed to be hard for him to say exactly what he wanted and she detected a bit of nervousness in his manner even beyond his usual reserved way. "My sister...Alice...is needing a girl to help her bake at least three days a week, uh, I mean...this summer. I heard her talking to Mom about it just this morning." He looked at Carrie as if to assess her reaction. Carrie smiled pleasantly, sensing there must be more he wanted to say so she waited for him to continue. "I'll bet she'd give you first chance if you're interested," he finished, looking at Carrie now more directly. Carrie wondered how John Mark could be so sure his sister would want her to work at the bakery.

"Well," Carrie began, trying to conceal her excitement, "I'm flattered that you thought to tell me, and I'd be pleased to work for Alice if Mom and Dad agree, but are you sure she would want me? I mean, I don't have any experience in a big kitchen or anything. I enjoy cooking at home but I don't suppose it's the same as what Alice would need."

"Oh, I wouldn't doubt she'd be real glad to have you alright," he said. "She needs to get someone soon so she's got time to train them before too late in the season. I heard her say if she doesn't get someone she knows soon she'll have to advertise for help. Eileen's too busy with other work and you'd be an obvious candidate, especially if Luke's coming over there to work. Besides, our family thinks a lot of you." With that John Mark looked away, seeming suddenly embarrassed at his last statement.

A long silence followed and he finally looked back directly at Carrie. With all the evenness he could muster he said, "I didn't want to tell you in front of the others since they were all making such a big deal about Homer working for us. I was afraid they'd start in on you and embarrass you. But it wouldn't hurt to let Alice know if you're interested, and the sooner the better."

Carrie's expression nearly betrayed her excitement at the thought of John Mark's concern for her feelings. In her shyness though, a simple "Thanks" was all she could say as she looked at him. For the first time she seemed to notice his beautifully clear green eyes as he spoke sincerely to her. John Mark nodded as he turned to walk away and after a few steps he looked back as if the conversation shouldn't have quite ended yet and said, "See you at church."

Disappointments

The day after the picnic was a difficult one for Carrie. She had been so excited on Friday to go to Birch Lake Farm and be with her friends and then to top it all off, true to John Mark's suspicions, Alice had called to talk to Carrie's parents concerning the job at the bakery. Now Saturday was here and Carrie felt as though she had been plummeted down a steep hill. All the fun of yesterday was behind her and her parents had delivered the news to her at breakfast that they thought it would be best for the Brooks family as a whole if she didn't take the job with Alice this summer.

"I'm sorry, Carrie," Dad had started, "Mom and I talked the job situation over carefully and we would love to let you work for Alice. This is a very tough decision. But we suggest that you consider waiting until next summer. But we'll let you pray about it and make the final decision."

"Dad!" Carrie cried with a rare burst of emotion and obvious disappointment, "What's wrong? Don't you think I can do the work?"

"No, dear, that's not it at all. In fact we know you can easily handle the work, but Mom definitely needs you at home this summer. With Addy to care for, it's going to be an extra difficult task to tend the garden, can, freeze and so on, and Mom just really would like your help. Plus," he continued, "I discussed this at length with Alice. She called last night while you and Luke had gone to the library. She needs someone to work at least twenty hours a week and not any less. If it was a situation of needing you just once or twice a week, it might be different. But this way, we just don't think it would work out." Dad looked truly sorry.

Carrie felt badly about the situation but tried to conceal her deep disappointment when she saw the look on her parents' faces. As she watched sweet little Addy innocently grabbing for anything she could reach on the breakfast table, Carrie realized what Dad meant. Addy was really going to be active this summer and a curious infant would require a lot of attention. As was the case with many of the families in the church, Carrie knew her family depended on the garden all summer long and then they ate of its harvest all winter in the form of canned goods. Her mother would have difficulty handling it all alone this year especially late in the summer and early fall when the canning began to overlap the preparations for another school year.

"I hope you understand, dear. It's not that Mom and I don't want you to work or that we're trying to prevent you from having fun. We just think it's the best way to do things for this summer. In fact, your Mom and I both are sorry it doesn't work out differently because Alice Henderson would be wonderful for you to learn from. She's such a fine Christian woman and she's definitely a great baker and business manager. It would be very educational for you as well. I told that to Alice when I talked to her." Dad continued with a smile, "However she assured me that next spring she plans to ask you again if you have to turn her down now. She's determined to hire you as her assistant eventually. That shows that she really thinks a lot of you." Carrie was feeling a little better at this thought.

Mom spoke next, "Alice told Dad she's really desperate for the help or she'd just go on another year without you. But since she has to get a girl, if you don't accept, she's going to hire a student with the understanding that the job will only be for one summer. She'll offer it to you again next year!"

"Carrie, we're very pleased to know that you're well thought of. Alice told me you were her first choice because she knows you have good Christian character. That says a lot, princess," Dad beamed.

"John Mark must have known Alice would like to hire me," Carrie thought to herself, then asked her parents, "What about Luke? He was basically offered a job too."

Luke had been pushing his bits of sausage around dejectedly on his plate as he listened to his parents give Carrie the disappointing news, feeling certain he'd be next. Now he looked up, sure that he already knew what Dad's answer would be.

"Yes," Dad said slowly, "it's a little different situation with Luke's job. We're recommending Luke go and see Mr. Henderson about the job, but the difference is, Carrie, that Luke's job will be even more part time than yours would have been."

Luke's countenance changed immediately. "Yes!" was his enthusiastic reply as he shot out of his chair, his fork dropping and crashing to his plate. He looked at his sister who was trying bravely to conceal her feelings and blink back tears and he suddenly felt concerned for her. He quickly sat down, tucked his napkin on his lap and dropped his gaze. He resumed his eating but this time with more gusto, using the duty of finishing his breakfast as something to keep him from absolutely beaming with pleasure at the thought of this new job.

"Son," Dad continued, "it will have to be understood that you are not to neglect your duties here at home just because you take a part-time job. Do you understand?"

"Yes, sir!" Luke said between bites.

"And you'll still be expected to help your Mom when you are home. One of your main duties will be keeping the lawn mowed and the garden weeded."

"Yes, sir. I can handle that," Luke said with real pleasure in his voice. He scooped another helping of sausage on his plate, his excitement being the impetus for his improved appetite.

"Good," Dad added, "that shouldn't be too hard because I also talked to John Henderson last evening and he said that you'll only be needed on Thursday afternoons for about three hours to help pick fruit and load the truck for Farmer's Market. Then they'll need you to help John Mark and Homer run the booth on Fridays. So you see, son, it's very part time." Luke nodded, his happiness a bit deflated by the discovery of how very part-time this job really would be.

"It would be different for you, Carrie if they had only needed you that long," Mom said in a comforting tone. Carrie looked up and managed a wan smile. She really didn't want to let her mother see her feelings of disappointment. Mom didn't deserve to feel badly over this situation, Carrie reasoned. "I'll try to make the best of it," she thought bravely.

"Pray about it though, Carrie," Dad added, "Ask God to advise you on this. We'll honor your decision either way, ok? Then let Alice know one way or the other at church on Sunday."

Later, when Carrie was alone outdoors hanging the laundry on the line, she again began to ponder the very disheartening prospect of spending the whole summer at home when everyone else seemed to have something exciting to do. It seemed so unfair. She knew Mom needed her, yet her own desires were getting in the way of cheerfully surrendering her plans for the summer months. A few tears slipped out of her eyes and rolled down her cheeks. Feelings of deep disappointment seemed to linger around her, threatening to make a permanent claim on her attitude. Maybe she should accept Alice's offer and just promise to keep up all her duties here at home like Luke had been cautioned to do.

Suddenly she remembered how she had prayed about becoming a virtuous woman like the example in Proverbs 31. Maybe following this model was going to be more difficult than she had realized. Here she was barely beginning to practice being a keeper at home according to the scriptures and she was already dissatisfied with the prospect. "Dear God," Carrie began to pray, "I feel so left out. I feel disappointed about the job situation with Alice this summer, especially when all my friends will be working at one thing or another." At this point the list of friends whom Carrie knew had summer jobs quickly flashed through her mind. Darla Harris was going to be a cashier at the Everly Garden Center's large booth at Farmer's Market. And now Luke and Homer would be at Blooming Hills with Eileen and John Mark. "Please, Lord, help me to be content staying at home and helping Mom. I know she really needs me, yet I'm so disappointed. Please help my feelings change. I don't want Mom to feel that I don't want to help her. I thank you, dear God, for hearing my prayer and for understanding. I make a commitment today to help Mom this summer with cheerfulness even though I might not always feel like it. Lord, I'm asking You and depending on You to help my feelings line up with my actions. In Jesus' name I pray, Amen."

As she whispered the last words of her prayer, Carrie felt more peaceful about her situation. Although the sting of the disappointment was still fresh, she had the distinct feeling that this burden would be easier to bear now that she had turned it over to the Lord.

Later that day after Carrie had finished her few chores, she decided to choose an outfit for church. Mom and Dad had instilled in Luke and Carrie at an early age their responsibility to prepare for Sunday school and church as much as possible on Saturday. This meant selecting an outfit, seeing that it was ironed, then studying the Sunday school lesson as well as trying to get to bed at an early hour to be rested for a busy Sunday.

As Carrie looked through her closet, she felt another wave of discouragement attempt to engulf her. Her dresses were few in number and they were getting old. The green checked pinafore was almost too short. The last time she wore it she had felt uncomfortable. Surely it would be even shorter now. Next she considered her blue denim jumper but the denim was so heavy that Carrie was sure it would be too warm for tomorrow. The weather had been quite warm lately and the forecast for Sunday predicted temperatures in the low eighties.

She heaved a heavy sigh and slid the hangers to one side. Next in line was the flowered dress Mom had made her last year for spring. One of Carrie's favorites, she had worn it often but now it was beginning to show some wear and since she had gotten slightly taller in the last year, it seemed to be shorter than she liked.

Finally the choice came down to a skirt and blouse or the yellow dress she had worn last week. Carrie resigned herself to the fact that she would wear the yellow dress again since both of her skirts were showing definite signs of wear and, to tell the truth, she was just plain tired of them.

"I had hoped to earn some money this summer," Carrie thought, "to spend on clothes." Now she knew there was no hope of that. How could she ask for dresses when she had just heard Mom and Dad talking about getting Luke some boots for work? And just last week she had heard Dad tell Mom how he needed a new Bible. The binding was completely gone on his and they had tried to glue and tape it back together. Without Mom working outside the home, Carrie's family had learned to be careful how they spent their money. Carrie knew that ten percent of all their income was immediately set aside to be returned to the work of the church as her parents believed strongly in tithing. She also knew God had always faithfully provided for their needs. Remembering this, she decided to trust Him for some clothes as well. She breathed a quick prayer and decided to make the best of her wardrobe selection. She again committed her feelings to the Lord and asked Him to help her be content with what she had. Even in her discouragement she felt that God was with her and that He was helping her to keep her attitude from being completely unacceptable. She remembered the prayer she had prayed earlier that day, asking Him to help her feelings line up with the way she had committed to behave, and the thought strengthened her.

That evening Carrie went to her room earlier than usual. She had decided to spend a little extra time studying the Sunday school lesson as her teacher, Elinore Winfield had announced last week that she planned to ask a student to help with the discussion each Sunday to encourage class participation and to help the girls learn teaching skills. Carrie wanted to be well-prepared in case Miss Winfield called on her.

Carrie looked up each of the verses and read them carefully. She read the entire lesson through once and then re-read it, this time making notes in her book. She was surprised to find the theme was very timely for her, speaking directly to her present situation. The lesson text was taken from Matthew, chapter six and the title was "Peace and Trust in God's Provision." The verses seemed to address Carrie's concerns and dilemmas very directly. Jesus was teaching his followers not to worry about their daily provisions; clothing was even mentioned specifically!

As Carrie studied, she could hear the Saturday night noises of the Brooks household echoing through the halls. Mom was bathing Addy. Dad had a praise tape softly playing as he finalized his sermon, and Luke was polishing his shoes and opening and closing drawers in his room across the hall as he got his Sunday morning clothes ready.

After a while, Carrie heard a soft knock on her bedroom door. "Come in," she said.

Her mother opened the door and peeked around the corner, "Carrie, can we talk a bit?" she asked gently.

"Sure, Mom," Carrie smiled. Mom came in and sat down on Carrie's bed.

"I just got Addy in bed and I wanted to talk with you a little about a few things," she began. "I know you were disappointed today about what we said about the job situation for the summer."

Carrie's gaze dropped and her mother knew that meant, "Yes."

"Your dad and I are both sorry it doesn't work out more conveniently."

"I know, Mom. And I want to help you, I really do, but I had so hoped I could make a little money this year." Mom nodded in understanding as Carrie continued. "I have prayed about it and I asked God to help me have a good attitude, even though I'm disappointed. But I've decided I won't accept Alice's offer, I'll be here to help you, and that's a nice situation too, Mom."

"I'm so pleased to hear that, Carrie!" Mom replied, brightening considerably. "The Lord will honor your prayer, I'm sure, because it's His will for you to have a good attitude always, even in difficult circumstances. Getting our will and attitude in order is half the battle, dear. I think now that you've decided to accept this situation and you've been so mature about this you'll even find yourself enjoying this summer, not just enduring it," Mom added with a twinkle in her eye that actually did seem to be contagious. Now Carrie felt a spark of hope that suggested maybe Mom was right and this arrangement wouldn't be so bad after all.

"Carrie, I know you were anxious to have a little spending money, but is there anything in particular that you were wanting to save for?"

"Well, Mom, look in my closet," Carrie began, strolling over to the open door. "I don't want to complain, yet almost all of my dress clothes are getting too short or worn out. I was going to save up for some new things."

Mom followed her daughter across the room. Pushing the hangers to the side one by one, she took a long look at the few clothes in Carrie's closet. Finally she spoke, "I see what you mean. I'm sorry I didn't realize this, dear. I've really had to neglect some things since Addy was born and I guess I didn't keep up with your wardrobe. I know you've gotten taller this past year and I suppose we can't expect things to fit forever. Why don't you and I make it a priority to find some new things for you this summer?"

"How, Mom?" Carrie asked. "I know Luke needs work boots and Dad needs a new Bible. I can probably get along with these things if you can't spare the money."

"Don't you worry about how we'll do it. You just leave that to me. God always meets our needs as He promised and shows us what to do. I've got a couple of good ideas!" Mom smiled. "I know you're getting to the age where you want to put some thought into your appearance, and it's only normal and right that you should." Mom was still smiling, but suddenly became more serious with her next statement. "I noticed that Homer was paying a lot of attention to you yesterday at the picnic."

A long silence followed, then Mom spoke again, "Carrie, you are such a nice young lady. Young men are bound to be attracted to you. We've committed to allowing God to lead our family where our children's relationships are concerned rather than dating like most people do. You know that." Carrie nodded her understanding. "Still, it's not too soon for you to begin to pray for God's will in this area of your life. If God chooses for you to marry and have a family, then we should be praying for discernment and for this young man, whoever he is, to be developing Christian character. After all, I wasn't too much older than you when I met your father. So please consider including this in your prayers, ok?"

"Ok," Carrie replied, too shy about the matter to admit she already had.

Distractions, Contentment, and a New Old House

Sunday morning was a bustle of activity with the family all involved in last minute preparations for church. Mom was dressing Addy while Carrie was loading the crock-pot with potatoes and meat for Sunday dinner. Dad packed his sermon notes and double-checked the announcements as Luke packed the diaper bag in the car and hunted furiously for his Bible that seemed to be misplaced again. At the last possible moment Luke finally located his Bible and the family set off.

Carrie was rather quiet as they rode the few miles to church. She was thinking over the theme of the Sunday school lesson— peace, trust, and God's provision. She was lost in her own thoughts and failed to absorb any of the discussion of the rest of the family. As she pondered the fact that she faced a summer without a paying job and she was longing for new dresses, she absent-mindedly played with Addy whose car seat was sitting between her and Luke. As Dad pulled the vehicle into the parking lot of Maplewood Christian Fellowship, she suddenly was jolted out of her daydreaming remembering that the senior high students were taking turns being greeters this month.

"Dad!" Carrie cried, as she grabbed the back of the front seat,

"Was it my turn to be greeter today?" She couldn't remember if it was this Sunday or the next and the thought of being late was an embarrassing one indeed. She looked around the parking lot and saw a few cars already there.

"No, I don't think so, Carrie. Calm down. We're here in plenty of time anyway," her father replied.

"I heard John Mark Henderson and Kirk Davis volunteer last week," Luke reassured her. Carrie sunk back in the seat and drew a long breath of relief. It was not a regular occurrence for Carrie to be irresponsible. She was usually organized and it disturbed her a bit to think she could have forgotten such an important commitment.

"I guess I've been pre-occupied with my own concerns more than usual lately," she thought to herself.

True to Luke's statement, as the Brooks' entered the church, Carrie saw John Mark and Kirk each holding a stack of bulletins, ready to shake hands and welcome people.

Kirk Davis was seventeen and attended Blue Creek Community High School. He was a popular boy who excelled in sports and seemed to be the topic of many girls' discussions. His athletic accomplishments were a frequent item in the sports section of the Blue Creek Herald during the school year. Carrie had overheard her parents talking to Tom and Ginny Davis once about their son, Kirk. Lately they had been concerned with some of the friends he had chosen to spend time with at school. When Carrie saw him standing there with John Mark, her first thought was, "Maybe John Mark can be a good influence on him. I haven't remembered to pray for Kirk like I should have." Again Carrie felt convicted as she remembered how much time she had spent praying for her own situations and thinking about herself. After all, being home schooled, she realized she wasn't even faced with many of the same pressures that other students her age had to deal with. Even though Carrie was glad her family had chosen to home school, she realized some families weren't convicted that way or for one reason or another they couldn't make the necessary sacrifices for such an arrangement to work. She made a new determination to include the needs of others in her prayers.

Luke was first to step forward and briskly shook hands with both boys. Mom greeted each of the boys and went on to the nursery to put Addy's diaper bag on the shelf. Luke stayed and talked to Kirk and John Mark awhile. Dad passed the little group with a quick greeting and handshake and began to attend to the Sunday morning details of the church service.

As Carrie stepped forward, both of the boys seemed eager to greet her, each holding a bulletin out for her. The moment was somewhat awkward while Carrie stood there not knowing whose bulletin to accept. The look on her face must have indicated embarrassment and John Mark recognized it. He turned slightly and looked at Kirk to see what he was going to do. But Kirk continued to smile, his hand extended and holding a bulletin toward Carrie. After a few seconds, John Mark politely pulled back his hand and let Carrie accept the bulletin from Kirk. Luke watched the whole scene, half amused, half astonished that anyone would be so anxious to greet his sister. He decided to keep his comments to himself instead of further embarrassing Carrie with a thoughtless remark.

After she had taken the bulletin and greeted both boys, Carrie went off to her Sunday school room. She was glad for the solitude of the basement room where the senior high girls' class was held. She was the first one there and she was relieved to be able to sit alone in the quiet little room for a few minutes and recover from the episode at the door. Something that would not have bothered most other girls had left her a bit flustered and she committed anew to work on overcoming the shyness that often seemed to plague her, causing her to feel ill at ease. She felt her face begin to cool and she knew she must have blushed a scarlet red in front of the two boys.

"How kind and mature of John Mark to decline the way he did," Carrie thought to herself. She knew though, that this was typical of John Mark's personality: even-tempered, thoughtful, restrained. At any rate, she was glad he had saved her from further embarrassment by just letting Kirk Davis hand her the bulletin and not forcing her to make a choice.

Soon other students began to enter the room and within a short time, the bell rang, indicating the beginning of the Sunday school hour. Miss Winfield began the lesson with a prayer and then she asked Miranda McCavitt to lead the discussion by giving her thoughts on the lesson. Miranda was one of the quietest girls in the class and like Carrie, rather shy, but she had obviously studied the lesson and with the teacher's help did a nice job of summarizing the theme. Miss Winfield then took over with some thoughts of her own. Elinore Winfield was well liked by all the girls. She was a woman of about sixty years of age who had never married but had spent her life as a missionary. She had returned home to Maplecrest a few years ago to help her aging parents and was devoting her life to their care and the work of the Maplewood Christian Fellowship. She taught Sunday school and was active in the ladies' sewing circle. She loved to bring beautiful bouquets from her garden to the church each Sunday while her flowers were in bloom. Carrie admired Miss Winfield. She was always cheerful and was truly a woman of a meek and gentle spirit. "She is what Mom would describe as 'gracious,'" Carrie thought.

Miss Winfield began with a story of some of her experiences on the mission field. "I think of contentment, trust, and God's provision each time I remember India, girls," she began. "India is where I got some real lessons in these things. That's not to say that I'm always perfect when it comes to being satisfied and peaceful, but I do look at things a lot differently since then. In some of the places I worked, conditions were very poor. The Bible verses on trust became real to me then as I battled my own will and some very real doubts day after day." Having deep respect for Miss Winfield's wisdom, the girls all listened intently. "I have other areas of my life where I've had to learn to be content and exercise my faith also," she went on, her voice changing slightly as if to indicate a bit of a painful memory. "You might be surprised at this, but it wasn't always my desire to be a single woman, you know. It's probably hard for you to believe, but once I was young like all of you," she smiled, "My greatest hope was to marry and have a family. But it wasn't to be that way."

Miss Winfield continued, "There was a young man who had asked me to marry him shortly after I graduated from high school. I was so sure this was God's will for me that I accepted. We were to be married in two years when he finished college." The girls quietly listened, eager for Miss Winfield's explanation. "One day I received a letter from him breaking the engagement. He apologized politely but said he had had a change of heart and asked to be released from the commitment." Carrie thought there was a certain distance in Miss Winfield's eyes as if the telling of this was still not easy, even after all these years.

"I was crushed, of course, but I realized over time that this man was not God's best for me for several reasons. Eventually, I saw that I had no one to blame but myself, realizing that I had not sought God on this matter as diligently as I should have. If I had been more diligent to seek the Lord's perfect will, I would have seen some of this man's character flaws from the start. God was actually sparing me from much heartache in later years. Oh, but I didn't see it that way at first!" she confided, "Instead, I felt cheated and disappointed and I was not always very happy until I fully realized the faithfulness of God in this matter. But through it all, as I saw God's will unfold for my life, I learned contentment—contentment in being single, trust in the Lord's provision, peace in my heart even in a hot, humid mission hut far from home, and now contentment at home with aging parents. We must each exercise faith everyday if we are to live the Christian life to God's glory."

Miss Winfield paused thoughtfully and looked down at her Bible that was opened to the scripture text of the day's lesson. "Paul also spoke in one of the epistles some words that have become real and precious to me—he told of learning to be content-- and now, looking back, I wouldn't trade my life for anyone's. It's been a good, rich life full of excitement and blessings from God. I've come to realize I haven't missed a thing! And now I can say to you that you, too, can experience God's peace in all your circumstances. If you walk with your hand in Jesus' hand, there is no situation in which you cannot be peaceful and satisfied."

As Miss Winfield finished speaking, she looked around at her students who had been listening so eagerly. Carrie noticed her face radiated with a genuine smile of happiness, one that only God could give. "She looks so young for her age," Carrie thought. "She has a brightness and zeal that some of the other women her age are lacking."

Carrie was again surprised to see how God had so quickly begun to answer her own prayers. It was only yesterday she had prayed about her troubling circumstances and here was a specific Sunday school lesson the very next day. But still Carrie felt a twinge of apprehension. She thought it might not be coincidence that the subject of marriage had come into a lesson on trust at just the time she had begun to ponder and pray about this for her own life. Was God trying to use Miss Winfield's testimony of singleness to prepare Carrie for the same thing? Somehow that thought was a little disturbing. What did it all mean?

Seconds later, the bell rang to announce the end of Sunday school and the beginning of the worship service. The classroom doors opened and out poured children of all ages, in a hurry to join their parents before the service started.

As Miss Winfield dismissed the girls and Carrie exited the classroom, she felt someone grasp her elbow from behind. It was Eileen who had just come out of another class. She and Carrie were one year apart in school and so they would not be in the same Sunday school class until next year.

"Can you sit with me today?" Eileen asked hopefully. She hurriedly continued, "Homer and some others from First Church will be here today to do a presentation, you know."

"No, I didn't know," Carrie replied, surprised. "A presentation for what?"

"They're going to sing and do a skit to help promote the joint Bible school in two weeks. I'm surprised you didn't know!" Eileen looked at Carrie quizzically, not believing the pastor's daughter could have missed this exciting fact.

Carrie instantly realized that it was her pre-occupation with her job, clothes, and life in general that prevented her from hearing this too. As they made their way to the sanctuary, Carrie saw that Eileen was right. Several youth from First Church were in the foyer, Homer included, and the whole place seemed to be buzzing with more activity than usual.

Carrie caught her mother's eye and motioned for permission to sit with Eileen near the front where other youth were rapidly filling the pews. Lately she had been sitting with her mom in the front bench to help with Addy. It would be fun to sit with her friends once again, especially today. Mom waved her approval and Carrie and Eileen made their way to the front, taking a seat behind a row of other teens.

In a few minutes, the service began. As pastor, Dad sat in the front behind the pulpit with one of the elders whose turn it was to give the announcements. After the offering was taken and the singing was finished Dad welcomed the four young people from First Church and announced that they were here to encourage participation in the upcoming joint Bible school to be held in two weeks. It was the first time the two churches had joined hands to reach the area children.

Homer was the obvious leader of the group. He played the piano while the two girls sang the first song. Next he sang a song about committing your life to the Lord. His beautiful, clear voice was so pleasant and the song so touching that Carrie felt deeply stirred in her heart. She thoroughly enjoyed the program, especially when the four young people invited the children up front for a puppet show and short lesson, a feature from the upcoming Bible school. Carrie enjoyed watching the delight on the faces of the little children as Homer and the others used the puppets to tell Bible stories.

During the last part of the service, baby Addy fell asleep and Mom was able to listen more carefully than usual to her husband's sermon. From her seat across the aisle, she glanced occasionally at her two oldest children. She was pleased to see the way they were growing up. As she watched them sitting among the others their age, she realized she was glimpsing the future. Just as they were sitting among friends this morning, someday they would take their place in the church and in their generation. Would she have prepared them well enough? As the thought crossed her mind, she breathed a quick prayer for grace and wisdom. Though her heart was filled with motherly concern for all of her children, lately her thoughts centered on Carrie. She prayed to the Lord daily on all her children's behalf but for some time now Carrie's future had been a most pressing concern.

Carrie's parents had never been through a courtship like they hoped their children would experience. Their relationship had begun with a few dates in their late high school years. Later after college, they dated more often and were eventually married. There was no experience to fall back on that was like the standards they were setting for their children's lives. She wondered if it would all work out. Would Carrie find a suitable husband or more accurately, would a suitable young man find Carrie? Mom wondered if she and Dad been right as they decided to teach their children to avoid traditional dating and rely more on God to lead them to a spouse of His choice.

There were some occasions when Mom thought she noticed certain young men showing interest in Carrie. She found herself quite often having to recommit her own heart to the standards she and her husband had set, reminding herself that in the long run this would be best for her children even though things had been different in her generation. A different world called for radical answers. Sometimes she was tempted to doubt her own convictions, especially when some people in the church were still satisfied with the traditional ways of thinking about such matters.

After the church service, Carrie and Eileen went outside to visit with their other friends. There was always so much to talk about. The boys usually stayed in one corner of the churchyard and often they'd begin a game of catch. The girls gathered in opposite corners or talked and laughed while they walked about the grounds.

This particular Sunday the weather was typical of late spring. The sun was shining, a light breeze was blowing, and the air was scented with flowers. Today Eileen and Carrie walked leisurely around the perimeter of the church property. Knowing Carrie had told Alice she couldn't accept the job offer, Eileen was expressing her disappointment over the fact that her friend wouldn't be able to work at Blooming Hills this summer. Carrie was bravely trying to forget the matter and be satisfied with her decision, so she decided to honestly share her struggles with her friend.

"Eileen, I really would have loved to be at your place all summer, but I just can't. It isn't even solely my choice. I prayed about it and I felt God showed me that following Mom and Dad's advice would be a blessing in the end. I'm trying so hard to be content with the whole idea. Let's not talk about it anymore. It will make it easier to forget, ok?"

"Sure," Eileen replied, "I guess you're right. I'm sorry."

"It's such a beautiful day," Carrie said, "Let's not waste it with sadness. After all, this is my favorite time of year!" she said dreamily as she drew in a deep breath of the sweet air. "May is my namesake, you know. Carrie May Brooks," she said decidedly as they walked on. Eileen smiled at the thought.

"Look at all the beautiful flowers around the church. Let's pick a bouquet," Carrie suggested and she pointed at the hedge on the east edge of the church lawn, a veritable wall of white bridal veil bushes and honeysuckle in full bloom. The hedge separated the churchyard from the little, old cemetery next to it.

Maplewood Christian Fellowship's building and grounds seemed to grow out of the surrounding farmland like an oasis. The church was a white frame building in the middle of newly plowed fields. If you stepped off the edge of the church lawn on the west, you stepped into a row of Carl Parker's corn. The north border was a pleasant stand of oaks and the south border was County road 65. The church looked as if it had been placed there as an afterthought, or maybe it had been there first, and appropriately, life grew up around it. Whatever the case, Carrie wasn't sure, she just knew she loved this place in every season but the season of late spring was her favorite.

The girls walked and talked as they each gathered arm-loads of the lovely scented sprigs, laughing and enjoying the glorious day and the blue skies.

Mr. and Mrs. Brooks were outside now on the steps, chatting with the people as families readied to go home. Carrie waved at her mother from the end of the hedge and held up the generous bouquet. She noticed some of the younger boys had begun a game of catch on the ball diamond. Luke, Kirk, John Mark, and Homer were gathered near Kirk's new car and were inspecting it with interest.

When Carrie and Eileen had picked their armfuls of the scent-drenched blossoms, they turned and walked back toward the parking lot. With a renewed sense of peace lighting her countenance, Carrie radiated with joy. Little did she realize that in the eyes of one young man that day, the yellow dress she had so dreaded to wear again only contributed to the lovely image she cast in his eyes as she walked across the lawn, her arms brimming with the pink and white flowers.

Even from a short distance as Mom stood on the steps of the church building, she noticed the look of admiration in the young man's eyes as he stole a look at her daughter. In her heart, she wondered if he could be the one Carrie would marry. From that day on, she mentioned his name in prayer before the Lord asking God's guidance and will for the young man's life, for even at this early age, she could see a unique character in him that was very Christ-like.

After dinner, Carrie and Luke gathered up the dishes and quickly washed them. They soon joined their parents for some relaxing time on the front porch. Mom was rocking Addy, hoping she'd fall asleep. Presently Dad laid the magazine he was reading down at his side and cleared his throat as if to prepare to speak.

Luke and Carrie had been discussing plans to take a bike ride, but they both stopped and looked at their father at this rather obvious signal that he had something to say. It was a few moments before Dad spoke. Carrie glanced at her mother. She noticed Mom was looking at Dad with a satisfied, knowing smile. Mom appeared to already know the information that he was about to report.

Dad began with carefully selected words, "Children, your mother and I have some good news to tell you." There was a pause and Mom kept looking at Dad with that same pleased smile. "We're going to move out of this house!" Dad said, smiling broadly. "We're going to a bigger house in just a few weeks!" Dad looked at Luke and Carrie as if he expected them to show great excitement at the news. Instead, they both appeared to be shocked. Neither said a word in return but stared speechlessly at their parents.

Assessing their looks as less than excited, Dad glanced quickly at Mom whose happy expression had changed to one of mild concern. Looking quickly back at Luke and Carrie, he continued, "You know we've been feeling crowded here especially since Addy was born. In the new house, we'll have a lot more room."

"Where is this place?" Luke asked, his curiosity finally overcoming his shock.

"Well, it's the Olmstead house on the west edge of Maplecrest. It's old and needs repair, but I found out yesterday morning that Travis Olmstead is willing sell it to us. I asked him awhile back if he would consider selling since he's the only family member left and it's getting difficult for him to manage that farm all alone." Luke and Carrie listened intently to their father's explanation. "He has wanted to get out from under the care of it for a long time, but he didn't think anyone would want it because it needs work. He's going to move to the senior citizen apartments in Blue Creek."

Carrie swallowed hard as she thought of leaving the only house she had ever lived in. "At least it's only across town," she tried to tell herself after her mind stopped reeling. She remembered the contentment lesson of earlier in the day and amidst her sadness and shock, she found the self-control to thank God it wasn't some place clear across the world--some uncomfortable place like Miss Winfield had described this morning.

Mom was adding details now as Carrie was pulled back into the conversation at the mention of her name. "Carrie, you'll have a beautiful room, a lot larger than the one you have now! We'll all be able to stretch out. You won't have to give up your bedroom when company comes anymore, dear," Mom was saying as she looked at her daughter with a hopeful smile, as if she wanted her to share her excitement. Carrie was trying hard to sort through her thoughts about this news. She was thinking of her familiar room with all its cozy comfort. It was painted the most beautiful shade of soft lavender; a shade she had chosen when she was a little girl. What about her big sunny window and the soft carpet she had helped pick out only a year ago? What about all the pleasant memories? This house held many memories for Carrie. How could Mom think a bigger room was all that would matter?

"I can't think which house you're talking about," Carrie said shakily when she finally spoke.

"You know," Dad started, "It's the old house on the highway just west of town on the south side of the road. It's white with green shutters. There's a couple of barns and an old iron fence surrounds the yard."

In her mind, Carrie began to get a vague picture of the house Dad must be referring to. She wondered if her parents could really be serious. The only place she had in mind had always seemed old and rundown, overgrown and dilapidated. What would the Brooks family want with a place like that? The questions in Carrie's mind didn't remain unanswered for long.

"We decided to buy the house because we will have much more room. Another reason is the cost. We'll actually be paying less to live there than it costs us for this house. Because it's old and needs work, we can get it for a very reasonable price." Dad sounded so positive.

Luke broke in, "What about the work, Dad? Is it good enough to move into? How much needs to be done?"

"Well, son, some things we'll have to work on gradually, but it's good enough to move in right away and we can deal with the other repairs later. After all, Travis is living there. Plus, it's sound and solid and has some beautiful features. Besides, I discussed this with the elders this morning and they said we'd organize several church workdays to get the main things done. They were only too glad to help since MCF has never provided their pastors with a parsonage. They feel it's the least they can do and I'm so glad they're willing to help."

Mom added her own list of positive remarks next. "Another good thing is that we'll have a huge yard—over eight acres, actually, and we'll be able to have chickens and a cow. We'll enjoy having our own eggs and milk. You know we have always wanted to have a bigger garden and you kids wanted to raise some rabbits. Now we'll be able to do all of that. It's really like a dream come true for us." Mom was absolutely glowing at the thought of realizing some of the family's desires. But to Carrie, all that didn't matter now. She had talked about having some pets, a few rabbits, maybe even a horse, but it had been easy to talk about moving when there didn't seem to be much chance of it actually happening. Now that it came right down to it, she felt a strange quivering feeling inside and none of those things seemed very enticing at all.

"We are scheduled to go tomorrow to take papers to the bank and you two can see the house then, ok?" Dad explained.

Luke, the scientist and budding farmer was beginning to catch the enthusiasm for the move now. "Sure!" he said happily as he thought of all the exciting possibilities that life on the farm held.

A nod and "Yes" was all Carrie could choke out, as she managed an artificial smile. Deep inside, she felt an intense sadness. When the little group on the porch finally broke up and headed in the house, Carrie made her way to the top of the stairs where she shut the door behind her as she entered the little room that had been hers for so long. She lay on her bed and looked out of the big window at the familiar view of the back yard and bravely pushed back tear after tear, refusing to cry them as they pressed at her eyes.

Settling Into Summer

When Carrie awoke on Monday morning, she felt a little disoriented. She lay quietly in her bed for a few moments, and then turned to see the clock that read 8:30 a.m. Why was she in bed so late? She flung the quilt back just in time to realize that today was actually their first day of summer vacation. Mom must have let her sleep in. So she covered back up and closed her eyes for a few seconds, still not ready to shake off her slumber. For the next few minutes, she lay in bed relaxed, but not asleep, yet she had the distinct feeling that something was not right. It was an unsettled feeling. In her grogginess she tried to wake up her mind enough to pin an event to this feeling. Suddenly she remembered—the new house! The new, old house. A sickening sensation washed over her as her mind recalled the disappointment of Sunday afternoon. Now it was all clearer. She had spent a large portion of the previous afternoon alone in her room, trying to deal with her disappointment. Then she had gone to bed early and her last thoughts before drifting off to sleep had been troubled ones concerning the move.

"I must have been pretty tired out from all my sorrow to have slept so long," she reasoned. Now she knew what her father meant the many times she had heard him refer to being emotionally tired. He often spoke of this after preaching or after counseling people in difficult situations. Now she was experiencing it first hand. It was a kind of exhaustion that wasn't cured by sleeping because she didn't feel refreshed, even after ten hours of rest.

Before she tried to get up, Carrie remembered to pray. She

quietly asked God to help her accept this move and to even be cheerful about it. Carrie's prayer was truly a prayer of faith because her heart felt anything but cheerful and her attitude about it all was not as good as she would have liked. Her mind kept wandering back to Miss Winfield's remarks in the Sunday school class. This seemed to her like a repeat of the lessons on trust that she thought she had learned a short time ago concerning the job situation.

She sat up in bed and reached over to the nightstand where her Bible lay open to the Psalms. Carrie knew that her daily Bible reading today was in chapter thirty-seven. She was eager to read the portion for the day, hoping there would be some nugget of truth for her to hold onto during this difficult time. Lately, Carrie had been learning how the scriptures could be so precious to her and she was much more careful to concentrate on each word, reading and re-reading them carefully in her search for comfort. So this morning, she eagerly searched the passage with the fervor of a hungry person hunting for a sustaining morsel.

After diligently reading the chapter, Carrie noticed that verse four seemed to stand out to her. She spoke the words aloud, "Delight thyself also in the Lord and He will give thee the desires of thine heart." Carrie read the verse again and again, hardly able to believe how timely the sweet promise was for her situation.

"This is what I need to do—delight myself in the Lord," she thought. "I've been praying and hoping He would give me the desires of my heart, but maybe I haven't been delighting myself in Him like I should have. It seems I've been so disappointed lately by so many things. Maybe it's because I've set my own plans and desires above my love for God. If I delight myself in Him, maybe my desires will change to match His will and I'll be happier."

Carrie felt tears of joy escape her eyes as she realized what this meant to all her recent trials. She remembered the lesson Miss Winfield had given only yesterday and this verse today seemed to speak to her in the same way.

As she finished her Bible reading, she prayed earnestly asking God to teach her what it meant to delight herself in Him.

"Thank you, Lord, for meeting me this morning with this word. I know You meant it just for me. Teach me to find my joy in serving You and not in my circumstances. Dear Lord, help me especially today to be pleasant and cooperative as we go to see the house. Help me to see the good in this move and to concentrate on the fact that it must be Your will and not dwell on my unhappiness about leaving here." Carrie continued her prayer remembering Kirk Davis as she had committed to do along with her other regular prayer concerns. As she got ready for the day, her heart was lighter and everything seemed new and alive with fresh hope and possibilities.

The more Carrie pondered the house situation, the more she was sure it must be God's will for her family to move to the old Olmstead place if her parents felt He had led them in that direction. So she was ready to delight herself in the Lord by being a model of thankfulness and obedience concerning the plan.

The family gathered for breakfast a bit later than usual this morning. On Monday mornings, Dad's day off, everyone usually slept in a bit. Today, since Mom had really been generous because of summer vacation, Luke too had taken advantage of the extra time to relax, emerging for breakfast later than everyone else.

Carrie's parents immediately noticed a difference in her countenance and although she hadn't shared a word about her new-found strength, her parents continued to observe a real change in her attitude throughout the day.

After lunch, the family prepared to meet Travis Olmstead at the bank where Mom and Dad would sign all the necessary papers for the sale of the house.

When the lunch dishes were done, the family headed downtown to meet at the bank. Luke and Carrie watched Addy during the long wait while Mom, Dad and Mr. Olmstead met with the banker behind large glass windows in an office at the end of the hall.

Luke seemed to fidget the whole time. He thumbed through every magazine in the lobby, some more than once. Occasionally, he would stop to ask Carrie a question or get up to get a drink from the large water cooler. Although Addy slept during most of the wait, Carrie too wished they would hurry since the little girl was showing signs of waking. Carrie could only see the back of Dad's head in the far office and was not able to tell exactly what was taking place. "I kind of wish we would have just offered to watch Addy at home," Carrie said to her brother with a slightly worried look at the little girl who was beginning to squirm. Luke nodded his silent assent and went back to reading a magazine.

Finally, after about a half hour and many magazines later, Luke plopped down on the lobby couch and folded his arms as he said impatiently, "What could be taking so long?"

"I don't know," Carrie answered, "I had no idea it would take this long, either. But why are you so impatient?"

Luke looked at his sister as if she should know the answer to that question. "I'm anxious to see this new place!" he replied. "I'm looking forward to moving. I've never had it as good as you as far as rooms go, you know. My room's even smaller than yours and besides I'm looking forward to everything else about the new place too. Think of the fun we'll have! Chickens, cows, rabbits; I can't wait!" Luke, the farmer at heart, was all smiles at the thought of it.

Carrie smiled at her energetic brother. His love of science naturally connected him to a love of animals and plants. Luke would be right at home at this new place. But a twinge of the old disappointed feeling tried to steal over Carrie as she thought how easy this move would be for Luke and how happy he would be on Thursday when he went to Blooming Hills for his first day of work. But there was an equal and balancing feeling of peace in Carrie's heart when she remembered how God had so graciously provided her with scriptures to soothe her disappointments. It was a comforting thing to realize that the God of all the universe was watching your life and caring about all the small details--caring enough to work out the events and situations in order to lead you. He even caused scriptures to speak to your heart at just the right time!

Suddenly Luke looked straight at Carrie, who seemed to be lost in her thoughts and said, "Hey, Carrie, this has all happened so fast, I forgot to ask. What's going to happen with our old place when we move out?"

"I don't know," Carrie said thoughtfully. "I was pretty surprised too, I didn't think to ask either." Carrie gave a little laugh and Luke chuckled too as they realized how they had each been so preoccupied as to have forgotten to ask their parents such an obvious question.

Luke spoke next, "Must be they're going to sell it. They'd never have enough money to buy another house if they didn't, would they?"

"I don't think they would. You're probably right, Luke. But

I wonder who they'll sell it to? It seems like Dad would have said something or brought someone through to look if they were selling."

"I don't know," Luke said as he pondered the thought. "Everything else has been a surprise so far."

Just then they heard a door open at the end of the hall and they saw their parents and Mr. Olmstead leaving the little office. Mom, Dad and Mr. Olmstead were smiling and the bank officer was shaking Dad's hand vigorously. Everyone looked pleased.

Carrie heard the banker say to her father, "See you tomorrow at 10:00." With this statement, Carrie really began to wonder what could be going on.

As the group approached Luke and Carrie, Addy began to stir more as she heard her mother's voice. Carrie and Luke both were anxious to ask questions, but realized it would be impolite and this was not a good time. Mom scooped Addy into her arms just in time to delay some oncoming crying. Carrie was relieved that the little girl had slept until her mother was finished in the office.

Mr. Olmstead looked directly at Luke and Carrie and asked enthusiastically, "How would you like to come over and see your new home?"

"Yes, sir" Luke replied with equal vigor while Carrie nodded politely.

"We'll meet you there in a few minutes, Travis, " Dad said, holding the big door open for the group as they exited the bank.

Once the Brooks' were all in the car, Luke looked at Carrie knowingly and then asked their parents the question that was burning in his and his sister's minds. "Dad, what's going to happen with our old house? I mean are you going to sell it or what?"

"Well," Dad answered, "It's already sold. We sold it to First Christian Church. Actually, we'll be selling it to them tomorrow at 10:00 a.m." Dad looked very pleased. Carrie was astounded at the news and Luke looked surprised too.

"When did all this happen?" Carrie asked.

"Remember about a month ago when Pastor Keene and Helen Williams came over with a few people from First Christian?"

"Yes," Carrie answered.

"That was the night we were headed out to the roller skating party," Luke commented.

"Well, Helen Williams is the treasurer of First Christian and the others were members of their parsonage and finance committees. They looked at the house and were very impressed with it. They are buying it to use as a parsonage for their church."

Carrie smiled at the thought. She was happy to know that another pastor's family would be using her home, especially a family as nice as the Keenes'.

"That's a nice idea, Dad. Maybe Alicia will get my room," Carrie suggested hopefully. Dad knew Carrie was referring to the Keenes' eight-year-old daughter.

"Well, I don't think so, dear," Dad replied. "Pastor Keene and his family won't be moving in."

Luke and Carrie looked at each other, puzzled, but Dad soon went on, "Gerald and Mary Keene are going to be moving this summer. They've requested a transfer from their church conference. Gerald's mother is getting older and she needs someone to look after her. Since she lives so far away, Gerald can't see to her needs as well as he'd like. About six months ago, he asked to be transferred as soon as possible to a church near where she lives in New York, if one became available. One did open up and they're going in two weeks. This is partly why we didn't mention it to you. We felt we had to keep it confidential until the committee made their decision and the people of First Church learned about Pastor Keene's move. I understand the congregation has known for some time now but the committee didn't make a final decision about the house until last week. Normally with a family decision such as this, your mother and I would have liked to include you in praying about it. But we really believed it was a positive move for all of us and we wanted to surprise you. I hope you agree," he said with a certain enthusiasm in his voice.

"Wow!" Luke answered, "Looks like everybody's moving! Who will be the pastor at first church after they leave?"

"Well, they're not sure yet, as I understand it. For this summer they'll be having a variety of new seminary graduates filling the pulpit, young men who are out of college and seeking an appointment to a church. That's where our house comes in," he continued. "For quite some time, the parsonage committee has realized the need for a more suitable home for the pastor. The house they're now using as the parsonage, where Keenes' live, is quite small and it makes it difficult for First Church to accommodate a pastor with a family. Besides, the old parsonage is too far from the church to be really convenient and was beginning to be in need of serious repair. The committee felt that in the long run our house would be more suitable for several reasons."

Mom spoke next, "To us it seemed like we were getting crowded, but imagine what it was like for the Keenes'. Their home had three bedrooms too, but they're all quite small and there was no extra room for guests, not to mention the yard was small, as well."

"That's right, " Dad added, "Our house doesn't have guest space either, but the lot is so big, they plan to add on an office and an extra bedroom. They couldn't have done that at their old location."

"So, no one will be moving in right away?" Carrie asked.

"No, dear, but they're still going to begin work at our house in about three weeks because they want to get started with the new addition as soon as possible so they're ready when they do get a pastor," her mother said, then added with excitement, "Look, we're almost there!"

"Now, children, please be careful what you say while we're here. Don't make any unkind remarks or show disappointment in front of Mr. Olmstead while we're in there today, ok?" she instructed. "After all, the place does need work so it may look a little impossible at first, but try to imagine the way it could be instead of dwelling on its present condition. Your father and I feel sure we'll be very happy here if we just get some work done on it."

Carrie thought of sweet, old Mr. Olmstead. He seemed so eager for her and Luke to see the place and like it. She steeled herself for anything and tried to imagine the worst possible condition of the house, thinking that if she was well prepared it might be easier to conceal any disappointment she felt.

As they drove in the driveway, Carrie heard Luke draw a deep breath as he sized up the exterior condition of the house. Carrie had purposely kept her eyes lowered to this point, almost afraid to look. Her family usually went out of town the other way and she had never really paid much attention to this place. She honestly couldn't remember much about it. But now hearing Luke's sigh, she slowly looked up, filled with apprehension, but determined not to show any dislike.

When Carrie's eyes beheld the sight out of the car window,

dislike was not what she felt at all. Sure enough, this was the house she had thought her parents meant, but today it looked different to her than it ever had before. It surprised her to detect an unexpected pleasure sweeping over her. In the initial shock of learning about the move, she had really imagined it to be worse than it was. She actually loved this place!

She had never really looked at it before but now she felt her heart give a little leap at the sight of the old structure and a smile began to pull at the corners of her mouth. If you could love a house, it was love at first sight and true love it was! The tired condition of the old home did not alter Carrie's devotion at all! She didn't seem to notice its many faults. She looked right into its past at its once glorious features and there was a definite sense of home and belonging that was immediately obvious.

She felt a little overwhelmed as her eyes tried to drink in a myriad of things at once. There were double bay windows, several quaint peaks with gingerbread decorations and a circle drive that Dad was pulling the car around just now. A short way behind the house, there stood two faded red barns, one large, one small. They were such a part of things that their foundations seemed to melt into the landscape with an aged dignity. Between the house and the barns was a small stone building, an old milk house with rambling vines creeping slyly up its corners.

But to Carrie the crowning delight was the long wrap-around porch whose intricate features seemed to be delicately carved out of the house. Around the pretty façade were what Carrie thought must be dozens of white bridal veil bushes in the glory of their full bloom! The flowered bushes clustered like a wide lace petticoat around the house. She marveled at the loveliness of her favorite flowers growing in profusion right there before her eyes! She wondered if God had once looked into the future and pre-arranged for these to be here just for her! Their old house had only one of these pretty bushes in the front yard, but it had always been her favorite. What a comfortable feeling it gave her to think of God caring to include this pleasure for her by prompting someone to plant all these long ago! And standing on the west side of the porch was Mr. Olmstead, motioning them in with a sincere smile.

The next hour or so was like a dream for Carrie. As she toured the house and grounds with her family her love of the place was fixed. She found all the rooms to be an exciting discovery, for each and every nook seemed to have a personality of its own.

Luke was equally taken with the prospect of life here on the farm. His real interests lay in the exploration of the barns and outbuildings, the fences and fields. Even the prospect of being responsible to mow the imposing lawns didn't daunt his enthusiasm toward his new home.

As the Brooks family reluctantly left the circle drive of the old farm a while later, a much-relieved Carrie was chattering excitedly to her mother about new paint, wallpaper and curtains. A house she had barely noticed before was now vividly etched in detail in her mind and occupying a corner of her heart with equal intensity, a corner not to be challenged by another home for several years.

Busy, Busy, Busy

The next few weeks were a blur of activity for Carrie and her family as they cleaned their old house thoroughly, carefully packing all their belongings and readying for the move.

One of the first tasks was to hastily plant a garden at the new farm. Travis Olmstead kindly decided that the last chore for his old tractor was to be the plowing of a garden plot for the Brooks family. He then happily turned the old piece of equipment over to its new owners, the Brooks.

The entire Brooks family set aside a Tuesday evening for planting. Mom and Carrie prepared and packed a meal to share with Travis that night. The old gentleman was touched by his new friends and ate heartily, commenting on how good it was to taste home cooking and enjoy conversation at mealtime. The kitchen table and a few chairs were some of the only pieces of furniture not yet moved to Travis' new apartment.

After dinner, Travis asked the family to come with him to the parlor, where he stopped in front of the old piano and gently laid his hand on the yellowed keys as he spoke, "Mrs. Brooks, do you play piano?" he asked.

"Well, I can play some," she admitted shyly.

"No one has played this since my wife Annie died." His gnarled hands lovingly stroked the beautiful instrument and for a moment he seemed transported back in time. His eyes were misty as he recalled the memories it stirred. "I bought this piano for Annie as a wedding present sixty-three years ago. She was quite a musician, my Annie. Times were kinda hard then, but I got it pretty reasonable. I bought it from the preacher and his wife. They were moving on and couldn't take it with them. I had it brought in here and surprised her with it when we moved in." He paused awhile, then added, "Now, I'm moving on and I can't take it with me so I'd like to give it back to the preacher and his wife." His usually gruff voice took on a tender note. "That is, if you'll have it. It's never been moved from this room since the day I brought it here and it seems like it belongs here. It's sort of a shame to move it now." He paused again and looked at Carrie's mother who was blinking back tears. "I'd like nothing better than for you to have it," he said.

"I'd be pleased to have this," Mom replied with a quiver of emotion in her voice. She reached out to touch the pretty wood, lovingly worn with years of careful polishing and joyful use. "It's beautiful," she said with deep sincerity.

"Well, sit down and play us a little tune," he suggested, breaking the silence after a moment. Mom carefully pulled out the piano stool and sat down. She gingerly touched a few keys, explaining that it had been a long time since she had played anything, but with a little coaxing, the gathered onlookers were able to persuade her to try a song. She opened the only book on the piano, an old, brown hymnal and after thumbing through its ragged pages, she chose number fifty-eight, "Great Is Thy Faithfulness." She played it through with a skill unharmed by years of little practice. Dad sang the words as Mom played on. The old piano was out of tune from long disuse but its chords rang clear and sweet and the instrument had the promise of fine quality within its tones.

At the closing notes of the hymn Dad saw Travis gazing heavenward with tears in his eyes. All fell silent for a time, then the older man began to speak, "I'd forgotten that old song", he said. His voice caught a little in his throat as he went on, "They played that song at our wedding. Annie used to love it. We never missed church, you know. We always went every Sunday, but after she died…" his voice trailed off for a moment. "I didn't go back. I suppose I was disappointed with God." His eyes dropped, as if he was ashamed. "Maybe it's long past time I went back. I probably wouldn't know a soul there anymore," he said. "But you folks have been so good and kind to me, it sorta restores my faith in God."

Carrie was blinking back tears now as she thought of this gentle old man alone for so many years, avoiding the God he so desperately needed. Dad laid a hand on Travis' shoulder and spoke with sincerity, "You'd be welcome at our church any time, Travis. I hope we'll see you there soon."

"And we want you to feel welcome to come back here and visit your home anytime," Mom added.

"Thank you," was his reply. "You've given an old man a lot of happiness," he said with a smile. "Now let's get at that garden!" he exclaimed, as if he suddenly had all the vigor of youth returning to him.

By sunset, the five workers had most of the large garden planted. Travis stood again on the west porch and waved a pleasant goodbye as the Brooks' van pulled slowly out of the drive. Carrie thought Travis seemed different now. She was sure she saw a hope in his eyes that hadn't been there before. It was marvelous the way surrendering to God could change a person's outlook. Carrie had experienced that firsthand. She made a promise to include Travis Olmstead in her prayers too.

A few days later on a Friday morning, Mom presented Carrie with some good news. Luke had left a few hours earlier in order to make it to Blooming Hills in time to be of assistance with the truck going to Farmer's Market. With Dad already headed off to the hardware, it was just Mom, Carrie and Addy left in the kitchen. While they were cleaning up after breakfast Mom asked Carrie with a smile, "How would you like to work on that promise I made to you a few weeks back?"

"What promise?" Carried questioned.

"Remember I told you we'd work on getting some new dresses for you?"

"Yes," Carrie replied, brightening at the thought.

"Well, it's only about a week until we actually move and I can't do any more packing until the last minute anyway, so I thought we could go shopping today in Blue Creek. That is, if you want to," Mom finished with a teasing twinkle in her eyes.

"Great, Mom! But can we afford it? I mean, especially right now with the new house and all?"

"Yes, Carrie. Here's what I have in mind. I thought we could go to the thrift shops and maybe to a few garage sales. Then if we can't get enough nice, quality things, we'll go look for fabric and buy enough material to sew up some dresses ourselves."

"I think that's a great idea, Mom. When will we leave?"

"As soon as you can get ready and the babysitter gets here, dear. I already arranged for Jenny Cox to watch Addy for us all day so we can really do some shopping. Jenny has offered several times and so I finally decided to take her up on it. I thought we'd go to Farmer's Market too since this is Luke's first day there. Then we'll meet Dad for lunch about noon, ok?"

"Mom, I'm so excited!" Carrie exclaimed. "I'll get ready this minute!" Carrie flung the dish towel over the drying bar and hurried off to finish combing her hair. By the time she had come back downstairs, Mom was ready and Jenny Cox had already arrived. Mom kissed Addy good-bye and left a few final instructions with Jenny and they were off.

Carrie could hardly contain her excitement while they rode to Blue Creek. Mom had wisely brought along a copy of the Blue Creek Herald with all the Friday garage sales circled in red ink.

"Carrie, there's a newspaper in the back seat; will you get it?" Carrie turned to the backseat and reached for the paper. "Look in the classified section. I circled several garage sales I thought we might check out. Check the addresses and tell me if there's any on Highway 80 before we get into town."

Carrie read the circled ads diligently but replied that all seemed to be city addresses. As they continued to ride along toward Blue Creek, Carrie's mind was filled with hopes of finding some new clothes. Her mother changed her train of thought completely with her next statement.

"Carrie, I forgot to tell you that Dad said you and I should be thinking about some of the color schemes we'd like for the different rooms at the new house. He can get the employee discount at the hardware and so we might as well paint or wallpaper as many rooms as we can. He's given me a decorating budget and the less we have to spend on each room, the more rooms we can finish this year."

"What a neat idea, Mom! I didn't know we'd be able to do anything like that so soon." Carrie was so pleased to discover that some of the rooms could get a fresh facelift for she had been decorating and re-decorating the rooms at Travis Olmstead's old house in her mind ever since she first saw the place. Even though she loved the place as it was, she could envision its splendor if it only had a woman's touch. "I've got a lot of ideas already, Mom. I've been thinking about my room, of course. Is that selfish?" Carrie stopped and looked at her mother thoughtfully.

"No, Carrie, I don't think it is," Mom replied, "In fact, Dad and I decided that it's best to first paint and fix the rooms that you and Luke will have since you're getting to the age where you may not be at home for too many more years. We want you to have as much enjoyment as possible out of your new home."

"Thanks, Mom." Carrie replied.

"Speaking of leaving home, Carrie, I was wondering if you've thought anymore about what God is calling you to do after high school?" Mom asked seriously.

"Not really, Mom. I've been praying about my future like you asked me to, but I don't think God has shown me any definite direction yet." Carrie answered honestly.

Mom nodded thoughtfully. "Well, there's no need to feel pressured dear. You're still young. It's wise to pray and seek God's direction at your age, but it's not uncommon to be undecided. I didn't pray much about my future when I was a young woman. You've heard me say how it was for me growing up."

Carrie nodded as her mother continued. "Even though we went to church regularly we didn't give much thought to including God in our decisions. It was very different from the way you're growing up. Dad and I want things to be different for you and Luke and Addy. We've accepted Jesus as our Savior and Lord and that means we live differently. It's more than just attending church; it's a lifestyle."

"I understand, Mom," Carrie agreed.

"I'd have been able to make better decisions if I had prayed about them first, Carrie. I don't mean to say my life has been bad or anything like that. It hasn't. It's just that I could have made some wiser choices and avoided mistakes had I been seeking God's will instead of just my own. It's a wonderful feeling to know you're in God's will. It gives a person such a peace and sense of security-- much better than floundering around depending only on yourself. Do you understand what I mean?"

"Yes, I think so," Carrie answered.

"But I do think there's too much emphasis put on trying to

do something immediately after high school anyway. It's not that necessary to have everything all planned out at the tender age of eighteen," Mom said, her eyes twinkling. "And besides, Dad and I want you to know that you'll always have a home with us as long as you want. Just because high school gets over doesn't mean you have to leave home. Your father and I actually prefer the thought of you staying home with us until God calls you on to something else-- maybe marriage, maybe some kind of ministry." Mom glanced at her daughter who seemed to be listening intently. " I just thought if you were sensing any direction, maybe we could tailor some of your home school classes to fit what you'd like to pursue. Does that seem good to you, Carrie?"

"Yes, it really does, Mom. It fits just what's in my heart." Carrie was glad, actually relieved, to find out that Mom and Dad felt the same way about her future that she did. It took a great burden off her shoulders to know that her parents meant to guide and protect her. She wondered how other girls who didn't come from a Christian home must feel. There must be so many decisions to make so quickly. How could anyone make good choices when they had to make them hastily? Maybe that's why so many young people went to college straight out of high school, then dropped out a year later. And what about those who married and were divorced in such a short time? Yes, it was all beginning to make sense, Carrie thought. Without God, your future was uncertain at best. And for a girl, without your parent's leadership and protection, life could be filled with extra pressure and uncertainty. Carrie silently thanked God for such loving parents.

"Mom, courtship, the way our family defines it, really fits in with this, doesn't it?" Carrie asked after a pause.

"Well, yes, I believe that's exactly the case. You are not on your own; you're part of a loving family that's looking out for your best interests and praying with you, trying to discern God's will for your life instead of pushing you out of the nest. And that certainly includes praying about a husband."

Carrie looked out at the many pretty farms passing by her window and was silent as these thoughts sank deep in her mind and heart. The conversation ended for several minutes until the two women reached the outskirts of Blue Creek.

"Let's go to a few sales before we go to Farmer's Market." Mom suggested. "Where's the first one?"

Carrie scanned the page and her finger stopped at one listed on the north side of town that had advertised, NICE CLEAN CLOTHES. "Let's try this one on Farmington Avenue first," Carrie suggested. "102 Farmington Avenue is the address."

Chris drove a few blocks until they found the right street and then they hunted for the one hundred block. Carried spotted the house first and directed her mother to the correct place.

As they parked and walked up the driveway, much to Carrie's delight, she saw several racks of clothes neatly hung along one end of the garage. A pleasant looking woman was receiving money from some previous customers as Mom and Carrie walked in.

Carrie and her mother began looking through the racks of hanging dresses and skirts. Carrie noticed a pretty pink dress in her size with a price tag of $3.00. Mom looked it over carefully and checked for tears and stains. They decided it would be a good buy and moved on to the other clothes on the rack. Soon Mom came across another dress in the same size. It was a pretty, soft brown floral print with ruffles. Carrie's eyes lit up immediately as she pulled the dress from the rack and examined it closely. It too had a price of $3.00.

"May I get this one too, Mom?" she asked.

"Yes, I think that's exactly what we're looking for," Mom smiled. As she continued to search the racks she also found two skirts in Carrie's size and a blouse to match both of them. The two women agreed that they had better take these as well.

When they went to the table to pay for the clothes, a friendly woman greeted them. "Hi! Is this all today?" she asked as she totaled the purchases.

"Yes. I think so." Mom answered, "We're so pleased to find these things for my daughter," she said, turning to indicate she was speaking of Carrie. "She's really in need of dresses and skirts and these are just her size."

"How old are you?" the woman asked Carrie.

"I just turned sixteen," Carrie replied politely.

"Is that right?" the woman said with a smile, "My daughter turned sixteen just a few months ago. The clothes were hers. I wish you could meet her. We just moved here from out of state and I'm hoping she can meet some girls her age."

Mom smiled pleasantly as the woman continued, "My

husband's company transferred him to the new Arlington Plant in Blue Creek. We've lived here for about six weeks, but it's been a little hard to meet people since we home school and our children don't attend the Blue Creek schools."

Mom and Carrie both looked very surprised and smiled enthusiastically at this bit of news. "Are you serious?" was Mom's surprised reaction. "We home school also! Welcome to the area!" At this, the woman's expression changed to one of happiness and excitement. "I'm so glad to meet you," Mom went on, "Let me introduce myself. I'm Chris Brooks and this is my daughter Carrie. We're from Maplecrest, about ten miles north." She went on to tell the names and ages of the other Brooks children.

"Well, let me introduce myself," the lady said, "I'm Sarah Melvin. My daughter that's about your age is Amanda," she informed Carrie. "We also have an older son in college in Texas. He's named, Trent, after his father. He's studying Bible because he hopes to be involved in the ministry and missions in some way. Our youngest is Paul. He's twelve." At this Carrie and Mom really began to feel a kinship with this new lady and from what she had told them it had become obvious that she and her family were Christians.

Mom spoke again, "He's interested in ministry? That's interesting. My husband is a pastor."

"Really?" Sarah asked. "What church does he pastor? We've been looking for a church but haven't settled on one yet!"

"He's pastor at Maplewood Christian Fellowship. It's about five miles from Maplecrest, out in the country on County Road 65. Actually it's located about halfway between Maplecrest and Homewood and that's why it's called Maplewood. We'd love to have you visit," she said warmly. Sarah Melvin looked very interested as Mom went on. "There are several families from Blue Creek that attend there. There are also several home school families."

"I don't believe we've heard of your church yet," Sarah said. "We've not met any other home school families yet, either," she added. "Actually we've only been to two different churches because the move has been so hectic. We went to the same two churches twice each and then missed two Sundays as well. That's the reason for this garage sale-the fact that we had sort of a quick move, I mean. Once I found out we were moving, there wasn't even time to clean closets or anything. We packed in such a hurry. When we started settling in and putting things back in closets we discovered we'd outgrown some items."

"I'm so glad you had these things for sale just when we needed them," Carrie said.

"And I'm glad we met you," Mom continued. "Please do come to visit our church as soon as possible; and by the way, there's a very active home school group called "Fellowship of Christian Home Schools" in the area. We refer to it as "FCH." The activities are over for this school year, but we'll be having a planning meeting in August for the upcoming year. You'd be more than welcome to attend."

"I'd love to get involved in something like that," Sarah beamed, "And I hope we'll see each other again."

"I do too," Mom replied, "My husband's name is Roger Brooks. If there's anything we can do to help you settle in, please give us a call. We'll be moving to a new house ourselves in just two weeks, but we'll still be in the Maplecrest listings--the phone number won't change. I know already how much is involved in just moving across town. I can't imagine how you feel moving out of state!"

"Actually I have been sort of lonely," Sarah said in a more serious tone. "It's so far from family and we left a lot of lifetime friends back in California. It's a funny feeling not to be able to pick up the phone and call someone you know that's close by. And with Trent off at his first year of Bible college, I feel like we're scattered all over. But it was a real career promotion for my husband and we do like this area so far."

"I've never experienced anything like you're describing before," Mom said sympathetically. "I hope you won't feel lonely anymore," she went on. "Now that we've met, you can call us anytime and we'll introduce you to a lot of other families you'll really enjoy. Let me just write our phone number down for you," Mom said as she pulled a slip of paper and pen from her purse.

"I'm so thankful! I think the Lord ordained our meeting today," Sarah said with heartfelt gratitude. "And I want you and Amanda to meet as soon as possible," she added, directing her comment to Carrie. "She's gone to the Farmer's Market to apply for a job today. I'm so sorry you missed her."

"I'm sorry too," Carrie said genuinely. "I hope she'll find the job she's looking for, though," she added.

"She thought it might be a way to meet people and fill up her summer," Sarah said. "She's lonely too. It's been difficult for her and Paul. They left a lot of friends as well."

"Well, we're headed to Farmer's Market today too," Mom informed her. "It's a big place, but maybe we'll see her."

"She's a tall blonde," Sarah said, "and she's wearing a green blouse and a blue jean skirt. She has glasses and wears her hair like mine. Do introduce yourselves if you see her!"

"We will," Mom assured her as they started down the driveway toward their car. They waved good-bye to their new friend, Sarah.

After they were in the car, Carrie commented to her mother about the incident. "I feel like we've known her a long time, Mom. She was so easy to talk to and we only just met!"

"I know," Mom replied. "I think it's because we're Christians and so automatically there's a natural bond between us. Isn't it great the way God works?"

"Sure is!" Carrie agreed. "I hope we see her daughter at Farmer's Market today."

After stopping at two more garage sales that offered only partial success in the search for clothing, the two ladies decided it was time to head for Farmer's Market. Carrie felt a familiar wave of excitement wash over her as her mother turned the car from the side street where the last garage sale had been to the main thoroughfare of Blue Creek. She knew that Farmer's Market was on the south end of town near the city limits. Carrie had always loved going to the market since she was a little girl. The market was such an exciting place with so many things to see. For a moment she envied Luke who occasionally would be spending whole Fridays there this summer. Then she remembered her commitment to contentment and realized that actually she would see more of the market than her brother whose work would keep him near the Blooming Hills booths most of the time.

She felt a smile tugging at the corners of her mouth as she thought of what a great day it had already been. New clothes, time alone with her mother, new friends, and now Farmer's Market. What more could she ask for?

As they reached the outskirts of Blue Creek, the beckoning site of the Farmer's Market grounds came into view. Men with orange sticks were waving cars from the highway into the large parking areas. "Dad's going to meet us here for lunch in about an hour," Mom said, interrupting Carrie's thoughts. "We'll have quite a bit of shopping time before then if we get right at it. I thought we'd start on this end of the market and work the other way," she said, pointing out the directions as she pulled into a parking space. "We're eating at Golden Garden on the north end, so we'll start shopping at the south door, ok?"

"Oh, Mom!" Carrie replied excitedly. "Are we really going to Golden Garden?" Carrie's eyes lit up with anticipation as she thought of lunch at one of her favorite booths. Golden Garden was a large booth area offering Chinese cuisine. Carrie loved the food as well as the atmosphere. Amidst the country setting of the Farmer's Market, Golden Garden was uniquely decorated like an Oriental garden with a tiny waterfall, lovely exotic plants and Chinese lanterns. She had often remembered eating there with her family on market days.

As they stepped out of the car, Carrie drew a deep breath. She noticed the familiar smells, sights and sounds of this fascinating place. She saw people hurrying and scurrying everywhere. Some were customers eager for a bargain; others were vendors, eager for a sale. Enticing aromas filled the air, everything from doughnuts to pickles to sausage.

They walked along the rows of outdoor vendors, stopping occasionally to inspect their wares. Most were small farmers with only a truckload of produce to sell for the day. Carrie's mother picked up an occasional item to inspect the quality.

As she and her mother entered the main building, they were greeted with the familiar din of vendors yelling out prices and customers shuffling along. Once inside, Mom's first stop was at the booth of the cheese and sausage man who had a large chalkboard suspended over his meat case with the specials for the day. Most of the vendors inside had permanent booths that they kept year after year. These were the larger, more established businesses like Blooming Hills Orchards, Golden Garden and the Meat Market. Mom contemplated the selection only a moment before she had decided on a few pounds of fresh ground hamburger.

"May I help you, ma'am?" the clerk asked.

"Yes. I'd like three pounds of that burger if I may pick it up later when I'm ready to leave," Mom replied.

"Certainly, ma'am." He smiled broadly as he scooped up a generous portion and placed it in a red-checkered paper tray. After carefully weighing and re-adjusting it, he wrapped it in white paper, sealed it with tape, and marked the price. "And you are…?" he inquired as he prepared to mark her name on the package.

"Chris Brooks," she replied.

"Oh! I'm sorry I didn't recognize you. I guess I looked at your daughter and was thinking she was much younger. You have really changed since last summer, young lady," the kind gentleman said to Carrie. She smiled shyly. "You're much taller than I remember just last season. And, didn't you have a boy too, Mrs. Brooks?"

"Yes," Mom answered. "He's working for Blooming Hills this summer. We expect to see him here today. We also have a little girl named, Addy. She's just a year old; maybe you never met her."

"Well, I'll be!" the butcher exclaimed again. "They sure grow up fast."

"Well, thank you for holding my purchase," Mom said as she paid for the meat. "We must keep going since we've got a lot of shopping to do. It's nice to see you again."

"Good-bye and thank you! Good to see you again!" The man waved as they headed off to other booths.

Soon they were nearing the busy Blooming Hills booth that was really the size of three booths combined. Talented Alice Henderson had designed and painted a new sign that stretched the length of the counters and was beautiful as well as eye-catching. Alice's new baked goods and homemade fruit products were attracting a good deal of attention from shoppers at the far end of the counter. Beautiful cartons of berries filled the shelves along with other seasonal products around the remaining area.

Carrie immediately caught sight of Luke and Homer aboard the truck which was backed into the loading dock and brimming with lugs of fruit stacked higher than Homer's head. They had an assembly line of sorts going as they passed the fruit boxes to John Mark who was stocking and rearranging the shelves as customers carried the plump ruby-red strawberries away. They seemed to be very busy and Carrie tried to catch Luke's eye to wave but he never looked up from his work.

As Mom and Carrie passed the counters, John Mark was

placing a fresh box of berries out for sale. When he saw them, he smiled his familiar pleasant smile. He waited as Carrie and her mother made their way to the counter where he stood. "Good morning, Mrs. Brooks, Carrie," he said politely. "May I help you?"

"I think I'd like to have two quarts of these nice berries today," Mom answered.

"Yes, Ma'am," he said as he found a basket for them which would hold the two boxes. As Homer and Luke realized that their assembly line had come to a halt, they looked to see what had happened to John Mark. Luke waved proudly from the tailgate of the truck as he caught his mother's eye. Homer happily waved a hearty greeting to Carrie and Mrs. Brooks.

John Mark noticed Carrie's gaze as she waved to the boys on the truck. He calculated her expression and gestures carefully, unbeknownst to her. As she and her mother moved along to speak with Alice, he returned to his work but continued to investigate Homer's behavior for a clue to his friend's thoughts until Carrie and her mother were out of sight.

As they passed the Everly Farm Market booth, Carrie waved at Darla Harris who was busy waiting on customers. She knew they didn't have time to stop and chat even though Carrie would have liked to talk to Darla. After several more interesting booths and a few purchases, the ladies made their way to Golden Garden to meet Dad.

The typical noon-hour line was already forming at the cash register as busy workers brought steaming plates of food to the front of the counter. Dad was already there in line and motioned for them to join him. "Hi, ladies," he smiled as they approached.

"Hi," they chorused and then exchanged small talk of their purchases as the line moved forward.

"Why don't you give me your orders and go claim that table by the fountain?" Dad suggested with a wink. Mom and Carrie took his advice and hurried to the table by the pretty water garden. A large potted palm secluded the table from the market and the rest of the Golden Garden area. Carrie thought this was the most elegant dining spot in the whole market.

As they sat down, Mom said, "I think I'll run across the aisle to the booth that has the discount cards while we wait for Dad. Ok, dear?"

"Ok," Carrie replied, glad to rest a moment and watch all the people going by. While she waited for her mother to return, Carrie enjoyed the pretty sounds of the trickling fountain. From her secluded spot between the fronds of the big palm, she watched the other customers strolling by. Suddenly she noticed John Mark Henderson walking down one of the aisles. "It must be his turn for lunch," she thought. She knew that John Henderson allowed his workers to eat anywhere they wished during their day at Farmer's Market and as a fringe benefit, Blooming Hills paid for their meals.

As Carrie watched John Mark, she noticed that he seemed pre-occupied, almost nervous. "How very unlike him," she thought. "I wonder if there's anything wrong?" Carrie thought he seemed to be looking for something or someone. At one point she saw him look directly at her and she wondered if he could see her between the leaves of the huge palm tree. She felt instantly embarrassed and as soon as their eyes met she quickly looked down at the table, hoping if he had seen her that it wouldn't appear as if she had been slyly watching him. She felt the same awkward feeling she had felt that Sunday in church when John Mark and Kirk Davis had both offered her a bulletin at once. She hoped her mother would return soon but she didn't want to look up again to search for her in case John Mark was still looking her way.

Nervously, Carrie fidgeted with the tablecloth. In moments, Dad appeared with a large tray of steaming Oriental delicacies and Carrie felt very relieved. She occupied herself with helping him set the plates out. "Where's your Mom?" her father asked.

"Oh, she went over to look at the discount card booth. She said she'd be right back."

"Ok," Dad replied.

Carrie looked toward the booth. She saw that her Mom was headed back across the aisle to Golden Garden and John Mark was nowhere in sight. She began to feel more relaxed again. Mom returned and sat down next to Dad and they bowed their heads to pray before the meal.

Carrie and her mother filled Dad in on all the details of the morning including their new-found friends, the Melvins. Carrie was savoring a bite of the delicious egg roll when her father spoke, "Hey, John Mark, won't you join us?" Carrie swallowed hard and looked up to see John Mark Henderson standing, tray in hand, a few feet away, seeming to search for an empty seat amongst the crowded tables. Dad gestured broadly toward the unoccupied chair by Carrie.

"Here's an empty seat!" he offered.

Carrie glanced around and noticed that in the last several minutes while she had been busily engaged in the pleasant meal and conversation with her parents, the restaurant had really filled up. John Mark, who had decided on Golden Garden for lunch, suddenly found himself without a place to sit. Carrie barely looked up as he accepted her father's invitation and took the only seat left, the one right next to her.

He politely greeted Carrie and her mother for the second time that day. Then John Mark removed his baseball cap, bowed his head, and silently thanked God for his food. Carrie's mother felt a stir in her heart as she noticed the young man's reverence and was pleased at his obvious spiritual dedication. Carrie barely said a word for the rest of the meal and she picked at the remaining food, her appetite having left her. She felt unusually conscious of every move she made and it seemed it took extra effort to do everything from sipping her tea to tasting the cookies without fumbling clumsily.

Carrie was relieved that her parents and John Mark carried the conversation during lunch. She wondered why it seemed so difficult to join in. After all, this was only John Mark Henderson, an old friend and Eileen's brother! "Really, Carrie," she told herself, "you're being ridiculous." But the awkward feelings never left her during the rest of the meal until John Mark politely rose and excused himself saying he'd better hurry since Luke and Homer, who were covering for him, were waiting for their lunch breaks. As he cleared his tray from the table, he bid them each good-bye and Carrie managed to look up directly at him to give a polite reply.

"Well, are you two coming down to the store to choose some paint today as long as you're in town?" Dad asked after John Mark had gone.

"I thought we would," Mom replied with a smile. "Our other shopping has been so successful, we may as well continue!"

"Great," he said. "I'll see you there then." He rose and took his tray, but not before stooping to give his wife a quick kiss on the cheek and a soft, "I love you."

"How nice," Carrie thought. "Dad is always so polite to Mom and he doesn't mind showing affection."

"We'll be looking for items especially for Carrie's room today," Mom said to him before he left.

Dad winked at Carrie as he turned to leave and said, "Good, I'm glad. Don't forget to look for the manager; he'll give you a good deal!" With that, he left and Mom and Carrie gathered their packages and purses and set out to shop the remainder of the Farmer's Market.

As they strolled toward the end of the market, they again passed the large Blooming Hills booth, this time on the opposite side of the enormous aisle. Carrie noticed a girl who fit Amanda Melvin's description talking to Alice. Mom was looking at some homemade quilts at a booth a few feet back. By the time Carrie got through the crowd to tell her mother, she looked back only to see that the girl was already heading toward the large market entrance doors. "I guess if that was Amanda we'll have to meet her some other time," Carrie said disappointedly to her mom.

"Luke may have met her if she talked to Alice for any length of time," her mother assured her. "We'll find out."

As they neared the meat market, Carrie glanced back at the Blooming Hills counter to wave at her brother. Luke and Homer were hoisting empty boxes to John Mark, who was standing on the back of the large farm truck. From his bird's eye view, John Mark spotted Carrie as he turned to grab the next box. He smiled directly at her and gave a friendly wave. Luke turned and saw Carrie and his mother and waved a proud good-bye as they walked on.

Making a House a Home

Mom's statement that there would be many Farmers' Market Fridays this summer would prove to be true, but the next two Fridays, she and Carrie missed the market due to all the work involved in their move. Carrie was surprised at all that had to be done just to move one family across town. First there had been all the sorting and packing, now the work on the new house had begun. Many of the tasks fell to the two women during the day with Dad pastoring and working at the hardware and Luke at Blooming Hills for a couple of days each week.

As soon as Travis Olmstead was comfortably settled in his new apartment, Dad, Mom, Luke, and Carrie took every available moment to work at the new house. First everyone helped to wash all the walls and windows. Addy was the only Brooks not able to help out! Some of the girls from church took turns watching her so the family could work in the evenings.

Luke and Carrie became expert painters in a few short days with all the rooms that needed attention. Carrie helped Luke paint his room on one of his days off and together they were able to finish it in several hours. Chris and Carrie had chosen a plain off-white shade for Luke's walls. They planned to add color in the form of a bedspread, curtains, and carpet. Luke really was the typical boy and could care less about all the decorating. But he made a wonderful helper, since he was eager to finish and turn his attentions to outdoors projects on the farm.

Carrie had found some in-stock wallpaper at the Martinson hardware store and since it was from the previous season it had been marked, "Clearance." With Dad's employee discount, the cost was very economical. The only problem was there had not been enough for all the walls. Mom supplied the perfect idea when she suggested installing the paper on top of wainscoting. While Luke's room was under repair, Dad worked on installing the wainscoting in Carrie's bedroom. It was a pretty beaded wood that was finished at the top with an attractive chair rail. After it was all in place, they would paint it in the lovely shade of cream Carrie had chosen to match the paper.

Carrie was looking forward to learning the art of hanging wallpaper. She was so anxious to see her new room all finished. She had fallen in love with the paper at first sight. It was a beautiful summer green floral on a cream background. It reminded her of the subtle shades of her favorite flowers in May against a world bursting with green buds. She could imagine pretty lace curtains at the bay window, drifting in and out with a gentle breeze and a soft carpet beneath her feet, even a silky new bedspread with a lace flounce. But she knew some of these fancier finishing touches would have to be added a little at a time. Dad had even promised to build a seat in the bay window, an idea which Carrie thought was most romantic! She had dreams of lounging there with a favorite book, and leaning upon oodles of velvety cushions or sitting and looking out over the circle drive, waiting for someone to arrive...

It seemed to Carrie that things went a lot faster in the evenings when everyone was there to work together and Addy was well occupied and entertained. Many men from church had come to help in various ways and it had been a real blessing for the Brooks' family. This Saturday, a church workday had been scheduled for anyone who could participate.

Carrie was filled with anticipation at the thought of her girlfriends seeing her new room. In the days preceding Saturday, Carrie reminded herself not to be prideful about her beautiful new room when she knew that some of the girls were sharing smaller rooms with their sisters. They would love such a room as hers. "I don't think it's sinful pride," she finally determined, "I'm just so pleased to be moving here to a place that I love so much and I can't wait to share it with all my friends."

Saturday finally came and early in the morning the Brooks

family all headed across town to the new house. Each time they went there now, they took a load of items that they could temporarily do without to eliminate as much last minute moving as possible. Today's load had included a picnic table, coolers, card table, and lawn chairs, all necessary items for the dinner at noon. Luke was unloading the tables onto the lawn as a large truck from Blooming Hills, driven by Joe, turned into the driveway. He and John Mark were hauling some tables and chairs from the church fellowship hall. All the extra seating would be welcome at dinnertime.

Other cars and trucks soon followed and families of eager helpers streamed out in every direction. Carrie was glad to see the Melvin's arrive. The family had started attending MCF the Sunday after she and her mother had met Sarah Melvin at the garage sale. That was only a few weeks ago, but Carrie had introduced Amanda to other girls at church that first Sunday and with Amanda's friendly personality it seemed as if they had been friends forever. Pastor Stanford seemed to be the work foreman and was giving directions to folks and helping distribute supplies from inside the large barn where he was efficiently manning a table full of paint, rollers, brushes, hammers, and every imaginable tool. Carrie was amazed at how organized the whole event was. While she had been so absorbed in details and work on her room for the past few weeks, she had not realized the magnitude of this day and the planning that must have gone into it.

It was obvious by the turnout that the members of Maplewood Christian Fellowship had really outdone themselves in order to help their pastor and his family. Many of Carrie's friends were already there, but Eileen was still missing. Carrie felt reluctant to take the other girls up to see her room until Eileen arrived. It just seemed that Eileen should see it first since they were best friends.

Carrie stalled some of the other girls as long as possible. When she was about to run out of reasons not to take them to see her new room, she turned to head for the house where Mom would surely have a job waiting for her. Just then she heard John Mark calling her name. "Carrie!" he called from a distance, "Wait a minute," he continued as he trotted toward her. "Eileen told me to make you promise not to show your room to anyone else until she gets here," he said with his shy sideways grin, doing his best to imitate the intensity with which Eileen had delivered the instructions.

Carrie blushed seeing that John Mark was half embarrassed to have to relay this message but she also smiled, as she imagined Eileen's stern directive to her brother.

"She'll be coming at noon, Carrie. We'll all be back at noon. Dad says we're closing the orchards early today in order to get over here for at least the afternoon and evening." Carrie immediately realized this was a real sacrifice for the Henderson family on a Saturday in the peak of strawberry season.

"Good. That will be good," she nodded, "I mean we really appreciate the help." Carrie stammered uncomfortably, searching for the right words. John Mark walked a few steps backwards and looked down as he fumbled with his cap that he had removed when he walked up.

"I'll see you later," he said finally. Carrie thought something in the way he spoke sounded almost like a question. But he must not have meant it that way, she reasoned, because without waiting for an answer, he turned toward the circle drive where Joe was just coming around in the truck to pick him up. It seemed Joe never even rolled the big vehicle to a complete stop when John Mark hoisted himself adeptly up and into the passenger side.

Carrie noticed how the tall, athletic John Mark was really tanned from the farm work and today, seeing him sitting in the cab beside Joe, he seemed older and more mature than he ever had. Both fellows waved as they headed the vehicle back toward Blooming Hills but Carrie, although unconsciously, had returned her wave to only one.

Carrie had hoped fervently that the Hendersons would all be here to share the day and now it looked as if they would. Yet she was a bit uncomfortable around John Mark lately. For some reason, he seemed nervous around her too--more cautious with his words and shyer than usual. It made Carrie uneasy in return. She found herself having a hard time talking to John Mark for the first time in her life. She wondered why she felt this way yet she wondered if she was mistaken about his actions and had just imagined that he seemed different.

Carrie had to admit that she had begun wondering if John Mark could be the one she'd marry someday. As soon as the thought crossed her mind, she reprimanded herself for even thinking it. "I'm supposed to wait to be found," she thought, "not run ahead of God's plan."

"Carrie! Carrie!" Her mother's voice stunned her back from her daydreaming. "I've been looking all over the house for you. I was hoping you could assist Miss Winfield with the china cabinet."

"Oh, I'm sorry, Mom," Carrie blurted out as she realized she had been staring dreamily in the direction of the truck. She was aware of a half-smile on her face as soon as she heard her mother's voice and she wondered how long she had been standing at the edge of the driveway staring and day dreaming. How many others had noticed her? Quickly glancing to the right and the left, she saw that miraculously, no one was around except Mom. All the others were busy working on one project or another.

A wave of embarrassment engulfed Carrie. She looked down to conceal her face as she felt a blush rise slowly to her cheeks. Carrie was surprised at herself for letting her feelings, however mixed up and uncertain they seemed, show in such a large crowd of people. "Here I am standing and staring after a boy as if I had no sense!" she scolded herself, heading for the dining room as fast as possible.

Once in the tranquility of the dining room, Carrie found Miss Winfield busily unpacking dishes and wiping them off. Some of the other girls were helping her. "Oh, good, Carrie! You're here! We need you to tell us where the dishes should be placed in the cabinet," Miss Winfield said. "You do know how your mother had these arranged, don't you?"

"Yes," Carrie said as she selected a stack of plates that Grandma Brooks had given her mother. She began placing them neatly on the top shelf as all the other helpers continued to unpack.

Miss Winfield was talking cheerfully to the girls as she worked. She handled the precious dishes very carefully. As she read the manufacturer's locations on the backs of some of the older pieces, she nearly always had a story to tell of her travels to the different areas. Miss Winfield was truly an interesting person, Carrie thought. It seemed her missionary travels had taken her everywhere! Carrie listened to the stories with wonder and thought how appropriate it seemed for Miss Winfield to be in charge of unpacking the dishes. She was gentle and sweet, refined, proper yet full of colorful beauty, just like fine china. Carrie couldn't imagine her painting or hammering out there with the others.

In fact, Carrie could hardly imagine Miss Winfield ever being young. She was always dressed up in prim, starched blouses and well-tailored skirts. She must have always been this way; just the way Carrie knew her now. She had only known Miss Winfield's older years. "Miss Winfield would be a fine woman to model my life after," Carrie pondered as the older lady passed her a couple of china teacups made in England, another place which she had visited in her many travels.

Even as Carrie worked, she found herself glancing at the clock watching for noon. She inwardly reprimanded herself for thinking about John Mark Henderson's return. Or was it the fact that Eileen would be here at noon as well that she was really looking forward to? She wasn't sure. Her feelings seemed uncertain and all mixed up. She considered sharing this with Mom to get her advice as soon as the subject conveniently came up. But for now, she was determined to concentrate on the duties at hand and think no more of John Mark Henderson and his unusual behavior.

Near noon that day, the Hendersons arrived in two separate vehicles, with the farm trucks loaded with grills for the chicken dinner. Alice, her mother, Eileen, and Tommy came in their large van and soon began unloading fresh fruit pies Alice had baked that morning. Carrie watched the preparations with excitement from the dining room window.

The men quickly set up grills and Carrie could see her mother helping Joe carry large bowls of fresh chicken from the extra refrigerator in the back room to where the men were preparing to cook. Carrie had worked half the afternoon yesterday cutting and rinsing the enormous amount of chicken for the midday meal.

Soon Eileen burst excitedly into the dining room to find her best friend and request a tour of the new house. Seeing the girls' excitement, Miss Winfield kindly pronounced a short break time. Promptly Eileen and Carrie headed for the stairs followed closely by Alice, Amanda, and several other girls. When they all reached Carrie's new room, there was much chattering and excited talk as each girl exclaimed over the room and offered her congratulations to Carrie.

Soon the smell of grilled chicken wafted temptingly over the lawn signaling the start of dinnertime while a large array of salads, breads, pies, and cakes were lined up on a long table. Everyone gathered on the lawn and Pastor Stanford asked the blessing. Then the extensive line of workers formed to help themselves to the food. Carrie had been stationed at the end of the food table to fill cups of iced tea and punch out of gigantic coolers. She was glad for the job as it afforded her the opportunity to greet the many people who had come to help today.

As the helpers filed through the line, they quickly filled the tables and existing lawn chairs. Others sat on the grass with their plates in their laps or leaned against a shade tree here or there.

John Mark and Joe were two of the last people to get through the line. When they got to the drinks, Carrie filled a large glass of iced tea for each of them. Joe joined his wife, Katie, but John Mark lingered at the table.

"Carrie," he said and paused, "aren't you going to eat?"

"Yes, but I want to see that everyone gets all they need first," she answered with a shy smile.

John Mark looked around and studied the crowd for a moment. "I think they're all pretty well through the line," he said slowly. Carrie looked around and nodded in agreement. She waited for him to speak, not knowing why he was hesitating. "I thought I'd go eat up on the porch," John Mark said gesturing toward the house. "There's no chairs left anywhere else," he added. He looked at Carrie as if he expected her to know his thoughts. "Will you join me?" he finally asked after a long, uncomfortable silence.

"Uh...I suppose I could," Carrie stammered. She wondered if it was ok to sit with him for lunch. What would everyone think? "Or am I the only one 'thinking' anything?" she wondered. Carrie glanced around the lawn at all her friends. Her quick survey of the dinner guests proved that all the other girls were eating at a long table that was already full of people. They would never notice her absence.

"I'll wait for you," John Mark said in a rare and brave show of determination. He promptly turned and walked toward the porch.

Seeing no one else coming for food or drinks at the moment, Carrie drew several glasses of tea from the coolers to set out before she left her post. Just then Dad walked by and tapped her on the shoulder, "Why don't you get your meal and take a break? You've earned it!" he winked.

Her mother and Addy were dispersed among the crowd by now.

Luke was with some of his friends. With the family scattered, she saw no reason not to join John Mark on the front porch. After all, John Mark was just a friend, Eileen's brother, in fact. And if she really was not thinking of him as a boyfriend or future husband, then this would prove that she had really matured and was letting God lead any and all relationships, she reasoned.

So Carrie took a plate and began to walk by the food tables. But she suddenly realized that she was not even hungry for the sumptuous meal that had looked so delectable only thirty minutes ago. She went through the motions of preparing her plate but nothing looked appetizing now. She wondered what the problem was. "Grow up, Carrie," she scolded herself as she determined to be mature.

She walked to the porch where John Mark was sitting on one of the two patio chairs. He promptly stood when he saw her coming and politely pulled the other chair from its place at the far end of the porch.

"I made a little table," he said with his familiar grin. He had hauled two sawhorses from one end of the porch and balanced a wide board between them. Carrie smiled and put her plate down at one end. As soon as she sat down, he seated himself proudly at the makeshift table.

At the beginning of the meal, Carrie forced herself to speak to John Mark in a controlled, poised manner while inwardly her stomach quivered and she wondered if all eyes were on the two diners on the porch. She was glad at least that John Mark had chosen to locate the 'table' at the far end where the porch turned to wrap around the front of the house. Most of the others were seated out of sight over in the side yard. She needn't have worried, for everyone else was eating and chattering, paying little attention to them. Only a few little girls were sitting on the steps around the corner, laughing and playing 'tea party' with their food.

Carrie breathed a sigh of relief when she caught her father's eye as he glanced her way on his second trip through the food line. He smiled and waved rather knowingly at her.

"He sees me and approves!" Carrie thought. As she relaxed a little, she actually began to enjoy John Mark's company. She was surprised to find him so talkative. This was unlike him. In fact, she didn't think she'd ever heard him say so much at one time in all her life! And certainly her presence didn't seem to affect his appetite. He was heartily enjoying a plate heaping with food.

"Joe and I want to get started on the one barn roof this afternoon," he was saying to Carrie.

"Oh?" she replied. "I didn't know you knew how to roof," she said. Then she suddenly wondered if he might be embarrassed at her comment, thinking she didn't see him as very mature or capable.

But he only replied confidently, "Oh, sure. I've helped Dad many times with roofs. With a farm as big as ours there's always one building or another needing something."

John Mark went on to tell Carrie how he enjoyed working on carpentry projects. Much pleasant conversation followed. Carrie was impressed to hear him talk about his plans for the next few years. "As much as I enjoy the farm, I want to really put my future in God's hands," he explained. "Dad says I'll always have a job on the farm if I want it, but I don't want to just do what's convenient; I want to be sure it's God's will."

Carrie listened intently to John Mark as he expressed his feelings with obvious sincerity. "I plan to spend a lot of time in the next two years praying about my future and trying to discern God's will." Carrie nodded with admiration. She could hardly believe the maturity of this young man sitting with her. He was so unlike some others her age. He seemed to really be confident and spiritually sensitive.

Carrie was enjoying the conversation when Luke and Kirk Davis came walking around the east side of the porch, past the innocent little 'tea party' chaperones on the steps. When Kirk caught sight of John Mark and Carrie, he grinned and elbowed Luke jestingly. The two strode up on the porch and Kirk gave John Mark a friendly slap on the back. "You better get over there for more pie before Luke and I get it all!" he joked.

Kirk was used to being the center of attention and it was obvious to John Mark that he wasn't going to let up with the teasing until he had thoroughly embarrassed them. Not wanting to make Carrie uncomfortable, John Mark quietly got up to follow Luke and Kirk to the dessert. "I better take these guys' advice and claim that pie," he said more to ease any awkwardness for Carrie than anything. "Excuse me, please," he said quietly to her as he rose to leave. "Can I get you anything?" he added quickly as the two other boys went down the steps.

"No, thank you. I'm done. I better be getting back to work," Carrie replied sweetly. But before she rose, she lingered for several minutes reviewing the pleasant conversation in her mind.

When evening shadows closed in around the farm, the families began to pack their cars and prepare to leave. It had been a wonderful day and much had been accomplished. The house was nearly in tip-top shape and the barns and grounds had received much-needed facelifts. Even with some work still to be finished, Carrie could hardly believe the change in the property after today's work.

At the end of the day, Pastor Stanford gathered everyone in the center of the circle drive for a few words and a closing prayer. He told everyone to join hands as he asked God to bless this new house and the family that would occupy it. As Pastor Stanford thanked everyone for coming, Carrie glanced around at the faces of those dear friends who had given of their time for her family. She caught John Mark looking in her direction from across the circle as Pastor Stanford spoke. He smiled a friendly smile directed just at her. She looked down and smiled and thanked God for this day.

Summer's End

The Saturday workday had been a great success. Much had been accomplished with many hands working together. Even though the Melvin's were so new to the church, they came to help, indicating their intentions to make MCF their home church. Carrie was glad for her new friendship with Amanda, even when she had first learned that Amanda had been hired as Alice Henderson's new helper, the job Carrie had dreamed of. Amanda knew right from the start that Carrie would probably be taking the job next season and it was all right with her since she too had other plans. Amanda wanted to become a nurse someday and was hoping to get a co-op position at the hospital in Blue Creek by next year to complement her education. She intended to enroll in the pre-nursing classes at the community college in Blue Creek. It seemed God had worked out this arrangement with the Blooming Hills Bakery job right from the start. The way things were coming together; it was benefiting everyone, Alice, Amanda, and Carrie. There was no room for jealousy or hurt feelings since the girls realized God was working these details out for everyone's good. Amanda needed the job for just one summer, and Alice needed the help for the same amount of time! So Amanda was welcomed into the little circle of friends that included Eileen, Alice, and Carrie.

"What a wonderful blessing to have a close group of friends," Carrie thought one evening as she stood in front of her mirror in her new room, combing her hair into the new, more mature style she had been wearing on Sundays for the past several weeks. She was thinking about all the great times she and her friends had had this summer. Carrie thanked God for the new clothes she was wearing, clothes that had seemed to be such an impossibility back in May.

She also thanked God for her beautiful new room, the room that she would never have enjoyed if she had been given a choice about the move originally. "I'm thankful You have better plans for us than we sometimes have for ourselves, Lord," she prayed, acknowledging that this had been the most enjoyable summer of her life. She realized that all things had worked together for good to her this summer just like the Bible promised in Romans.

Carrie had learned that the summer could be wonderful even if she didn't have a job. In fact, she had been a big help to her mother in many ways. The two women had managed a large garden even in spite of the move to the farm. She had learned to make jams and jellies and how to can the fruits and vegetables for the family's winter meals. Truly it had been a fun summer for Carrie and a time to mature as well. Working diligently with her mother, she had gotten a good start on learning all the womanly skills involved in managing a home. Now with the beginning of school only a few days away for most of the home school families, last minute planning and book ordering had to be done.

Tonight was the annual FCH yearly planning meeting that was always held on the last Friday of August. A carry-in dinner was to start at six o'clock in the fellowship hall of Christian Assembly, a large church in Blue Creek. Carrie smoothed the folds in the skirt of her new dress as she checked herself in the mirror. She had a sense of serene accomplishment about this garment since she had made it herself this summer, a task she wouldn't have been able to handle even months ago. "It really feels good to be able to sew and take responsibility for my own wardrobe," she pondered. She was learning to see fabrics as potential garments and gaining a sense of economy and style as well. She smiled at the thought that this new dress had only cost around ten dollars. She remembered how the woman in Proverbs 31 was described as being "clothed with scarlet" and that "her husband has no need of spoil." Apparently that woman knew how to make her own clothes economically too!

Carrie had always loved to sew things for her dolls and make simple skirts for herself. But this summer she had been able to learn some finer techniques of tailoring from her mother, an accomplished seamstress. The well-dressed Miss Winfield would trust her dressmaking and altering to no one but Chris Brooks. Now, Carrie had learned many of her mother's sewing skills until Mom declared that at times she was sure her daughter was passing her in many of the finer techniques.

"As soon as Luke and Dad arrive from work, we'll be almost ready to go," Carrie thought as she hurried to finish pinning her hair in place. She attached a brown velvet bow beneath the neat braided bun; a bow she had made to match the plaid tones in the new dress.

A hint of fall was in the air now as a cool late summer breeze floated in her bay window. As Carrie glanced outdoors, the gentle breeze blowing over the rolling hills and the faded look of the garden at the west edge of the property seemed to speak of the end of the summer season. She knew the start of school was just around the corner and she was glad that she would soon be opening her familiar books.

Carrie sat at the pretty, cushioned window seat as she put on her shoes. Soon she saw her father and Luke turning into the driveway as they arrived from their jobs. She smiled contentedly as she thought how pleasant it was to be a keeper at home with Mom and Addy and to greet her father and brother at the end of the day. "I guess there's other summers for jobs," she told herself. "This is really the way I want to live my life though," she thought. "Staying home, cooking and sewing, greeting someone I love at the end of the day," she whispered, "I'm glad I was home this summer so I could discover the fun of homemaking. I might never have known that that's what I really wanted in life if Mom and Dad had just let me go my own way. Thank you, Lord for working things out just right." She breathed a sigh of happiness with her prayer, but as often occurred, a twinge of concern followed in her thoughts. "Is being a wife and mother and homemaker what God has planned for me? Maybe He has other plans. What about the need for missionaries like Miss Winfield?"

After a few minutes lost in her anxious thoughts, Carrie remembered to cast this care upon the Lord as she had been learning to do. This was only one of the valuable lessons she had learned this summer. After a quick prayer, she hurried downstairs where the rest of the family was gathering and taking care of last minute preparations for the meeting.

Carrie was quite excited to be going this evening and renewing old friendships for the school year. A lot of business and planning for the year's activities would take place tonight. She would probably see friends she hadn't seen all summer.

Carrie greeted her father as she passed the office. Dad was reviewing the messages on his desk. Luke was already in the shower and Mom and Addy were both ready to go. Carrie checked her casserole and turned the oven off. She was pleased with its appearance and delectable aroma. Two beautiful pies, one blueberry and one cherry; waited on the screened-in back porch.

Carrie began to pack the picnic basket with the family's dishes and food. Soon everyone was ready to go and the family headed for Blue Creek, enjoying pleasant conversation about everyone's day while they drove.

Once at the church, Luke and Carrie were having a great time seeing all their friends again and chattering about their summer vacations in the minutes preceding the meal. Carrie commented to Luke that it seemed like most of the families were in attendance tonight with a few new ones as well. With that kind of attendance for a planning meeting, it promised to be an exciting year.

Carrie was gathered in a chattering group of friends including her brother and Eileen, Darla and Tom, Amanda, Homer and John Mark when last year's board president, John Henderson, rapped on the podium for attention. "Welcome, everyone!" he said, "May we have silence while we have a word of prayer for the meal?" He called one of the fathers up to the microphone to ask the blessing. Then John gave directions for the food line and asked everyone to move through the line quickly so that the business meeting would begin no later than seven p.m. With that, everyone joined their families and moved through the lines.

Promptly at seven, John Henderson again rapped on the podium for silence and asked God's blessing on the upcoming meeting.

Luke and Carrie listened patiently through several reports from last year's committee members. They were anxious to hear Mr. Henderson announce the new business for the year. Finally, the time arrived and the first item on the agenda was the selection of board members. After that voting was through, the Student Activities Committee would be chosen. At the close of the board nominations and voting, a short break was given while the board members tallied the results.

Soon it was announced that all the board positions remained the same for this year. A round of applause followed and John Henderson announced that nominations were open for the Activities Committee. Only senior high students could nominate and vote on these positions according to the FCH constitution, the committee being comprised of senior high students only. The seven students with the most votes would be the winners.

A few minutes were allowed for voting and then the ushers for the evening collected the ballots. During the counting, two officers from last year's student committee gave year-end reports. John Mark passed by the Brooks' family table to collect Luke and Carrie's votes and votes from the Taylor family who were also seated with them.

Out of the corner of her eye, Carrie's mother noticed John Mark's polite demeanor as he patiently waited for one of the Taylors to finish writing. Mom glanced occasionally at John Mark and wondered if it was only her imagination that made it appear that he was gazing at an unsuspecting Carrie the whole time.

Eventually the Taylor boy finished writing and dropped his ballot in the offering plate. John Mark went on to another table. On his way back to return the ballots to the secretary, Homer, one of the other ushers, stopped quickly and whispered something to Carrie. Mom remembered with pleasure her days as a teenager, all the fun and friends and somehow she wished she could have heard what Homer said.

After the votes were counted, John Henderson announced the results. "This year's Student Activities Committee will consist of the following seven students." Carrie looked around and noticed the looks of anticipation on the faces of several friends as they listened intently to the list. "Homer Martinson." A smattering of applause and whispering swept the room. John held his hand up for silence and said, "Please hold your applause." He smiled and went on. "Timothy Cox, John Mark Henderson..." At this Carrie glanced at John Mark who sat with his arms leaned on the table and his head lowered shyly, smiling his typical sideways grin. Homer, on the other hand, was shaking hands with a friend at the table behind him.   "Carrie Brooks, Luke Brooks, Eileen Henderson, and Tom Harris. Congratulations students," he said with a smile. "Your first committee meeting is scheduled for next Friday evening at seven o'clock at Maplewood Christian Fellowship Church. Last year's adult sponsor, Evelyn Cox, will preside over the first meeting and assist you in choosing officers and a new sponsor."

Carrie was overwhelmed with surprise and wondered if she had only imagined hearing her name being read. But a quick glance at her mother disclosed otherwise as Mom beamed a congratulatory smile. Carrie sat stunned but smiling at the news. Luke shared her surprise but was a bit more vocal as Tom Harris, seated a few feet in front of Luke, leaned back on the legs of his chair and slapped hands with Luke in a gesture of triumph. Carrie was pleased but slightly embarrassed, feeling many eyes were on her also. She caught a glimpse of Darla who sat quietly at the next table with her family. The look on Darla's face spelled disappointment, Carrie discerned, yet Darla was bravely trying to conceal it as her younger brother enjoyed his victory.

For once, it seemed that the talkative Darla had nothing to say. Carrie felt sorry for her. It was true that Darla was always loud and somewhat forward. "But on the other hand," Carrie thought, "she seems to need attention and she thrives on being in the spotlight. How hard it must be for her to watch her brother and Luke and Eileen accept a position usually awarded to the older students."

It was unusual for three younger students to receive this honor. Carrie was especially pleased for her brother and her friend, Eileen. "It shows that other students respect their level-headed maturity; what an honor!" she thought. Yet her own election amazed her. "I'm not popular or outgoing," Carrie reasoned, "How could this have happened?" Still she was pleased at the thought of being on the committee with such a great group of students.

Carrie's thoughts were interrupted at the sound of Mr. Henderson's voice, "Thank you all for coming tonight. We are looking forward to a great year with the Lord's blessings." He dismissed with last minute announcements and prayer. As the families began to get up from the tables, Carrie still felt shocked and it seemed to take her forever to stand. In her stomach, she felt an excited shakiness and hoped the feeling would soon pass. Within minutes she was surrounded by friends who were congratulating her and before long it seemed the whole Activities Committee had gravitated toward the center of the room where the Brooks' and Harris' tables were.

Much excited discussion was going on with Homer at the center of it all. He heartily congratulated Carrie and all his fellow committee members with enthusiasm. John Mark smiled at Carrie with a look that said, "Congratulations!" which she promptly returned. Darla, for whom this must have been most unpleasant, managed a sweet smile and congratulatory words for Carrie and the others. To Carrie it seemed this was a real step of maturity for Darla and for the first time she actually showed a poise and grace previously foreign to her behavior.

On the way home in the dark back seat of the family van, Carrie rode silently, leaning against the window and watching the beautiful stars appearing one by one out of the late dusk. Luke dominated most of the conversation as he talked endlessly of plans and ideas for the school year. Carrie was smiling to herself, a smile the rest of the family didn't even notice as she happily thanked God for what she believed was going to be the best school year of her life.

School Days

As the summer swiftly rolled into fall, Carrie observed all the changes around her. The days were noticeably shorter. With each passing day, less produce came from the garden. Tall, stately Queen Anne's Lace flowers gently waved their heads in the early fall breeze, lining the road in front of the house and nodding lazily along the fences in the pasture. The emerald greens and vivid hues of summer foliage and flowers gave way to the muted and dusty shades of fall. The house and barns had been completely painted now and their fresh, clean colors offered a stark contrast to the fading landscape all around. A few ruby-red tomatoes still clung to their vines and scattered pumpkins and squash were now making their debut. School had begun and Carrie was enjoying her studies more than ever. Luke was already deep into his science book as well as other subjects. All was going well for the Brooks students.

A few weeks before, the first planning meeting of the Student Activities Committee had been held. Homer had been elected president, to no one's surprise. However, being a junior, he refused to accept and suggested that Timothy Cox, who had been elected vice-president take the position instead. Timothy insisted he would only accept if Homer took the vice-presidency. Timothy had described it as an Aaron and Moses relationship since everyone knew that Homer was the obvious public speaker and had the personality for that portion of the duties. All the committee members and the sponsors agreed and so the arrangement was made official with a vote of the members.

Carrie, the group's new secretary, recorded the minutes and the vote in her official notebook. Everyone had agreed that Carrie was organized and well able to handle the SAC records and correspondence. John Mark was chosen to serve as treasurer, which was an obvious compliment to his factual, trustworthy nature.

That first meeting had been a buzz of excitement and plans, everyone bursting with new ideas. Evelyn Cox had been the group's adult advisor for two years now and she wished to step down. So the members of the SAC unanimously voted to replace her with Miss Eleanor Winfield. Miss Winfield happily accepted the position when she was approached with the request. Even though she had no children of her own, she was very interested in the young people and their activities and was quite liked and respected by them. It had been Carrie's suggestion to include her and a fine one it was. However, Miss Winfield agreed to the position only if she could have assistants and she suggested that they be Roger and Chris Brooks.

At first, Dad had been reluctant to accept since his two jobs already kept him so busy. He finally accepted when Luke prodded him with the thought that there would be Mom and Miss Winfield as well and he probably wouldn't have much to oversee with their capable help.

Many activities had already been planned for the school year. One of the largest events was to be the Spring Science Fair, Luke's idea. Miss Winfield had suggested a career day with a missions emphasis that was to be held in November. Numerous field trips and programs were scheduled as well.

After the second meeting in early October, the year's events were clearly etched in the calendar. But of all the exciting events that were scheduled, Carrie found herself anticipating one far above all the others. Her father had come to the second meeting with a folder of flyers and information regarding a youth character training seminar. The teachers were a husband and wife team and their three children from another state who traveled the country teaching about Christian family living and godly relationships.

At the October meeting, Dad had encouraged the committee with his recommendation. "I have a burden on my heart for young people in this generation," he began, "and so because of this I wish to make a suggestion for this committee to consider. I have some information on a family ministry that teaches about character and relationships from a Christian perspective. I'd like to see us invite this family to do a three-day seminar in late March, if that's agreeable to you."

Miss Winfield nodded in approval as Dad passed a few leaflets to Timothy to circulate around the table. "Having attended some teaching sessions from this ministry several years ago, I can personally recommend this seminar. The Holcombs brought fresh insight that eventually revolutionized my thinking on some issues. I believe them to be scripturally sound as well."

The committee members looked with interest at the information. "I thought it would be nice if FCH took an active part in sponsoring this event since so many youth would be reached this way. Even if you're not interested, I believe I will recommend to our elders at church to sponsor this event once again. I just thought this group would be an obvious co-sponsor. I would have offered to include First Christian Church as well if there would have been a pastor in place."

First Church was still without a pastor and the gentleman presently serving in an interim position was scheduled to move on by Christmas. The long drawn out pastoral search was a growing concern at First Church as it seemed to be unusually difficult to find a suitable replacement for Pastor Keene. Some of the members were becoming disheartened and as a pastor himself, Dad realized it was not the time to further burden the elders with extra decisions.

"Possibly we could include First Church by using their building on Saturday for the seminar. I am suggesting that we have the first few sessions of teaching during Friday classes, then some more sessions on Friday night, and all day Saturday. Then the father, Gary Holcomb, will bring the message at our church on Sunday morning. Does this sound like something the SAC would like to sponsor and take part in?"

Miss Winfield was the first to speak, "I heartily recommend we take Pastor Brooks' suggestion. I feel this is an area where training and information is much needed by our local families. It is obvious that by FCH helping to sponsor this event more teens will be made aware of these character classes."

Carrie understood what Miss Winfield meant. It was widely known that many of the young people were already paired off in dating relationships, even with others who were not Christians. Some parents were expressing concern for some teaching concerning relationships and how to follow God's leading in finding a future mate.

Even though Carrie knew clearly where her parents stood on this issue, she was curious to hear this couple explain the concept and ways to live out a courtship arrangement that would honor God. Still, Carrie felt a little embarrassed as her father presented the idea. She felt herself blushing a bit and hastened to lower her eyes, busying herself with her secretarial notes. She thought she detected slight embarrassment and reluctance to talk about the subject on the part of some of the others as well. All the committee members respected her father's suggestion though and decided to schedule the seminar for the third week in March.

After some other planning and general discussion, the committee's attention turned to classes that the group would offer for the year. It had been an FCH tradition for the past five years to conduct classes once a week at one of the local churches. The committee decided to schedule the classes for Fridays this year as attendance had been down last year. Last year the classes had been held on Monday and that was thought to be a probable cause for the lack of participation. Many suggestions were given and it was finally decided to run four classes each Friday beginning in November and lasting through April.

Parents had volunteered to teach Spanish, Art, Music, and State History. A special Home Economics class would also be offered by Alice Henderson. Carrie was given the job of coordinating the time slots and confirming the teachers. A list of costs and supplies for each class was to be typed up and entered in the FCH newsletter by next week.

After a word of prayer, the meeting was adjourned and refreshments followed. "We have cookies and drinks to enjoy this evening," Miss Winfield announced after the business meeting was over. "Carrie was kind enough to volunteer to provide refreshments for us, so let's all remember to thank her. This caught Carrie off guard and she felt her face color again as she politely accepted the thanks of her friends, excusing herself to the kitchen to help serve the items.

As she placed the large sugar cookies on plates, her fingers fumbled and she felt rather clumsy from embarrassment. Although she was well liked by others, Carrie's shy personality often made her feel awkward in public situations and she hoped, that with age, determination, and God's help, she would be able to improve on that. Her mother often encouraged her to participate in group situations in order to gain poise and combat the shyness that seemed to hinder her.

Everyone on the committee enjoyed the cookies immensely and each thanked Carrie as they left. Carrie and her family locked the church after the last committee members had gone.

On the way home, Addy drifted off to sleep almost instantly, being tired from the activity of the evening and all the playful attention she had received. Carrie dreamed quietly about all the upcoming events, especially the courtship teachings, although the missionary conference and career day captured her thoughts as well. The rest of the family was quiet during the drive home. Dad had a praise tape playing and everyone was enjoying the music. Carrie drifted off to sleep in the car, but her last thoughts were happy ones as she remembered the sincere look of admiration on one young man's face this evening. He had waited until she was alone to compliment her on the sugar cookies she had made.

With the arrival of November came the anticipation of the Career and Missionary Day. One of the Fridays had been set aside for this event. Miss Winfield, who had a real heart for missions, had been tireless in planning and organizing the day.

Luke and Carrie arrived at First Christian Church that day in the family van, driven by Carrie, the newly licensed driver. Much activity was already obvious as the parking lot hummed with people.

"I hope we're not late, Luke," Carrie said with a concerned look as she parked the vehicle. "We were supposed to be here early to set up. I had no idea so many people would be here already."

Luke glanced at his watch, "Nope. We're ok. Homer said for committee members to be here by nine a.m. and it's only eight forty-five." He looked around, surveying the parking lot and sizing up the situation. "Looks like only Homer's here ahead of us. All the rest of these people must be the speakers and missionaries."

Carrie breathed a sigh of relief as she pulled her purse and notebook from the back seat. "We still better hurry," she said, tossing Luke the keys. He opened the back door and retrieved the pile of cardboard signs and supplies he and Carrie had agreed to bring and followed his sister to the back entrance.

As they entered the church fellowship hall, they saw Homer and Miss Winfield already busily organizing and directing the participants. "Oh, Luke! Carrie! I'm so glad you're here," Miss Winfield said, somewhat breathlessly. "Carrie, can you begin taping the signs up at the different tables, please?"

"Yes, Miss Winfield," Carrie agreed and promptly set to work. Luke located Homer and was soon engaged in helping to move chairs and haul items in from the parking lot. Before long the whole committee had arrived and by starting time at ten o'clock, all was in order and the seminar began.

The event was well attended with over forty students registered. Carrie found many of the different careers presented to be quite intriguing. Each speaker representing a certain career was given time for a short presentation; then during the one hour lunch break the speakers were available to answer questions at their display tables.

Many of the girls flocked to the teacher's and nurse's tables. Carrie was pleased to see several boys questioning Pastor Everton from Blue Creek Community Church. An architect, a doctor, and a lawyer, drew much response also.

After a fine lunch served by the First Church Ladies' Missionary Society, the morning speakers were free to leave if they desired. The afternoon session was to include three missionaries in different forms of mission work.

After lunch, Carrie settled in to the comfortable church pew with Eileen by her side. For the next few minutes, students filed into the sanctuary and took seats near the front. Homer, Timothy, John Mark, and Luke sat in the front row on Carrie's left, nearest the podium. Promptly at one-fifteen, Homer stepped up to the microphone and introduced Miss Winfield, who gave an introduction to the missions part of the program. She highlighted some of her mission work overseas and gave her thoughts regarding the day's theme, "Hearing God's Call." At the end of her comments, she unveiled a large world map on the stage where she pointed out the mission base of the first speaker—the remote regions of the Indonesian Islands.

"It is my pleasure to introduce to you my dear friends, John and Deborah Clark, missionaries with the same organization I served under for twenty years." Applause followed as the couple stepped to the microphone. John Clark spoke for some time on answering God's call and then Deborah gave details of their work with children and villagers in remote jungle locations. Carrie was completely engrossed in the fascinating descriptions of life on the mission field.

Near the end of their presentation, she noticed John Mark who appeared to be deep in thought as he sat leaning forward and intently listening to their words. "I wonder if God is calling John Mark into missions?" Carrie pondered to herself. "It wouldn't surprise me," she thought, "he's a faithful servant and so spiritually mature." She remembered their conversation on her front porch the day the people of MCF came to help out at the Brooks' new house.

When the next missionary came forward, he spoke of his work in music with a Canadian Indian church as he pointed to a remote northern location on the map. Homer seemed to be intently listening to this presentation, seeing a new avenue of possibilities for his musical abilities. All the missionaries' presentations were very exciting and each piqued the interest of the students in one aspect or another.

When all the presentations were concluded, the missionaries stayed in the church fellowship hall and many students took advantage of the time to get some questions answered. Miss Winfield was beaming with pleasure at the interest with which her friends and fellow missionaries were received. She approached Carrie and Eileen who were talking in a corner of the fellowship hall. "Girls, isn't this wonderful? There seems to be so much interest in the presentations! I'm just delighted." It was obvious that Miss Winfield had a heart for missions and on this day she was in the height of her glory. Her enthusiasm was contagious and Carrie had to admit to herself that during the talks she had felt a certain warmth in her heart for the regions afar off, a drawing that she had never experienced to this extent before.

That night at home in her bedroom Carrie lounged on the window seat dad had built, looking into the distance and pondering the strange new feelings she had experienced today. "What a fine thing to take God's love to spiritually dark places," she whispered aloud. "What greater thing could one do with their life?" She wondered if her thoughts indicated that God had spoken to her today. Her mind was drawn to Miss Winfield's wonderful example. "Twenty years in mission work and now she's helping young people by teaching Sunday school and working with us home schoolers. And she's still able to be faithful to her aging parents and care for them. What a full life she has," Carrie thought. "Maybe she couldn't have accomplished all that if she would have married as she had intended." Carrie felt a slight shiver with that thought. "Here I've been praying for a husband and thinking how much I'd like to be a keeper at home. What if that strange nudging I felt today is God's call to the mission field?" Carrie had to admit this thought was unsettling, yet she couldn't deny how her heart had been strangely warmed at the missionaries' words. Would I have the courage to obey God if He was calling me to missions? she wondered. Could I give up my own dreams and hopes of a home and a family?

Carrie prayed for a long time that night before she crawled into her bed and wrapped up in the downy comforter. She was determined to listen closely to God.

The Watch

This particular Christmas season was glorious for Carrie. It was a picturesque time with snow glistening on the countryside. The fir trees were blanketed with the freshly fallen white fluff. Carrie often took time to enjoy the beautiful view from her window seat as she marveled at the wonders of God's creation.

School was in full swing with a Christmas choral program coming up soon, under Homer's able direction. Carrie was thoroughly enjoying her school year and had found a new sense of peace in the increased prayer time and Bible reading she had begun.

Mom detected maturity in Carrie that pleased her heart. She thought of her own teen years and was humbled at the difference between her daughter at this age and her own teen years. She often thanked God for the difference, praying daily for the Lord's guidance on all her children, but realizing that Carrie was currently facing some turning points in her life as she listened for God's direction.

Early on a mid-December Saturday morning, Carrie rose and began to work in the kitchen on baked goods for the holiday season. Because she delighted in cooking and baking, she was making endless varieties of cookies and breads for gift baskets this year.

She spent the entire morning baking delicious treats, a project that warmed the farmhouse kitchen and scented it with spice. The entire family commented on the tempting aromas that wafted from the kitchen as dozens of cookies were stacked in ever-growing piles on the counter tops. Luke had tested his share of the delicacies already and was feeding a shortbread cookie to Addy while he held her on his lap.

At two o'clock Carrie pronounced that she was finished as she dried the last pan from the dish drainer. She turned to Luke and Addy who were seated at the kitchen table suspiciously close to a loaf of sweet nut bread. "There, I'm done!" she announced, wiping her hands on a dish-towel. "I'm going to spend the rest of the afternoon finishing my new dress so it's ready for tonight," she told a disinterested Luke. "What time do we need to leave?" she asked matter-of-factly.

"Uh, I don't know," Luke muttered between bites of cookie. "Check the invitation. Six o'clock, I guess," he said, more interested in pastries than parties.

"Oh, Luke!" Carrie said in an exasperated tone as she walked to Dad's office to check the bulletin board. The invitation Luke had received as an employee of Blooming Hills Orchards read:

WE REQUEST THE HONOR OF YOUR
PRESENCE AT OUR FIRST ANNUAL EMPLOYEE
RECOGNITION BANQUET TO BE HELD AT
BLOOMING HILLS BANQUET ROOM AT 6:00
P.M.,
SATURDAY DECEMBER 18.
PLEASE BRING A GUEST.

"Oh, boys!" Carrie laughed as she walked back to the kitchen, invitation in hand. "It starts at six, Luke. We'll need to leave here by five-thirty, maybe sooner with all the snow."

"Ok, whatever," Luke mumbled.

"Make sure you're ready on time," Carrie instructed.

Luke looked a bit insulted and answered, "Whose party is this anyway? You act like it's yours. You wouldn't be going if it weren't for me. I can always ask somebody else, you know!"

"I'm the one with the driver's license," Carrie reminded her brother.

"Ok, ok." Luke conceded with a smile. "You win. I'll be ready by five forty-five, but not a minute sooner and I won't tie my tie 'til we get there 'cause it's uncomfortable!"

Carrie was filled with anticipation for the evening but she also understood Luke's fifteen- year-old, boyish reluctance to spend Saturday evening at a banquet with his sister and wearing a tie! Still, she was secretly thrilled when Mom and Dad had insisted on Luke attending out of respect to the Hendersons and suggesting that he take Carrie as his guest. Carrie knew that Alice had personally created the beautiful invitations and that "PLEASE BRING A GUEST" written on them was intended to honor the single employees that may want to bring a close friend. Alice told Carrie at church the week before that she and Eileen had thought and thought and written and re-written the invitations hoping the proper wording would prompt Luke to consider bringing Carrie and that Amanda would bring her brother Trent who was home for the holidays.

Artistic Alice had done a beautiful job with the invitations and was hard at work decorating the newly finished banquet room with a delightful wintry theme. The Henderson men had taken a few weeks during this off-season to finish the interior of the newly added section just in time for the banquet. Alice's bakery had flourished beyond everyone's expectations in its first season. It was her hope to add the banquet room as an extra moneymaker to be rented out or used as a future restaurant if the bakery and dessert counter continued to thrive. Being only a short distance off the main highway, the location was perfect for a facility such as this.

The employee recognition dinner was to be the first event held at the new banquet hall. Carrie was as excited to see the new room as she was to go out for dinner. She had heard Eileen talk about the new room for weeks. Now the day was finally here.

Carrie worked diligently for the rest of the afternoon putting the finishing touches on her new green velveteen dress she was making for winter. She was tacking an ecru lace collar to the high neckline as Mom passed by her room. "Knock, knock!" she called from the doorway.

"Come in," Carrie replied.

"The dress is looking beautiful, honey! I'm so proud of you and the way you've improved your sewing."

"Thanks, Mom."

"I was wondering if you'd like to wear Great Grandma Haywood's pocket watch tonight. It would look so lovely on that green dress!" Mom pulled a beautiful antique gold pocket watch and chain from her apron pocket and dangled it for Carrie to admire. Carrie had seen the watch many times. She knew it was a cherished possession of her mother's family. It was usually kept in a little velvet bag in the top of Mom's chest of drawers. Although Carrie knew the history of the watch, her mother seemed to love telling it once again.

"This watch is very special, you know, dear. Great Grandpa Josiah Haywood presented it to Great Grandma two weeks before their wedding day long, long ago. She wore it on her dress the day they were married."

"I remember the story, Mom," Carrie said, recalling the old brown-toned picture in the big oval frame that hung above her grandmother's fireplace mantle. The two young people in the picture were posing so formally and the lady had a chain pinned to her white dress. Grandmother had told her that it was Great Grandfather Josiah and his bride, Molly. When Carrie was just a little girl, she loved to gaze at the picture and the lady's beautiful lacy dress.

"He was intending to marry Grandma for some time, but times had been hard and he had determined not to take her as his wife until he could make his little farm a profitable business," Mom recounted sentimentally. "He asked her father if he could court her late in the fall one year in hopes that they could marry in the late spring of the next. But her father insisted that Grandpa get one complete crop in to prove he had money enough to support a wife before they could marry. My momma used to say that her papa, Josiah, claimed he'd really learned to pray that winter and he worked very hard to get in a good crop as early as he could in the spring. Still much depended on the weather, especially in those days." Carrie smiled as she listened, hand sewing all the while.

"A couple of times through that next summer, conditions seemed to threaten the young farmer's crops, but every time, God saw him through and blessed his hard work. By the end of the season, his harvest was especially bountiful. After all the crops were harvested and sold, Grandpa Josiah had a sizeable nest egg to start off married life. So he went to town to deliver his harvest and put his money in the bank. Then he visited the general store. He saw this watch and decided to take it to his bride as an engagement gift since he had been so profitable."

Carrie stopped a moment to look at the beautiful watch. The details of the heartwarming account behind the elegant piece of jewelry made it even more precious.

Mom went on with the story, "Grandpa showed the watch to Grandma's father and asked if he might give it to her and request her hand in marriage. Her father happily agreed and said he surely must have had a good year in order to afford such a gift. That evening he presented it to her and asked her to marry him. It's been the property of the oldest Haywood daughters ever since. It was given to my mother, then me. Some day it will be yours, but I thought you might like to wear it tonight," Mom concluded, hopefully.

Carrie beamed happily. "It will really look nice against this green fabric," Mom said, encouragingly. "See? There's a bar pin on the end of the chain where you fasten it to the dress and then slide the watch into a watch pocket if you choose, or you can hook the watch directly to the pin if you wear it without the long chain. In the pictures Grandma always wore it with the chain gently draping and the watch was apparently enclosed in a pocket at the waistline of her dresses."

"It's beautiful," Carrie sighed. "I'd like to wear it with the chain attached, but this dress doesn't have a pocket."

"I know," Mom agreed, "but if you'd like, I can show you how to put a pocket in the front of the dress. If you have a little scrap of the fabric, it won't take long at all."

Carrie hurried to her box of fabric scraps in the closet to search for the rest of the green material. Upon locating the leftovers, the two set to work immediately and by five o'clock Carrie was dressed and ready to go. She looked especially elegant in the green dress; the color was very becoming to her. There was a distinct personality to Carrie's clothing. She was at all times very modest and took care to see that her clothes fit well and were clean and pressed. She enjoyed wearing old-fashioned styles that were the epitome of modesty and femininity. Her tastes and style set her apart from the others her age that were often drawn to the immodesty of the latest trends. Her clothes made a statement about her gentle personality and were attractive without being showy. They set her apart in a positive way. It could be honestly stated that she was clothed in scarlet and her inner beauty, a gentle and quiet spirit, shone through.

As Carrie stood in front of her mirror adjusting the lace collar, Mom entered the room once again with the watch in her hand. "I'll help you pin this on," she offered. Carrie smiled, watching in the mirror as her mother pinned the lovely filigree bar to the high collar of the new dress. "Now arrange the chain like this," Mom said as she adjusted the chain and secured the watch into the little pocket. "Make sure the pocket is kept buttoned until you wish to look at the watch to see the time."

Carrie unbuttoned the tiny pocket and removed the watch again so Mom could show her how it worked. "To open the watch you gently press the winder at the top." As she demonstrated, the lid of the watch popped open to reveal a lovely face with delicate Roman numerals and slender hands.

"I love it, Mom! It's really pretty. Thank you so much!" Carrie cried as she hugged her mom. She took the watch in her hand and closed the lid, tracing the beautifully engraved flowers. There was even a tiny bird amongst the leaves. She carefully buttoned the watch into the new pocket.

"It looks so old-fashioned!" Mom exclaimed. "Even though the pocket wasn't in the dress pattern it's as if it belonged there!" Carrie happily agreed and quickly finished pinning her hair into the upswept style she had been wearing on special occasions. She hurried downstairs to find Luke; his lanky frame lounged in the living room rocker with a book propped on the knee of one leg that he had slung over the chair.

"Luke!" she said astonishingly, "You'll wrinkle your suit! Sit up!"

"You're really getting bossy lately," he muttered, shifting his position and sitting up straight. He closed the book he was reading and looked at his sister. Suddenly it was as if he'd never seen her before. Even Luke was moved to compliment, "Wow, Carrie! You really look nice."

"She's growing up and becoming a fine young woman," said a deep voice from the hall. It was Dad who was just entering the living room. His eyes twinkled with admiration as he gave his daughter a kiss on the cheek. "You really do look nice, dear," he said. Addy stood up from where she had been playing with her dolls and toddled over to Carrie. She reached out to touch the pretty fabric of Carrie's new dress.

"Ooohhh!" she said slowly, smiling.

"Thank you, sweetie!" Carrie said, stooping to kiss her little sister. She knew the little girl's exclamation indicated that she thought the dress was pretty.

"We'd better get going, Luke," Carrie announced. "It's five-twenty."

"Ok," Luke assented. As he raised his tall frame from the chair, he grabbed his suit jacket, which he had slung over the back of the sofa. Even in Carrie's high-heeled shoes, Luke now towered over his petite sister by several inches.

By now Mom had joined the family in the living room. "Don't you both look nice!" she exclaimed. "So grown up! Roger, can you take their picture?" she asked excitedly.

"Let me get the camera," he said as he opened the desk drawer.

"Oh, please!" Luke moaned, "Do we have to?" he pleaded. But no one seemed to pay any attention to his protests.

Carrie was getting her winter coat from the hall closet when her mother noticed and said, "Oh, no, dear! You can't wear that coat when you're all dressed up! How would you like to borrow my cape?"

"Great idea, Mom," Carrie agreed. Mom's cape was rose-colored wool lined with a satiny fabric. It was very nice for winter Sundays and special occasions. Mom hurried upstairs to get it.

As soon as the pictures were taken, Dad gave a few quick words of instruction to Luke and Carrie. "This is the first time that I know of for you two going anywhere alone in the van. Please be careful. It's a wintry night but if you drive sensibly, you'll be fine. Luke, you are to be polite and gentlemanly to everyone...and that includes your sister. Do you understand?" Dad asked with a hint of stern authority in his voice.

"Yes, sir," Luke replied seriously.

"I'm sure I wouldn't have to tell you all these things; it's just a reminder."

"We understand, Dad. We'll be careful," Carrie assured her father.

"Don't forget to thank Mr. and Mrs. Henderson!" Mom called as her children left into the frosty evening.

The banquet room was everything Carrie had imagined and more. Alice had done a beautiful job of decorating the long tables. There were fresh evergreen boughs everywhere mixed with holly berries and silver-sprayed thistle. Even the tables were decked with lace cloths. Several tall taper candles arranged among winter greenery sparkled on each table, casting a twinkling, star-like romance around the room. No detail had been overlooked and the warm glow of the holiday season was evident.

Joe and Katie greeted Carrie and Luke at the door. A florist's box of several identical corsages waited on a table next to Katie. She reached for one and announced to Carrie that all the ladies were to receive one this evening.

"Oh, thank you!" Carrie graciously replied. Luke hung his coat and Carrie's cape and talked with Joe as Katie adjusted the pretty flowers on Carrie's dress. The lovely corsage was an arrangement of two deep red roses, waxy green holly leaves, and white baby's breath with a cream-colored stain ribbon. Carrie thought it was the prettiest corsage she'd even seen and no combination could have set off her hunter green dress any better. All the while Katie exclaimed over the elegance of Carrie's new dress. She was also quite interested in the unique watch that Carrie wore. Katie listened intently as Carrie gave the watch's history.

Eileen rushed over to Carrie as soon as she spotted her friend and began exclaiming over Carrie's new dress. "Oh, Carrie!" Eileen whispered excitedly as she slipped her arm in Carrie's and whisked her off to the table where the punch bowl sat. "That dress! Is it new?"

"Yes," Carrie smiled.

"It's wonderful! Did you make it? It's exquisite!" Eileen didn't even seem to stop for a breath. "I've never seen one like it! Leave it to you to come up with the best styles! And what is this, Carrie?" Eileen said as she pointed at the lovely, gold pin with the gracefully draping chain attached.

Carrie removed the watch from the pocket for Eileen's inspection.

"Oh, Carrie, I've never seen anything so intriguing!"

As Carrie pushed the little winder the lid sprang open to reveal the faithful face of the old timepiece. Eileen was enamored with the item and reluctantly allowed Carrie to close it and put the watch back in the pocket a few moments later.

"Let's have some punch," she finally said after she finished exclaiming over Carrie's watch.

"Alice and I made this punch. It's been chilling all afternoon.

I hope you like it!" Eileen was rosy-cheeked from the warmth of all the preparations she had been assisting with until Carrie had arrived. She looked as though a cool glass of punch would be welcome. Carrie filled two cups and handed one to her friend.

"So, did you and Alice work on this all day?" Carrie asked, sweeping her hand in a circle to indicate the decorated room.

"All day!" Eileen lamented. "And Katie helped too! I only got away to get dressed about forty-five minutes ago. We cooked and cooked and cooked. Then we decorated. Then we cooked some more!" Both girls laughed. "I saw to it that you and Luke will be sitting with our family," Eileen said excitedly. "I arranged all the place cards, so I got my choice."

Carrie was pleased to hear that she'd be next to her friend, as she was feeling a little awkward being at such an occasion for the first time without her whole family. Luke was not a bit intimidated and had already found his circle of friends and visited the hors d'oeuvres trays twice. Carrie smiled to herself as she noticed him socializing with his friends, balancing his plate of appetizers in one hand.

"We did all the food and decorating ourselves, but we hired some staff from Blue Creek Catering Service to serve and clean up so all of us can sit down and enjoy the meal and program," Eileen was informing Carrie.

Soon Homer Martinson arrived with Amanda Melvin and her brother Trent. Apparently Homer hadn't brought a guest but all three had driven together. Homer and Trent joined Luke, John Mark and the other guys while Amanda joined the girls.

Carrie felt as though her senses were overwhelmed as she tried to take in all of the sights and sounds in the large room. The sumptuous odors from the kitchen were mouth-watering. The decorations were exquisite and the happy chattering of friends continued to mount to a crescendo of laughter and good will. Within minutes Alice emerged from the adjoining kitchen and spoke to her father who then stepped to the head table where a small lectern, festively draped with fresh greenery, had been placed.

"May I have your attention?" John Henderson began, "Welcome everyone! Welcome!" The crowd became quiet as John continued. "I'd like everyone to find your places please, so we can get started." The guests quickly moved to the tables. Carrie, with Eileen by her side, was seated at the end of a long table of Hendersons. Then Homer and his guests and Luke seated themselves on the opposite side of the table near some of the other farmhands as each employee located their place cards.

When all were seated, John continued, "The Henderson family is honored by your presence this evening as we celebrate the end of the harvest for the year. We are thankful first to God who has given us such a bountiful season and we praise Him for doing so."

As Carrie listened to Mr. Henderson's words, she ran her fingers over the shape of the watch concealed in the velvety pocket in her lap. "What a coincidence!" she thought, "This watch was originally purchased because of a bountiful harvest and here I am wearing it for the first time at another celebration of the same!"

As Carrie sat, somewhat awed by the coincidental circumstances, she listened to Mr. Henderson continue. "All of our family wish to thank each one of you who are employed here at Blooming Hills Orchards for your hard work and dedication this year." His comments continued on this order until he called John Mark to the podium to offer the blessing for the meal.

John Mark rose from his chair where he was seated next to Alice and moved to the microphone. "Let's pray," John Mark began in his devoted way. He bowed his head, but it was a moment before he spoke.

"Dear Lord, we come humbly before you tonight to offer our thanks and praises for this abundant year. You have graciously blessed us with a good harvest and we glorify Your Name. Father, we want to thank you now for each one who is here tonight and ask your blessing upon them. As we partake of the meal that has been prepared for us, we remember Your goodness to us, Your faithful provision for us in all things, especially Your gracious love in providing salvation for us through Your son, Jesus Christ. May we be ever mindful of your love to us. For all these things we thank you and ask you to bless this food to our use that we may glorify Your name in our generation. Please guard and guide our lives in all we say and do. In Jesus' Name we pray, Amen."

Carrie was again amazed at John Mark's quiet maturity, the ability of the otherwise shy young man to stand up and take his place in spiritual matters. When it came to things of the Lord, John Mark seemed to suddenly lose his shy reserve and have no problem speaking. "What a beautiful prayer that was!" she thought.

No sooner was John Mark seated than the waitresses began arriving from the kitchen with steaming platters of roast beef and bowls heaping with fluffy mashed potatoes and golden yellow corn. A tossed salad had been placed beside each dinner plate and the tables were dotted with baskets of Alice's homemade bread. The waitresses served coffee, tea, and ice water. Fancy dishes filled with spicy apple butter, another of Alice's new Blooming Hills products, followed the baskets of bread being passed around the tables.

Carrie found herself thoroughly enjoying the evening as she joined in the pleasant conversation of friends. The Hendersons were a warm, hospitable family who made all their guests feel very welcome and important.

A short time later when the waitresses emerged from the kitchen with large trays of assorted fruit pies, Carrie found herself nearly too full to accept a slice. Upon Eileen's urging, she finally decided on a piece of cherry vanilla cream. Everyone was passing compliments to the Henderson sisters, the confectioners.

After the meal, Mr. and Mrs. Henderson rose to the microphone. Mr. Henderson called each employee forward and together they thanked them and presented each one with an envelope and a small wrapped box. When Luke returned to the table he opened his envelope as others had done. It contained a lovely card, a twenty-dollar bill and a gift certificate to the Blue Creek Christian Book Store. The little box held an assortment of Alice's fruit preserves. "What a generous gift!" Carrie thought as she inspected the card. Leave it to the Hendersons to be generous.

A time of informal singing followed as Homer was invited forward to lead Christmas carols on his guitar. All the warmth and merry feelings of the season rang out with the age old verses of song as the company sang them one by one.

"This evening was thoroughly delightful," Carrie dreamed later as Luke helped her with her cape when they readied to leave. As she stood in the coat room talking with Eileen and the other girls, Luke offered to start the car and warm it up. As Carrie gave her brother the keys, Luke submitted good-naturedly to some teasing from Alice about not driving off without a license.

Mr. and Mrs. Henderson were making the rounds of the departing guests, shaking hands and thanking them all for coming. Soon they came to Carrie. Mrs. Henderson, with her typical friendly sincerity, took Carrie's hands in hers and warmly thanked her for attending the dinner.

After the Hendersons left Carrie, and passed to some other guests, Carrie overheard Trent and John Mark who were standing in one corner of the coat room. They were deep in a serious discussion about missions. Trent was finishing his last semester of school and planned to leave for South America in April. John Mark was listening intently as Trent gave an enthusiastic description of his upcoming duties in the Amazon regions. "We really need guys to commit to the South American areas. Pray about it," he added, putting his hand on John Mark's shoulder. "Let me send you some information on the missions teams when I get back to school," Trent was saying.

Carrie could see John Mark nod as he smiled and wished Trent well, promising to pray for him also. Just then Homer walked up and suggested that their carload leave soon since it appeared to be snowing more heavily just in the last few minutes.

Carrie felt a little uneasiness at the thought of driving in the snow but with Luke along she trusted there wasn't much real danger. But upon checking outside, Mr. Henderson saw that the snowfall had indeed been quite heavy in the last few hours and a fresh blanket of powder lay on the already existing inches with more heavy snow rapidly falling.

Mrs. Henderson insisted upon calling the Brooks house and letting Luke and Carrie's parents know that they were on their way home as Mr. Henderson commissioned Joe and John Mark to follow them to Maplecrest in one of the farm trucks. He then told Homer that he would personally drive Amanda and Trent back to Blue Creek so that Homer would not have to drive from Blue Creek to Maplecrest alone after dropping them off. Homer was to follow Luke and Carrie in the caravan to Maplecrest. Although the teens all insisted they'd be all right, Mr. Henderson wouldn't take "no" for an answer and the young guests all left together into the wintry night.

Everyone arrived home safely but what had started as a picturesque snowfall turned into a raging winter storm that continued for almost twenty-four hours dumping several feet of snow on the countryside. Carrie couldn't remember such a storm in all her life for it caused churches to be cancelled the next morning and schools were closed for almost a week. By the time the county had dug out from the deluge it was time for the area schools to be on Christmas vacation.

The Christmas choral program that had been scheduled for Wednesday evening had to be cancelled and there was no time to reschedule it. Luke and Carrie were sorely disappointed. Their disappointment was second only to Homer's since he had worked so hard to prepare for the event.

Carrie spent the days diligently finishing the semester's book work but inwardly she was sorry to be missing church and the chorale and the company of her friends at Friday classes. She had to admit that she had grown very fond of the busyness of the Activities Committee and she looked forward to Christmas vacation ending so that the pace would pick up again.

Winter

Home school events filled the winter with activity. The FCH Eagles basketball team went undefeated during the regular season. Luke was a player on the junior varsity team and so the Brooks family attended all the games. Fridays were filled with afternoon classes and evening basketball games.

Carrie often helped with the concession stand at the home games. The FCH group rented the Homewood Christian School Gymnasium for the home games. The two groups coordinated their athletic events accordingly and it worked out well for both organizations.

By March tournaments had begun and FCH was doing well so far with two wins and five more games to play before the state Christian school finals began. The third game in the series proved to be the final one for the Eagles. They lost to Bennington Christian Academy 62-65. The FCH Eagles were glad to have done as well as they did considering it was the first time the little home school group had won their league title. Even with the close loss to Bennington, there was a sense of rejoicing among the FCH teams and fans.

With all the excitement of tournaments, March was passing rapidly and soon it was time for the weekend of courtship and character teachings that had been scheduled by the Student Activities Committee. The Friday that began the three-day seminar finally arrived and Carrie found herself excitedly looking forward to the beginning of the sessions.

When Carrie and Luke arrived at Friday classes, several of their friends were already at the church. Carrie and Luke went to State History class for the first hour. After State History, Luke went on to his music class and Carrie went on to Alice's Home Economics class. Alice was doing some lessons on food preparation. All the girls in the class were enjoying this unit greatly since there was a time of snacks and fellowship following each class allowing the girls to taste the items they had prepared.

After the second class, Carrie gathered her books and headed for the sanctuary as soon as Alice dismissed everyone. As Carrie and Eileen made their way through the halls, many of the other students from various classes were moving toward the auditorium as well. Carrie and Eileen found a seat in the sanctuary where they watched the others file in. They chatted awhile as they waited. Carrie double-checked her notebook to be sure she had plenty of paper to take notes. This beginning session was to be directed especially for teens with scriptural studies and practical applications.

Carrie glanced at her watch and saw that the class was to begin in five minutes. "Eileen, I believe I'll run out and get a drink before it's time to start," Carrie said as she stood up.

"Ok," Eileen replied. "Hey! What do you suppose happened to the group from Spanish class?" Eileen asked as Carrie started away.

"I don't know," she answered. "I'll look for Luke out in the hall. He's not here either," she said. With a quick glance around the room, Carrie realized Eileen was right and only a few of the students from Spanish were in the auditorium. When Carrie reached the hall, she saw Luke and Amanda heading for the auditorium along with a few others. As she passed the Spanish classroom she saw John Mark and the teacher discussing something but heading toward the door. Carrie took a quick drink at the fountain and then made her way back toward the sanctuary.

Suddenly Homer passed Carrie. He was heading for the sanctuary on an almost run, thinking he was late. Before anyone could yell, "Watch out!" Homer had collided with John Mark who was coming out of the Spanish class doorway at just that moment. Books, papers, and notebooks flew everywhere. Carrie stood back, staring at the two friends.

After a moment, Homer and John Mark began to laugh and the others who saw the sight giggled as well. Still smiling, John

Mark reached his hand over to his friend and helped the big, muscular Homer off the floor where he had unceremoniously landed in a seated but sprawled position.

The boys began hurriedly scooping up papers, knowing they were pressed for time. Both boys stuffed the myriad of papers back into their backpacks and notebooks and made their way to the sanctuary. Carrie followed them as she headed back to her seat where Eileen waited. Homer and John Mark were still smiling when they found a seat together by Luke down in front of Carrie and Eileen. They were whispering and laughing as they related the incident to Luke, who was now quietly sharing in the laughter. Just as Carrie finished explaining the incident to Eileen, Miss Winfield stepped to the microphone and introduced the Holcombs and the teaching was underway.

Carrie found herself very interested in the information that the Holcombs presented. Most of the students were taking notes and seemed to be quite absorbed in the class. A handout of scripture verses and an outline of the Holcombs Friday presentation were passed around.

Carrie was a bit annoyed at Luke as she watched him from her seat two rows behind. She thought he seemed a bit disinterested in the class. Although he was polite and not at all disruptive, she didn't see him taking any notes at all. On the contrary, his two companions were obviously interested. Homer was diligently writing and flipping through the pages of his Bible as he followed along and John Mark did likewise with his usual quiet seriousness. He was closely following his outline and writing notes on the front of a paper. "Oh, well," Carrie thought, "Luke's younger than the others. It's probably not a topic of great interest to a freshman boy whose mind is not yet concerned with girls, let alone marriage."

When four p.m. arrived, Carrie was amazed at how rapidly the hour had passed. She had enjoyed the class so much that she was sorry to see it end. She had been so absorbed in the information that she hadn't noticed her Dad who had arrived from work in time to hear the last half hour of the Holcombs' presentation. She was surprised when Miss Winfield called him forward to give announcements and close in prayer.

The students were folding their papers and putting their notebooks away as soon as Pastor Brooks dismissed the assembly. The usual visiting followed where everyone socialized, some for the last time until the next Friday.

Carrie and Eileen moved toward the front where the boys had been seated. Eileen tapped her brother on the shoulder and indicated they needed to leave for home. "We better get going too," Carrie said to Luke.

"I'm going home with Dad," Luke replied, with a tone in his voice that seemed to ask his sister to respect his maturity.

"Ok," Carrie agreed.

Homer, who was standing a short distance away, suddenly looked bewildered as he thumbed through his backpack.

"Wait, John Mark! I believe I've got your Spanish book here," he said. John Mark turned around and checked his books.

"Sure enough," he replied as he traded Spanish books with Homer. "I guess that collision is responsible," John Mark grinned.

"Oh, sure," Homer teased, "You were trying to get my notes for that test next week!" He jostled his friend good-naturedly as the little gathering dispersed for another week.

The Return of May

The courtship and character seminar was a huge success for the young people in the home school fellowship and youth groups. Carrie was glad for the teaching and information that the Holcombs gave. Because of the seminar and the excellent teaching, several of Carrie's friends had made decisions to commit to relationships of purity, allowing God to direct their lives even in their choice of future mates. Carrie knew that the Martinsons, the Hendersons and others were already solidly committed to let the Lord lead in their children's lives concerning relationships and marriage. Traditional dating was not what they encouraged. Now several new families had decided to make similar commitments. Some of the people Carrie knew had been dating for a few years now and she had seen how emotionally attached they became, making their lives difficult when they broke up with one another. All things considered, Carrie reasoned that missing the temporary fun of a few dates was little to sacrifice to be free of the heartaches that she knew some of her friends had experienced.

Shortly after the weekend of the Holcomb's seminar, planning for the Student Advisory Committee began with all the spring activities and graduation just around the corner. Busy April swept into May with the swiftness of a gusty spring breeze, and before long, graduation was upon them. All the committee members had worked diligently with the seniors to plan the graduation and the details were progressing well.

As the day of the commencement ceremony approached, Carrie often reflected on how quickly the school year had passed. She thought how amazing it was that next year at this time she would be a graduating senior herself! To Carrie, this had been the best school year ever. Being a member of the SAC had been wonderful. All the activities made unforgettable memories for her, but Carrie still wondered often about her future. She prayed daily about it, but still she felt uncertain as to what God might be calling her to do.

She was quite sure that in her heart she just wanted to stay at home and be like her mother, a homemaker. Yet there was still a warm spot in her heart each time she considered foreign missions. She experienced an unsettled, yet excited feeling each time she thought of herself as a senior, knowing in a very real sense that next spring after her own graduation, a new chapter of life really would begin.

For the time being, at least one thing was sure--at the end of school this year she would be joining Alice's staff at Blooming Hills. How excited she was about that! She and Alice had already spent much time after church on Sundays discussing the details of Carrie's employment. "It's going to be so much fun," Carrie thought. Working for Alice, earning money, and being with all her friends for the summer. What could be better?

Alice was an enthusiastic young woman, full of ideas and projects, fun-loving yet gracious and solid in her Christian faith. And she was Carrie's good friend as well, much like Eileen, only older. But age didn't seem to matter to Carrie's circle of friends. They all got along well in spite of age differences. Alice was four years Carrie's senior, and Eileen was closer to Luke's age. Yet they all were good companions. Having been raised with good character and manners helped them all to be mature and able to relate well to others of all ages.

"Yes," Carrie thought, "Alice will be an excellent role model," and she looked forward to the summer months when she could spend more time with her, for she truly admired the older girl.

On the afternoon of graduation, Carrie was quite busy. Such an exciting evening it promised to be. The SAC was working dili-gently with a group of parents and volunteers to decorate the gym at Homewood Christian School, where the ceremony was to be held this year. So much had to be done before the evening. A few hundred chairs had to be set up; flowers needed to be arranged, streamers hung, and the stage decorated.

The twelve graduating seniors had chosen blue and silver for their class colors and the white rose as their class flower. At three p.m. when the final bouquet was in place and the last silver streamer affixed to the basketball hoop, Miss Winfield heaved a sigh of relief as she stepped to the stage and tested the sound system. "Thank you all," she said over the microphone, "for a job well done!" She smiled as her voice echoed in the near-empty gym. "Everyone sit down for a much-deserved break," she directed. "Oh! And don't forget, Carrie and John Mark, you two, as honor guards, need to be here by six-thirty. We will be going over last minute details and lining up early. Also, Homer, since you are vice president and Timothy is a graduate this evening, you'll be representing the SAC and we will need you here early too. By the way, I guess the sound system is working well," Miss Winfield joked as she finished giving the instructions that resonated loudly across the room. As her voice echoed all through the gym, she stepped down from the platform and smiled a tired but satisfied smile. She slumped into a chair in the front row next to Chris Brooks and some other moms who were following her advice to take a break.

Carrie and her friends were chatting near the back of the gym as they excitedly discussed the upcoming evening. The girls were commending Carrie's choice of flowers for the bouquets. Large bunches of fragrant, white, mock orange blossoms spilled from baskets on the stage, while peonies dotted amongst them provided color. Carrie had borrowed all these from Miss Winfield's profusely blooming gardens. A large bouquet of white roses was ordered from a local florist and now graced the platform just under the podium. Carrie and some of the other girls had made blue and silver bows to attach to the first several rows of chairs, reserved for graduates and their families. Altogether, the room looked festive, yet distinguished and Carrie's sense of artistic décor was largely responsible.

Later that afternoon as Carrie began getting ready for the ceremony, she put on her new spring dress she had sewn just for the occasion. In keeping with the class colors, she had chosen a soft, blue voile print and lined it with white cotton. The dress was a beautiful, old-fashioned design with slightly puffed sleeves, a sweeping skirt and deep flounce at the hem. The tiny silver buttons Carrie chose were shaped like rosebuds. Delicate white lace adorned the sleeves and neckline. Carrie's appearance was formal yet very spring-like and sweet, reflective of the elegant young woman she had become.

Soon the entire Brooks family was dressed and ready to go, Luke in his new suit and Addy in her new summer dress. But Carrie was ready first and stepped outside a moment before everyone else. She stood on the porch that was now surrounded by white blossoms and took a deep breath of the sweet late May air.

"My favorite time of year," she reminded herself. "I wonder how it will feel to step out here next year on an evening such as this and know that I'm to be the one graduating?" she romantically wondered aloud.

She walked to the east side of the house and leaned against the porch rail; gazing dreamily over the pasture and the distant fields, now green with spring. Blossom, the Brooks' new milk cow wandered slowly to the fence, the bell that Carrie had insisted on draping around her neck clanging out a tune with each of her plodding steps. She stopped at the part of the fence closest to where Carrie stood and stared at the girl with her big, brown eyes as if to say, "A penny for your thoughts, Carrie."

Carrie chuckled at Blossom's inquisitive look and answered as if she had actually heard the cow speak, "Oh, I'm just thinking about growing up, girl. I was wondering what I'll be doing this time next year. I was wondering what my future holds—missions, courtship, marriage, career? But I guess you don't have anything like that to think about, do you?" Blossom continued to stare as she contentedly munched some green grass.

The screen door opened and Mom came out followed by the rest of the family. "Who are you talking to, Carrie?" she said from the other side of the porch.

"Just Blossom," Carrie smiled in answer as she picked up her purse and joined the rest of her family who were now ready to leave.

When the Brooks family arrived at the gym a short time later, a few of the seniors and SAC members were already there. Homer was busy going from place to place checking last minute details in Timothy's stead. Miss Winfield met the Brooks' as they entered the school and breathlessly declared, " I'm so glad you are here! Pastor, will you please take charge of the boys' dressing room and see that everyone's caps and gowns are correctly adjusted and they're all ready to line up by six forty-five?"

"Yes, I'll be glad to," Dad answered as he transferred Addy to Luke who would be her somewhat reluctant caretaker for a good share of the evening.

"And, Chris and Carrie, I hope you'll do the same for the girls," Miss Winfield requested, motioning down the hall to the classroom marked, "SENIOR GIRLS."

"Sure, Miss Winfield," Carrie said, pleasantly.

"If you need anything, I'll be around here somewhere," Miss Winfield assured them. "I have to help the ushers and the musicians and so on," she said as she hurried away to dutifully attend to all the details.

Carrie and her mother found the dressing room buzzing with the nervous, hurried preparations of several senior girls fixing their hair and changing their shoes, busy with all the last minute details before donning their caps and gowns. A large vase of long-stemmed white roses sat on the teacher's desk. Carrie knew from rehearsal that each girl, including herself, was to receive one to carry tonight. Mom and Carrie immediately busied themselves with helping the excited girls.

When six forty-five arrived everyone was ready. A few of the girls were already in tears. A good share of hugs and sentimental words were being exchanged amongst the group. After checking the progress in the gymnasium, Mom quietly opened the door and announced that it was time to line up in the hall.

As each girl filed out of the room, Mom handed her a white rose from the vase that sat on the desk. The boys were already waiting outside their dressing room and Miss Winfield was giving motherly advice as she adjusted a cap here, a boutonnière there. When she saw that the girls were ready; she raised her hand for quiet and then announced that it was time to line up.

"Now everyone take your places just as we practiced yesterday," she coached in a whisper. With that, Homer popped in the door and said, "I gave the signal for the band to start the music at six fifty. At seven sharp I'll start the graduation march on the organ and that will be your cue, ok?" he asked.

Somehow Homer had creatively arranged for several of the students from the Christian school to join with some of the home school students to play their stringed instruments for about an half hour ahead of the ceremony. Soon the lovely music floated into the hall where the graduates waited.

Miss Winfield waved acknowledgement from down the hall where she was helping the graduates find their places. Before he stepped back into the auditorium, Homer winked at Carrie and said, "You look very nice! Lead them down the correct aisle, ok?" he teased.

"Ok," Carrie answered back, blushing. Just then she saw John Mark enter the hall from the boys' dressing room. He smiled as he walked toward her. "He looks very distinguished," she thought to herself as she noticed his new suit. John Mark was wearing a nice deep blue suit that complimented the class colors and Carrie's dress very well. It was unusual to see John Mark Henderson so dressed up. Even though the Henderson family was financially well off, they were not ones to dress in fancy formal attire. They were mostly seen in their farm clothes and even church was less than formal at Maplewood Christian Fellowship. So to see John Mark in a suit was a real surprise.

Carrie thought he looked different in some other way too and suddenly she realized that the loose shock of hair that always hung mischievously over his right eye was obediently combed in place. How mature it made him look! Suddenly she realized she had been staring and she quickly lowered her eyes as he greeted her.

"You look very nice," he said shyly but sincerely.

"Thank you," Carrie answered in like manner. The two were somewhat alone for a few minutes at the front of the procession while Miss Winfield and Pastor and Mrs. Brooks checked details, answered questions, and gave final instructions.

While they waited, John Mark said, "Well, I guess next year it'll be us in caps and gowns." Then he added in his characteristically serious manner, "That is...if the Lord tarries."

"Yes," Carrie smiled, wishing she could think of something more to say.

A pause followed and John Mark looked up and said, "Does it frighten you, Carrie? I mean, graduating and being out of school."

Carrie paused a moment before she spoke. "Sometimes," she said slowly. "Why? Does it scare you?" she asked back.

John Mark looked uncertain. "Sometimes, I guess," he admitted.

"Yet I know that God has a purpose planned for me in life. I just have to find it and live it." Carrie nodded her understanding as he went on. "Sometimes I wish God would just drop a sign in front of me that read, "John Mark! Do this… or do that," he smiled. "But I know that's not the way God works, so I keep praying…and listening and trying to discern His will."

"I know," Carrie agreed. "I don't know what God has for me either."

"Well, sometimes I think I'll just stay on farming," John Mark continued. "Sometimes I'm drawn to missions. I still have to spend a lot of time praying about it."

At that moment the strains of the graduation march at the able hands of Homer Martinson and the other musicians wafted through the doors. Dad said a quick prayer of blessing on the graduates and then he and Mom exited the hallway and found their seats. John Mark quietly opened the big door and he and Carrie led the procession slowly and ceremoniously into the gymnasium just as they had practiced.

Carrie found herself filled with a variety of emotions as the graduation ceremony unfolded. She thoroughly enjoyed the whole program that evening even though certain moments were marked with sentimental tears. Later that evening, alone in her room Carrie sat in her beloved window seat with the windows opened to the warm, late spring breeze. She gazed out over the fields that were bathed in silvery moonlight as she pondered her earlier conversation with John Mark in the hallway of the school. As she thought of all the changes she'd face in the next few years, she was relieved that at least her immediate future was planned; working for Alice.

She Sees a Field and Buys It

Carrie's first week of work for Alice was a happy one. Having cheerfully taken her parents advice last summer in not taking Alice's job offer, Carrie found that the timing was just right for her this year and many added blessings were hers.

This summer the garden at Blossom Lane, the name Luke had recently given the Brooks' farm, was already well established with strawberries, raspberry bushes, and grapes. Addy was a year older and took less care than last year and it would be easier for Chris to care for the garden alone since she had had Carrie's help pruning and coaxing the tired masses of tangled old berries last season.

During the winter, the final touches had been put on the house and all the rooms were now done. Yes, it was like starting fresh this year with a lot of the work already behind the Brooks family as far as the new property was concerned. Blossom Lane was now a productive little farm complete with Blossom, the milk cow, a pig, and several laying hens. New chicks had arrived this spring and were being fattened for butchering. Luke was instrumental in taking care of the animals and farm chores at Blossom Lane even though his Blooming Hills job took up a good share of his time.

Today after work, Carrie, Alice, and Eileen had planned to go to Farmer's Market for supper and shopping. The first week of work at Blooming Hills Bakery had been one of diligent preparation for the upcoming season when tourists and customers would flood in with the ripening of the first strawberry crop. Alice had suggested to the girls that they visit Dottie's Fabrics, one of the permanent booths at Farmer's Market to find fabric for work dresses and aprons. So after a hard day's work on Friday, Alice announced that the little store would be ready to open by the middle of next week and declared a Friday evening holiday for her workers.

"I think we're finally finished, girls," she announced. "Let's go to Farmer's Market and I'll treat us all to supper like we planned. Then we can look for some fabric at Dottie's."

"Ok," Eileen and Carrie agreed as they headed for Henderson's big farmhouse to change their work clothes and freshen up. Alice followed, carrying a golden custard pie to the house for her family to enjoy over the weekend. Most likely her brothers would have it all finished off before Sunday. Custard happened to be Tommy's favorite and he was a growing boy with an appetite to rival John Mark's.

On the way to Blue Creek, Alice shared her ideas with the others. "I set back enough of the profits last year to buy fabric for curtains for the bakery and work outfits for us." Carrie and Eileen eagerly exchanged smiles. "Eileen, you'll be working with me in the bakery more this year so you're included in this. I thought I'd like to get red gingham for pinafore aprons; enough so each of us could have about three. Then I thought we'd make the curtains out of the same fabric."

Excited, Alice continued to spell out the plans without waiting for their approval although her tone of voice continued to ask for their acceptance. "How about if we get three contrasting fabrics in a good cotton for the dresses and we'll each have three uniforms?" Eileen and Carrie nodded their agreement as she went on. "Here's the pattern I thought we might use," Alice said as she pulled a worn envelope from her purse. Eileen passed it to Carrie, the seamstress, who immediately recognized it as one of Alice's everyday dresses.

"This will be great, Alice," Carrie said, "The style is perfect for work." The dress featured a simple circle collar with button front bodice attached to a slightly full skirt with a deep flounce at mid-calf. The apron was a pinafore with ruffles on the bib that crisscrossed in back where a large bow was tied. Carrie could easily envision this pretty outfit being made up in the fabrics and colors Alice suggested and was anxious to shop for the sewing supplies.

When the girls reached Farmer's Market, as usual it was crowded and noisy with activity. In the late afternoon most of the people coming to the market were whole families making an evening of shopping. The girls headed straight for the Dottie's Fabric display as soon as they parked the car. They made one short stop at the Blooming Hills booth where John Mark and Homer were just getting ready to leave for home.

"Hi, guys!" Alice waved. "Did you get all the work done today?" John Mark brushed his hands on his jeans as he walked toward the girls, Homer following close behind.

"Yeah, we're done all right! He just about worked me to death!" Homer joked, smiling at his friend.

John Mark grinned and addressed his sister; "We were just putting the finishing touches on the new shelves." The boys had been working for a few days on revamping the large booth and getting everything ready for the first fruit of the season. Some new carpentry work had to be done on the existing shelves so that all would be ready in time. Many of the other owners of permanent booths were doing the same at this early date. The farmers who had potatoes, onions and earlier spring vegetables for sale were already in business and several of the permanent booths were open as well.

"We're going to shop for fabric and then go to dinner," Eileen told the boys.

"What did Luke do today?" John Mark asked Carrie.

"I think they were checking fields and doing some sorting on boxes and lugs. Maybe they were spraying trees too; I'm not sure. They weren't back from the orchards yet when we left."

Homer spoke next, "Well, if I wasn't such a mess," he said, gesturing to his work-worn clothes, "I'd join you girls for dinner. I'm starved!" he said and whistled. "How about you?" he said to John Mark.

John Mark shyly jostled Homer, "I don't really feel like going fabric shopping right now, do you?" he teased with a good-natured grin.

"Well, maybe...." Homer joked. "Especially if there's a SALE!" he squealed in a girlish voice. The two boys laughed at their joke.

"Ok, you two," Alice scolded, "that's enough teasing. We'll see you later. C'mon girls," she said and led her employees away as she smiled and added, "Let's go shopping!"

When they arrived at the Dottie's Fabric booth, the girls set to work looking for suitable dress material. Alice found the red gingham she liked for the aprons and then they began trying to match up some prints for the dresses. After a good deal of looking and comparing the girls finally settled on three different prints. The first was a white background with a fine, red stripe decorated with cherries and strawberries. The second was a small, red floral on white, and the third a red and white dotted Swiss.

The girls made their large order to the sales lady at the cutting counter, who assured them that it would take quite some time to measure and cut all the different pieces. So Alice suggested they go to dinner while they waited for the lady to get all the fabric ready.

They decided to eat supper at a booth called "The Seafood Market", where fresh fish and seafood were the specialties. They enjoyed a leisurely supper before returning to Dottie's Fabrics to pick up their purchases.

When they reached Dottie's, they saw that the sales lady had neatly piled each separately cut piece of dress and apron fabric for the girls. Alice had purchased the entire bolt of gingham for aprons and curtains and the rest of the bolt was set aside with their order as well. Next they spent several minutes at the notions racks selecting enough buttons, thread, and lace to complete the dresses. When all was calculated, Alice paid by check from her business account and the girls carried the myriad of sacks to the car.

"Can you have at least one dress and an apron done in time for our first day of the season?" Alice asked Carrie on the way out.

"Oh, sure. I don't see why not," Carrie answered, anxious to get to work on the new fabric.

"Eileen and I will work on ours tomorrow and try to get one outfit done for each of us. I'd love it if we could get the curtains done for the seating area too," she added hopefully.

"Oh, I'm sure we can, Alice. I'll help. Maybe if we all work together...." Carrie suggested.

"I know!" Alice suggested enthusiastically. "We'll work on them Monday and then if we're not done by supper, could you stay for the evening and we'll try to get them finished?"

"I'll ask," Carrie said, "I don't know why not, unless Mom needs me for some reason."

"Which print shall we make up first?" Alice asked.

"How about the one with the cherries and strawberries," Eileen suggested.

"Yes! Since it's strawberry season, that's perfect," Carrie agreed and so it was decided.

The girls chattered excitedly about the dresses, the bakery and all their plans until they finally reached the Brooks' farm. Alice pulled her car into the circle drive to drop Carrie off. Carrie thanked her for the supper and the new dress fabric as they divided up the thread and buttons and checked to see that Carrie's items were sorted into a separate bag.

"We'll get our dresses and aprons cut tomorrow and we'll bring the pattern pieces to church on Sunday for you, if that's all right. Will that give you enough time?" Alice asked Carrie.

"Sure, no problem," Carrie replied as she walked toward the back door. She turned and waved to her two friends and hurried into the house to share the excitement of three new dresses with her mother.

By the next Wednesday afternoon Alice, Carrie and Eileen had hung the last new curtain in the bakery restaurant. Everything looked so pleasant and inviting. The girls were tired but satisfied as they reviewed their work. "What a change from last season!" Alice sighed. "It was only a simple bakery last year, now it's looking almost like a full-size restaurant! I can hardly believe the difference! God has really blessed me!"

Carrie and Eileen agreed. The Henderson men had spent even more time during the winter after the Christmas banquet installing new carpet, a new ice cream freezer, tables and other equipment for the thriving enterprise. With more room, Alice was adding ice cream treats to the menu as well as a shelf of old-fashioned candy jars behind the cash register. The new carpet, curtain, and tables completed the atmosphere. Alice's decorative eye had given the place a clean, country kitchen look. It was very appealing and promised to boost business even more.

"This reminds me of the phrase, 'she sees a field and buys it,' from Proverbs 31," Carrie quoted. "You saw this opportunity for business and you made the best of it."

Alice smiled and answered, "The glory should go to the Lord." Carrie nodded knowingly at her friend.

When Carrie went to work on Thursday morning, it was with

great anticipation of the opening day of Blooming Hills Bakery. All the dresses and aprons had been finished, even though it had meant some late nights and help from mothers. The girls had decided to wear the striped dresses with the fruit pattern print and their checked aprons for the bakery's opening day.

Thursday was also the first day that the Blooming Hills fields were going to be open for picking strawberries. With the customers would come bakery business and the girls were ready. Alice had several strawberry pies ready for sale, whole or by the slice and displayed in the cooler.

Eileen was helping with other baking and Carrie was waiting on customers, dipping ice cream, and keeping the front area under control. Business was slow in the morning hours, but as soon as the people that were picking berries began to come in from the fields, Carrie found herself quite busy. Several mothers came in and purchased ice cream cones for their children. Carrie also weighed out a lot of the bulk candy, with peppermints and gumballs competing for top sales.

At one o'clock in the afternoon, Alice came out from the kitchen to check on Carrie. "Whew!" Carrie said as Alice entered the dining room. "The last hour has really been busy!" she told her. "This is the first lull I've had."

"Take a little break," Alice suggested. "Eileen and I are cleaning up and doing a load of dishes. We'll soon be done for the day."

Carrie flopped in one of the chairs and opened her lunch bag that Alice had kindly thought to bring out from the cooler. They both sat and rested a bit while Carrie ate her sandwich. "I suppose business will only get heavier in the days to come since Dad and Joe put up a new sign out on the highway last night. It says, 'Visit Blooming Hills Bakery for Mouthwatering Seasonal Specials,'" Alice said proudly.

"Oh, good!" Carrie said finishing a bite of sandwich. Just then Homer, Luke and John Mark came in the front door looking tired, hungry, and a bit dirty.

"Hey, no one's here and the help's all sitting down on the job!" Homer teased, looking at Carrie.

"We've got the place all to ourselves," John Mark added. "Hey, Alice, is it ok if we eat our lunch in here since you're not busy? It's so hot out there."

"I suppose so, as long as you order something," Alice teased.

"No problem with that!" Homer said, enthusiastically, surveying the menu.

The boys sat down at a far table and Carrie told Alice she'd get their orders as she stood up from her lunch break. She crumpled up her lunch bag and wiped the table where she had been sitting.

"I'll finish helping Eileen," Alice said as she pushed open the doors to the kitchen and disappeared. Carrie walked over to the boys and took their orders just as professionally as if they were non-family customers.

"Wow!" Luke said, "You're just like a real waitress!"

"Well, I hope so," Carrie said, "Since that's what I am! Now what can I get for you?"

"I'll have a chocolate malt," Luke decided.

"Me too," John Mark agreed. "But I'll have just a little extra chocolate, please," he added with a grin.

"I'd also like a piece of strawberry pie," Homer thought to add as Carrie was walking away.

Carrie prepared their orders and efficiently delivered the items to their table. Meanwhile other customers had come in. She was kept busy serving for the next half hour.

When the boys had finished their lunches, they rose to leave and met Carrie at the cash register. Each boy came to pay his bill in turn, Homer being first. "Tell Alice that's great pie," he said as he handed Carrie a five-dollar bill.

"No," Carrie said in a whisper, waving his money away. "Alice says it's all free to you guys since it's our first day." The surprised boys told Carrie to thank Alice, and Luke and John Mark complimented Carrie's malt making as they headed back to work in the fields.

Before John Mark went out the door, he turned to Carrie and added in a way that would become familiar to her over the summer, "May I please have fifty cents worth of peppermints? I'll pay for these," he added.

"Sure," Carrie replied as she weighed out the red and white pinwheel designed candy.

"Thanks," John Mark said as he handed her a fifty-cent piece and unwrapped one to pop in his mouth. "They're my favorites. Would you like one," he offered politely.

"No, thank you," Carrie blushed.

He smiled at her and put the candies in the pocket of his jeans as he headed out the door and back to the hard farm work that was putting muscles on all of the boys.

The rest of the week went quite smoothly at Alice's bakery in spite of increased business by the day. By Saturday afternoon, strawberry season was in full swing and the three girls had to admit they were anxious for five o'clock when the orchard would close for the weekend. The first week had been a huge success and Alice had sold out of pies and several varieties of ice cream and next week would likely be the same. The three tired girls finished the final cleaning on Saturday afternoon to close up shop for the week.

As Carrie hung up the last towel and grabbed her purse from the shelf, she wearily, but happily told her friends that she would see them tomorrow at church. Luke had just walked in from the fields with Homer and the others. He headed immediately for the bakery. As the bell on the door rang, Alice and the two girls looked at each other, stunned. "Not another customer!" Carrie gasped. "I thought I locked the door after that last family left!"

"We'll just have to tell them we're closed," Alice said decidedly as she pushed the big swinging door open and looked out into the dining room. "Oh, it's just Luke," she announced as Carrie and Eileen followed her out to the front.

"Are you ready to go home?" he asked to his sister as he flopped down on a stool at the end of the counter.

"Yes, we're finally done," Carrie said.

Luke looked very tired. "You must have put in quite a day," Eileen commented as she looked at the bedraggled young man.

"We sure did," he agreed. "Customers everywhere!" he sighed. "I recounted one lady's order two times because she insisted I was charging her for two quarts of extra berries. Then I had to ask two other ladies to quit switching rows as they were picking and to "please stay on a row and pick it clean!" I think I spoke to five different children about trampling the plants and so on and so forth." Luke's voice trailed off. The girls giggled and assured him they were tired too as all five of them left, turned out the lights and locked the door. Carrie remembered to turn the sign to "CLOSED" as she stepped out into the early June evening.

The Stranger

On Monday, Carrie took her turn working the kitchen while Eileen handled the dessert counter and cash register. Carrie enjoyed all aspects of the job so far, but she preferred the variety of duties involved in working the front to the monotony of the baking. The job at Blooming Hills was very positive for Carrie in many ways, not the least of which was how it challenged her to overcome her shyness as she worked with the customers. Waiting on tables and working at the front counter gently nudged her to stretch her wings a bit. However, the kitchen work offered her time to be with Alice and they worked well together, sincerely enjoying each other's company.

While they baked dozens of pies, much of the girls' discussion centered on their futures. Carrie was surprised to learn that Alice, whom she had always thought of as so decided and established, was herself still praying about her future and seeking God's will for her life. It surprised Carrie to hear Alice speak of the bakery as a stepping stone, just a place to be for now until the Lord revealed other plans. Alice even confided to Carrie that she hoped to have a home of her own someday, a husband and children, leaving the work at the bakery to someone else.

When John Mark came in on his afternoon break, he purchased the last of the peppermints from his sister Eileen, completely emptying the jar. She restocked the jar as soon as business let up for a few minutes. Eileen promptly told Alice to add a re-order of peppermints to the list for the deliveryman. She also announced that strawberry pies were selling rapidly and that she had served five individual slices with vanilla ice cream just in the last hour.

Many of the strawberry customers stopped in for pie, coffee, or ice cream, making the week a busy one for the girls. Finally by Thursday, Alice and her staff noticed a slight slow down in business. Eileen and Alice were baking and actually managed to get caught up on pies for the first time in days. And it was a good thing too since Thursday meant baking a double amount of pies so they could be sent to Farmer's Market on Friday. Because of the thriving business in the bakery, Katie had agreed to go to Farmer's Market tomorrow in Eileen's place.

Carrie was taking care of the front and found a bit of time to straighten things up, restock some items, and just get everything fresh and in order once again. As she was wiping the glass on the ice cream freezer, the doorbell rang and a customer stepped in. Carrie looked up from her work and greeted the tall, blonde stranger. His friendly smile was immediately likeable. He strode up to the counter and swung his lanky frame onto one of the stools as he studied the menu above the counter.

"May I help you?" Carrie asked pleasantly.

"Um, yes," he said slowly. "I believe I'll have a slice of strawberry pie and a cup of coffee…for starters," he added with a teasing sparkle in his eyes.

"Ok, just one moment," Carrie said as she turned to get a cup for his coffee. She wondered who this stranger could be. She knew he was no one she had ever seen before and he certainly didn't look like the strawberry-picking types who had comprised a large share of the bakery's business so far. He was well dressed in a suit and tie and looked very professional.

As Carrie served his pie and poured his coffee, she glanced out the window to the parking lot where his car was parked. She noticed it had an out-of-state license plate. She saw that he was studying one of the maps of the area that several of the local businesses provided for tourists. Carrie felt a bit uncomfortable being alone in the room with this only customer even though he seemed friendly enough. She wished Eileen or Alice would pop out of the kitchen for some reason.

She busied herself with meaningless tasks for a few minutes until the man spoke suddenly, "Miss!" he said, startling Carrie,

"May I please speak to the manager?" Carrie felt her stomach sink, noticing he had only taken a few bites of his pie.

"Yes, sir," she said timidly as she headed for the kitchen door. Carrie was filled with jitters hoping there wasn't anything wrong with the food or the service. She stepped into the kitchen and summoned Alice, all the while keeping her eye on the gentleman through the porthole style window in the kitchen door.

In whispered tones, she quickly explained to Alice that a customer had asked for the manager after only a few bites. "Hurry!" Carrie pleaded. She went back to the dining area, not wanting to leave the front counter unattended. Alice dusted the flour off her hands and apron, following quickly behind Carrie, who upon entering the dining area, was relieved to see that more customers had come in. She began to wait on them while keeping one ear open to Alice's discussion with the tall stranger.

"I'm the manager, sir," Alice said pleasantly. "Is anything wrong?" The man laughed softly and shook his head. At this, Carrie thought she caught a look of relief in Alice's eyes.

"No, Ma'am!" he said definitely. "I just wanted to ask who made this incredibly delicious pie. I haven't tasted anything so good in ages!" he smiled. "My compliments to the chef!" he added.

"Thank you, sir. I made it," Alice replied shyly. "Well, my workers and I made it, I mean. It's an old family recipe."

"It's…wonderful!" he said, taking another bite. "Strawberry pie is my favorite and this is most assuredly the best I've ever eaten."

"Thank you," Alice repeated, blushing at his enthusiastic praise. "We grow the berries here on the farm and the pies are made fresh daily," she added. "Would you like more coffee?" she asked, recovering her poise.

"Yes, thank you," he smiled as he cleaned up the last crumbs of pie from the plate. Alice poured another cup of coffee for him.

"I'm new in the area," he said, tapping on the map he had been studying. "I was just out driving around trying to get to know the countryside when I saw your sign on the highway. The thought of home-baked pie was just too much for me and I couldn't resist stopping in."

"I'm glad you did, sir," Alice said, replacing the coffee pot to the counter.

"My name is Steve Creighton," said the stranger. Alice paused, thinking that the name sounded familiar, all the while trying not to let him see her quizzical look.

"Pleased to meet you, Mr. Creighton," Alice said turning around to face the gentleman.

"I'm the new pastor at First Christian Church in Maplecrest," he continued. "I just moved in a week ago."

Alice looked surprised, knowing she had heard the name somewhere. It was all coming together now as she remembered Homer's excited news of the church finally getting a pastor.

Carrie turned from her post at the cash register with new interest as she busied herself behind the counter, eager to hear every word.

"And I'm Alice Henderson," she replied brightly. "I knew I'd heard your name somewhere! One of your parishioners works here at the orchard. Homer Martinson," Alice informed him.

"Oh, yes! Homer! Is this the place? I remember that now. He's the talented musician, isn't he?" the pastor asked.

"Yes, " Alice replied, "That's Homer! He works part-time for us and also part-time for his father's business, Martinson Hardware Stores."

"Oh, yes; I remember" Pastor Creighton said. "There are so many names and faces. I'm trying to put them all together," he laughed.

"Oh! This is Carrie Brooks," Alice said, remembering her assistant who was looking quite busy, diligently wiping the counters. Carrie stopped and walked over to Alice who continued to introduce her. "Carrie's father is Pastor Roger Brooks of Maplewood Christian Fellowship where we attend. It's right down the road a few miles," Alice said, gesturing in the general direction of the church.

"Oh, say, I think I passed it on the way here! A large white building with a bell in front?" he asked as he shook Carrie's hand.

"Yes," Carrie nodded with a smile.

"Pleased to make your acquaintance," he added to Carrie who was now relaxed from her earlier trepidation concerning the tall stranger's request to see the manager.

Carrie asked Pastor Creighton how he liked his new home and then informed him that it had been her family's home until recently when First Church bought it.

"I'm really enjoying the house," he said, "It's more than

adequate and really nice inside. Just like new actually with all the new improvements I hear they did."

Carrie smiled. "Excuse me," she said as she hurried to the cash register where the other customers were waiting. Alice and Pastor Creighton continued to talk as he finished his cup of coffee. Finally he stood up to leave. He complimented Alice once again on the pie as he paid Carrie.

"I hope you'll stop in again," Alice said as she began to head back to the kitchen.

"You can be sure I will," he smiled. He chatted just a bit more before leaving.

Alice and Carrie glanced at each other as Pastor Creighton pulled his car out of the parking lot and onto the road. The girls thought this pastor seemed young in comparison to the last few men to fill this position at First Church. But Steve Creighton had told them that he was just out of seminary and eager to pastor his first congregation.

Just as the two stood reviewing Pastor Creighton's words, a flour-dusted Eileen burst from the kitchen with an annoyed and questioning expression. "Hey, where have you been?" she said to Alice. "I'm up to my elbows in pie crusts and the oven's buzzing with more waiting to come out!"

"Oh, I'm sorry!" Alice apologized as she hurried back to her baking. "Carrie and I were just talking to the new pastor from First Church."

"What?" Eileen asked with a puzzled look, "And you didn't call me and introduce me?" She finished her sentence with a pout. "Where is he?" she asked as she leaned around to see out the dining room door.

"Oh, I'm sorry. He already left," Alice said sincerely. "I forgot. I guess we got to talking." Carrie smiled at the thought of Eileen, the outgoing, friendly type who hated to miss a new acquaintance, even if he was a pastor probably ten years her senior!

On Friday at Farmer's Market, Katie completely sold out of Alice's pies by noon. It was such a busy day at the Blooming Hills booth it was as if the Hendersons couldn't bring enough pies or pick enough fruit to keep up with all the demand. Meanwhile, back at the bakery, Alice and her workers were still busy as well. Another day with several customers went by and Saturday afternoon saw the girls closing the bakery for another week with record sales.

Carrie found her summer speeding by; her days filled with her job at the bakery and her chores at home. Many excited discussions occurred each evening around the Brooks' dinner table with Luke and Carrie always brimming with details of work. The latest discussion this week centered on the meeting with the new pastor. Carrie was surprised to learn that her father hadn't even met Pastor Creighton yet. Carrie had talked to him only briefly when he had visited the bakery to pick up pies and a few other items. Dad said he intended to try to meet with him within the next week.

The next Tuesday afternoon Carrie was serving bakery customers when a familiar face entered the dining area. Pastor Creighton smiled and waved as he sat down at a table and waited for Carrie to take his order. "Hi, Carrie?" he smiled hopefully, trying to remember her name as she arrived at his table.

"Yes. Hello, Pastor Creighton, what can I get for you today?" she asked, pleasantly.

"Well, I'd take another piece of that strawberry pie and a glass of iced tea," he smiled.

"I'm sorry," Carrie started, "We're completely out of strawberry right now."

"Oh," he said, disappointed. "What other kinds do you have?"

"Well, I believe we have custard, chocolate cream, lemon, coconut, and cherry."

"Umm...I believe I'll try custard today," Pastor Creighton decided.

"Thank you," Carrie said as she wrote the order on the ticket. In a minute she returned with a tall, cold glass of iced tea and a generous slice of custard pie.

"Looks great!" Pastor Creighton said as he picked up his fork and spread his napkin on his lap, preparing to enjoy his dessert.

Carrie walked away and tended to some other customers at the cash register. When they left, Carrie went back to Pastor Creighton's table and gave him a refill of tea from the pitcher. "Is everything ok?" Carrie asked.

Pastor Steve smiled and then said, "Well, actually, umm...could I speak to the manager?" Carrie's smile suddenly turned to a look somewhere close to shock.

"Sure, I'll get her," she answered, failing to notice the twinkle in his eye as she turned toward the kitchen. Carrie went into the kitchen closing the double doors behind her. "Alice! Pastor Creighton's here. He ate a few bites of pie again and asked to see the manager!" she whispered, her face clouded with a worried look.

"Ok," Alice said bravely and smiled, though she was rather puzzled. She stopped to wash her hands and then went out to the dining room. Carrie quickly checked through the window to see if any new customers had come in. None had so she turned to assess Eileen's reaction. Eileen was popping a pie into the oven as she hurried to get a glimpse of the new pastor. She bustled to the doors and nearly pushed Carrie aside as she looked out into the dining room.

"What do you suppose he wants with Alice again?" Carrie whispered as the two girls peered out through the double doors.

Eileen didn't seem to hear Carrie at all. "He's tall! And he looks young!" she exclaimed.

Carrie could see Pastor Creighton was smiling as he spoke with Alice. He didn't seem upset about anything! Eileen turned to go back to baking pies, seeming to be satisfied just to get a glimpse of him.

Just then three customers came in and Carrie knew she had to go serve them. She went out into the dining room to take their orders as soon as they sat down at a table near Pastor Creighton. After a minute or so, Carrie noticed that the pastor rose part way out of his chair and gestured to Alice to sit down as he held the other chair out for her. Alice was smiling and didn't seem a bit disturbed, so there must not be anything wrong, she deduced.

Carrie brought three glasses of water to the new customers and handed them a menu. "I'll give you a few minutes to decide," she said politely and went back to the counter.

The restaurant area was small enough that she couldn't help passing Alice and the pastor on her way back to the front. She got the pitcher of iced tea and asked Pastor Creighton if he cared for anything else, "Just a little more tea, thank you," he said holding his glass toward Carrie.

She filled the glass and started away but stopped and hesitated as she looked back at Alice. "Can I get you anything?" she asked her almost as an afterthought.

"No, I don't think so, Carrie, but thank you." Carrie went on to the next table to get the peoples' order, wondering all the time what Pastor Creighton was telling Alice.

"Are you ready to order?" Carrie asked pleasantly to the three customers, a young boy and his grandparents.

"Cherry pie with vanilla ice cream, please." the little fellow answered decidedly.

"And you, ma'am?" Carrie asked, turning to the grandmother.

"Umm…" the woman said, pausing as she studied the menu. A long silence followed.

As she waited for the woman's order, Carrie could not help overhearing Pastor Creighton at the next table. He was asking Alice, "Do you serve meals here?"

"No, not yet," she replied, "But we're considering expanding the menu for next year to include at least soup and sandwiches."

Carrie wrote down an order of custard pie when the lady finally decided and continued to wait on the grandfather's order. She heard Pastor Creighton continue, "Well, then could you recommend a good restaurant around here? A fellow gets tired of his own cooking after a while you know, especially when he's not very good at it," he chuckled. Smiling, Alice hesitated a moment. Soon Carrie heard her name a few of the more popular area restaurants.

Finally the grandfather gave his order and Carrie was off to prepare the food. When she passed Pastor Creighton and Alice's table she could hardly believe her ears! He was asking Alice to join him for a dinner at the restaurant she had recommended! What would Alice say?

Carrie knew the Henderson family didn't really approve of dating the way most people defined it, yet Alice was older and he was a pastor after all. Would Alice accept? "Is he asking her for a date?" Carrie wondered. Even though she was curious, she forced herself to keep her mind on her work and not deliberately crane her ears in Alice's direction. She couldn't help what she'd overheard, but she didn't intend to become a busybody.

Just having to walk by the table to serve the other customers made Carrie feel like she was intruding. But the other people must be served. Carrie saw Alice lower her eyes and fidget a bit nervously with the placemat in front of her while speaking to the pastor. As Carrie passed the table carrying a tray loaded with desserts for the other customers, she heard Alice explaining sweetly,

"That's very flattering of you to ask, but I'd prefer if you spoke with my father first. You see, my family believes in something we call courtship, for lack of a better word." Alice hesitated a moment, not knowing whether this man would understand what she meant. "I suppose you may wonder why a woman my age would ask you to speak with her father." At this, the pastor nodded slightly, seeming to ask Alice to explain. "I could accept your invitation. It's not like my parents would punish me or anything like that." Alice smiled. "They've raised me to follow God and they trust my judgment. But I've voluntarily placed myself under their leadership. Even though I'm out of school and could conceivably be out on my own living somewhere else, I would rather not accept such an invitation from a gentleman without their prior consent. I hope you understand," Alice finished sincerely. Even after her explanation, Pastor Creighton seemed to be struggling to conceal his complete unfamiliarity with this concept.

"Well, so that was Alice's answer!" Carrie thought, "I'm proud of her. She honored her family's convictions even when her parents weren't around to watch her actions. That's true obedience from the heart," she observed. "After all, Alice is twenty-two years old and I know she'd like to marry someday. She easily could have accepted his invitation and not told Mr. and Mrs. Henderson at all."

Carrie's thoughts were awhirl for Alice's sake as she set the desserts in front of her eager customers. A few seconds later, on her way back to the counter, she hoped she had remembered to be polite to them having been so preoccupied with the happenings at the next table!

Now four more people had come in and seated themselves at the table across from the little boy and his grandparents, forcing Carrie past Alice and Pastor Creighton once again. Carrie almost felt sorry for the pastor who looked a little confused as he stared at Alice, not knowing what to say. He fumbled with his fork and took a bite of pie and a sip of tea rather nervously. Alice was speaking again and she appeared to be explaining her family's convictions to the bewildered pastor.

Out of the corner of her eye, Carrie saw Alice rise from her chair. She took Pastor Creighton's empty pie plate but was still talking with him as she stood by the table. By the time Carrie filled the latest orders, the first customers had finished, leaving their payment on the table along with a generous tip. Carrie cleared their table and could hear Alice saying, "My father will be glad to speak with you, if you choose. I hope you understand, Pastor Creighton."

Carrie took the dishes and hurried to the kitchen not lingering to hear his reply. She pushed open one of the double doors and placed the dishes in the big dishwasher. Somehow she felt a bit breathless and embarrassed. Eileen looked up from her crust rolling across the room. "What is going on? Every time that Pastor Creighton comes in I get stuck out here alone! What does he want with Alice?" she asked in exasperation.

Carrie was glad her back was turned to Eileen as she arranged the dishes in the machine. Her reddening cheeks would possibly betray Alice's personal business. Carrie couldn't lie and she wished she hadn't heard a thing. What should she say? Would Alice want Eileen to know? Many questions raced through Carrie's mind in a few flashing seconds. She started to reply slowly but honestly, "Well, for one thing, I think he really likes the pie and wants to compliment Alice," she started, hoping that would be enough to satisfy Eileen's curiosity.

"Well, is he going to do this every time he comes in?" Eileen retorted.

"No, I doubt it, Eileen," Carrie replied. "After all, he's been in a few times and just picked up something to take home." Just then the swinging door opened and Alice entered. Carrie turned to face her. She had a slight blush to her cheeks and her eyes met Carrie's with a knowing look as if they shared a common secret. Carrie thought it looked as if Alice was smiling slightly as she leaned against the kitchen wall. Carrie picked up a fresh cloth to wipe tables and headed rather hurriedly for the door.

"What's going on?" Eileen demanded. Before passing through the door, Carrie glanced nervously at Alice, wondering what she would say to her curious sister. "What did Pastor Creighton want to tell you?" Eileen demanded again, as if she felt left out. She seemed to realize there was something to be "known" and she was the only one who had failed to find it out.

"It's ok," Alice said, seeing Carrie's worried look. "Pastor Creighton called me out to compliment me on the pie, Eileen. However, I think he had another reason as well." Alice blushed once again as she continued, "He said he's tired of his own cooking and could I recommend a good restaurant around here."

Carrie shifted from one foot to the other nervously, but Alice's gestures seemed to ask her to stay for a few seconds longer, "I checked out the other customers," she said, indicating that Carrie didn't need to hurry back to the dining room. "Anyway, when I told him that Schenkel's in Blue Creek was a favorite that I'd recommend, he asked me if I'd like to join him for dinner on Saturday night."

"Alice!" Eileen exclaimed as if she was scolding her sister. "You know what Mom and Daddy have always taught us about dating!" Alice held her hand up for Eileen to calm down.

"I know, I know. I didn't accept."

"What did you do, Alice?" Eileen asked, now smiling with girlish curiosity. Carrie relaxed a bit now and managed to smile as well.

"Well, basically; I told him our family was committed to something more like an old-fashioned courtship and that I wasn't going to accept his invitation without my parents' knowing first. Then I told him he was welcome to speak with Daddy," Alice replied matter-of-factly. "And, it wasn't exactly easy to explain that," she added.

Eileen had stopped her work and was listening intently with her arms folded. She looked as if she was enjoying this immensely. "So what did he say to that?" she probed with eager anticipation.

"Well, at first I don't think he knew what to say," Alice replied. "He seemed sort of nervous. I felt kind of sorry for him. I tried to explain what I meant by courtship and he said he understood." Alice smiled as if that was all there was to say.

The kitchen was silent for a moment as the girls looked at one another. "Well, is that all?" Eileen said, finally breaking the silence. "I mean is he going to talk to Mom and Daddy or what?"

"I don't know," Alice smiled, "I guess that remains to be seen."

"You don't even know him!" Eileen reminded her sister.

"I realize that, so I'm not going to worry about it," Alice assured her. "If he does call, Daddy will know how to handle the situation. I'm glad my parents' will take care of it; at least I don't have to handle something like this alone. This is one of the nice things about an arrangement like this, wouldn't you say? It was a bit embarrassing explaining our convictions to him, but what's really more awkward—explaining my convictions or having to go out alone with someone you barely even know for a whole evening, wondering all the time what to talk about?" With that Alice went back to her work, apparently unruffled by the whole scene.

Carrie went on out to the dining room with a new admiration for Alice, a new determination to be contented with letting the Lord bring her a husband some day, and a real wondering about how this whole situation would turn out. Later that evening alone in her room, Carrie wrote the events of her day in her diary. The incident with Pastor Creighton took up a good deal of space. Carrie wrote, "I'm so impressed with Alice's calm faith." On the last few lines she added, "She's taking it all in stride, putting herself in her parents' hands. What if Pastor C. is the man she'll marry? How will she know in her heart that he's the one?" At the end of the entry under "Prayer Requests" Carrie wrote, "To know who I'm supposed to marry and be sure about him when and if the time comes."

Several weeks went by and the three girls at Alice's Bakery had neither seen nor heard news of the new pastor, Steve Creighton, except some general conversation from Homer about First Church and the new minister.

Eileen had found a few secret opportunities to whisper an excited question or two to Carrie over the past few weeks. "What do you suppose will happen with Alice and Pastor Creighton?" "I wonder what Mom and Daddy will say to the whole thing?" And finally the question Eileen most wanted an answer to, "How do you think Alice feels about Steve Creighton?"

One day when Eileen and Carrie were alone in the kitchen rolling out pie crusts, Eileen asked Carrie, "Has Alice said anything to you about how she feels about Pastor Creighton?"

Carrie looked up form her work, "What do you mean, Eileen?"

"Oh, Carrie, you know what I mean! I'm so anxious to know what's happening! You know, if he's going to court her or not. Has she told you anything?" Eileen pressed her friend for details.

"Well, Eileen, maybe there's nothing to tell."

Eileen looked disappointed. "So you mean you don't know any more than I do?"

"No," Carrie smiled, "If there was anything to know, don't you suppose you'd know before me anyway? After all, you're her sister."

"I know, but she thinks of you as one of her closest friends. I'm just her little sister. Sometimes I think she just sees me as a pest." Carrie smiled at Eileen's assessment of the relationship.

"I don't think that's the way it is, Eileen. I've never seen her give you any reason to feel that way. And besides, you're just a few months younger than I am. If she thinks of me as a close friend, I'm sure she's not holding your being younger against you when it comes to sisterly confidences."

Eileen was silent for a while. Finally she spoke, "Oh! I just can hardly stand the suspense! I'm anxious to see how something like this really works out! When Katie and Joe got married, I guess I was too young to care. I didn't pay that much attention."

"Well," Carrie began, "I guess I'm curious too. After all there aren't too many families around here committed to courtship, it's kind of a "new" old idea, so there's not very many examples. But as far as Alice is concerned, you have to remember that she doesn't even know Pastor Creighton, other than the brief contact we've had with him here, and neither do your parents. I'm sure there's no point in wondering how she feels about him. She probably doesn't feel any way about him. If anything, she's probably been praying about it. That's the first step anyway. And truthfully, Eileen, that's what you and I should be doing too—praying for Alice instead of wondering and whispering behind her back."

Eileen was silent. She wore a slightly pouty look as she shoved a couple of peach pies into the oven. She knew her friend was right. Carrie had reminded Eileen of a most important ingredient in a godly relationship—prayer. Eileen realized that Carrie was exhibiting a much more mature attitude toward the situation and consequently she felt a bit shamed. The girls worked on in silence for a while until Alice entered the kitchen. "How's it going, girls?" she asked cheerfully.

"Fine," they chorused. "We've got all the bread raising and we're just starting the pies," Carrie announced.

"Good, good," Alice remarked, assessing the progress in her kitchen. "How about you relieving me out front for a few hours, Carrie? It's been really busy this morning and you know I sort of prefer the kitchen work and I know you enjoy the dining room too."

"Ok," Carrie answered. She washed her hands and went out front where a few tables were filled with people Alice had already served. Peach season was bringing in yet another wave of customers and a boost in business just as had been the case with each successive type of fruit crop all summer.

Carrie knew that peaches were the last crop before school started and their ripening marked the end of her full time career at Alice's bakery. In two weeks she would be dropping down to part time hours as her senior year commenced. "Senior year!" Carrie thought it still sounded unreal as she whispered the words to herself again and again throughout the day. She anxiously looked forward to all the fun that she hoped was in store, while she was also saddened by the thought of spending less time at the job she had grown to love.

About four o'clock, Alice came from the kitchen with a stack of clean plates still warm from the dishwasher. While she was placing them in orderly fashion on the shelves, the familiar ring of the doorbell sounded as more customers walked in. This time it was John Mark, Luke, and Homer who had just finished in the orchards for the day.

The three boys, tanned from the hard work in the sun, strolled up to the swivel stools at the counter and sat down. John Mark was the first to speak. "Are we too late to get something to drink, Ally?" he asked directly to Alice.

"No, we'll serve you. But Carrie, you'd better lock the door and turn the sign now," Alice advised.

"Ok," Carrie answered as she headed for the door.

"What can I get you fellows?" Alice asked sweetly.

"A nap!" Luke said as he dropped his head to his hands. All the others laughed knowingly.

"I agree, Luke," Homer added, "But before the nap I'd like a chocolate soda, please!" Everyone laughed again and exchanged small talk as Carrie helped Alice fix the final orders of the day. By now Eileen had come out from the kitchen with two fresh peach pies to be placed in the glass case as a head start for tomorrow's morning customers. She greeted the boys and joined in the talking and laughter.

"Hey, Eileen, are those peach pies?" Homer asked between sips of his soda.

"Yes, fresh from the oven!" she replied.

"Could you box one up for me, please? Pastor Creighton asked me last night if I'd bring one back and drop it off on my way home. I almost forgot! He really loves peach pie, I guess."

Carrie tried not to show her surprise but she found herself exchanging a hurried glance with Eileen who looked a bit surprised as well. Carrie saw Eileen steal a glance in Alice's direction in hopes of summing up her reaction to Homer's statement. But gracious Alice did not allow herself to betray any feeling one way or the other. She simply went on, wiping the counter and taking care of all the details she would normally attend to at closing time. "Sure, I'll box the pie," Eileen replied, "I'll do it right now."

After the boys finished, they rose to pay and John Mark typically bought a handful of peppermints from Carrie as he left, once again offering her a piece of the candy as had become his custom. This time Carrie graciously accepted one of them.

Luke was the last in line. "I'll wait for you in the car, Carrie. Take your time. I think I'll try to get a little nap in," he grinned.

"Ok," Carrie chuckled as she closed the cash register.

After the boys left, Alice asked the girls to finish the final closing. Because she was teaching a children's class at prayer meeting tonight, she hoped to get a little extra studying and preparation done. As soon as she left, Eileen looked at Carrie and said, "So that's the way Pastor Creighton is! He won't come in here anymore because of what Alice told him! I'll bet he's too embarrassed to face her."

"Well, I had to wonder too," Carrie admitted. "It does seem kind of odd. Before he always stopped in himself and now he sends Homer instead. I admit I thought the same thing. But, maybe we shouldn't be too critical. Let's give him the benefit of the doubt. It could be that he's real busy. Or maybe he just feels awkward because he doesn't understand the convictions Alice discussed with him." Eileen listened to Carrie's remarks. "Courtship is an unusual concept to a lot of people. I mean, think how you'd feel if you were in his shoes."

"I suppose so," Eileen admitted as they left, turning the lights out and locking the door behind them.

As soon as Luke and Carrie reached their home, they knew it was time for chores. Even though they were tired from a long day at Blooming Hills, they understood that the rest of the family still counted on them to do their chores at home. Luke went to the pasture gate to lead Blossom in for milking and Carrie went up to the porch where Mom was sitting on one of the rockers with a bowl of late beans in her lap. She snapped their ends rhythmically as she greeted Carrie. Carrie pulled up a chair and began helping as she and Mom talked over their day. Addy was asleep on the porch swing with her doll. "Your sister played hard today," Mom said, motioning toward the little girl. Carrie smiled. How Addy had grown! Carrie felt like she had missed a lot this summer in some ways but that she had experienced a lot in other ways.

"How was your day, honey?" Mom asked.

"Oh, fine," Carrie replied. "We worked hard as usual. I'm kind of sorry to see it all end in a week or so."

"It was a good experience for you, wasn't it—working for Alice, I mean?"

"It was great! I loved being around my friends so much. I'm really going to miss it, yet I'm really looking forward to my senior year," Carrie's eyes sparkled at the thought. "It's really exciting, but a little scary too. Being done with school sort of feels like a big step."

"It is, dear, but it's a step that most everyone gets to at one time or another," her mother replied.

"I've been praying a lot about what to do after high school, yet I still don't feel I've gotten any clear direction from God." Carrie's usually happy voice trailed off on a concerned note.

"That's ok, Carrie. Maybe you're supposed to keep on just as you are for a while. God will speak to you all in good time. A lot could happen in a year, you know," Mom wisely reassured her daughter.

Carrie nodded and the two headed for the kitchen with the prepared beans. Carrie picked Addy up and carried her to the living room and laid her on the couch to finish her nap. Then the supper preparations began.

Before the evening meal, Dad read a short devotional. The discussion around the table centered as usual on the activities of everyone's day. Carrie listened as always to her family's conversation but she found her self keenly interested when her father mentioned First Church's new minister. "I finally got to talk with Pastor Creighton today," he began.

"Oh?" Mom replied. "What's he like?"

"Well, he seems to be a very likeable fellow. I met him for lunch. We had a nice talk and I know it's going to be good working with him from time to time." Carrie swallowed hard and listened intently.

"He is very well-liked at First Church I hear," Mom added. "I saw June Harris last Friday at Farmer's Market, her sister attends First Church you know. She gave a glowing report of Pastor Creighton. In fact, she just couldn't say enough about him." Carrie found this easy to imagine, as June Harris could be as zealous in her demeanor as her daughter Darla.

"He's been working really hard during his first few weeks here and decided to take the day off today," Dad remarked, " so he was free to meet me for lunch."

Carrie sat shocked, but silently continued eating. With her father's last statement, she now realized that what she and Eileen had hoped—that Pastor Creighton was too busy to make a trip out to Blooming Hills Bakery for his own pie—simply was not true. He had avoided coming there for some other reason! Carrie felt disappointed in the new pastor now. Maybe he wasn't a man of high character after all. It looked as though he wanted the delicious baked goods but wasn't willing to face up to Alice and Mr. and Mrs. Henderson. Carrie wisely determined to keep her thoughts to herself as she realized from experience how damaging it could be to a church to have people speak ill of the pastor. She was not about to be a gossip or busybody and undermine Pastor Creighton's ministry. After all First Church had gone long enough without a pastor and she sincerely hoped this new man could help the church in a positive way to recover from the months without a senior leader. After all, it was Homer's church and she wanted her friend's church to be strong as much as she did her own.

When Friday arrived, Carrie found it difficult to work with the knowledge that an important evening lay ahead. Tonight her family would make the trip to First Church where the FCH annual planning meeting would be held. Carrie tried to conceal her excitement at the thought of another round of elections for the Student Activities Committee. She had to admit it had been such fun to be a part of the committee that she wished last year's group could have just gone on and on. But that was probably too much to expect; in fact it was impossible. At least one member had graduated. So she kept trying to quell her excitement as she faced the possibility that she might not be re-elected. The group of students on the SAC had come to be such a part of her life that she wondered what a school year would be like any other way.

But when she awoke Saturday morning she happily rose with the knowledge that she was again a member of the committee. What an exciting evening it had been! Homer, Carrie, and John Mark were re-elected as well as Luke, Tom Harris and Eileen. The seventh member, replacing outgoing Timothy Cox, was Darla Harris. Carrie was glad for Darla. It would have been painful for her to be left out in her senior year. Darla seemed to have a need to be included. Carrie had noticed a softening in Darla's personality of late. Oh, Darla would always be Darla, but she had changed somehow in little ways and Carrie suspected the Lord had been working in Darla's life to smooth out the rough edges just as He had done in her own. So all in all, with the activities committee remaining basically the same, senior year promised to be as much fun as her junior year had been. Last year's members counted it a double honor that they had all been re-elected. It spoke well of their performance and felt like a stamp of approval of sorts to Carrie and the others.

During last evening's events, Carrie was even moved to reconsider her opinion of Pastor Creighton. He came to the meeting even when it didn't involve him just to show support for the home school families of First Church and to act as host. He was genuinely friendly and made a special point to visit the Brooks' family table and chat. He remembered Carrie and spoke well of her to her parents concerning her job, complimenting her abilities as a waitress. When he was introduced to the crowd by John Henderson and asked to pray, his words were sincere and devout. He prayed with the demeanor of one who had spent time with the God and knew Him as Lord and friend. How could anyone like that be of low character, flippant or insincere? Carrie was sure she must have been wrong and was determined to focus on his good qualities from now on.

The Note

As school began for another year, Carrie was only working now on Saturdays and this too would soon end with the last apple crop. The mornings were chilly and a hint of frost was in the air. The days were clear and sunny but each one was shorter than the last. It seemed the calendar pages flipped rapidly and November was soon upon the Brooks family. The Friday classes would start within days. Carrie eagerly anticipated taking the Spanish class this year, thinking it may be a logical step if she decided to pursue missions.

Biology was also being offered and Luke was the first one to sign up. He was becoming quite a capable farmer and was, in large part, the manager of Blossom Lane. His chickens were doing well and he was the proprietor of a small orchard that was becoming healthier and showing more promise with each season. He never seemed to tire of planting and coaxing all manner of new vegetables in the family garden. His experience at Blooming Hills had only served to whet his appetite for more in the business of farming. All winter he studied his science texts diligently and read endlessly of horticulture and animal science, books that Carrie found quite technical and boring. But science was Luke's favorite subject and understandably he seemed to excel in it.

On the first day of Friday classes, Luke and Carrie worked diligently to finish all their regular subjects in time to leave by noon. At lunchtime, they each grabbed a quick sandwich at the kitchen table where Addy sat eating a bowl of homemade alphabet soup.

She played as much as she ate, trying to find letters among the vegetables. Carrie laughed at her cute little sister as she ate the last bite of her sandwich.

"After today I'll help you spell something in Spanish with your soup, sweetie."

Addy just smiled at Carrie. Luke laughed as he scooped up his books.

"Oh, I forgot, Carrie!" Mom said, "I've got a new Spanish book for you! Don't take Luke's old one; it's falling apart." It was true. Luke's book had lost the cover and the pages were all loose. Before purchasing it for Luke at a used book sale last year, it had already been owned by several students. Mom went to Dad's office and opened a file drawer from which she drew out a fairly new Spanish textbook. "Luke's old book was really bad, so I borrowed one for you to use this year. Take good care of it; we have to return it when you're done with it."

"Where'd you get it, Mom?" Carrie asked as she put the book into her backpack.

"I borrowed it from Esther Henderson. John Mark used it last year."

"Well, thanks for thinking of getting me a newer one," Carrie replied. She remembered that John Mark had taken Spanish last year at Friday classes. She had seen him carry the book many times.

Luke and Carrie left for Friday classes with books in tow. It was great to see all their friends again and start in on the old routine. After the first hour, a fifteen-minute break was given and then the students switched classes. Carrie went to a First Aid/Health class while many others went to the Art and Drama classes. The first day of Friday classes was so busy that Carrie never even opened a book. Most of the teachers gave out a class syllabus and spent time giving overviews and getting acquainted with the students. Carrie was excited about all the classes and was even anxious to begin the assigned homework for Spanish, which consisted of reading the first chapter in the book. But that would have to wait until after tonight or even Monday since this evening the Brooks family was going out to dinner for a special treat. It was to be a family night. They planned to go to Farmer's Market one last time and eat at Golden Garden.

Today was the last market of this season. The businesses were closing since the produce was nearly done for the year. Pumpkins and cider were the only items most farmers had left and the permanent stalls were closing as well. Some of the booths were known to have fantastic sales at the last few markets of the year and Carrie and her mother hoped to find some bargains.

As the last class of the afternoon closed, Carrie began turning her attention to the fun evening ahead. She and some of the other girls gathered after classes and were discussing the probable bargains to be found at the market. As Luke and Carrie lingered with their friends, as usual an informal gathering of the closely-knit SAC group began to form in the foyer as other students left for the day. Carrie was glad for the chance to see Eileen for a few minutes and chat. Carrie was on a different schedule than her friend and they didn't have as much time to visit as they had last year.

"We're going to Farmer's Market one last time tonight," Carrie announced to Eileen, "And we are eating supper at Golden Garden!"

"Oh, really?" Eileen sparkled. "That sounds like fun! I'd love to be able to go once more, but I've got to help with the last of the cider making. Joe and Katie took the truck to market today and I guess John Mark is going to help Daddy with closing things up for the winter around the farm." Carrie knew that the coming of winter meant a new kind of work on the farm, the cleaning of machinery and the winterizing of buildings.

"Say, Carrie, Alice wanted me to ask you if you could come in to work one last time tomorrow and help her do a big bunch of pie crusts. She's going to freeze them ahead for pumpkin pies. I guess she's got an unbelievable amount of orders for Thanksgiving and she's trying to get a head start," Eileen explained.

"I think I could," Carrie said, "I'll ask tonight and then give her a call."

"I'll be working on cider and the last of the pumpkin sales. Plus we want to winterize the sales building so I won't be able to help her. It would be great if you could. She said she wanted to start at eight. That way with an early start, she could get done before too late in the afternoon. You know she never likes to work too late on Saturdays because of studying the Sunday school lesson and getting set for church."

Carrie nodded, knowing it was the same at her house. Everyone made an effort to limit their Saturday night activities in order to prepare for Sunday. It was a time to slow down from the week's work and to get ready for worship the next day. But little did the girls realize that they were partially mistaken in what they thought was Alice's motive for finishing early. There was another important reason as well.

When Luke and Carrie arrived home, Mom greeted them as they came in the back door and Luke set his books on the laundry table. He grabbed a fresh cookie from the kitchen counter while Carrie and Mom talked about all the news of Friday classes.

"Quickly finish your chores and get ready to leave for Blue Creek. Your father called from the store and said they were quite busy today and he'd meet us at the market at five fifteen to save driving home first. So we've really got to hurry," Mom directed. Carrie hurried to change clothes as Luke grabbed his work coat from the hook in the mudroom and put on his boots.

"I'll help you, Luke," Carrie called as she quickly headed up the open staircase. In minutes, she was out the door and headed to the barn to help her brother with the duties of feeding the livestock. Working together, they got everything done in time to get to Blue Creek and meet Dad at Golden Garden.

It was an enjoyable dinner for the Brooks. Each of the family ordered a different Oriental meal. Carrie was fond of the chicken dishes while Luke could make a meal of egg rolls. Dad liked chop suey and Mom's favorite was beef and peapods. Little Addy liked the crackers and cookies!

While the family ate, Dad quoted some verses from Ecclesiastes that spoke of everything having a time and a season. The Brooks' discussed the passing of seasons, evident all around them as farmers and vendors hustled and bustled to close down their market booths for the year. Dad related this to life and its seasons of change. Carrie and Luke heartily agreed, thinking back to the summer, now gone, but seeming to have been only yesterday.

After dinner, Luke and Dad went to the booths that interested them, while Chris and Carrie took Addy and shopped for things of interest to women. Dottie's Fabrics was having their annual "End of the Market" sale. The two women bought several yards of fabric for winter clothes and other sewing. While they were at Dottie's they met Amanda and Mrs. Melvin who were shopping for fabric as well. Carrie and Amanda chatted exuberantly about Friday classes, while their mothers talked of church and home school.

Later, Mom and Carrie put a wearying Addy in the fold-up stroller they had brought along. They stopped at a few more booths and made a purchase here and there. They passed many businesses already closed for the season. As they strolled past the Blooming Hills booth, Carrie thought how strange it looked all quiet and closed, no longer the hub of activity buzzing with eager shoppers. Only a small section was still open with the last of the cider and pumpkins. The large, prominent Blooming Hills counters looked lonely and deserted. It gave Carrie a funny feeling as she reflected on Dad's words about change and seasons in life. How she preferred to see the booth alive with people as it was in the summer!

Changes. Carrie pondered them for the rest of the evening. She was quieter than usual as she and her mom and Addy drove home. Luke and Dad were following them home in the pickup. By the time they arrived back at Blossom Lane it was already nine o'clock. After the car was unloaded and all the packages brought in and put away, Carrie excused herself to her room to relax awhile and read devotions before bed.

Carrie put on the new nightgown that she had made this summer and curled up comfortably in her favorite spot—her alcove window seat. She turned off the ceiling light and flipped on her soft reading lamp that sat atop a pretty dressing table near the window. She decided to open her Bible to the third chapter of Ecclesiastes and read the verses that Dad had quoted at suppertime. She read them slowly and then prayed to God about her own life. "Dear Lord, I thank you for today and all the wonderful experiences. I pray that you will guide me in the seasons of my life. You have been gracious in guiding me so far through many changes. Please help me to recognize when I need to change. Help me to hear Your directions, dear Lord."

Carrie continued praying, thinking of her senior year and all the changes that may await her in the spring. When she ended her prayers, she reached over to the nightstand where the pile of schoolbooks she had carried upstairs earlier lay near her lamp. She chose the Spanish book first and eagerly thumbed through the pages, enjoying the colorful pictures of Spanish speaking areas of the world.

As she turned a page near the center of the book, a piece of paper fell out on her lap. She turned it over and instantly recognized it as one of the typed handouts given at Friday classes the day of the character-building seminar last March. She had been given one just like it that day during the first hour class. It was simply a note about the FCH board meeting and the Holcombs' presentation on Saturday and Sunday. This one must have been John Mark's. But there seemed to be something unusual about this piece of paper. Carrie noticed several of the letters on the page had been circled-one here, another there. At first it seemed that the circled letters were just random doodling. But why would someone circle a bunch of letters?

Upon closer investigation Carrie noticed that the circled letters formed a pattern of words. She sat up straight and spelled out the first few words slowly, whispering them to herself. But as she read on she could hardly believe what she saw! "My...heart's...d-e-s-i-r-e...i-s-t... No, no, that's not a word," Carrie thought to herself and went on with her spelling. "i-s...is...t-o...to." Again she repeated the first line, "My heart's desire is to...."

She began to decipher the next line, "c-o-u-r-t-a-n-d-m-a-r-r-y," Carrie stopped suddenly, wondering what, if anything, the next line would reveal! "My heart's desire is to court and marry?" What in the world was this anyway? Her fingers touched the next few circled letters one by one. "C…" She was nearly scared to read any more, but she took a deep breath and continued. "a-r-r-i-e." Could it possibly be? "Carrie?" Her heart skipped a beat and she felt as if there were butterflies in her stomach as she read on out loud. "B-r-o-o-k-s." So that was what was spelled here! "My heart's desire is to court and marry Carrie Brooks!" she gasped.

She stood up now and looked at the paper again. She retraced the letters carefully in complete awe of the message she saw. She read it again and again and there was no mistake; it clearly spelled out, "My heart's desire is to court and marry Carrie Brooks!" Suddenly she remembered that Mom had borrowed this book from Esther Henderson. It had been John Mark's Spanish book! Is this the way he felt about her? Carrie was shocked, yet pleasantly surprised. Still, she couldn't imagine John Mark actually sitting and doodling such a thing! But this was his book! Was it true? Could it be true?

Carrie sat down again and folded the paper and slipped it into her diary that lay on the nightstand. As she leaned against the pile of soft, fluffy pillows on the window seat, she pondered the meaning of the paper that she realized she hadn't been meant to discover. Her mind went back to the day when the papers were given out at the Friday classes. She remembered vividly in her mind how John Mark and the other boys were sitting a few rows in front of she and Eileen. Was this what John Mark had been doing when it had appeared that he had been so diligently taking notes? That didn't seem to match John Mark's serious nature at all.

"Oh, my!" she suddenly said aloud, remembering the crash in the hallway that very day! Papers had flown in every direction as John Mark and Homer scrambled to put everything back together. It was entirely possible that the note was written by Homer!

"Homer Martinson?" Carrie exclaimed. This revelation shed new light on the message circled on the paper. Now Carrie couldn't possibly know which young man had written the coded words!

Carrie thought hard--as hard as she could to remember the sequence of events that day almost nine months ago. Slowly she was able to piece most of it back together. She remembered how Homer had traded some books with John Mark before they left the auditorium that day--books that had gotten mixed up in the shuffle in the hall. That being the case, the paper might be Homer's. But, the note had been passed out during first hour and either one of them could have done the writing and then stuffed it in the wrong book by accident during the crash in the hall. Homer could have written it during the Holcomb's seminar and then forgotten it when the books were traded!

"Oh, my!" Carrie breathed. "What will I do? I don't know how I can face either one of them again!" She couldn't help wishing she knew what had really happened and who the mystery author truly was! Her mind was a whirl of thoughts as she processed the meaning of it all and the shock of knowing that someone had written such intentions about her.

She turned her light off and flopped down on her bed. She lay staring through the darkness at her ceiling, illuminated only by the dim moonlight sifting through the lace curtains. Carrie's thoughts still raced long after she lay down and she found it impossible to drift off to sleep. After awhile she began to pray, "Dear Lord, I feel so stirred up about this." She paused and thought about that statement. "Yes, I am "stirred up," but it's a happy sort of unsettled feeling. At least I **know** there's someone out there who's thinking of asking to court **me** someday." Then she continued her prayer. "Please Lord, help me to quiet my heart and my thoughts. I've tired so hard to put my life in your hands and not worry about my future, when I'd be courted; even if I'd be courted. Now this feels like it changes everything! How will I listen for your direction with this knowledge ever present? Help me to rest, Lord, from my own thoughts and questions, Amen."

As Carrie lay still, she soon remembered the theme of the chapter she had read tonight—to everything there is a season—and how she had prayed to God about being able to hear His direction concerning changes. A few moments later, she had found the paper. Maybe this incident was to prepare her for a big change—the knowledge that someone was thinking of her as a wife! But on the other hand, maybe this paper was just the mindless doodling of a teenage boy and meant just about as much. Carrie finally drifted off to sleep with the assurance that she had re-committed her life, her thoughts, and her whole self to the Lord. She slept a very sound, peaceful sleep.

Someone's "Courting"

When Carrie awoke on Saturday she rose from her bed with a strange feeling of excitement. No one knew about the paper she had found except herself and the Lord. Maybe the writer of the circled letters had realized by now that his "secret" paper had slipped through his hands and he was living life with the same unsettled excitement as he searched frantically for it. "No," she thought to herself, "boys don't think that way. The person who wrote it has probably forgotten it by now—whoever he is," Carrie determined as she went about her morning activities. "But I am committed to praying for him in case he hasn't changed his mind!" she determined with a smile.

Carrie finished her chores early and headed off to Blooming Hills to meet Alice at eight. When she drove up the hill to the orchard buildings near the bakery, the first person she saw was John Mark. He was working around the barns and probably had been up since sunrise. Upon hearing a car, he turned from his work and saw that it was Carrie driving in. He smiled and waved at her. His bright flannel jacket was a vivid color against the crisp, blue of the autumn morning sky. Carrie felt a quick nervous jolt as she remembered again the mysterious paper and realized it would be silly to try to avoid John Mark just because of the note and there was no use trying. She waved back, attempting to be as poised and natural as always but feeling she had somehow failed and her actions would eventually betray her curiosity.

As she parked the car, she gathered her purse and looked

cautiously in John Mark's direction. He had gone back to his work and seemed like the old John Mark—nothing different. "Well, why shouldn't he?" Carrie thought. "Nothing is different," she reassured herself. Carrie watched him diligently working as she had seen him do so many times before and she scolded herself for her ridiculous suspicions. "John Mark Henderson could not have written that note. It's just not like him. He wouldn't sit idly day-dreaming anytime, but especially not during the Holcomb's teaching and definitely not during a class. It must have been Homer. Fun-loving Homer. Homer? Homer Martinson?" Carrie still couldn't imagine it. It was more believable that Homer Martinson would sit doodling such a thing, but Homer wanting to marry her? "Unbelievable!" Carrie decided aloud and dismissed the idea. Homer wasn't the husband type. He was...well, just Homer!

Carrie remembered some times when John Mark had been unusually kind and it had seemed as though he would have liked her in a boyfriend-girlfriend sort of way had they not both been committed to waiting for a courtship. But no, it was not to be that way and she reminded herself not to dwell on this whole matter. It might not be easy, but she'd try.

As she entered the bakery, Alice greeted her cheerfully from behind the cash register. "I'm so glad you could help me today, Carrie!" she smiled as she eagerly took her friend by the arm and steered her toward the kitchen where the counters were already lined with pie tins and ingredients, rolling pins and bowls.

"Eileen said you really needed the help and wanted to get done before too late this afternoon."

"Yes," Alice smiled.

"I don't blame you," Carrie continued, "I like to have a little extra time on Saturday afternoon to wash my hair and study the Sunday School lesson too. It's so awful to be rushed on Sunday morning."

Alice quietly smiled and hung her head shyly. "Carrie," she began, "that's not really the reason I need to get done early."

"Oh?" Carrie said. She noticed the pleasant smile Alice wore as she began to explain.

"I didn't tell Eileen that **that's why** I needed you today. I hope you weren't misled."

"I guess she didn't say you **did,** come to think of it," Carrie admitted. "I guess we both just assumed that."

Alice continued to smile. "I didn't tell Eileen yet, but tonight Mother and Daddy have invited Pastor Creighton over for pie and coffee about seven o'clock." Alice's smile widened now as she watched Carrie's face change from questioning shock to a knowing smile in the few moments it took her to realize what Alice must be about to say next.

Alice went on happily filling in the details. "Carrie, he met with Daddy a couple of times after that day that I told him I wouldn't date him; remember that?" Carrie nodded, excited to be the privileged confidante in this matter. "At their first meeting, Daddy explained how we feel about letting God lead our relationships and all and then he told him he could pray about it and come back to talk again if he felt led."

Carrie felt breathless with excitement as she waited for Alice to go on. "Daddy said Pastor Creighton contacted him a week later and asked to meet with him again. He told Daddy that he had been thinking and praying about the whole matter and he was willing to honor our family's convictions. He said he could certainly see the wisdom in Christians being led by God's Spirit when it comes to relationships like this. That's when he also told Daddy that he had been praying for a wife for over a year and a half and his parents had been praying along with him, but they'd never heard of anyone having an old fashioned courtship. He told them he had met a girl that he was interested in and they were thrilled."

Alice was beaming now with the happy news. Carrie stood speechless, but smiling, sharing her friend's joy.

"My parents found out that Pastor Creighton's family has so much in common with us. He told Mom and Dad so much about them. They felt very positive about their conversations. They'll be coming for a visit next month during the holidays and we'll get to meet them then. They're anxious to see their son's new church."

"Oh, Alice, I hardly know what to say!" Carrie finally answered. "I'm so happy for you!"

"Thank you!" Alice said, continuing to explain. "That's why Pastor Creighton didn't come in anymore after his second visit. He said he felt he shouldn't come here until Mom and Dad and I had time to pray about all this and give our final approval."

Carrie saw it all fitting together now. She and Eileen had been so wrong about the Pastor in their original assessment! He was actually a man of the highest character. He wouldn't attempt to see Alice even in a business association until her parents agreed. "How noble!" Carrie thought. She had a new admiration for the chivalrous Pastor Creighton.

"Well, anyway, I got ahead of myself," Alice continued. "Then Daddy asked me if I felt I would like to pray about whether or not Pastor Creighton might be God's choice for me. I agreed to pray about the matter and I did for several weeks. I felt such peace about the whole thing and I had to admit I was quite drawn to him and would like to get to know him better. So here we are! And tonight he's coming over for his first visit—dessert and coffee."

Alice took a deep breath and sighed, the sincere smile still radiating from her face. Carrie just smiled back and shook her head in awe. The two girls finally burst into laughter mingled with happy tears as they hugged each other and Carrie congratulated her friend again.

"I guess we better get to work," Alice admitted after a moment, "Enough of the celebrating for now!" So the two girls set to the tasks of baking.

After working together rather silently for several minutes, Carrie looked up from her pie crusts and said, "Maybe you better tell Eileen!" Both girls burst into fresh laughter and giggles knowing how Eileen hated to be left out of news.

"You're probably right!" Alice agreed. They talked about how the perky Eileen might react with such a surprise thrust upon her. Carrie confided to Alice how the two had pictured Pastor Creighton as being a coward at first because he sent Homer for his pies. Upon hearing this, Alice promised to take time to tell Eileen at lunch hour before she heard it from anyone else.

As Carrie worked, she was filled with the good news of a courtship possibly beginning and she was glad to be seeing how it would all work out, yet she was almost bursting trying to hold in the incident of the note. She wished she could tell Alice, yet she knew she better not, especially since it could have been John Mark who wrote it. No sense exciting more peoples' suspicions.

At noon the bakery's big kitchen door swung open as Eileen came in during her lunch break. She greeted her sister and Carrie as she pulled a stool up to the counter by the big sinks. They chatted a few minutes about general matters. Carrie couldn't wait to hear Alice tell Eileen the news. Soon Alice did. Carrie watched Eileen a little nervously as the story unfolded. She wondered what her friend's reaction was going to be.

Eileen stared with disbelief as Alice explained. She looked from Alice to Carrie as if to confirm the report. Carrie smiled back at Eileen who began to smile too. "You mean we were wrong about him?" she said to Carrie.

"Yes, I guess we were! Aren't you glad?" Carrie replied. Eileen just laughed and shook her head in awe. Alice went on giving the details with an excitement that was contagious and soon Eileen was up from her chair and hugging her sister enthusiastically.

"This is so romantic!" she cried. "I can't believe it!"

"Slow down!" Alice said. "He's just coming to visit. We're just beginning to talk and get to know each other; nothing too serious—yet."

But Eileen couldn't be subdued and she chattered on about how exciting this all was. "Do John Mark and Tommy know? Do Joe and Katie know?" her questions came one on the heels of the other.

"I don't know," Alice admitted. "I'm letting Mom and Dad take care of John Mark and Tommy. I wanted to tell you and Katie because you're my sisters and we're so close. I told Katie last night."

As the three talked together joyfully, Eileen continued her breathless questions, completely ignoring her remaining lunch that lay on the counter. Finally she declared, "I've got to get my work done so I have time to get properly dressed for tonight! What are you going to wear, Alice?" she asked without waiting for an answer. "See ya later!" she added as she sped out the door and back to her work.

Alice and Carrie looked at each other in surprise, "You'd think it was her courtship!" Alice laughed as she and Carrie exchanged yet another happy smile.

The next day at church Eileen was all smiles as she approached Carrie immediately after the service. She had kept her exuberance bottled up all during the morning and now she couldn't wait another second to tell Carrie the events of last evening.

"Let's go for a walk!" Eileen begged her friend as she took Carrie's arm and whisked her outside. Carrie laughed, barely having time to agree. Before she knew it, they were walking the edge of the church grounds as they had done so many times before. Today though, the weather was cool and they had stopped to put their coats on in the foyer before heading out.

Eileen chattered excitedly as they walked. Carrie had to admit to herself that she was anxious to hear of the important evening. "Pastor Creighton seems very nice!" Eileen was saying, as they stepped outside. "He played checkers with John Mark for awhile and I made popcorn. Then we all ate the apple pie that Alice had made and we even had homemade ice cream! We visited a lot and had such fun!" Eileen finally stopped to take a breath.

The rapidly drying stalks in the cornfield that bordered the church grounds, rustled in the breeze and the brisk fall day seemed to whisper of the winter that soon would come. As the girls turned the corner of the church property, Alice caught up with them under the tall oaks at the north edge of the lawn. The fallen leaves crunched beneath her feet as she approached. Gray November clouds rolled across the sky allowing the sun only partial command and creating alternating patterns of sunshine and shadows on the country church.

"I suppose you've filled her in on all the details already," Alice said to Eileen, teasingly. Both girls smiled back sheepishly. "Eileen already knows this, but I want to ask a favor of you, Carrie," Alice began, her face alight with a new glow. As they strolled along, she explained her feelings to Carrie. "I wanted you to know that Steve is coming over to visit with me, but I thought it might be best if we don't just randomly announce this to everyone and get a lot of unnecessary gossip started. You understand, don't you?"

"Oh, sure! I really do, Alice. I won't tell a soul if you don't want me to," Carrie assured her.

"Thank you, Carrie," Alice said. "It's not like it's really a secret or anything, but other than my family and you, I don't want to be the one to tell it around. I want Steve to do the telling, if and when he chooses." Carrie thought it sounded so strange to hear Alice refer to Pastor Creighton as "Steve," and understanding her concern over the matter, Carrie vowed that if the news slipped out, it wouldn't be from her lips.

As they walked along the east lawn past the cemetery and back toward the church house, Carrie couldn't help missing the lovely green and white hues of the flowering hedge that now looked stark and bare. But, sharing in Alice's excitement, life was so wonderful for now Carrie knew she could patiently wait for May when the blossoms would return.

The news of Alice and Pastor Creighton's courtship was soon public knowledge in the Maplecrest and Homewood area. Carrie didn't have to keep Alice's confidence very long for the pastor was not at all secretive about the relationship. He seemed to be extremely happy to have been allowed to court such a wonderful young woman as Alice Henderson and when he asked her to accompany him to a Sunday evening service at First Church in early December, the news told itself.

When the Christmas week arrived, Pastor Creighton's parents and younger sister and brother arrived from Oklahoma to visit him for the first time since his appointment to First Church. Carrie suspected that their visit had as much to do with meeting Alice Henderson as with seeing their son.

Through Eileen's efficient reporting, Carrie was privileged to watch the relationship unfold. The two young girls were drawn deeper into a commitment to order relationships in their own lives this way as they saw Alice's happiness. They knew that the Hendersons had been praying for Alice and that Steve Creighton was just the kind of godly man they had hoped to have to for a son-in-law. It had become so evident that Alice and Pastor Creighton were obviously fond of each other. He treated Alice with the utmost respect and manners at their every meeting, according to Eileen's faithful observations and reports!

In Carrie's heart, she found herself hoping that someday this same joy and excitement could be hers, for to her it seemed that this plan of courting instead of dating was indeed a most romantic concept. After all, God had worked out all these details for two people who never would have met any other way but through the hand of God in answer to many prayers. Pastor Creighton was chosen as a minister in Maplecrest many months and many candidates after the pastoral search began. He came from quite a distance away—another state, in fact—and just happened to see Alice's bakery sign one day. It had to be more than chance! And to top it all off, he liked his pie so well that he called for the manager, never realizing it would be a woman, let alone a single woman who had been praying for God's choice of a husband! Yes, it was too wonderful to be anything coincidental! The thought of putting one's life into the hands of God who could work such intricate details was not only wise, it was an exciting adventure, Carrie reasoned!

Another quiet observer of the unfolding events of this courtship took great courage from this whole matter. Carrie's mother's concerns over such things were greatly laid to rest and her faith was strengthened by Alice's experience. She felt her commitment to courtship for her own children grow greatly as she saw the wonderful workings of God and was encouraged in her own walk with the Lord. She now saw how all the details of a relationship like this could work out. As a result, her prayers for her own children grew more fervent and specific. And this was as it should be. Alice and Pastor Creighton's Christian example was like the sharpening of iron to others' convictions.

One particularly clear evening late in March, Carrie Brooks sat in her window seat watching the early spring dusk fade into night. This morning Pastor Steve had left one of First Church's elders in charge of the service and had come to church at with Alice. Together with Mr. and Mrs. Henderson, the couple announced their engagement to the congregation of Maplewood Christian Fellowship. It had been a happy moment as the congregation shared the joy of not only the young couple but the Henderson family as well. Carrie thought that this was a moment she would never forget as everyone had stood and joined in hearty applause following her father's lead.

Everyone gathered around Steve and Alice at the close of the service and laid hands on them and blessed them as Pastor Brooks prayed for their future. Steve and Alice both absolutely beamed with pleasure as friends and family greeted them after church. Much hugging and hand shaking went on with the women shedding a few tears as they greeted Alice.

Carrie was sure she had never seen Alice look so beautiful, the joy of being in love and being in God's will shone brightly in her face. And all the while, Carrie watched and observed the strong love that was evident between them. After church, amidst the vibrancy of a sea of people, Pastor Steve would occasionally steal a glance at Alice. When their eyes met, Carrie noticed a devotion and magnetism so strong that it pierced through the others in the room as if they weren't even there. Then Alice would look back, smiling a smile that was different than all her others. As long as Carrie had known her, she had never seen Alice smile quite that way. It seemed to be something she had reserved only for him, a part of her countenance that only became observable with Steve Creighton's presence.

Carrie now sat pondering these thoughts as she looked out into the night sky. The last rosy patches of the spring day were quickly giving way to nightfall. A growing number of stars were popping out against the darkening sky and the moon rose with silvery swiftness to accompany them. Carrie's thoughts mingled with prayers as she watched the silent, but lovely display of the heavenly lights. She was surprised to hear herself softly say, "Just think! If God has a man chosen for me to marry he could very well be watching these same stars tonight—even if he lives miles and miles away. God knows him and knows how to bring us together!" Thinking of the newly engaged couple, this dream now became believable and Carrie felt a sense of peace previously unequaled as she gazed heavenward. And even though she had supposed her last statement had been just a romantic thought, a young man was doing that as well.

Events of Spring

With spring advancing daily, the end of the year events were now on the horizon for the home school families. Carrie, Luke, and the rest of the SAC spent many hours preparing the spring banquet, the last event before graduation. Being on the SAC had been a privilege mingled with fun and hard work and this year's banquet promised to be spectacular.

Carrie, Eileen, and Darla commandeered the decorating while the boys chose the location and set the order of program. It was to be a carry-in dinner in the only facility large enough to accommodate the growing event-the Homewood Christian School gymnasium that the SAC had rented for the evening.

As May approached, Carrie worked diligently on her new dress. The garment that she had often dreamed about and then carefully designed, would double as her graduation dress only weeks later.

Carrie and her mother had chosen a soft, off-white fabric that was delicately sprigged with faint rose buds. Carrie bravely tried a pattern that she had never sewn before. The capable little seamstress added a few touches of her own, sewing the pretty bodice with soft ruffles from front waist to back waist. She opted for a square neckline and puffed three-quarter length sleeves in anticipation of the warm weather rather than the high collar and tight fitting cuffs of her favorite winter dress. A pretty pink sash adorned the waist and was the finishing touch to the ankle-length gown. Only days before the awaited Saturday, the dress was done.

On the day of the banquet, Carrie's morning was filled with

duties. She hurriedly finished her chores and then helped her mother with the food for the carry-in meal. As soon as she could, she washed her hair and set out her dress, shoes, purse, and all she needed to remember to take to the banquet. All this was done amidst last-minute phone calls and hurried work on a few late-assembled crepe-paper roses for the stage.

Miss Winfield, once again the SAC chaperone this year, had suggested they all arrive ninety minutes before the banquet in order to attend to the details of the evening. The SAC members were planning to meet at the Brooks' farm at four-thirty and ride together. The little group had grown so close with the many duties of working together this year that this was just another excuse for a happy gathering of good friends. During the school year the SAC members had gone beyond just being acquaintances. Through much time spent in devotions and prayer at their meetings, they had grown together as a team of Christian young people committed to serve each other and their home school group. Under Miss Winfield's direction they had learned to work as a team. She taught them the importance of prayer and discernment in making their decisions, a lesson she had learned years before while working on mission teams.

The members of the group took genuine interest in each other's lives and upheld one another daily in prayer, remaining accountable and helping each other in their spiritual walks. Their closeness radiated to the activities they planned, causing many of the FCH families to comment on the supreme organization and quality activities that had been provided for the year.

Luke finished the evening chores early and came in the back room, hanging his work jacket on its familiar hook. He removed his boots and headed through the kitchen where Mom was washing Addy's hair. Little Addy lay on the counter with her head rested on a towel as her mother scrubbed the long auburn curls in the big farmhouse sink. Addy smiled at her big brother as he passed. "I go too," she announced proudly.

"I know, sweetie," Luke smiled. He headed for the staircase, bounding up with his long legs clearing two steps at a time. Once atop the stairs, he turned and knocked at the first door on the left, Carrie's room.

"Yes, come in," she answered from within.

Luke opened the door and stuck his head in, "I did your chores," he informed her. A surprised but pleased smile lit Carrie's face as she said, "Well, thank you, little brother!"

"I thought you'd need the extra time to get ready, so I just did them."

"I really appreciate that. I guess I owe you one," she smiled.

"I gotta hurry and get ready," Luke said, heading down the hall.

Carrie smiled to herself as she thought about how much Luke had matured even since September. He had really taken an interest in the home school activities and had become a vital part of the SAC. He no longer just endured these events that he once would have considered "girl stuff," but now took an active part and even seemed to look forward to them as evidenced by his eagerness to get ready for this evening. He was beginning to be noted in the family for his lengthy preparations with his hair and his meticulous attention to detail concerning his attire. He always polished his shoes, straightened his tie carefully, and never allowed a wrinkle in his clothes. Carrie was proud of her little brother who had grown into such a fine young man. God was developing in him a very sensitive spirit that the whole family noticed and appreciated. Luke was dependable and considerate of others as well as sharp in his appearance.

"How good God has been to us Brooks," Carrie said to herself as she mentally enumerated the blessings her family had recently enjoyed, especially the new farm and the love everyone shared. "What an exciting time of life this is!" she thought. "Next week I'll finish my studies and the week after that is graduation!"

Carrie breathed in the fresh spring breeze from her open window as she looked out across Blossom Lane Farm. The cow and her calf were in the pasture. The fields and hills were greening now with the approach of summer. The full, lush bridal veil bushes skirting the porch were laden with buds waiting to burst into frothy whiteness and the very air held the promise of life, joy, and the blessings of God.

Any apprehension Carrie had felt concerning her life after high school had now faded away, for she had her immediate plans following graduation in two weeks now confirmed. With her parents' blessing, she had decided to go back to work for Alice at Blooming Hills for the season and continue to pray and receive direction from the Lord for her future. It would be so wonderful; her old job back, all the gang together again, and her whole life ahead of her!

Alice would really need her this year as she and Pastor Creighton's wedding was planned for October. The preparations were sure to take much of Alice's time in the next few months. Yes, with the wedding on the horizon, this was likely to be the most exciting summer yet!

Carrie glanced at the clock on her desk and saw that she had only an hour before all the SAC members were to arrive at her house. Luke passed by, rapping on her door. "One hour to be ready, Carrie!" he called, alerting her to the time.

It was almost time for all her friends to arrive when Carrie put on the elegant new dress and twirled around in front of the full-length mirror in her room. Pleased with the fit of the garment, she stepped into the hall to call for her mother to come tie her sash. At that very moment, Luke headed down the stairs, all dressed and ready to go. He looked especially grown up in his sage green suit. As usual every hair was in place and his shoes shined to perfection. He smelled of pleasant cologne. Carrie complimented her brother as he passed by.

Soon Mom was upstairs to help Carrie tie the sash. The two women tied and re-tied the ribbon until it was just right. "You have really done a fine job on this dress, sweetheart," Mom said to her.

"Thanks, Mom," Carrie smiled.

"You know, I can hardly believe you're graduating in just two weeks. It seems like only yesterday you were Addy's age." Mom's eyes looked misty as she smiled at her daughter. "You've grown up to be a fine young woman and I'm very proud of you!"

Carrie's eyes thanked her mother silently. "I know this banquet is one of the last highlights of high school for you. Don't work the whole evening away just because you're on the SAC." Carried nodded her understanding. "Do remember to enjoy yourself. It'll be something you'll always remember," her mother wisely advised. "I better run along and finish getting Addy ready. I love you!" she added as she hugged her daughter one last time.

Carrie fixed her hair, then took it down and put it up again another way, disappointed with the first style she had chosen. Soon she heard a car pull up in the circle drive and she saw John Mark and Eileen get out as she peeped out from behind the curtain. "Oh!

I'd better hurry!" she scolded herself. Soon after their car drove in, another followed and it was the Harris' car with Tom, Darla, and Homer. Carrie could hear footsteps on the front porch below as the door opened and her father began talking to the friends as they entered the front hallway. Their laughter and chatter floated up the stairs. As she fumbled nervously with her uncooperative hairpins, Carrie thought she heard Luke invite everyone to take seats in the parlor.

Before long, Homer was seated at the old piano and he had everyone participating in some joyous singing. Laughter and clapping followed the first tune. "How like the close little group," Carrie thought with a smile as she heard Tom Harris say rather loudly, "How about another song, Homer?" Soon strains of a second melody wafted up the stairs to Carrie's room as she quickly secured the last strand of hair into the style that had finally suited her. She hurried to put her shoes on, not wanting to keep the others waiting any longer.

As Carrie took a final check in the mirror, she realized she had forgotten to wear Grandma Haywood's watch that had now become a signature part of her attire for her most important events. She hurriedly took the watch from its place on her mother's dresser in the room across the hall and pinned it on the new dress. She took a deep breath to regain her composure after all the hurrying. Down in the parlor Homer's clean baritone voice led the group in "Little Church in the Wildwood" as Carrie hurried back to her room, picked up her handbag and stepped out into the upstairs hall. She stopped to catch her breath from all the hurrying and smiled to herself as she listened to the pretty singing for a moment. These were the voices of her friends which she had heard many times before as they had worked and played, sung and prayed together time and again for nearly two years now.

The young people in the parlor were having a fine time as they waited for Carrie. Homer, the able entertainer, had easily involved everyone in the room and a mood of celebration prevailed. But if anyone had been paying very close attention they would have noticed that one of the young men didn't seem to be as involved as his friends were in the singing. He seemed pre-occupied, even a bit nervous as he repeatedly glanced in the direction of the open staircase that emptied into the hall in full view of the big parlor doors. Someone did notice—Carrie's mother. Due to the infectious enthusiasm of the singing, she and Dad had joined the happy little gathering around the piano. Although he didn't realize anyone else was looking, Mom noticed the young man's frequent, wondering glances toward the stairs.

Her heart was strangely warmed as she watched him, realizing that her suspicions about him might really be true. He was probably anxious to see her daughter. And nothing could have pleased her more.

In a moment, Carrie appeared at the top of the stairs and Mom's careful eyes quickly noted the young man's response. Having kept a diligent watch on the stairs, he soon caught sight of Carrie. Mom watched him as he stopped singing and his wondering glances changed to a slow half smile, a smile mixed with adoration as his eyes beheld her. With the hearty singing continuing all around him, he began walking slowly toward the stairs. He held out his hand to the lovely young lady as she descended the last few steps, the little scene still unnoticed by everyone else. Carrie accepted his gentlemanly assistance and gracefully stepped down the last few steps. Though for a moment he was silent, his eyes spoke a volume of words as he gazed at her. She too was silent, but smiled gently in answer.

Mom's heart skipped a beat for her daughter as she saw the significance of it all. Though the moment seemed to last forever, in reality it was only a few seconds until John Mark finally spoke. "You look very nice tonight, Carrie," he said.

"Thank you," she replied as he continued to gaze at her. After a moment, he let go of her hand.

"I'm looking forward to this evening," he said as he gestured in true gentlemanly fashion to invite her to lead the way back into the parlor.

Mom watched John Mark Henderson, the serious young farmer, as his eyes followed Carrie. He seemed to be totally taken with her as if she were the only other person in the room, or possibly in the whole world. It wasn't long before the others realized Carrie had arrived and was ready to leave, so Homer ended the song with a flourish, everyone clapping as he rose from the piano stool to take a bow. Luke slapped him on the back, all in good fun and someone suggested they be off to the banquet.

Carrie scooped up an armful of crepe-paper roses from the parlor chair, the last decorations to be placed in the gym. The pink roses seemed to match the blush on her cheeks. Darla took a few, as did Eileen. The girls made a lovely picture all dressed up and carrying their oversized bouquets! Soon the boys were loading the Harris' car with all the last minute supplies.

Mr. and Mrs. Brooks stepped onto the porch with little Addy as they watched the group split up to ride in the two vehicles. Luke and Carrie, John Mark and Eileen were in the Henderson car. Homer, Darla, and Tom took the Harris' car. Carrie smiled back and waved at her parents as John Mark came around to the passenger side to open the door for her. She gracefully sat down in the back with Eileen as Luke doubled up his lanky frame, ducking as he slid in the front seat. Carrie saw her dad cast a quick little frown at Luke for not remembering to open the door for Eileen. Carrie smiled to herself as she noticed Luke give a little wave to Dad acknowledging that he realized his mistake.

As the cars turned out of the drive, Mom's eyes filled with misty tears. Dad and Addy turned and went back into the house but Mom lingered awhile on the porch. She watched the cars fade into the distance as she leaned dreamily against a porch post. Her thoughts carried her back many years while her hands twisted a bud from one of the sprawling bushes beneath the railing. She held the sprig of leaves and stood gazing and remembering.

If what she had seen in the hallway indicated a developing relationship between John Mark and Carrie, how different it would be from her own young adult years. She knew a different style of courtship was to be the pattern and she silently thanked God for revealing this plan to her and her husband. She sighed as she realized how much more romantic it might have been to have her own teen and young adult years more like Carrie's promised to be. Although she had nothing to regret in her own life, the idea of really allowing God to lead your relationships seemed to be a better alternative. "It's so wholesome and very, very romantic," she thought as she pondered it all. She saw it all so clearly now and any doubts she had had before seemed to float away into the sultry evening. Mom realized that years of mothering seemed to be coming to a culmination like never before, feeling in her heart that this afternoon she had witnessed the results of some of her prayers. The future remained to be seen, but she felt it definitely looked bright.

The Spring Banquet turned out to be the FCH event of the year. The warm, balmy evening was a perfect setting for the spring theme of the choir's selections. The stage was decorated with the roses Carrie and the girls had made and several randomly hung tin foil stars gave a heavenly twinkle to the room as they caught the light from a hundred or more tiny candles placed on the tables.

The annual spring banquet was traditionally the most formal FCH event of the year and most of Carrie's friends were wearing new dresses. Normally, it would be unusual to see all the boys in suits. Many parents were commenting about how nice all the young people looked tonight, especially in their formal attire. Nearly everyone was taking pictures and the atmosphere was festive indeed.

The junior class was designated to help the SAC with cleanup. It was a very easy job as all the families took their own dishes home making the kitchen work minimal. The Homewood principal had suggested that the decorations be left intact for an upcoming function at the school. Only the candles and folding chairs were to be put away and the floors swept at the close of the evening.

After the program most families lingered awhile to talk before leaving. No one seemed to want the lovely evening to end. John Mark left the small group of friends he was with and walked across the gym to where Carrie was standing near the door with some of the girls. Her friends were just leaving and she was soon alone.

John Mark gave her a shy smile, "Would you join me for a walk in the school courtyard? Some of the others went outside--it's so nice this evening."

"Thank you," Carrie answered, "I think that would be nice."

John Mark held the door for her and the two walked out to the courtyard area where many of their friends were talking and enjoying the warm, spring evening.

"It was getting kind of stuffy in the gym, I thought," John Mark said, shyly.

"I agree," Carrie replied. A long silence followed as they strolled along the pretty cobblestone paths constructed and maintained by the high school science and building trades classes. The lovely area was filled with little gardens and flowering trees, shrubs, pathways, and benches for students to enjoy. Each year the various classes sponsored projects to add to the courtyard for their studies.

"Hello," John Mark said as they passed Amanda Melvin and Emily Turner.

"Hi," Carrie smiled as well, feeling a little self-conscious thinking she had seen the girls cast a slightly curious look in her direction. Carrie was wondering why John Mark had asked her to go walking with him. She knew there was nothing improper about it; many others were out here as well, yet, there had been something undeniably different about John Mark tonight. It had all started with the incident in the hallway before they left her house. Carrie knew she would never forget the way those few moments had made her feel. Yet could she have been wrong about it all? Was that hallway scene just a gentlemanly show of John Mark's good manners? Was she making it out to be more than what he had meant it to be?

Suddenly one memory raced to the forefront in Carrie's mind as she and John Mark strolled along. "The note! The note with the circled letters! Maybe it was John Mark's after all. Maybe that explains his behavior tonight. It must be!" Carrie thought, "It must be!"

She had to admit she had been hoping for these many months that John Mark had been the writer of the note and that someday he would openly declare his love for her and ask to court her, just like Pastor Steve had done with Alice. Still she had tried to leave it all in the Lord's hands and she was satisfied that she had done a pretty good job of it too.

Thoughts and questions raced through Carrie's mind as they walked on in silence, their only words an occasional greeting to others as they passed. "Is he going to ask to court me or something like that?" The abrupt question in Carrie's mind caused a sudden nervous wave of emotion to engulf her.

She immediately felt the color rise to her cheeks as she looked around, now even more conscious of what others must be thinking.

"No, Carrie, don't be so silly," she told herself. "No one thinks a thing of John Mark walking with you. It's not a bit out of the ordinary for two SAC members to be together. Our group is always together," she assured herself. And indeed, of all the others strolling the courtyard no one, except Amanda and Emily, really did seem a bit curious about John Mark Henderson and Carrie Brooks taking a stroll. She breathed easier now as she assessed the few others in view and found no one looking with unusual interest in her direction.

As they approached a little stone bench alongside the walkway, John Mark gestured for Carrie to sit down. Ever the gentleman, he waited for her to be seated first, and then he sat down beside her. He smiled at her but said nothing for a few moments. Carrie felt someone should speak; the silence was almost embarrassing, yet she couldn't think of anything in particular to say. Finally she spoke. "I can't wait to get back to work for Alice in a few weeks," she said pleasantly, feeling relieved that she had found something intelligent to say to break the awkward silence. "It was such fun last year with all the friends together."

John Mark just smiled back, then dropped his gaze. He seemed to be studying the ground as he pushed a stone around the sidewalk with his foot. "That's one of the reasons why I asked you to take a walk with me tonight." John Mark said softly, still looking down. His voice sounded unusually serious and his familiar sideways grin had been replaced by a more somber expression. Carrie thought she sensed a certain sadness in his voice, almost as if something was wrong. She waited, expecting him to explain.

"What are your plans for after the summer?" he asked, not at all seeming to answer the questions in her mind.

She wondered how to respond. Was this leading up to a courtship proposal? "We're only just graduating! If this is going to be some kind of proposal what will Mom and Dad think?" Thoughts raced through Carrie's mind. "How old were Joe and Katie when they got married?" she wondered. "Does age matter?" Carrie's anxious thoughts tumbled one over the other in split seconds.

After a short pause, Carrie found herself answering, "I...I'm not sure," she said, honestly. "I just plan to work for Alice and wait on the Lord to instruct me further. My parents and I have decided that's best for now," she continued. "There! That was a true and satisfactory answer," Carrie thought. "If he asks to court me, I'll just refer it back to Mom and Dad. He knows that I would anyway." At this a measure of calmness returned to her being.

"Does the future ever seem...well, frightening to you?" John Mark asked, searching for the right words.

Carrie thought a moment, "Not frightening exactly. I guess just unsure and sort of unsettled."

"I guess 'frightening' wasn't the right word; 'unsettled' describes it better," John Mark said, rephrasing his thoughts.

"Do you feel unsettled?" Carrie asked.

John Mark nodded, "Yes, just a bit; excited but unsure." He was smiling now. Feeling the need to explain his comments, he went on to say, "That's one of the reasons I asked you to take this walk with me tonight. I've got a big change just ahead of me, Carrie."

Carrie listened intently, almost breathlessly as she searched John Mark's face for a clue to this puzzling conversation. She felt a strange quaking feeling in the pit of her stomach.

John Mark leaned forward, his elbows on his knees, his hands clasped together as if he were about to say something very serious. He looked down at the ground as he spoke, "I was hoping you'd...I was wondering if you would....well....pray for me in the coming months?" He looked directly at her now as if awaiting an answer.

She stared back, not knowing whether to answer, "Yes," or wait for him to explain.

"I'll be moving just after graduation," he finally said.

"What could he be talking about?" Carrie thought. Surely the Hendersons weren't leaving the area. They owned a well-established business and a lot of land. "He must be leaving to go to college... or missions!" Carrie's ideas whirled as dangerous scenes of faraway places raced through her desperate thoughts. Emotions and questions flooded Carrie's mind as she stared speechlessly at John Mark. She hoped her face didn't betray her feelings of shock and disappointment.

Sensing her questions, John Mark went on, "Dad bought a farm over near Bixley. He had a chance to get it for quite a reasonable price and he wants me to farm it." He paused a moment. "It needs a lot of work to get it productive, so he's going to send me to work it."

Carrie tried bravely to look pleased for John Mark's sake. She knew another farm meant more income for the Hendersons and also this was proof of John Mark's reliable maturity. His father trusted him enough to make a new investment "productive." But Bixley? It seemed so far away. Like the end of the world, in fact! Why, it was way over beyond Dalton Corners! Carrie could remember being there only one time in her whole life! Once her family had gone to Grandma Haywood's a different way and passed through Dalton Corners and Bixley. It was miles from here!

"So, I'm kind of unsure. I mean I hope I can handle my own

farm. I love farming, but being completely in charge of a whole farm is another thing," John Mark was saying.

Carrie felt numb as she began to realize how far off target her thoughts had been. A creeping embarrassment began to steal over her. She managed to say some words of encouragement and give her consent to pray for her friend.

John Mark seemed relieved to have shared his concerns with a friend and to have received her support in prayer as he continued on with the details, not noticing her shocked feelings. "There's a farm house there. I'll be living in it and working to fix it up during the winter. It's pretty rough." Even as he described its dilapidated condition, he seemed pleased and Carrie was struck with a feeling of near shame at not being able to feel happy for him. Instead, she seemed only able to nurse her own regrets at the news.

Carrie couldn't wait to get back into the gym and head for home, all the while desperately hoping John Mark had not sensed her incredible embarrassment and disappointment. The rest of the walk was a blur to her. On the way home, she fought back tears as she sat quietly in the dark backseat. Eileen chattered on about the wonderful banquet but Carrie's ears caught only the words of Luke and John Mark in the front seat as John Mark broke the exciting news about his farm to Luke.

Luke was on the edge of his seat with excitement for his friend. "Great!" was his enthusiastic assessment, "Your own farm! Wow! What a dream! I'd give anything to be in your shoes, John Mark."

Carrie swallowed hard as the lump in her throat grew with her painful emotions. Still feeling the embarrassment of misconstruing John Mark's intentions, she shrunk into her thoughts as the others in the car talked on. She agonized within herself wondering if somehow the look on her face had betrayed her feelings when John Mark had broken the news. "Could he somehow tell what I was thinking?" she wondered in fear, shuddering again at the thought.

Soon they were at Blossom Lane and Luke and Carrie thanked them for the ride. Pleasant good-byes were exchanged with a congratulatory slap on the shoulder from Luke to John Mark.

When they went in the house, Luke was brimming with the news of John Mark's farm. He reported it to his father as he flopped down in Dad's big office chair. Carrie was thankful it was late and she wouldn't be noticed if she just went hurriedly to bed.

As she rounded the corner to go up the stairs to her room, her mother called from the living room, "Hi, dear. Great banquet! You all did a good job!"

"Thanks," Carrie replied unenthusiastically.

"You sound tired, dear," Mom said.

"I'm headed straight for bed," Carrie called as she went up to her room.

Safely behind the door, Carrie let her tears fall as she put on her nightgown and slid into her bed. As she leaned back on her pillow, she gazed out at the May night, staring at the stars in the black sky. They seemed to stare back at her. Hot tears spilled from her eyes and rolled down her cheeks. She felt a mixture of sadness, disappointment, and embarrassment. How could she have suspected John Mark wanted to court her? "Just because I think and pray about a courtship some day doesn't mean the thought ever even crossed his mind. Maybe God has other plans for him--and for me," Carrie told herself. "How silly I've been...how childish!" she scolded herself. A new wave of shame and embarrassment engulfed her as she thought once again, "What if John Mark suspected my feelings? What if he somehow could tell what I thought?"

Carrie lay awake a long time suffering with her mixed up feelings. Sadness over the SAC breaking up forever, John Mark going away, and embarrassed at herself for misreading his intentions all tormented her. "I have only myself to blame for the way I feel. I should never have let my heart get ahead of God's plans for my life," she reminded herself softly, but sternly. "I thought I was so grown up. I was so concerned about how a courtship would work out that I forgot to do the most important thing—keep the thoughts and intents of my heart stayed on God and wait for His timing."

Graduation

After the ordeal of Friday night, Carrie made a new commitment to keep her heart and mind from straying to thoughts of John Mark, or anyone else for that matter, falling in love with her. She worked diligently to finish her final work in school and even amidst the year-end activities of the SAC, she was careful not to look for any more clues to John Mark's feelings. After all, if he had listened very well to the Holcomb's teachings, he would be turning any intentions of courting Carrie over to the Lord anyway until he was prepared to support a wife. "No good will come of dwelling on it," Carrie kept reminding herself.

Graduation soon arrived for the home school group. One May evening Carrie found herself waiting in the hall of Homewood Christian School just as she had last year only this time she was the graduate instead of an honor guard. On this particular evening as she stood there in cap and gown, she experienced a myriad of feelings, everything from happiness to apprehension—"excited but unsure" as John Mark had called it. But when an exuberant Miss Winfield gave the signal to start the graduation procession, Carrie was glad she wasn't at the head of the line. After the honor guards, Amanda and Homer were first and she followed with the others including John Mark and Darla Harris.

The graduation ceremony was beautiful as well as meaningful. Parents gave diplomas to their graduates, a touching gesture which left few dry eyes in the auditorium. Mom was filled with a mother's bittersweet joy as she lived this moment that she had waited for so long. All the years of dedication and hard work had come to an end for the first of her students and she felt as much a sense of accomplishment as Carrie did but with a tiny sense of sadness at finally reaching this landmark.

Many tears and hugs followed the ceremony as parents and friends moved through the receiving line. Carrie was proud to have her father and mother standing next to her to receive guests. Miss Winfield was especially touched as these students from her Activities Committee moved on to another chapter in the lives to which God had called each of them. Her love and commitment to the students was evident this evening; she was as proud of them as any parent.

Carrie's graduation reception followed the ceremony. Mom and Dad had ordered a lovely cake from Alice. Luke had cleared out and cleaned the big barn and set up tables for guests. Beautiful ribbon decorations adorned the porch that was also set with a few tables and chairs as well as a gift table. The women had wisely thought to put the gift table on the porch so that all the items wouldn't need to be carried to the house at the end of the evening.

Carrie and her mother had made gallons of punch earlier that morning which Luke now served to guests as Carrie graciously accepted gifts from friends. It was a memorable party with so many of the Brooks family's friends in attendance. Darla, Eileen, and Amanda helped Carrie open and record all her gifts in a special remembrance book. The girls enjoyed admiring the gifts and talking of their plans for the future.

At the end of the evening Carrie thanked the last of her guests as they left one by one. One of the last to leave, John Mark Henderson strolled across the lawn and up to the porch. Carrie was standing at the gift table near the steps where she had plucked a few sprigs of the white spirea whose heavy branches now nodded their perfume into the evening air. She was pressing one of the flower clusters into the remembrance book when John Mark approached, smiling pleasantly. He stood on the lawn and leaned against the porch rail, "Hi, Carrie," he said.

"Hi," she replied and looked back down at the book. "I was just pressing a few of these flowers into my graduation book. They're my favorites, you know. When I first found out we were moving here I was sad, but when we drove up to look at the house that first day, these were here in full bloom welcoming me and I loved them so. I don't know if I could ever really feel at home anywhere without them now."

Then as if John Mark should have known all she had been thinking since their conversation on Friday evening, Carrie added almost with a note of warning in her voice, "I want to remember this day just as it is; flowers, music, friends...." With this her voice trailed off, and she suddenly realized she had rattled on without poise in facing John Mark. Since the incident at the banquet, Carrie now realized how important it was to keep her feelings in check for now she was uncomfortable talking to her old friend. It seemed like a certain ease in their friendship was gone. She hoped he wasn't going to mention a lot more about the farm and his move. She had to admit that subject was slightly unsettling to her.

John Mark listened to Carrie politely, then spoke, "I just wanted to take a moment to ...say, well... congratulations on graduating and everything."

"Thank you," Carrie smiled back sincerely. "Congratulations to you too."

"Thanks. I was also hoping to talk to you for a minute in case I didn't get a chance again before I leave next week," he said rather hurriedly as if he feared losing his courage to speak.

"Oh, I'll be at your party tomorrow," Carrie quickly assured him, hoping to ward off any more unpleasant information he may be about to share concerning his move.

"Oh, good, but I was afraid it would be so hectic tomorrow that I'd miss you. What I wanted to ask was..." Carrie took a deep breath, unnoticed by John Mark and braced herself for whatever he was about to say next. "Please don't forget to pray for me. You promised, you know. I'll really need it," his eyes searched hers for approval.

"I will," Carrie said, honestly. And quite to herself she thought, "I surely will. Praying for you will be good for me as well." For she knew that praying for someone was a sure way to get your feelings adjusted toward him. It caused you to desire the best for the other person—it was a totally unselfish endeavor. "Yes, John Mark Henderson, you can count on me for that," she thought silently.

"It's been a really fun year. I sort of hate to see it end," John Mark was saying. "It's been great working with you on the SAC for two years now. You've been a good friend to me and to Eileen and Alice. I'll sure miss everyone around here."

"Well, Bixley's not the end of the world, " Carrie found herself saying, immediately realizing her statement was contrary to her true feelings.

"Yeah, I know. I'll be back for church every Sunday that I possibly can," John Mark replied and with that he began to walk away. But halfway across the lawn he turned and waved as he called back, "God bless you, Carrie. Good bye!"

Seeing him there as he crossed the lawn brought an old memory vividly to the surface. Carrie saw in her mind's eye a picture of John Mark a few years ago the day the church people had helped the Brooks' move into the new house. John Mark had come to the picnic that day and now he was walking away just like he had then. As she watched him, she wondered if this time he was walking away in a much more permanent sense. In some ways, not much had changed since the day of the picnic, yet there were times when it seemed to her that her whole world was changing, maybe a little too fast.

Back to Blooming Hills and Beyond

In a few days, it was time to go back to work for Alice and after a week or so the graduation parties were all over. Somehow with the conclusion of the last party, a new feeling settled in with Carrie Brooks. It was the sense of having arrived at a new stage of life and being at least temporarily settled. It was the realization that high school had really come to an end and adult life had officially begun.

This week the Hendersons were in a whirl of work and activity getting everything ready for John Mark's move. Carrie's help was especially valuable to Alice at the bakery because the move was causing Joe and Katie and even Eileen to be tied up helping John Mark. A few trips to Bixley had already been made to transport some farm equipment that John Mark would need. His father had decided to spare some of the older implements for him to get started so the boys had driven the items to their new home. The final move of John Mark's earthly belongings was scheduled for tomorrow.

Saturday finally came and for the first few hours of the morning, Luke, John Mark, and Joe had been loading John Mark's bedroom furniture, clothes and books onto the truck. Homer worked in the orchards racing to keep up with the customers and to help the other hired hands with various duties around the farm.

Meanwhile, Carrie worked hard in the bakery, diligently attempting to think of everything as normal. She tried to put her feelings for John Mark aside. Lately she prayed often, read more in her Bible and busied herself in service to others in order to keep her mind and heart from straying to courtship and romance. Alice could completely rely on her in the restaurant and bakery with no instructions needed and it was a good thing today since she was constantly interrupted with one thing or another in all the busyness of the move.

When three o'clock finally came, John Henderson closed the orchard for the weekend and gathered everyone around the large farm truck that held his son's things. Everything was packed and ready to go. "I thought it would be good if we could all gather around John Mark and pray a blessing on him as he leaves," John announced to the employees who had all gathered to say goodbye.

The group circled John Mark and the men laid hands on him as they took turns praying for the young man's future, the new farm, and his protection. Several of the men led out in prayer including Homer and Luke and after a while John Henderson closed the prayer. When the bowed heads lifted, some eyes were misty, even Eileen's. In motherly fashion, Mrs. Henderson looked proud, but sad.

Joe, Katie, and John Mark climbed into the cab of the truck and were soon off for Bixley. Carrie helped Eileen and Alice pack coolers of food in the van as Mr.and Mrs. Henderson readied to leave, following the truck. Carrie and Alice had worked quite a while that day preparing a meal for the movers to eat tonight at John Mark's new home.

As soon as the others were gone, Carrie and Luke headed home where their own evening chores waited. "I sort of envy that John Mark," Luke was saying as they drove. "Getting his own farm! Wow! I'd love it!"

"Let's not envy anyone, shall we?" Carrie reminded her younger brother. "There are plenty of blessings to go around for all of us. You live on a farm and you'll get to work it real soon! In fact your chores are waiting for you right now you know," she reminded him with a bit of a stern sisterly tone. Luke just looked at her, slightly annoyed at her air of superiority. He wondered at what seemed to be a slight agitation in his sister's voice.

John Mark didn't make it back for church the next morning and there seemed to be an empty spot in the row where the boys always sat during the service. As Carrie noticed the empty seat, the same old suspicion about the permanence of John Mark's departure engulfed her for a brief moment. She decided it was just a fearful thought and tried to dismiss it, realizing that life was bound to change for everyone in her graduating class.

After church Eileen told Carrie about the evening at John Mark's, yawning between sentences. All the Hendersons looked tired. It had been a late night for them by the time they unloaded everything, helped John Mark get settled, and drove the long distance home from Bixley.

Even Alice was at MCF this morning for the first time in two weeks. She had taken a few Sundays to join Steve at First Church but was too tired this morning to get up early enough to be ready in time for him to pick her up.

"I guess we got John Mark all settled," Alice said to some of the girls after church.

"We never got home 'til twelve–thirty a.m.!" Eileen added with a note of adventure in her voice.

"Does he have a nice house?" Amanda Melvin asked.

"Oh, it's nice enough, I guess," Alice said.

"I don't know," Eileen contradicted. "I think its sort of run down. It looks like it needs a lot of work to me." The curious girls listened with interest as the Henderson sisters explained.

"Well, you're right about that," Alice admitted. "But I think it's good enough for a man. They don't usually care about decor and all that." All the girls laughed, agreeing with Alice.

"But, I'd say the farm's really got potential," the practical Eileen went on.

"John Mark will be able to put it in order soon enough," Alice said confidently.

"I hope John Mark won't miss too many of the church activities now, being so far away, I mean," Darla said, almost with a hint of scolding in her voice.

"Oh, I think he plans to come to church every Sunday unless there's unforeseen circumstances," Alice assured her.

"Well, I see he's not here today," Darla continued, probingly.

"He called this morning." Alice quickly informed her, coming to her brother's defense. "He hadn't located his alarm clock and he woke up late. Then he couldn't find half of his stuff. He was going to try to make it to the little church down the road from his house, though."

His house! Carrie thought that sounded strange indeed! The John Mark Henderson whom she had grown up with lived in the big farmhouse at Blooming Hills! To think of him owning his own house! But she said nothing and just continued to listen to the others.

"The little church is really quaint," Eileen said dreamily. "You know the song about the church in the wildwood? Well, if that church could be seen, I think it would look like this one. It's not more than a quarter mile from his house but it's so much hillier around Bixley so you can't see it from his place."

"That's right," Alice agreed, "It's a pretty little brick building, very old-fashioned with a beautiful stained glass window and a tall bell tower. It's nestled between two hills and a creek runs along the one side."

"Oh, that's right!" Eileen said with enthusiasm. "And there's this pretty stone bridge over the creek right before you get to the church! It's so serene. I'd love to have my senior picture done there!" All the girls expressed their delight at the thought and went on talking and exchanging news until the families began to leave one by one. As usual, the Brooks' were the last to leave.

Dad locked the big doors while Carrie and Luke turned off the lights. As Carrie stood in the now quiet sanctuary she noticed that the Sunday morning ritual of locking up seemed to be different today. She shivered as she looked around the empty room. The church was not just a building; it was really the people and when they weren't here the building seemed so cold and empty. The moment reminded her of the feelings she had been battling lately. With everything changing gradually, Alice getting married and John Mark leaving, feelings like loneliness and exclusion, even self-pity, wrestled for control of her emotions. But as Carrie looked around the sanctuary, several bold banners that decorated the room caught her eye. Each displayed a Bible verse that she had memorized as a child. "All things work together for good...In all thy ways acknowledge Him and He shall direct your paths...I will never leave thee nor forsake thee…" As Carrie read the banners, the truths written on them began to comfort her heart. She managed a smile as she walked out of the sanctuary with the knowledge that no matter how her circumstances changed, God's promises never would.

As the summer sped by, Alice's wedding drew closer and closer. Early in October she and Carrie began making the frosting flowers for the wedding cake and putting them on trays in the big bakery freezer. Alice spent a good deal of time planning the menu for the reception and ordering the food. Carrie found herself happily drawn into the busy preparations. She helped Alice design the dresses for the wedding as well.

One Friday evening, Carrie and all the Henderson women planned to go shopping for fabric. What a wonderful evening it was sure to be! John Mark had pulled up the hill and into the drive about six p.m., just before the women left. For only the second or third time since he had moved, Carrie got a few minutes to speak with him. He was planning to spend the weekend at home for a change. His old home that was! How good it seemed for everyone to be together again if for only a few minutes, Carrie thought. Even Luke was there because he had worked after school today and hadn't gone home yet. Already being off to college for the year, Homer seemed to be the only one missing from the little group.

As they all stood talking in the parking lot outside Alice's bakery, John Mark asked, "Anyone heard from Homer lately?"

"Amanda Melvin told me she received a letter from him only last week," Carrie offered. "I guess he's doing well but all his studies are really keeping him busy. He'll be home at Christmas."

"Oh?" John Mark said, "Well, then, how's Amanda?"

"Fine," Carrie added. "She's doing well in her schooling too. She'll be getting her nurse's degree by next summer." Amanda was taking nurse's training at the Blue Creek Community College. She hoped to use her skills in mission work someday since Trent had really impressed upon her the need for missionary nurses.

Just then Dad, who was coming home from a long day at the hardware store, started up the drive to pick Luke up. He waved a hearty hello from the car, especially directed at John Mark who returned the greeting. "How are you doing, John Mark?" Dad asked.

"Fine, thank you, sir," John Mark replied, walking over to shake Pastor Brooks' hand.

"Great! How's farming?" Dad continued speaking to John Mark from the car window as Luke hopped in the passenger side.

"Oh, it's going very well, actually. I've been able to get a lot of work done and I hope to be able to do some things to get more production out of it by next year."

"Good. Sounds fine. I hope to get over to visit you before winter."

"Thank you, Pastor," John Mark said politely.

"We'll see you later tonight?" Dad asked Carrie.

"Yes," she smiled.

"You ladies have a nice time," Dad said to Carrie and Eileen, who stood in the drive by John Mark.

"Ok, Daddy," Carrie waved as her father's vehicle pulled away.

"Well, Carrie, I guess we better get ready to go. Alice will be waiting," Eileen suggested to her friend as she headed for the house. John Mark stood in the driveway with Carrie a moment.

"It's great to be back for a few days. I've missed...everyone," he said and looked down shyly. Carrie felt the same quick flutter of emotion she had experienced that evening of the banquet when she had talked with John Mark. "I guess I better get my stuff out of the truck and get settled." John Mark grabbed two huge duffle bags from the seat of his pickup.

Carrie concealed a smile as she headed across the big parking lot toward the Henderson's house where Alice, Eileen, Katie, and Mrs. Henderson were piling into the family car. She untied her checked apron, folded it neatly and placed it in the front seat of her own vehicle as she passed by. Alice's foresight in choosing fabric and patterns allowed her work dress to double as a nice everyday dress when needed.

Mrs. Henderson pulled the car around and picked Carrie up before she reached the house. As she slipped into the back seat, she heard Eileen say saucily, "Well, John Mark's home! I see his laundry coming!" All the Henderson girls laughed at the sight of John Mark lugging the obviously over-stuffed duffle bags into the house.

"If he stays over in Bixley for long, he'll be hunting for a wife just to do his laundry!" Katie joked. Everyone but Carrie laughed again. She sat shyly smiling, not knowing exactly how to respond.

"Now, girls," Mrs. Henderson interjected, " You know the reason John Mark brings his laundry home. If he did have a wife, she wouldn't have a wash machine! Nothing's hooked up around his house. He's got plenty of construction to do on that place yet.

I'm sure a washer and dryer are the least of his worries, very low on his list of repairs and improvements. Besides, when he looks for a wife, she'll be a very special girl I'm sure, whoever she is. You all should be praying for him instead of laughing at him," Mrs. Henderson said good-naturedly.

Carrie sat quietly in her seat as she listened to the women of John Mark's family and she fought the urge to speculate in her mind whether or not she might be the "very special girl" for John Mark but she was determined still to guard her heart and wait on the Lord.

As October ended, so did the last of the Henderson's fruit crops. A few varieties of apples and some pumpkins were about the only items left and there were fewer customers each day. Carrie and Alice took the extra time to work on the dresses for the wedding and see to all the last minute details. The time before Alice's big day was swiftly running out.

Carrie was excited to see the wedding approach. She, Eileen, and Katie were to be the bridesmaids. John Mark, Joe, and Pastor Creighton's brother were the groomsmen. She was thrilled to be included in the many fun preparations that were daily taking place.

Alice had decided to close the bakery at the end of October as usual. She would continue to run it in the spring, even though she was going to have to drive to work everyday from Maplecrest where her new home, the First Church parsonage, would be. Pastor Steve and Alice decided she should continue working at the bakery since it was a family enterprise. They agreed that her duties as a pastor's wife would come first and that someday soon they hoped to be blessed with children, then she would definitely be done working. So with this in mind, Alice made a special effort to prepare Eileen and Carrie to take added responsibilities with the ordering and planning, knowing that in the near future she would probably say goodbye to the profitable little business she had built.

Carrie was very capable help and Eileen promised to be a proficient successor when the time came. She was a true farm girl at heart. Eileen loved all the seasons and knew each crop well, what to look for in the different varieties of fruit and how to prepare them in the bakery. She was a good worker, trustworthy and amiable with people. Yes, Eileen was the obvious successor and with Carrie's help, Alice would never have to give a second thought to the future of the bakery.

Alice had decided early in the season not to pursue adding more restaurant selections to the menu this year. It had been a wise decision with the wedding occupying a major portion of their time lately. There was always next spring for that and the less there was to learn, the easier it would be for Eileen and Carrie if Alice couldn't always be available.

But with all things considered, something had been bothering Carrie lately. She knew there was plenty of work to do until Alice's wedding in two weeks, but what about after that? She had been wondering what she would do all winter once the bakery closed. She would miss the money and although her mom would be glad for the extra help at home, Carrie knew she would miss her job. Other than the holiday pie orders and an occasional banquet, the bakery wouldn't operate during the winter. So for the past while Carrie had been seeking and wondering what God would have her to do.

She began to wonder more seriously again about missions. "Dear Lord, do You have a place for me in missions?" She would often pray. But nothing seemed to be right or fall into place as she checked different options in mission work. She and her parents prayed specifically about two openings in Central America that had interested her and matched her skills, but none of them felt a peace in their hearts about either option. This made Carrie sure she was not to pursue either assignment. It was beginning to look like she'd be a "homemaker's helper" for the winter, as Mom called it. This was all right with Carrie and Mom liked the idea too. There was always the church office work to help with. Carrie had become so proficient in office skills that her father found himself depending on her more and more even with her job at Alice's bakery. She had become a real blessing to him as she lifted the burden of the church's clerical duties off her Dad's shoulders.

One day Dad arrived home from the hardware with good news. "Carrie," he called as he walked in the kitchen door.

"Yes, Dad?" she answered from the living room.

"I've got something to tell you that you may be interested in," he explained.

When Carrie turned to see her father approaching the room, she noticed he was smiling. She stopped her cleaning, laying the dust cloth down as he addressed her.

"What is it, Dad?" she asked.

"Well, I have something I want you to pray about until Friday and see how the Lord is leading you."

"Ok, Dad!" Carrie smiled with interest.

"It seems Martinsons have purchased the old warehouse that adjoins the hardware in Blue Creek where my office is. They are planning to open a farm supply division and eventually incorporate the two businesses into one. The office space in the old warehouse is a lot larger than the little office I have at the hardware now," Dad explained. "You remember Ralph Martinson's aunt, Etta Van Buren, don't you, Carrie?"

"Yes," Carrie replied, remembering the older lady her father spoke of.

"Well, Etta has been the bookkeeper and office manager for years at the main offices in Maplecrest. She is going to be in charge of setting up new offices in the warehouse area over the next several months. They are going to hire a part-time helper to assist her in getting everything ready. Eventually my office will be moved over there too. As soon as I heard about the job, I thought of you." Carrie listened eagerly to her father's explanation. "I mentioned you to Ralph right away, and he told me to have you come in and see about it if you're interested. You've gotten so good with all the clerical tasks for church, I thought this just might be the thing for you this winter while you wait on more permanent directions from the Lord."

"It sounds great, Dad!" Carrie said, excitedly. "What are the duties? When would I start? Do you know how much it will pay?"

"Whoa! Wait a minute!" Dad cautioned. "First you'd better pray about it. I did mention your name to Ralph when we talked about it, and he told me you can have the job because no one else even applied, but you'll need to be sure how you think God is leading first. Ralph said they'd have to start an ad in the paper on Friday if you decide you don't want the job. That's why they'd like to know by the end of the week. I told Ralph you'd need a few days to pray about it and then maybe you'd be in to see about the duties. I think they need someone about three days a week to help with whatever Etta needs to complete the transition."

"It sounds perfect, Dad!" Carrie said enthusiastically. "I will pray about it though and I'll let you know how I think God is leading me. Will you and Mom pray for me too, Dad?" Carrie asked.

"Yes, of course we will, Carrie. In fact we already do. We pray for you and your brother and sister daily about a number of things. That's partly why I was pretty sure you'd be interested. It seems like an answer to what we've already been praying about. Do you see what I mean?" Carrie nodded in answer to her father. "In fact, it may eventually lead into something more permanent." Carrie listened with interest as her father explained. "Etta has been the secretary and bookkeeper at the main office for years. Since she's getting older, she's been talking about retiring in the next few years. If you already had your "foot in the door," so to speak, you might be considered for her position when and if the time comes, assuming you were interested and had the necessary skills. Maybe there would even be a full-time office position that would open up with the new farm supply division."

"It seems like a lot to think about all of a sudden," Carrie admitted.

"I know, and I want you to understand, no one actually mentioned full-time employment in the future, but I just think it could be a possibility. Ralph often has moved existing employees to better positions when they opened up. So, if you decide to take this job, you could always consider enrolling in some business classes at the community college in the future. Of course, if it ever came to that—being offered a more permanent job, I mean—you'd probably have to choose between your job at Blooming Hills and the position at Martinson's. But, I'm getting a little ahead of myself. Something like that would be a while down the road—if it happens at all—and God very well may open up some other opportunity for you in the meantime. We'll make a special point to pray about it as a family tonight at supper."

Later that evening the Brooks family prayed for Carrie and the new job possibility. Carrie went to bed that night with a feeling of peace about the new job. She slept soundly and awoke with renewed vigor and purpose as she sought God's will in the matter. Her prayers were filled with anticipation as she specifically asked God to answer. On Friday morning Carrie awoke with a joyful feeling. She remembered to take a few moments to pray before she joined the family for breakfast.

"Dear Lord, I thank you for this day, even though it is still early morning and everything is so dark I can't even see the day yet! I feel You've led me to this job. It's something to be thankful for even though I can't see all it's details yet. I feel You want me to proceed with the interview. If I've heard You wrong, please make that clear to me even this morning. In Jesus' Name I pray, Amen."

When the family gathered for breakfast, Carrie waited with anticipation for her father to bring up the subject about how they felt God had answered their prayers. Dad read a scripture and then prayed as usual. As they ate, he began to talk about the new job. "Carrie, I'm curious to know how you feel about applying for the job at Martinson's now that you've had several days to pray about it."

"Well," Carrie began, "I felt good about it from the start. I wouldn't be afraid to pursue it," she said cautiously, hardly daring to check her parents' expressions; for she so hoped they would be thinking the same thing as well. "I haven't felt God say 'no.' I'm sure of that. I really have peace about it, Dad. I'd like to apply. I'm anxious to know what you and Mom think after praying about it."

Mom was smiling as she helped Addy with her cereal. Soon Dad replied to Carrie, "Your mother and I prayed all week about this," he began. "We think it would be an excellent opportunity for you for several reasons. First, it is only part-time. Your mother still appreciates you being at home to help out with Addy. You've even been a real help to Luke from time to time with his schoolwork."

Luke was busy eating his cereal and seemed to be removed from any concerns about office jobs.

Dad went on, "Another good thing about this job is that you'd be traveling to work with me and saving one of the vehicles here for your mother." Carrie nodded her agreement. "It's good in another way too. You'd be in a good environment there at the office. I think that's a real positive thing to consider. Some job situations you could get into might be difficult just because of the atmosphere, if you understand what I mean. We never have to be concerned about that at all when you work for Alice either. That's something to really be thankful for." Carrie nodded her agreement again. "Alice is such a good sister in the church and a fine role model. I'm really glad you are getting to learn from her skills. It's really good for you and Luke both where the Henderson family is concerned. They care about you kids and your Christian walk and so it's been nice that you could both work there." Carrie agreed with Dad's comments. Realizing the same things, she had often thanked God for her job at Blooming Hills.

"So I guess, with all that, we're saying we believe this job is an answer to prayer for you," Dad concluded.

Carrie could hardly contain the excitement she felt as she tried to finish her breakfast. The only problem she could see was the possibility of someday having to decide between the Blooming Hills job she had grown to love so much and the new office position. But she decided to let God take care of those details. She remembered the lessons she had learned in Miss Winfield's Sunday school class so long ago; concerns about daily provisions and the affairs of life should be committed to the Lord.

"If you'll get ready as soon as you're done eating, you can ride into Blue Creek with me to work and we'll see about the details of this job. You'll have to fill out an application and some paperwork, and then I'll show you around the office and the new store area."

A Wedding

The following Tuesday morning, Carrie awoke to her alarm ringing loudly, signaling it was five-thirty a.m. and time to be up getting ready for work. After going to work with her father on Friday and getting oriented to the duties of the job, Carrie was anxious to start even though this week she would work only two days because of the exciting events near the end of the week—preparation for Alice's wedding! This week, she was especially thankful that this new job was only part-time and that the Martinson's were glad to be flexible with her hours to accommodate her schedule.

As Carrie readied for work, her mind was spinning with thoughts of the busy week ahead of her. Today was the first day on her new job. Thursday she'd be back at the bakery helping the Henderson women with all the food for the wedding and Saturday…oh! Saturday! Carrie could hardly wait! One of her best friend's weddings! "What could be more exciting?" she had thought. She was glad she had finished her dress last week and the only details to be completed for Alice's special day could all be done from Thursday on.

When Dad and Carrie left for work, Mom kissed her daughter good-bye, wishing her well on her first official day at the office and Luke promised to pray for her during the day as he did his schoolwork. Luke held Addy as he and Mom waved to the two setting off in the car.

The first two days of the new job were great, Carrie thought.

She had no trouble handling the duties. She especially enjoyed working with Etta and anticipating that the empty warehouse building would one day be a thriving store, knowing that she would have a part in making that happen.

By Wednesday noon, Carrie had really given a woman's touch to the old office area in the warehouse. She had swept the floors, dusted thoroughly and even arranged much of the papers and supplies in her dad's office next door; a job the men at the hardware never seemed to find time to do. Now Dad's office was tidy, organized, and ready for the transition. In the warehouse office, Carrie hung a few pictures from home and even a vase with dried flowers now adorned the large windowsill that looked out over the parking area. The room was ready for the office furniture that would be coming soon. The hardware had been especially busy this morning. So when Carrie had finished all the jobs Etta had left for her, she watched the phones for her father in his office while he tended to customers out front.

When Dad popped his head in the door at lunchtime, he was moved to exclaim, "Wow! Carrie! What a wonderful difference you've made in this place." The piles of sales receipts and purchase orders previously stacked on the desk for lack of time were now neatly filed, giving the area an air of calm organization.

"Any phone calls?" Dad asked Carrie.

"A few," she answered. "The company that supplies the snow shovels called to give a proposed delivery date on that backorder. Then there were a few salesmen…. one from the lawn and garden supply and one from a paint company. And…oh! Alice Henderson just called too."

"What did Alice need?" Dad asked with curiosity.

"Well, she said she's really swamped with work on last minute details for the wedding and she wondered if there was any way I could help for a few hours after work. I told her I'd ask you."

"Sure, Carrie, that's no problem. In fact, why don't you call Etta and if she doesn't have any more for you to do, ask if you can be done for the day and then go help Alice right after lunch. You've done such a tremendous amount of work in two days. I don't see why you can't leave early today. It looks to me like everything's in order around here."

"Thanks, Dad," Carrie beamed.

When Carrie called Etta at the main office, she was given permission to be finished with her duties for the week. She politely thanked her supervisor and wished her a nice weekend. Then she promptly proceeded to dial Blooming Hills Bakery.

After several rings, a breathless Alice answered, "Hello, Blooming Hills Bakery."

"Alice?" she began, "This is Carrie. I'm calling from work. Etta said I can leave early to help you if you need me."

"Oh, praise the Lord!" Alice cried. "Yes, I certainly do need you. When can you come?"

"Whenever you want," Carrie replied.

"I'll send who ever can get a moment free over to pick you up immediately, if that's ok." Alice said.

"That's fine," Carrie answered.

"Have you eaten lunch yet?" Alice asked.

"No, we were just getting ready for lunch break," Carrie started.

"Well, just plan to eat here if you want. We're all working out here in the banquet room and Katie fixed a big pot of soup!"

"Ok," Carrie replied.

"I'll send someone over to the hardware to get you. It'll probably be fifteen minutes or so," Alice said.

"Ok. Thanks. Bye," Carrie replied and hung up the phone. She turned to her father who was waiting for the report. "Alice sounds almost desperate," Carrie chuckled. Her father smiled knowingly. "I think that's the first time I've ever heard her sound so flustered. She said she needed me immediately if possible, and that everyone's eating there while they're working in the banquet room so I can just eat there if I want. I hope that's all right with you, Dad," Carrie said, suddenly remembering they had planned to go out together for lunch.

"Of course, it's fine with me, sweetheart. It sounds like she really needs you. If Alice Henderson is that flustered, it must be a stressed situation," he smiled. "All the Hendersons are usually so calm, even under pressure. You go and help her out. We'll go out to lunch next week when you're back to work. Do you need me to run you over there?" he questioned.

"Thanks, Dad!" Carrie hugged her father. "But Alice said she'll send someone over to pick me up in about fifteen minutes."

"Ok. I'll run next door to the doughnut shop and get a cup of coffee and a sandwich. I'll bring it back here and wait with you."

"Great, Dad," Carrie said.

As Dad left, the phone rang and Carrie answered it and handled the call as efficiently as usual. In a few minutes, Dad was back with his lunch. He sat down at one of the desks and began sipping his coffee. One of the other employees was handling the front of the store while he and Carrie were on break. It afforded them a few moments to talk and enjoy each other's company, resting from their busy morning.

Soon Eileen came in the front door of the hardware. Carrie saw her and motioned for her to come back to the office.

"Hi, Carrie! Are you ready?" Eileen asked as she walked through the office door.

"Yes, I am!" Carrie grabbed her coat and purse and readied to leave.

"Hello," Dad said to Eileen.

"Hello, Pastor Brooks," she replied with a polite smile.

"So, you're the chauffeur today?" he teased.

"I got my license recently," Eileen answered proudly.

Pastor Brooks nodded between bites of his sandwich. "Well, I hope you two can be a real help to Alice today," he said to the girls. Both of them smiled and turned to leave.

Once they were in the car, Eileen filled Carrie in on all the details of what was going on with the wedding preparations.

"Alice was a little flustered this morning. The restaurant supply truck came and some of the food order for the wedding was messed up. They accidentally sent the wrong items. They're sending another truck out with the correct order, but she got a little upset and now she's feeling like with the setback, we'll never get everything done." Eileen talked incessantly until they were halfway to the orchard. Then rather suddenly, she turned to Carrie and with a new look and tone of voice that Carrie had never quite heard from Eileen before, she rather coyly declared, "John Mark just got home a few minutes before I left to pick you up."

Eileen looked directly at Carrie for a second as if to study her reaction before returning her eyes back to driving. When she was satisfied that there had been no change in Carrie's demeanor, she went on. Her next statement seemed to probe further, "He barely said hello to me and then asked where you were."

Eileen looked at Carrie again with the same curious, questioning look that seemed to be asking for a response from her friend. Recognizing the nuances of Eileen's voice and look, Carrie shifted uncomfortably in her seat. She replied as nonchalantly as she possibly could, "Oh? I'm glad he was able to come home in time to help Alice out."

Between watching the road and checking the rearview mirrors, Eileen studied Carrie.

Carrie thought her friend seemed somewhat annoyed at not discovering any clues in her behavior. So Carrie took the first opportunity to change the subject as soon as she could think of something about which to converse. "Your dress is done, isn't it?" she asked Eileen.

"Yes, I finally finished it last night. But not without ripping out the one sleeve twice," Eileen said. "I almost called you for help. Alice and Mom could've helped me but they've been so busy they hardly know which way to turn. I got it done though, with a little persistence."

The girls talked on until they reached Blooming Hills. They parked the car and quickly headed in. When they stepped into the banquet room adjoining the bakery kitchen, Carrie saw most of the Hendersons from oldest to youngest working and scurrying on one project or another.

The long tables were filled with dried flowers that Alice and Katie were arranging for the bouquets. Tommy was tying birdseed and rice into fabric squares for guests to toss at the bride and groom and John Mark was hauling some of the church's folding chairs from one of the Blooming Hills trucks into the large back doors.

Alice looked hurried, but happy. She was glowing with the pleasure of it all even amidst the frenzied work. "Oh, Carrie! I'm so glad you're here! I hardly know where to start you working. I need you...everywhere!" she exclaimed.

"I'll do whatever I can, Alice," Carrie said as she put a comforting hand on her friend's shoulder. "Don't worry, it looks like you've got a lot of expert helpers here. We'll get it all done," she reassured her.

"I guess I've come to depend on your help more than I realized," Alice confided.

"That's ok, Alice. Where should I start? Shall I help Eileen in the kitchen?"

Alice bit her lip and looked as if she was deep in thought. "No, not yet anyway. I suppose Eileen told you about the mix up with the truck," she rolled her eyes in dismay. "I think I need you most at the flower arranging. If we can get all the bouquets and corsages assembled, then we can clean up this room and the men can set up tables."

"Ok," Carrie agreed. She pulled up a chair by Katie and set to work helping group the bridesmaids' bouquets. Alice had dried dozens of tea roses from her mother's garden in the summer and Katie was assembling them with baby's breath and greenery. Carrie couldn't help thinking how beautifully the muted shades of the flowers would compliment the maids' light brown velvet dresses on the day of the wedding. Such an eye for beauty Alice had.

As Carrie worked and chatted with Katie, her mind continued to wander back and reflect on what Eileen had said on the way to Blooming Hills. It seemed pretty obvious to Carrie that her friend was suspecting something about her and John Mark. But had her suspicions arisen from John Mark's actions or had Carrie given Eileen some reason to question what so far had been just an old friendship? She became increasingly aware of Eileen's curiosity, for she seemed to look in Carrie's direction each time she popped her head out of the kitchen for one reason or another. Carrie decided to be very careful to give her no further room for suspicion. She was determined to remain neutral in her attitude and behavior toward John Mark Henderson. After all, he was simply a good friend, her brother's pal, and Eileen's brother. Nothing more.

Later when John Mark found a moment to rest, he came up to the table where Katie and Carrie were working. He pulled up a chair and greeted Carrie as he sat down. "Hi, Carrie!" he said in his typically shy tone, yet obviously glad to see her.

"Hello, John Mark," she replied, trying to be friendly but unemotional.

"I heard you got a new job. Do you like it?" he went on.

"Yes, it's fine, thank you; although truthfully, I haven't had time to form much of an opinion as yet."

John Mark went on trying valiantly to draw her into a conversation, which was not an easy task for the usually quiet young man. He was discouraged to find himself doing most of the talking. Carrie tried so diligently to be polite, even friendly, without doing anything to arouse any more suspicions in Eileen.

When the somewhat disappointed young man finally excused himself to Carrie and Katie, Carrie felt she had failed miserably in her attempt at nonchalance and may have even given John Mark the impression that she was avoiding him. She was glad when the last bow was tied onto the flowers and they were placed in boxes to await the wedding, for then, Alice dismissed her to help Eileen and Mrs. Henderson in the kitchen.

Several pitchers of punch had been made and Eileen was pouring them into decorative molds for ice rings. Carrie began helping Mrs. Henderson who was in the process of baking the layers of wedding cake to be frozen until Friday afternoon when Carrie would help Alice decorate the cake.

It was a fun but busy afternoon that came to an end when the last huge bowl was washed and hung above the large counter area of the bakery kitchen. Alice heaved a sigh of relief and all the ladies clapped spontaneously and laughed with joy for a long day's work completed.

It was only then that Carrie noticed her stomach growling and realized in all the busy excitement she had forgotten to eat some of the soup they had served for lunch. "Oh, well," she thought to herself, "I'll just wait for supper now." With thinking about Eileen's strange comments and all the hurried preparations of the afternoon, Carrie had simply forgotten to eat.

"Thank you all," Alice said gratefully. "This really helps out! What would I do without all of you?" Everyone smiled and Carrie assured Alice she wouldn't have missed all the fun for anything.

Carrie spent the next two days working at Blooming Hills as she had done all summer, only now the bakery was closed for the season and all the work focused on Alice's wedding. Great quantities of potatoes were peeled for salad. Carrie spent Thursday afternoon mixing and molding hamburger into meatballs for the wedding reception while the rest of the ladies of the Henderson family worked on various other foods for the meal.

The days leading up to Alice's wedding were such fun for Carrie as she worked with the Hendersons to get the many preparations finished. She watched how they related to each other even under stressful time constraints. They exemplified a Christian family and were still kind to one another even when it got late and everyone was tired.

On Friday, even Steve Creighton came over to help with the decorating. As soon as the cake was completely finished, Alice and Carrie began to vacuum and tidy up the banquet room. Steve helped Luke and John Mark set up tables and chairs in the arrangement Alice suggested while Mrs. Henderson, Katie and Eileen measured paper and covered each table, decorating it with dried flowers. With the many hands helping, the work was light and by two-thirty every last detail was finished.

Alice was delighted with the results and went to the house early to get ready for the rehearsal which was to be held at the church at six p.m. Carrie headed for home to get ready also.

The rehearsal dinner was being prepared by the ladies of First Church. Carrie was excited for Alice and Pastor Creighton, but she had to admit to herself that she also looked forward to this evening. It promised to be a nice time with Homer home for the weekend. He would be at the dinner since he was singing in the wedding. With Pastor Brooks performing the ceremony, all of the Brooks' had been invited to the dinner as well. Even with the excitement of this evening, it was Saturday that Carrie really anticipated.

Finally Saturday arrived and when Carrie awoke in the early morning, she was filled with excitement. There was no time to lose today in preparing for the wedding. Recently, Pastor Brooks had found a used car for the family to have as a second vehicle. Today Carrie was especially glad for the car as she packed all her things in the backseat. She needed to be at the church early with the other bridesmaids. The rest of the family would come in the van a little later.

Last evening had been so wonderful even if it was only the rehearsal that Carrie couldn't help smiling to herself at the memory of it as she drove to the church. Homer, Eileen, Luke, John Mark— everyone together again, just like it had been that first summer at Blooming Hills. Carrie fondly remembered the rehearsal. Homer's solo was exquisite. His violin music had been absolutely beautiful as the bridesmaids walked slowly down the aisle. It was obvious that even a short time at school had begun to hone and polish his already fine skills. And then, the look on Pastor Creighton's face when Alice had walked down the aisle! It was a moment Carrie thought she would never forget! He had looked so in love as he watched her. Everyone noticed his jubilant smile and Carrie could see his eyes shine with joyous tears.

"How good it is to be a Christian," Carrie thought. "We don't miss anything. We have everything; we have all things in Christ!"

It was obvious that the courtship, which occurred in the most orderly fashion between Steve and Alice, had not destroyed romance as some worldly people may have thought, but just the contrary. A strong love was built between the two as they sought to live in God's will. This truth was obvious in the shining expressions on every face last night. Carrie remembered each part of the evening from start to finish and thanked God for being able to be part of it. Carrie's group of friends had all sat together in the fellowship hall for the dinner and Pastor Creighton's younger brother, Brad, was happily welcomed into the gathering.

The ladies of First Church served a delicious dinner. The first course was an elegant salad followed by roast beef, baked potatoes, vegetables, homemade rolls, and pies. Everyone had a wonderful time visiting together and getting to know Pastor Creighton's family.

Carrie was so glad, for it seemed that John Mark had given her a second chance, so to speak. She felt more comfortable talking with him in the presence of the others, not having to worry about Eileen's suspicious attention. He didn't seem to be at all dissuaded by what Carrie had feared was cool, impolite treatment she had given him earlier in the week at Blooming Hills. She hadn't meant to be rude at all in her attempt to appear normal and casual. And he had apparently not taken her as such for he was pleasant and talkative last evening—as talkative as John Mark Henderson ever was!

Carrie thought the wedding day turned out even more glorious than the day before had been, if that was possible. The weather was typically late autumn. It was cool, but sunny. The church was a bower of bouquets—the work of Alice's hands—dried roses, German statice, baby's breath, strawflowers, dried delphiniums; all arranged in breathtakingly beautiful displays. A small bouquet tied with a bow adorned each pew at the center aisle.

When Carrie arrived, she paused a moment at the sanctuary to behold the lovely decorations before she made her way to the basement to Miss Winfield's familiar, old Sunday school room where the bridesmaids had gathered to dress. The room was a profusion of dresses, shoes, bouquets, and excited ladies. Only Alice and Mrs.

Henderson had not arrived yet, but they were due soon.

Eileen fairly squealed when she saw Carrie, "Isn't this the most exciting event ever?" She pulled Carrie into a friendly hug and the two girls laughed together over Eileen's exuberance. Katie was smoothing Alice's dress and veil that were hung on a room divider. It was the first time Carrie had seen the dress since it was finished.

"Isn't it lovely?" Katie said as she turned to the girls.

"Yes!" they chorused. Carrie ran her hand over the smooth satin, admiring it's every fold.

Soon Alice and her mother arrived and the countdown began. Everyone donned their dresses and then helped Alice, seeing that her hair was done just right so that her veil could be positioned correctly. A few minutes before the start of the ceremony, everyone was finally ready. Alice sat down on one of the Sunday school chairs and breathed a happy sigh. Mrs. Henderson's eyes were brimming with tears. "Let's pray," she suggested to the girls. They all joined hands asking God's blessing on this special day.

As soon as Mrs. Henderson said, "Amen," a knock was heard at the door. Alice answered it to find Chris Brooks. She smiled as she peeped in at the bridal party. "It's almost time, girls!" she whispered. "Roger told me to tell you to quietly make your way upstairs as soon as you're ready!"

"Thank you," Alice said softly.

"You all look so lovely," Mom complimented as she held out her arm for Mrs. Henderson and together they disappeared up the stairs. Alice looked nervous but excited, embracing each girl as they all passed in front of the full-length mirror to check their dresses one last time before leaving the room. Carrie was first in line, next came Katie, followed by Eileen and then Alice. The girls tip-toed quietly and when they reached the top of the stairs, Alice clapped her hand to her mouth and let out a muffled gasp as she saw how full the church was! Extra chairs had been set up to accommodate all the guests.

Homer started playing the music for the processional and perfectly on cue, the groomsmen filed out from the pastor's study with John Mark in the lead, followed by Joe, and Pastor Creighton's brother, Brad. Pastor Brooks took his place at the center with the groom as they waited for the ladies to enter the sanctuary. At the start of the second verse, Carrie began to walk slowly down the aisle just as they had practiced Friday evening. She tried diligently to smile and remain poised though she felt very jittery. Her bouquet trembled as she tried to steady her shaking hands. She hoped her nervousness was not evident to anyone else. Soon she reached the front and filed into her place at the end of the line. Her father winked approvingly at her. At this she felt relieved and knew that even amidst her nervousness she must have done well.

The others filed in, all in turn and finally Alice herself started down the aisle, escorted by her father. A rustling of people all rising to their feet, filled the sanctuary as Alice entered the room. Carrie's eyes drank in the scene. She was enjoying the excitement of the moment. She glanced to her left beyond the other bridesmaids to see Pastor Creighton's face as he watched his bride. His expression was the same as last night at rehearsal only now he looked even more serious. As she observed Pastor Creighton, her eyes caught sight of John Mark who was standing farthest to the left. Carrie's eyes met his for a moment. Instead of looking at his sister, the bride, he was looking at her! It must have been Carrie's look of mild surprise that caused him to turn his gaze away quickly. He looked dutifully back down the aisle as Alice approached.

Soon the ceremony began and Carrie was drawn into the touching music and prayers. Her father's sermon was a fine presentation of the message of salvation as he described the relationship between Christ and His church and likened it to a marriage. And then it seemed to Carrie that just as swiftly as it had begun, the wedding was all over. Her father was introducing Pastor and Mrs. Steve Creighton and the congregation was applauding as Homer played the strains of a joyous march on the piano.

The newlywed couple walked down the aisle and each of the bridesmaids and groomsmen followed in turn. When Carrie reached the center where her father stood smiling at her, there was John Mark offering her his arm. "Funny," she thought, "I didn't remember practicing the recessional this way." But she slipped her arm in John Mark's as all the other girls had done with their escorts. How strong and steady he seemed! How glad she was to have his help, as she still felt shaky in the whirl of it all! Together they walked down the aisle and out to the foyer where the receiving line had formed. As they took their place in the line, he released her arm and gave her his familiar, sweet smile. Already the rows of family at the front were being ushered out.

Soon it was time for the short trip to Blooming Hills banquet rooms, the only facility large enough to hold all the guests for the reception. The food and fellowship were wonderful and Carrie had the time of her life being seated at the front table with the bridal party. The elegant reception was reward enough for Carrie as she watched everyone enjoy the fruit of her labors—the pretty decorations, the delicious food, the delicately assembled cake.

A microphone was placed at the head table and Pastor Brooks acted as host. He said a few words about the couple and then Pastor Creighton took the microphone and gave a moving testimony of how he had prayed for a Proverbs 31 wife like Alice. He told everyone how the Lord had arranged their meeting and how the courtship had taken place. Several of the women were teary-eyed as he related the story. When he finished everyone applauded the happy couple.

Many people were taking pictures and Carrie felt she had smiled for a thousand photographs by the end of the day. But she and the others girls made lovely subjects in their pretty velvet dresses with the lace collars as they stood next to the groomsmen all in suits with their matching brown ties—gifts from Pastor Creighton.

When the new Mr. and Mrs. Creighton finally left amidst a second deluge of rice and birdseed, a shower of the last golden leaves of autumn swirled around them, driven by a wayward gust just as they got into their car. Carrie drew in a deep breath and sighed at the loveliness of it all. It was a scene that she thought rivaled her beloved May for beauty.

She was glad that several couples from First Church had offered to help with cleanup and she was free to go home for she longed to curl up in her familiar window seat and relive the glorious day with a soothing cup of tea.

The Quilting

On Tuesday it was back to work in Blue Creek for Carrie. The same sensation of finality that had come over her at the end of high school when the last graduation party was over seemed to steal its way into her thoughts again today. It was a feeling of settling into a routine that somehow she knew was not to become permanent.

Carrie worked diligently for Etta, assisting her considerably with the new office set-up. Although she was practicing contentment by doing the tasks at hand with a willing heart, whether it be her job for Martinson's or helping her mother with the housework, there remained an empty spot in Carrie's heart—a feeling that she couldn't name yet she could sense its presence from time to time. It was a knowing that while for the time being she was doing God's will, that there was a calling to something more; a knowing that this stage of life with its various duties was not her final destiny.

With the coming of the weekend, Carrie experienced a feeling of isolation. Luke had been invited to John Mark's farm for the weekend. He was to leave on Friday afternoon to help his friend with some last minute tasks around his place before winter. Carrie found herself feeling rather lonely with her brother gone, Alice married and living in her own new home, and Homer and Amanda both back at school. At least she could call Eileen and for that she was thankful. But the fact that everyone else her age seemed to be busy moving on with their own lives and into various ventures left

Carrie questioning her situation once again.

But Carrie had learned to wait on the Lord. She knew that being in a desert place in one's life could be fruitful if handled properly. Past experience had taught her to redeem the time wisely. Although she couldn't deny the tender ache she felt, she didn't allow herself to dwell on it. Rather, she turned her attentions to Bible study and filled her lonely hours with prayer and service to others, mainly her mother.

However, when Sunday finally arrived, Carrie was glad to have Luke home again. He and John Mark had come back in time for Sunday school. It seemed livelier and happier around the Brooks house with Luke back today.

"How was your weekend?" Dad asked Luke later that day during Sunday dinner.

"Great, Dad!" Luke replied, enthusiastically between mouthfuls of mashed potatoes.

"What all did you do over at John Mark's?" Mom asked.

"Oh, lots of stuff. Friday we painted the front porch rails—even after it got dark we just turned the porch light on and finished it quick. We also replaced some rotten boards on one of the barns. Umm, then Saturday we hooked up water to his back room so he can do laundry." Luke laughed at the thought of it. He went on eating voraciously between sentences.

"You must not have eaten at all over there the way you're going after those potatoes!" Dad joked. Everyone laughed including Luke.

"There was hardly time," he admitted. "We really kept busy. We did go to Dalton Corners on Saturday night and picked up a pizza though!" Luke smiled. "Oh, and we had to plant a whole bunch of these dumb bushes," he went on. "Sometimes I think that John Mark's been over there in the boondocks alone too long. I can't figure him out."

"Why? What do you mean?" Mom asked her son.

"Well, the last thing we did Saturday afternoon was go out to the edge of one of his fields where an old house used to stand. I guess it was torn down long ago. Only a few little stones from the foundation were left. He said we were going to uproot this one bush. A really big bush, I mean. And he kept saying how we had to be so careful. It took about an hour just to get it dug up! It was huge!" The family continued to listen with interest.

"I thought that was kind of weird," Luke went on, "I mean, he doesn't even have the bathroom all modernized and he's worried about some stupid bush? I admit it was in the way of what he's got planned as far as that field goes, but really! So, anyway, we loaded it on the truck and brought it back to the house. Then what do you suppose he did?" Luke asked, looking around the table at everyone. The family all stared back at Luke who went on to explain. "I'll tell you what he did; he took it off the truck and we split it into a zillion pieces and planted all these little sticks of bush all along the front porch. Now is that strange or what?" Luke asked.

"Well, I don't know," Mom sympathized. "That is how you transplant shrubbery," she added with a woman's understanding, yet she too seemed a bit bewildered by the thought of John Mark caring even the least little bit about landscaping when he had a whole farm to put in order.

"Did you ask him why he was doing it?" Dad questioned as he poured another glass of water.

"Yeah, I did. I said, 'Hey John Mark, what's going on here. Are you going to become a flower farmer or what?'" Everyone laughed at the idea of it. "He just said it had to be done before too late in the fall so the bushes would bloom in the spring. I still thought that was strange," Luke added, shaking his head. "But it seemed like it was really important the way he acted, AND...he was buying the pizza!" Everyone chuckled at Luke's sense of priorities.

A moment later Dad seemed to take the thoughts straight from Carrie's mind as he said, "I'd really like to see John Mark's farm. I'm going to have to get over there on a pastoral call soon. It seems it just hasn't worked out so far. Maybe we can all go as a family sometime before the holidays."

Carrie thought how much fun it would be to see John Mark's farm, for she had often wondered what it was like. It sounded to her as if he was putting great care into the property as well as trying to make the farm productive. She hoped silently that her father would soon plan the trip.

With winter rapidly approaching, Carrie and her Mom were now finished with the canning and freezing and turned their attentions to sewing and needlework projects.

One Friday afternoon early in December, Dad had arranged for the entire family to drive to Bixley to visit John Mark's new home. Mom and Carrie had intended to take John Mark a package of bread and cookies from their holiday baking. Carrie had worked with special care to decorate the delicious treats. But when Friday finally came Dad and Carrie came home from the hardware early only to find Mom tending to Addy who was ill with a fever and sore throat. Under the circumstances, Mom knew she had to keep Addy home for the evening. Although Carrie had looked forward to the trip to Bixley more than she cared to admit even to herself, she laid aside her own desires and offered to stay home to keep her mother company since the long drive would mean the men would be gone for most of the evening.

Even though she had looked forward to the trip all day, Carrie decided that the gray, blustery, afternoon was no fun to venture out in anyway, and resigned herself to the fact that she still was not going to get to see John Mark's farm. Carrie comforted herself that with the early approaching darkness; she wouldn't really be able to see the grounds, only the farmhouse anyway.

At about four o'clock when Luke finally finished his weekly assignments, Mom handed the two men the big basket filled with baked goods and Carrie waved to them from the bay window as the car pulled out of the drive. She fought back feelings of sadness at not being able to go; all the while knowing she had made the right choice, especially for her mother's sake.

Determined to be cheerful, she helped her mother stir some noodles into a big pot of bubbling chicken broth that had been simmering on the kitchen stove. The rich aroma filled the kitchen and warmed the house as well as Carrie's spirits. Maybe it would be a nice evening just to be here at home with Mom and Addy, cozy and warm.

Mom had set up a quilt in the parlor only days before and she and Carrie intended to quilt on it after supper. As soon as the dishes were done, Addy drifted off to sleep on the couch. Carrie built a fire in the pretty marble fireplace. It soon cast gentle warmth into the parlor where Carrie and Mom pulled chairs up to the quilt frame and began the intricate stitching. "Yes, this will be a pleasant evening," Carrie thought. The wind howled outside and reminded the women that they could be thankful to be in where it was warm, satisfied to have left the visiting to the men.

"It is good to be with Mom and have her all to myself," Carrie reasoned. As the women stitched they talked and laughed, enjoying each other's company. "What pattern is this?" Carrie asked her mother as she deftly worked her needle in and out of the fabric.

"This is an old pattern called the 'Double Wedding Ring,'" her mother replied. "I like it because it uses up so many little scraps," she told Carrie. Carrie nodded and went on with her work.

"What will we do with this one? Is it for missions?" Carrie asked after awhile.

"Well," Mom said slowly, a smile pulling at her lips, "I pieced it with the idea of adding it to your hope chest some day," she answered.

"Oh," Carrie said quietly and kept looking down at her work. "Thank you, Mom. I really love it!"

"I'm glad," Mom smiled.

The two women stitched on for a while in silence. It was Carrie who spoke next, "Mom, when you were my age, what were you doing with your life? I mean...did you have a job or what?"

"Oh, things were so different for me," her mother remembered. "I was going to college and I had dreams of a career. I didn't seek to please the Lord or include His will in my decisions. I was a Christian, but I was pretty worldly-minded I'd say, now that I look back on it. My deeper commitment to the Lord came later on. I'm glad you and Luke are already way ahead of me on that!"

"I see," Carrie nodded.

"Why do you ask, dear?"

"Oh, I don't know. I guess I just sometimes feel like there's something more for me out there somewhere. Don't get me wrong, Mom, I'm content being here with the family and I love my jobs at the store and Blooming Hills. But even after a lot of praying and seeking, there's still a little part of me that feels incomplete...as if God has more purpose for me, yet I haven't found it."

Mom nodded and looked thoughtfully at her stitching as she began to reply, "I think I know what you mean, dear." A short silence followed her words. "There was a time when..." Mom bit her lip as if she wished to retract her last half statement.

"What were you going to say, Mom?" Carrie asked innocently.

A look of concern crossed Mom's face as she looked up for a moment into her daughter's eyes. She said nothing and looked back down to the quilt. Her fingers traced a square of fabric that Carrie recognized as having been left over from the dress she had made to wear at the spring banquet and graduation.

"Oh, I was just thinking," Mom said slowly, "that there was a time when I thought John Mark Henderson…would ask to court you sometime after high school." She paused as she waited for Carrie to reply. The silence continued a moment longer, then she spoke again. "You're young yet, Carrie. There's a lot of life ahead of you. It could still happen. Or there may be some other fine young man who will see you as God's choice for his wife, and maybe you'll feel likewise when the time comes." Mom tried to sound hopeful having sensed a tiny bit of impatience in Carrie's earlier questions. "Here we are talking as if you're well on in years!" she chuckled. "You're young, barely out of high school. There's absolutely no hurry about anything. I'm sure God will show you His plans for your life all in good time. Your father and I have learned that that's usually the way it works. God reveals His will one step at a time."

So! Mom had sensed it too! She had noticed John Mark's attentions to Carrie! "It hasn't been all my imagination," Carrie told herself. A smile pulled at the corners of her mouth. But she fought to hide it. After a long pause, she found the courage to speak, "Mom, what made you think that about John Mark?" she asked.

"Oh, maybe I shouldn't have said anything about it," her mother apologized. "I've tried so hard not to put ideas into your head about boys. That way you wouldn't dwell on any one boy, dreaming of him as a future husband. I want you to be able to discern with a completely clear head if the time ever comes for a young man to ask for your hand."

She went on with concern in her voice. "It's just difficult for me at times to try to wait on God. I wasn't raised with the same convictions. Dating was the custom, you know. Back then it was pretty well accepted for girls to date several young men, never really intending to make any serious commitments, then some got interested in a person prematurely, not taking time to seek the Lords' will. It wasn't really the best plan because a lot of times, thinking back, some of my friends, even Christians friends, went out with guys who wouldn't have made very Christ-like husbands. So why bother to spend time getting emotionally attached with someone whom you don't even believe you could spend a lifetime with?" Carrie nodded her understanding as her mother explained. "Still, having grown up that way without any different kind of pattern, sometimes it's hard for me to let God have control. As far as John Mark, I guess I just thought he seemed extra attentive to you at times." Carrie nodded showing her understanding of what her mother meant. "It's probably just that he's very polite and quite a good friend of the family," Mom remarked.

"I thought I noticed the same thing too, though, Mom," Carrie confessed slowly.

Mom looked up at Carrie and gradually a smile spread across her face. "Really?" she said to her daughter.

"Yes!" Carrie replied. "I was always going to say something to you about it and sort of share my struggles with you. But I was kind of embarrassed and I decided long ago to let God have control of my thoughts where John Mark Henderson or any other boy is concerned," she added.

"I'm glad, Carrie. It's best, really," Mom assured her. "I hope I haven't been a stumbling block to you. Forgive me, please," she asked.

"No, it's ok, Mom. It's good to know you'll be making me accountable in this. I feel very relieved having my feelings out in the open with you. I've prayed a lot about God's will—even about John Mark Henderson. But I felt kind of silly wondering if he was interested in me. I thought it seemed like he was, but I didn't know how it seemed to anyone else, so of course I felt reluctant about sharing that." Mom smiled an admiring smile at her daughter, thankful for her maturity.

"Now you know how I've struggled to give my concerns to God and you can pray for me. Will you pray for me, Mom?" Carrie asked.

"I surely will!" Mom smiled as she affectionately squeezed her daughter's hand.

Over the winter the two women made many lovely items to fill a hope chest for Carrie. They completed tablecloths and pillowcases, comforters and doilies, often praying together about God's will for Carrie's future as they tucked each new item into an old cedar chest. Ever present was the double wedding ring quilt in the parlor, which the ladies saved for quilting on during the long winter evenings. It was nearly finished now and the edges were rolled up until the unquilted portion was just a narrow strip.

Of all her busy schedule, Carrie treasured most the days spent with her mother. She learned many skills of homemaking and received rich spiritual training as she worked with her mom, a real model of biblical womanhood. Still the gnawing feeling of being called to another mission never left her. It was easier though knowing her mother understood and was praying for her.

It was so different at Sunday school and church now. Most of Carrie's friends were off to college or like John Mark, pursuing careers elsewhere. Even Kirk Davis was gone to State on his second year of a football scholarship and was rarely seen around Maplecrest or Blue Creek anymore. Carrie received an occasional letter from Darla Harris who had taken a short-term missions assignment in Mexico, and Amanda often worked Sundays at the Blue Creek Community Hospital as part of her training, missing church meetings as a result.

And to add to Carrie's occasional feelings of isolation, the winter had been unusually hard weather-wise. The area experienced a blizzard in January that closed nearly everything for at least a week. Other frequent heavy snowstorms had caused traffic accidents and cancellations. There were many Sundays that John Mark never even made it home for church. But this Sunday promised to be different. The late winter days were coming to an end. Small signs of the calming weather gave hope to the snow-weary inhabitants of the area.

During last week much of the remaining snow had melted. Trent Melvin was home for the weekend on a missionary break, and he was scheduled to speak to the young people tomorrow at church. A fellowship dinner was planned after the service. Carrie looked forward to the day with great anticipation. Eileen had said John Mark was coming home this Sunday for sure. He didn't want to miss Trent's visit. All in all it seemed like a lot of excitement wrapped up in one day, Carrie thought, considering how dull much of the winter had been.

When Sunday finally came, it was a delight to Carrie. Sunday school and church were great with Trent back to visit. He had given an interesting presentation of his work abroad. It was thrilling to hear of people being saved and lives changed through the many branch projects of the large mission organization.

During his presentation, Carrie once again felt the old tug at her heart toward missions. She wondered again if there was a place for her in God's army of faithful mission workers. Apparently Trent's talk spurred similar feelings in others as well for Carrie noticed that many of the younger people spent time afterward conversing with him. But Carrie surmised that some of the giggling high school girls that were talking to him were not as sincerely interested about his work spreading the Gospel as they were smitten by his rugged good looks and adventurous spirit.

Eileen had volunteered to help in the kitchen with today's dinner, so Carrie was left standing in the foyer as Eileen made her way quickly to the fellowship hall right after the service. While Trent and Miss Winfield talked with others who were interested in the mission work, Carrie took a few moments to read the information and look at the pictures he had set up on display boards near the doors to the sanctuary. Drawn into the thrilling descriptions and interesting pictures of the native people, Carrie hadn't realized how long she had tarried there until a strong, masculine voice interrupted her thoughts. "Carrie Brooks!" She turned to see that all the others, even Miss Winfield, had already gone on to the fellowship hall for dinner and she and Trent were standing alone in the empty foyer.

"Hi," she said, shyly. "Oh, I hope he doesn't think I lingered here just to talk to him like those other girls did," Carrie thought to herself as she remembered how some of the girls would use any excuse to strike up a conversation with an eligible young man... especially one as tall and handsome as Trent Melvin.

"Can I answer any questions for you?" he offered warmly.

"Uh, well...maybe," Carrie fumbled for words. Oh, how she longed to overcome this uncomfortable shyness that seemed to limit her so! "If I could just be a bit more like other people, I could get myself gracefully out of situations like this," she thought, "or at least be more at ease when I find myself in them."

Seeing her slight confusion, Trent tried to rescue her, "I know you've been interested in missions for some time," he began.

"How does he know that?" Carrie wondered. The thought that he was aware of this slightly intimate detail of her life somehow made her a bit uncomfortable, for she didn't remember mentioning it to anyone but her parents and a few close friends. "Has Amanda told him?" she queried to herself.

"There are lots of positions opening up in these regions," he went on, pointing to the map. "There are new missions beginning in many of the little villages."

As Trent talked on, Carrie glanced from him to the display. She couldn't help wondering if it was hard at first for a tall, blonde, American with deep blue eyes, to be accepted by these dark-skinned, dark-eyed natives who he seemed to love so much.

"I have considered missions," she finally admitted. Trent smiled knowingly and nodded. "Nothing has ever seemed right, though," she said. "I haven't exactly felt peace about anything in that direction yet," she told him.

"I think I know how you feel," Trent assured her. "It was hard for me at first. It was a big step. Then after I took the step, I sometimes questioned myself. I got lonely at times. Still do. That's one drawback with mission work," Trent said honestly. "But you heard me say this morning that my position has changed a bit. I'm not out in the villages as much now. I've got a more permanent home by being at the main station; more westernized you might say. So now, I sort of have a feeling that I can settle down. Being far away now feels more homelike than it did to me at first. Still, my housing is kind of rough compared to what we're used to here in North America. But now that I'm in charge of some of the work at the main station, life is a little easier." Carrie nodded her understanding as she listened. "But it's also a trade-off. I miss the excitement of the day-to-day witnessing and work with the natives. People come into the station from time to time, but other times I'm the only one there and this job also keeps me alone, sometimes for long stretches of time."

Carrie looked thoughtfully at Trent and then back at the pictures as he went on. "It's hard to be in a completely different culture, I get to longing for someone who grew up like I did. You know, it's hard when you don't have anyone who can relate to you on your own cultural level—speak your language, share memories of home. For instance, on the Fourth of July I always miss being back here and no one could possibly understand that but another American." Carrie laughed along with Trent at this confession. "Sometimes I'm surrounded by people but very few have any reference point when it comes to understanding me." Carrie detected a slight sadness in Trent's voice at this admission. She looked at him with sympathy and then determined to pray more faithfully for him and others on the mission field. "But I guess it's the same for those I minister to. The situation is just flipped around. They have to learn to accept us tall, light strangers with different clothes before they can feel like listening to the Gospel we preach. That's why mission work like I'm presenting here takes commitment. It's a life choice—or should be."

Carrie was nearly astonished at his last few sentences. "It was as if he read my mind!" Carrie thought concerning his comments on the natives accepting him. "That's the second time in this conversation that he seemed to know about me or what I was thinking!" Carrie wondered how this could be, if it was only a coincidence, or maybe just her imagination. She had to admit she found it a bit unnerving.

But Carrie knew that what Trent was saying about mission work was right. "Going into these new territories," Trent stated, as he pointed once again to the area he had shown Carrie, "is going to require teams of dedicated individuals, even couples and families; people who are willing to live among the natives and learn their dialects and culture until they can find the keys that help unlock the doors to their hearts." Carrie could hear a gentle, pleading passion in Trent's voice that made him perfect for this job of recruiting new workers. "That kind of commitment isn't for everyone. Pray about it, Carrie," he added, "and I'll pray for you too."

"Thank you," she said honestly as she turned to make her way to the fellowship hall, leaving Trent standing in the foyer as he gathered up his brochures.

After dinner Carrie was once again aware of the impact that Trent's talk today had had on the young people as she watched several more gather around him to discuss the brochures he had handed out.

But the one who seemed most interested of all was John Mark Henderson. He and Trent spent quite a while alone in what seemed to be a deep conversation after their meal. It reminded Carrie of that evening at the Blooming Hills appreciation banquet when the two boys had huddled in serious conversation at Alice's newly-opened banquet room.

Today they talked and talked as Trent presented John Mark

with brochures that told of the various works of his organization. As Carrie watched from the far corner of the fellowship hall, she tried valiantly to push away the feeling of disappointment that was trying to creep into her soul. She wanted to be happy for John Mark if he was pursuing missions, after all, she had committed to pray for him before he ever left for Bixley, but there was still a part of her will that needed to be given completely to God. And truly, Carrie had to admit that Trent's love for his work and his enthusiasm to present the Gospel to unreached people was contagious. His words were nearly enough to make her reconsider if she had missed her calling the times when she had not gone on some of the missions she had considered.

She finally had to admit to herself that she had truly hoped John Mark would eventually approach her father about a possible courtship and today's events seemed to be pointing to quite a different future for the young man.

As the Brooks family drove home after dinner, Carrie's heart was not as light as it had been earlier in the day. The melting snow that had promised spring only this morning, now just looked muddy and dirty. The morning sun had given way to clouds that now threw a depressing half-light over the countryside. When the Brooks' arrived home, Carrie excused herself for a nap, as did the others, except Dad who was tending to a few details in his office.

For a while Carrie lay awake in her room staring up at the ceiling and thinking about her life. "Why can't I get some definite direction? When will this unsettled feeling end? How will I ever truly stop thinking of John Mark?" And now to add to her feelings of frustration and confusion, Trent's sincere words today plagued her afresh with thoughts of a possible call to work in foreign lands. But truly, her thoughts of John Mark Henderson were the real source of her restlessness, and she recognized that fact. Finally realizing that the only way she could ever be totally free of the relentless thoughts of him was to lay her heart's desires before the Lord; Carrie continued her prayers with deep passion. After a long time she felt some peace and her mind quieted a bit as she prayed, "Lord, I want to release my thoughts of John Mark Henderson to you once and for all." A few tears escaped her eyes and rolled slowly down her cheeks. "If he's to be a missionary, I ask that you bless his work and guide him to where you want him. I don't want to hold on to him in my heart anymore. I always tried not to, but today I realized that maybe a little part of my stubborn will still surfaces now and then."

Then Carrie drifted off to sleep. When she awoke and looked at her clock, she was surprised to find it was already four o'clock. She rubbed her eyes and glanced around the room. Addy, sat at the foot of her bed playing paper dolls and talking to the figures as she played. Carrie reasoned it must have been the little girl's voice that woke her up.

"Hi, Addy," she said with a yawn.

"Hi, Carrie. Did I watu' up?" she asked innocently.

"I don't know. Maybe. But it's ok, I've slept long enough," Carrie said, sitting up. "Are you having fun with your dolls?"

"Yup," Addy answered, busily arranging the dolls. "I woke up, but Momma's still asweep," she explained.

"That was nice of you to let her sleep," Carrie complimented her sister.

"Here," Addy said, reaching into her dress pocket and producing a chubby fistful of peppermints.

"Where did you get those?" Carrie asked.

"John Mart, he gave 'em to me," she said in her little girl voice. Carrie smiled to herself at her little sister's pronunciation of John Mark's name.

"He did?" Carrie said.

"Yup. And he said I could give one to you," the little girl continued. Carrie looked curiously at her little sister.

Addy soon went on supplying more details. "I went to see Daddy. He was busy. He said I have to go play quiet. Soooo..." she dragged the word out dramatically. "John Mart gave me these," she said, extending the peppermints to Carrie. "He talked to Daddy a long time. That's why I came up here, to play quiet," she said matter-of-factly.

"Was John Mark here?" Carrie asked, surprised.

"Yup," Addy said, dumping the peppermints on Carrie's bed. Addy scooped up her dolls and headed off to another room. Carrie sat pondering the little girl's words as she looked down at the candies, John Mark's favorites.

"So, John Mark was here a long time," Carrie said to herself, repeating her sister's words. "It stands to reason. Every mission organization requires candidates to go through their pastor first for a recommendation," she whispered, pondering her own words for a moment. "Sure…he came to see Dad before he left to go back home for the week! Well, it's a good thing I have turned this over to God," Carrie thought as she paused to reflect, surprised that her first opportunity to test her new convictions concerning her thoughts toward John Mark Henderson had come so soon.

Spring's New Promise

March passed slowly Carrie thought. It seemed spring would never arrive as the days wavered back and forth between sunshine and gray skies. When Carrie turned the calendar at the store to April, she sighed to herself as she looked out the big window. Even though generally, the weather had been warming up, today was rainy and dreary. But she reminded herself of the old saying, "'April showers bring May flowers.' I better endure the rain patiently since I do want to enjoy my favorite flowers next month. Besides, it won't be long now until I go back to work with Eileen." Even though Carrie had been a tremendous help in setting up the new office, there was still no promise of a more permanent position in the Martinson's store. Carrie had prayed about her circumstances and informed Etta Van Buren that she was planning to continue at Blooming Hills, since the office transition was nearly complete with no increase in hours available until the farm supply division actually opened. It seemed to be working out just right for everyone, though. Eileen would need Carrie back at the bakery just about the time the office work would be completely done.

Carrie was really looking forward to returning to her favorite job, working at Blooming Hills Bakery, and this time there was the possibility of it extending into a full-time job in the fall.

Just then, Dad came from the hardware into the new office to get a catalog from the files. "How's it going, Carrie?" he asked.

"Oh, fine," she replied. "I sure am anxious for spring, though," she added, looking hopefully out the window.

"I know what you mean," her father replied, "But remember the seasons do follow one another ever since God created the earth. So eventually spring will come just like every other year until the Lord returns."

"I know, Dad," Carrie admitted. "The rain today seems kind of cold and drizzly. I'm glad I don't have to be out in it. This weather makes you want to curl up at home in front of a cozy fire."

"Well, maybe this evening we can do just that," Dad offered. " Maybe we'll ask your mother to pop some popcorn after supper, or we'll have tea and dessert and the four of us can just visit. Luke's got Science Fair meeting tonight, you know."

"Oh, that's right," Carrie remembered. "That sounds great Dad. I'm already looking forward to it," she added, pulling her sweater tightly around her shoulders as she stared out at the damp day.

"I am too, sweetheart," Dad said, with a wink and disappeared out of the office.

That evening Luke left for his meeting as soon as he finished his supper. He was the Student Chairman of the FCH Science Fair committee and he took his responsibilities very seriously. Even the prospect of dessert hadn't detained him one minute longer as he hurried out the door.

Carrie had offered to milk Blossom for Luke, giving him a little extra time to make it to his meeting. After the dishes were done, she walked to the barn, enjoying the last moments of the day that was now fading lazily into nightfall. Today's rain had left the cool air smelling strangely pleasant even though the flowers were far from blooming yet, to nod their heady scents into the breeze.

Carrie worked in the barn and talked gently to Blossom. "You're the most contented creature, Blossom," she said. The cow turned and looked at Carrie with her big, brown eyes. "I used to really struggle with being contented, Blossom. I've really had a hard time with my will. I've wondered a lot about my place in life. But, I'm really doing better lately," she went on, as if the cow could understand every word. "I used to wish contentedness would come naturally to me, like it does to you, old girl. But now, I realize I had to go through a process of growing in order to gain any solid spiritual ground. I had to turn some things completely over to the Lord."

Carrie paused and was quiet for a while. Finally Blossom turned and stared at Carrie again as if to say, "Is that all?" Carrie couldn't help but laugh at the cow's look. She finished the chores and headed in to the house through the misty, drizzling dusk to start enjoying the relaxed evening Dad had promised. The smell of warm pie in the kitchen lured Carrie from the back porch as she hung her coat.

Mom was pouring hot water for tea into the good china teapot. "Wash up, Carrie. I'll take care of the milk and we'll sit around the fire and have our dessert in a little while," her mother said, motioning to the parlor.

Carrie happily followed her mother's advice. When she returned, Dad was setting up the folding table in front of the freshly kindled fire. The flames crackled as they licked the logs, sending a warm, radiating light throughout the room and dispelling the chill of the evening. Carrie helped Mom bring in the tea and dessert with Addy close behind. As the family sat down together and began to visit, Addy joined in, eating her pie and talking with the family. Soon though, she tired of the adult conversation, hopped down from her chair, and curled up on the couch with her doll. Finally sleep pulled at her eyelids as she drifted off for the night.

Dad and Carrie were filling Mom in on all the details of work at the hardware as the three enjoyed their tea in front of the cozy fire.

"Carrie, I suppose you're looking forward to going back to work at the bakery soon?" Dad asked.

"I sure am," Carrie bubbled. "I love the office job, don't get me wrong, Dad, but my first choice is still the bakery. I just really enjoy that work."

Mom smiled and nodded in understanding, knowing Carrie had become a very able helper in the Brooks' home when it came to the cooking and baking chores.

"So, is it still in the plans to open the bakery year around?" Dad asked.

"Yes, last I heard," Carrie replied. "Eileen plans to start work in a month or so, right before strawberry season to get everything set up. Then she plans to keep the restaurant open through lunch hours all year and run the bakery too, with Alice and me helping of course, after all, she's still got her senior year to get through."

"I hope she's not taking too much on," Mom said with concern.

"I'm quite sure she expects I'll help her, Dad," Carrie added thoughtfully. She looked at her father to assess his thoughts. "I talked with Mrs. Van Buren and she understands that I'll have to go back to the bakery here very shortly. She said it's probably going to work out just about right. Maybe just a slight overlap with my two jobs. She assured me we can work the details out." Mom and Dad nodded as Carrie continued to explain. "If the farm division had opened sooner, maybe Martinson's would have had more work for me and I'd have had to make a decision, but it looks like that will take a little more time. It seems like this is my best option, to go back to Blooming Hills hoping for full-time by fall. Do you think Martinson's would hire me back when the farm store opens if Eileen can't give me full-time employment by then?"

"Well," Dad started, clearing his throat. Carrie listened, waiting for his reply. He looked at his wife and a slight smile began to form on his face. Carrie looked from her father to her mother, still expecting to hear an answer. Mom was smiling too as she looked down at her lap where she had now laid the knitting she had been working on.

"I guess this is as good a time as any to tell her," Dad began, looking to his wife. Mom just nodded as she smiled the most interesting smile.

"Tell me what?" Carrie wanted to shout! But she didn't; instead she listened patiently and waited for her father to go on. In the split seconds between his pause and his explanation, Carrie's mind ran wild with all kinds of excited thoughts. "Maybe my hardware job isn't going to end after all! Did they decide they needed a permanent office girl? Did Etta Van Buren announce her retirement already? Maybe Mom is having another baby! What could be going on here?" A million questions and a million scenarios raced through her mind.

Dad saw the look of anticipation in Carrie's eyes and went on to explain, now more seriously. "Your mother and I have something important to discuss with you. It's worked out well for us to be home here tonight so we can discuss this alone…just the three of us."

A pause followed as her father seemed to gather his thoughts in order to speak very carefully. "Carrie, your mother and I were wondering what your plans are for the future. I mean, have you felt God giving you any particular direction for your life lately?"

"No," Carrie said slowly. "I have prayed a lot about it and that's what's been so disturbing to me for so long. I never seem to sense God leading me into anything...definitely...long term, I mean." Then she added, "It's bothered me some, to feel this unsettled compared to others my age. It seems like everyone else has found their calling. I thought I wanted to go into mission work, but you know how that's been--there's never quite been the right spot for me it seems."

Mom and Dad looked at her with understanding as she continued.

"I think my heart is really pure when it comes to missions, I'm really drawn to the idea, and I'd be willing to go if I knew God was definitely calling me. But as yet, I guess it isn't time. Somehow it's just never worked out. It's as if I was being held back for some reason." Carrie knew her parents understood what she was describing for they had often prayed with her about the different mission possibilities that had presented themselves over the last several months. She knew they had even sensed a bit of the frustration she occasionally felt concerning her future.

"I'm learning to be content with being at home and working at my two jobs, Martinson's and Blooming Hills." Carrie went on, " I'm thankful for the employment," she quickly added, "But I do hope that someday God will call me to something more—something where I feel I'm really making a difference. Somewhere I can be real a blessing to someone's life."

Carrie's parents smiled and looked so pleased at her unselfish response. "I want to tell you that for the last month or so your mother and I have been praying, and fasting occasionally as well, specifically on your behalf," Dad said.

"Thank you!" Carrie said sincerely.

"Carrie, what would your answer be if we asked how you felt about starting a courtship with plans to be married?" Dad asked with a smile.

Carrie's look of shock almost surprised her parents. It was quite a long moment before she gathered her thoughts enough to speak. Still bewildered, she asked, "I.... I'm not...exactly sure. What do you mean?" Her voice trembled a bit as she spoke.

"Well, there is a certain young man who has approached us asking permission to court you," Dad said, obviously pleased to deliver this news. "After praying and fasting, your mother and I feel quite certain that this is a real blessing from the Lord."

Carrie's mother was now looking up, directly at her daughter, her eyes shining with delight and a joyous smile lighting her face. Carrie couldn't help smiling a little as well, even in spite of the fluttering feeling in her stomach. Her hands trembled and she couldn't find her voice as she waited for Dad to explain.

"Who could it be? What if it's someone I don't even know well?" she wondered. "Who has approached Mom and Dad? What will I say? How should I respond?" And then she finally allowed herself to think, "Could it be John Mark?" She hardly dared to wonder about the last question that had bubbled to the forefront of her mind. Carrie's thoughts rapidly spilled one over the other until her father's voice broke the silence once again.

"Everything you've said to us here tonight only confirms this as far as I can see," Dad went on, looking at Mom who happily nodded her agreement.

Carrie's eager, questioning look brought her father to a full explanation. "Do you remember about a month ago when Trent Melvin was home on his missionary leave?"

At the mention of Trent's name, Carrie's heart sank, but she hoped her face didn't betray her emotions.

Just as Dad was about to continue, the doorbell rang loudly, its tones seeming to pierce the mood in the room. From where Dad was sitting in the parlor he could see the driveway, "Oh! I'm sorry, I really should get that," he began as he stood up. "It looks like Pastor Stanford's car. I forgot, he said he was going to drop by with some things for the church directory this evening. Excuse me for a moment, please. I'll be back as soon as I can," he said apologetically and headed for the back door.

The ringing doorbell had awakened Addy and Mom rose to cuddle her. "I think I'll take her up to bed and tuck her in as long as Dad's busy for a few minutes," she told Carrie as the sleepy-eyed little girl reached for her mother. Mom quickly added with an eager smile, "I'll be right back too!"

As Carrie sat alone in the parlor, a strange, helpless feeling engulfed her. "I have no reason to feel this way," she scolded herself. "Trent Melvin is a wonderful Christian man. He's certainly nothing to be depressed over! Why, most girls would be thrilled to be courted by him! Why do I feel so awful, then?" she asked herself.

She fidgeted with the hankie she had tucked in the pocket of the apron she was wearing and bravely pushed back the tears that stung at her eyes, and threatened to spill over uncontrollably. "Trent is kind and dedicated and I said I'd be willing to go into missions if I only knew where God wanted me to go. What's wrong with me?" Carrie thought. "Maybe it's just the shock of it all. Maybe I'll feel differently tomorrow or after I've had time to pray about it," she reassured herself. "After all, if Mom and Dad think it's God's will...well, they're pretty wise ..."

Carrie felt as if her world was crashing down around her as she glanced at the quilt in the corner—the double wedding ring quilt—now almost finished. A few tears escaped her eyes as she looked at it, remembering all the happy hours she and her mother had spent together as they worked on it, hoping and dreaming of her future with every stitch. It would never do to carry it to a home on the mission field, where hardship and difficult conditions abounded. "Who would need a quilt in the jungle anyway?" she told herself, remembering the pictures she had seen on Trent's display boards. She quickly dabbed the tears from her cheeks, not wanting her parents to see her disappointment.

All her years of preparation for homemaking---what good would it be? She'd seen the pictures of mission villages. The scenes of dirty, dilapidated housing danced through her mind as she wondered how one could build a pleasant home for a husband and family under such conditions. Then she scolded herself once again, believing her thoughts to be selfish. After all, missionaries probably got lonely too, in fact, she knew they did from what Trent had told her, and a wife would be a great comfort. She realized this could be a special calling if undertaken with a good attitude.

"Maybe it was his interest in me that I sensed that day in the foyer when I felt so uncomfortable. I must bear up and be mature about this. I could at least make an effort to get to know Trent better. It's so selfish of me to feel this way," she continued to scold. She took a deep breath and tried to compose herself. It was a challenge though, as the butterflies she had felt in her stomach moments ago had nearly turned to a feeling of sickness. The once cozy warmth of the fireplace now felt hot and stuffy.

"I thought I had prepared myself for a life of mission work?" she thought as she fanned her face with her hankie. "And after all, they don't expect me to marry someone I'm not in love with. Even though Mom and Dad want to help guide me; I know they want me to have the final say in a matter like this." Somehow though, even that thought was little comfort to Carrie.

Just then she heard the back door close as her father said goodbye to Pastor Stanford. Quickly she dabbed her eyes once again and tucked the hankie into her lap when she saw her mother coming down the stairs. She took one last deep breath and tried to create a settled, even pleasant look on her face, hoping her parents wouldn't notice the tears that had welled up, making her eyes glisten with a slight moisture.

Dad and Mom sat down again at the little table. It was Dad who spoke first. "I'm really sorry about the interruption. That was pretty important. I had asked him to bring that stuff to me or we wouldn't have been interrupted. Let's see if we can get back to our discussion. If the phone should ring, we'll let that go too, because this is important," he said, and winked at his daughter. "Now, where was I?" Dad asked as he started to speak.

Carrie tried to steel herself for her father's announcement. "Oh, yes, the day Trent Melvin was home…Well, after church that day, on his way back to his farm, John Mark Henderson stopped by to see me…." Dad went on, "I have to admit I thought he had come to see me on a pastoral matter, but his intentions were quite different. He asked for your hand in marriage!"

So, it wasn't Trent Melvin! It was John Mark after all! Years of John Mark's polite interest were now confirmed to be more than friendship. Even the note with the circled letters! It must have really been true after all! John Mark Henderson did want to marry Carrie Brooks! The wondering was finally over!

Dad looked a bit confused as he saw Carrie's eyes fill with tears, tears that she now allowed to fall freely down her cheeks. She lowered her head and began to tremble as she fumbled for the hankie once again. Her parents exchanged concerned glances as Mom reached over and placed a loving hand on her daughter's shaking one, a look of motherly concern clouding her face. "Is anything wrong, dear?" she asked after a moment.

"No!" Carrie said, smiling through her tears. She lifted her head and looked directly at her Mom and Dad. Both parents seemed relieved and their looks of concern were replaced with smiles. "No, everything's finally right!" Carrie said, "God has been so good to me!"

Both parents breathed a sigh of relief as a few happy tears escaped their eyes as well. "We couldn't be more pleased, Carrie," Dad went on. "There's no finer young man than John Mark Henderson."

At a loss for words in the emotion of the moment, Carrie could only nod her agreement. After a while she spoke between a few tears as well, "For a long, long time, I felt John Mark was interested in me, you might say. Mom knows that," Carrie said, exchanging a knowing smile with her mother. "I sometimes wondered if the thought of him was what kept me from realizing any definite direction in my life. So I tried diligently not to think about him. And Dad, this is the part that is so very strange…. just that Sunday that John Mark was here, I remember going up to my room after church and praying to God, releasing my feelings for John Mark once and for all. It all came about because I saw him talking up a storm with Trent Melvin that day after church. I'd seen John Mark act that way before when missionaries spoke. You know, really interested." Carrie's parents nodded their understanding, for they too knew John Mark to be a serious young man when it came to the work of the Lord.

"Even way back a few years ago when we had Missions Day at Friday classes, I could see that he was drawn to the Lord's work overseas. I figured he had finally decided to pursue missions and I needed to pray for him instead of wishing for things to be different. When I found out he had been here that afternoon, then I was sure he'd come to get your wisdom and a formal recommendation."

"Maybe I can shed some light on all this," Dad chuckled. "Which also brings up another important point in this matter. When John Mark was here he asked if your mother and I would agree to pray about this matter to see how we felt led about his intentions toward you. Then he told me that over this long winter he had prayed and fasted diligently about this himself. He told me that he has always had a heart for missions and he wanted to be sure of God's will. He assured me that he has never had any doubt at all about his affections for you, but he had a great desire to be sure that he was discerning between God's will and his own will in all of this."

Dad paused a moment and then went on. "A few things you

said this evening confirmed to me that this relationship is truly God's will. One is the fact that you said you there is a particular drawing in your heart toward missions. John Mark feels the same way you do about God's work abroad and he thinks he has finally discovered the role he is to play in serving God."

At this, Carrie again felt the shaky, fluttering tremors in her stomach as she waited for her father to explain. Would she, Carrie Brooks, become the wife of a foreign missionary after all? Maybe so, but somehow just the thought of being John Mark's wife changed the whole idea!

"John Mark told me that over the winter as he prayed and sought God, he felt very strongly that the Lord showed him that his part in missions will be financial," Dad said. "That is, he feels he wants to be the best possible farmer he can be so that he may direct large gifts toward supporting missionaries. He feels his farm is a gift, a blessing to be used for God's glory."

"Wow!" Carrie thought, "What a noble, unselfish idea!"

Dad continued his explanation, "So, John Mark told me that he wishes to court you with the intention of marrying you in the next short while if this season is productive for his farm—assuming you agree."

As Carrie looked at her father, the questioning expression she wore indicated that he should explain.

"He feels he could easily provide for a wife now, as things are with the farm, but he thought by asking you now, there would be time for a courtship while waiting for one more years' harvest. He would like to start off the marriage with the ability to give to missions right from the start. He said it's important to him to get off on the right foot, so to speak, with this vision of giving. He doesn't want it to get lost in other concerns and end up falling by the way-side. Do you see what I mean?"

"I think so, Dad," she said.

"Secondly, let me comment on something else you mentioned. You said that you released your feelings for John Mark that very day?"

"Yes, Dad. I did," Carrie replied.

"Well, I've often noticed that seems to be how it is. God grants us the desires of our heart when we've laid them all down for Him. That's when our desires have really become His desires."

Carrie nodded and was silent as she pondered Dad's words. "Thank you, Dad," she said softly.

Suddenly a surprised smile lit Carrie's face as she turned toward her mother. "This reminds me of the story of Grandma Haywood's watch!"

"Yes, it does!" Mom agreed with equal surprise.

Dad listened as his wife and daughter recounted the sentimental story, comparing the details to John Mark and Carrie's situation. There was a definite atmosphere of joy in the parlor as the women exclaimed over the story's similarities.

After a time of excited discussion over the last of the tea, Dad turned the conversation back to a more serious note, but still with a twinkle in his eye, he asked, "So, Carrie, am I to assume that you are in agreement with this proposal?"

"Yes!" she said sincerely.

"Fine," Dad said, and then added, "I would like to ask you to devote this week to praying about this matter one final time. I know you've probably prayed about this before; after all you've grown up knowing John Mark. You may feel pretty sure at this point, but we feel it's not a light matter and now that you know all the details, it would be good to search your heart and pray specifically."

"After all," Mom added, "with the financial vision that John Mark has, it will be important for his wife to be in agreement. You'll have to economize quite a bit and do all you can to help him be successful in giving. It may mean some sacrifice on your part from time to time."

Carrie nodded her understanding. Any sacrifice for John Mark seemed small in Carrie's eyes. Her heart was filled with thoughts of making a home together and using all the skills of homemaking that seemed to come so naturally for her.

"With your permission, Carrie, I'd like to speak with John Mark and give him some indication of how we're all feeling about this matter as soon as you've had a few days to pray. After all," Dad continued, "this is a young man who tells me he's prayed for you for a long time but he's been waiting patiently for God's direction. I know he's anxious to hear from us." Dad winked at Carrie as he reached across the table and took the hands of his wife and daughter and led them in prayer, thanking God for the their many blessings.

When Dad had finished praying, Carrie helped her mother clear away the dishes. Carrie's mind was spinning with the exciting news. She felt as if she was floating on a cloud. "How will I ever calm down enough to pray and really listen for God's thoughts on the matter?" she wondered to herself. Dad carried the card table out to the back porch. As he passed through the kitchen, Carrie stopped him, "Dad, does Luke or Eileen or anybody else know about this courtship?" she asked, almost as an afterthought.

"Oh, I should have explained," Dad began, "I'm not really sure. I don't know if anyone else knows except Mr. and Mrs. Henderson. John Mark told me he went to them first to get their insight and their blessing, but I don't know if he spoke about it to anyone else. He did tell me at one point that he didn't want to embarrass you if you decided not to accept him."

"Decide not to accept him!" Carrie thought. "Could John Mark really have thought I'd turn him down?" Carrie suddenly realized that all these years while she had been wondering how John Mark Henderson felt about her, that he had probably been wondering how she felt about him! He truly hadn't known! "This proposal must have been a real step of faith for him!" she concluded.

Finally she asked, "Well, Dad, do you happen to know how his parents feel about this?" Carrie asked shyly, yet believing it must blessed by them or John Mark wouldn't have proceeded this far with his plans.

"I certainly do. John Mark himself told me that very Sunday that they were quite pleased when he told them of his plans and they gave him their hearty blessing. He suggested that your mother and I may want to talk with his parents if we had any doubts or questions about him."

Carrie chuckled slightly at this, knowing that John Mark had always been well thought of by her family as were all the Hendersons and that her parents would likely have no reservations about John Mark at all.

Dad soon went on to offer more information, confirming his daughter's thoughts, "Of course, there were no doubts in my mind about John Mark's character whatsoever. I felt no need to make any inquiries of his parents. However, I will tell you that the very next Tuesday after the elders' meeting, John Henderson stayed late at the church and talked to me awhile."

Carrie's heart thumped nervously once again as she wondered what concerns John Mark's parents may have had to bring to her father about the whole matter. Did they find her unacceptable in some way? She turned and continued to help her mother with the remaining teacups while Dad explained, "John told me they were so pleased about their son's decision." At this, Carrie breathed a sigh of relief. "They had prayed long and hard for him to be blessed with a solid future. When the farm came up for sale in Bixley it was a natural addition to their business and they hoped it would help John Mark get started. In fact, John said there were times when he and Esther wondered what was taking John Mark so long to ask you! They almost suggested you to John Mark because they felt so strongly that you were God's choice for their son! Instead they decided to pray and fast for their son to have wisdom. And well... now you see where we're at!"

Carrie could not conceal her pleasure as she smiled with delight. Mom, too, seemed to be beaming with happiness.

"I would suggest that we don't say anything to anyone until you've had time to pray about it. Then I'll call John Mark with your decision. It will be his place to contact you further and share the news with others when he feels the time is right."

"I understand," Carrie agreed.

By the time Luke got home, everyone was heading for bed because of the lateness of the hour. Carrie thought it felt odd to have a matter which could not yet be shared with the whole family so she welcomed the chance to go to her own room and be alone with her thoughts. That night she lay awake for a long time in her bed. She spent quite a while praying and listening for God to speak to her heart. Happy thoughts flooded her mind. Was it really true? Yes! It was! John Mark Henderson wanted to marry her, Carrie May Brooks!

As she thought how wonderful her life was, she prayed for John Mark, so far away in Bixley, yet somehow Bixley didn't seem so far away anymore! She found the clock swiftly ticking the late evening away as she lay there thinking and praying, too excited to drift off to sleep. Finally she got out of bed and put her robe on as she walked over to her window. She wrapped herself in the cozy garment and curled up on the comfortable window seat. Her heart was so full of joy that she felt she could hardly contain herself. The bright moonlight cast silvery shadows over the countryside. The night sky had now cleared and was illumined by thousands of stars. Carrie gazed westward in the direction of Bixley.

"Bixley must be just about beneath that one beautiful, bright star in the distant west," she decided, truly knowing it was only a silly, romantic thought. "Maybe John Mark is looking up at this lovely evening sky and praying for me as well," she hoped. Even through the distant miles, it now seemed as if John Mark was closer somehow. She felt sure he was thinking of her too! The distance seemed to be shortened as in her mind she pictured him, somewhere at the farm, praying for her.

As she pondered the happy thoughts, scene after scene from the past paraded by explaining themselves one by one. It was all so clear now; the day so long ago at the house-warming when he had asked to eat with her, the note with the circled letters, the evening they were honor guards together, the Spring Banquet…Oh! How could she begin to thank God for this wonderful turn of events? She got back in bed and snuggled under the warm coverlet. "I always thought of courtship as God miraculously bringing two people together from miles apart through unusual circumstances, something like Steve and Alice. But now I see it's no less a miracle when God brings you someone you've known all along," she said quietly as she closed her eyes. "Thank you, Lord," she whispered as she drifted off to sleep.

The next day when Carrie awoke, she lay in her bed for a few moments and basked in the warm, spring sunlight that shone through her bay window. The weather seemed to be changed today. The skies looked clear and a pretty, warmer day was dawning on the horizon. How welcome was the sun, just now beginning to rise. Yet, even a cheerless, cloud-draped day could not have dampened Carrie's outlook on life now. Her first thoughts upon waking were of the wonderful turn life had taken last evening.

After a few moments, she arose and went to her window seat and sat looking into the western distance. A few stubborn piles of snow clung desperately for life here and there but spring was finally winning the battle. Carrie gazed across the rolling hills that grew more pronounced at the place where the horizon met the sky. Even amongst the rosy-blue dawn of morning, their outlines were silhouetted like a painting. Somewhere amongst those distant hills lay a little farm nestled cozily between a country crossroads. Even though she had never been there she had pictured it many times in her thoughts. This morning the little farm and its inhabitant were the object of her prayers. She wondered what John Mark was doing at that time of the morning. He had probably risen and was tending to chores, maybe praying for her while he worked.

Carrie spent a longer time than usual in prayer this morning. She poured out her heart to her Savior, thanking Him for the joy she felt. She tried to listen for His guidance, honestly humbling herself to His Lordship. She admitted to Him her difficulty in keeping a totally open mind and heart about this matter of courtship with John Mark Henderson. But she felt comforted with the thought that it was all right and quite natural to feel rather sure of all this already since she had always had tender feelings toward John Mark. She knew she had been diligent to guard her heart where he was concerned, plus their parents had already given their blessing; so the first bridges of decision had been crossed. She closed her prayer asking God to speak to her concerning a future with John Mark and dedicated herself to listen with a sincere heart in the next few days before giving her final answer to her mom and dad. Then, remembering the similarities of the story of the watch, just at the end of her prayer she quickly added, "Dear Lord, please bless the crops this season and John Mark's farm!"

With a peaceful feeling of contentment, she reached for her Bible and pulled the pages open where the ribbon bookmark lay. Today's reading was Psalm 16. She read, rather repetitiously, much like every other morning until suddenly one verse seemed to leap at her as if it were in bold-faced type. She read it once, then read it again, repeating the phrase aloud as the revelation of it embedded itself in her heart. "O Lord, You are the portion of my inheritance and my cup; You maintain my lot. The lines have fallen unto me in pleasant places; Yea, I have a goodly heritage."

"Thank you, Lord," was all Carrie could whisper as she sat, amazed, staring at the verse and repeating it again and again. It was God's answer to her, she believed. "Surely God has given me this verse to confirm my thoughts and feelings. The lines have fallen to me in pleasant places," she said aloud. Even though she had never been to John Mark's farm, the only way she had ever imagined it was pleasant. All the reports she had heard about it from others confirmed this, save the humble condition of the house. "Yea, I have a goodly heritage," she repeated. "Yes, if I marry John Mark, I will have a good heritage. To take the Henderson name would be an honor. The Hendersons are so well thought-of and respected," Carrie remembered. "John Mark's family have all been prosperous farmers for generations. They're respected because of their good character and Christian virtue. Yes, the Henderson name is a goodly heritage'and it would be mine," she reasoned.

She shut the Bible and clutched it to her heart as she closed her eyes and sighed dreamily. It seemed God had given her a special word in answer to her prayers and for this she was thankful. While Carrie and her mother worked throughout the day the two women often exchanged smiles that shared a common joy. Carrie's heart was light and every task seemed to be filled with a new delight.

As she worked at her various duties, she tried to imagine how it would be to do the same tasks in her own home—thoughts she had often entertained before only now they seemed to be a goal that was reachable. How happy she would be to cook and sew, wash and iron for John Mark! She prayed continually throughout the day and meditated upon the scripture God had shown her that morning.

As the week wore on, Carrie began to wonder if John Mark would be home for church on Sunday as usual. How would it feel to meet him for the first time knowing they had begun a courtship? Carrie felt the color rise to her cheeks just thinking about it. How would John Mark act? She hoped she could keep from blushing so obviously when she next saw him.

One of her biggest concerns was quelled when Dad talked with her on the ride home from work on Friday afternoon. "Well, we had a pretty good week at work, didn't we, Carrie?" Dad started.

"Yes, Dad!" she answered. "But I'm glad it's Friday!"

"Me too!" Dad agreed. "By the way, Carrie, since it is Friday, I was wondering if you'd had enough time to pray concerning John Mark's proposal? I'm sure he'll be home on Sunday and he'll be anxious to know of your decision. It would be best for us to call him ahead of time. It's hardly fair of us to expect him to come to church without knowing one way or the other."

"Oh, yes, Dad. I agree," Carrie quickly said, remembering her own concerns over meeting John Mark for the first time after he had asked to court her. "I've prayed about it all week. I even felt God speaking to me through my Bible reading."

"Oh?" Dad began, " Well, then, may I ask how you feel you've been directed?" he winked at his daughter.

"Sure, Dad," Carrie started, "I felt immediate joy about the situation, you know that," Carrie confessed, as a smile pulled at the corners of her mouth. Her joy was so great she found it difficult to contain. "The very night that you told me, I began praying. The next morning I prayed to the Lord, telling Him how difficult it was for me to have clear thoughts about this. I dedicated myself to pray and listen for God to speak, even in spite of the fact that my own desires would be to say, "yes" immediately!

"The very next morning my devotional reading came from Psalm 16." Carrie repeated the words to her father—the words that had so touched her heart that morning and that had danced through her mind a thousand times since, "the lines have fallen unto me in pleasant places, yea, I have a goodly heritage." As her voice softly finished the verse she hoped that her father would feel the same impact it had had on her when she first read it, and realize what it meant to her situation.

Dad listened knowingly to the familiar words. He smiled and nodded silently as he drove. After awhile he spoke, "I think that confirms what your mother and I thought." He turned to glance at his daughter, "Shall I call John Mark tonight and give him the good news?" Carrie nodded her approval with a wide smile and they rode on toward home.

All through supper Carrie was conscious of the fact that sometime this evening Dad would call John Mark and give him her decision. She knew what her father was going to do when he excused himself right after supper and went into his office, closing the big glass doors behind him. Carrie couldn't help wishing she could hear what Dad said and even more than that, how John Mark would reply.

Carrie had helped clear the table and Luke had volunteered to do the dishes so Mom could relax. While her brother worked in the kitchen, Carrie decided to quilt on the double wedding ring quilt in the parlor. Luke didn't seem to wonder at all about Dad's solitude and Carrie was glad he was occupied with the dishes and not asking a lot of questions. She was anxious to share her happy news with Luke, yet she hoped it could be done when the time was just right so Luke would understand why he hadn't been told right away. After all, he had always been such a good, kind brother and deserved to be treated with consideration since this matter concerned not only his sister, but also his good friend.

From her seat at the quilting frame, Carrie could see the back of Dad's chair as he sat at the desk. He didn't make the phone call right away and Carrie couldn't help wondering why he didn't. Then she saw him close his Bible and push it to the side as he picked up the phone. "He was reading some devotions," she thought to herself. "Or maybe he was reading Psalm 16." A tremor of excitement raced through her whole being as she once again thought of the words of the Psalm and how much it had meant to her to discover God speaking it specifically to her.

Her fingers trembled as she tried to stitch; the usually simple movements of needle and thread were suddenly difficult beyond belief especially since she couldn't help frequently glancing in the direction of Dad's office. It was obvious when John Mark answered, for Carrie saw her father lean back in his chair as he often did while talking on the phone.

Carrie's heart gave a little leap at the thought of their conversation and that same nervous excitement enveloped her being once again. It seemed like a long time while Dad was on the phone. Carrie anxiously waited for her father to emerge from the office. Finally, she saw him rise from his chair and instead of coming out he looked her way and motioned for her to come to the office.

Carrie lay her needle down at nearly the same place she had started, for her shaking fingers had accomplished very little while she had waited. She opened the big glass doors and entered Dad's office—a cozy room that smelled of leather and paper, like a library, Carrie thought, a pleasant, serene, place.

Dad motioned for her to sit down in the big, comfortable chair opposite his desk as he smiled at her. "I think we just made one young man very happy!" he declared. Carrie blushed, a wide smile covering her face. "He'll be home for church on Sunday," Dad went on.

"What did he say, Dad?" Carrie asked eagerly, but almost in a whisper.

"I told him your mother and I had prayed diligently about the situation and we felt that we could definitely give our blessing to a proposal such as this. Then he asked me how you had answered."

Carrie searched her father's face with eagerness as he paused. "I told him you were in agreement as well. And I explained to him how you had been praying and seeking direction as well, only never feeling completely settled."

Carrie waited as Dad paused again. "And?" she finally asked.

"Well, after I was all done explaining how you felt, he gave a sigh of relief and said, 'Thank God, and thank you, Pastor Brooks!'"

Inwardly, Carrie laughed to herself as she thought about John Mark and how he must have said, 'Thank God,' in his quiet way, yet with the familiar sideways grin and the ever-present twinkle in his eye.

"I told him to feel free to contact you by phone whenever he likes or he can come over to visit. Ok?" Dad asked.

"Yes!" Carrie agreed enthusiastically. "Can I tell Mom?" she asked as she rose to leave.

"Yes, that'll be fine. But remember, let's wait to tell other people until John Mark gives the lead in that area or until the two of you decide on that together."

"Ok, Dad," Carrie agreed.

It wasn't long before Carrie's happy news was revealed to the entire family. For, the next day about two o'clock in the afternoon a knock came to the Brooks' front door. Luke was the only one downstairs who was free to answer it. Words could not describe his surprised look when he opened the door to see a floral deliveryman holding a large bouquet of flowers.

"Delivery for Miss Carrie Brooks," the man said.

"Uh…thanks," Luke stammered with surprise as he accepted the package and closed the door. He turned and called to Carrie who was upstairs choosing a dress to wear to church the next day.

"Oh, Carrrrr….rrrrriee!" he yelled rather impishly.

"Yes?" came the voice from the second floor.

"You better come down here right away!" he called.

Luke continued to inspect the package as much as was possible in light of the tissue paper wrapping that concealed it from complete view. Poor Luke was nearly overcome with curiosity while he waited the few seconds for his sister to arrive downstairs.

Soon Carrie came walking slowly down the stairs. When she

turned and saw Luke she asked, "What did you want?" Luke looked at Carrie with a half-smile as if he expected her to explain. He stepped aside and gestured toward the package that sat on the hall table. Carrie's eyes lit up, "For me?" she questioned.

"Yeah, I guess so," Luke said curiously.

"Who is it from?" she asked.

"Well, now…," Luke slowly began, "that's just exactly what I was wondering," his voice trailed off teasingly as he tapped his fingers on the table right next to the package. "Why don't you open the card?" he suggested, making it obvious that he intended to stay until the secret was revealed. He pulled up one of the dining room chairs and sat down. He leaned back and folded his arms as an indication that he had settled in with no intention of moving until the mystery was solved.

Carrie wasn't sure whether she should open the card in front of Luke or not, for by now she had begun to realize that the package had probably been sent by John Mark. If Luke found that out, she would not have followed Dad's cautions to let John Mark tell this news. On the other hand, if John Mark had flowers sent to her door, surely he would not expect this to be kept from her family. "What should I do?" Carrie wondered as her brother stared at her with relentless curiosity while she inspected the package. On a sudden impulse, Carrie grabbed the package from the table and said, "Thank you, Luke," as she turned to head up the stairs to her room, leaving her curious and disappointed brother staring after her.

When she reached her room, she stepped in quietly and shut the door behind her. She hastened to her dressing table and set the flowers down. Her heart beat with excitement as she opened the envelope. A pretty, gold-embossed card with lacey edges fell out. On it was the unmistakable handwriting of John Mark Henderson. Carrie knew it well, for she had seen it many times when working with him on the SAC. The words read, "To Carrie, I hope you enjoy these flowers. They are sent with sincere affection and thoughts of you. Anxious to talk to you soon, John Mark."

Carrie's heart melted as she clutched the card tightly. She smiled through happy tears as she carefully peeled the paper away from the bouquet. Inside was a lovely arrangement of pink and white rosebuds among tiny white blossoms of baby's breath all set in a heart-shaped ceramic vase. She stared at the delicate flowers. They were the most beautiful she had ever seen. She read and re-read the card as she imagined the thoughtful John Mark carefully penning the words. "Oh, how kind and generous of him!" she sighed as she looked again at the blossoms. "And how very romantic!" she added.

After a while Carrie heard a knock at her door and Mom's sweet voice asking to enter. She quickly ushered her mother in and closed the door softly. "Look, Mom!" she whispered excitedly, leading her mother to the table where the flowers sat. As Mom read the card, a look of girlish excitement swept her face. When she finished, she hugged Carrie tightly and they chattered like best friends about the lovely gift and the excitement of this courtship.

"I'm sure Luke was anxious to see who they were from," Carrie said as she explained the arrival of the flowers. "You were sewing, Mom, and I wasn't sure what to do," she admitted. "Dad said it should be up to John Mark to decide when to tell everyone or that we should talk about it and decide together, so I haven't said anything to Luke yet. And, Mom, I've been wondering if Eileen or any of the other Hendersons know yet. It seems like if she knew she would have called me right away, knowing Eileen." Her mother nodded in her understanding way.

"I'm sure Luke is curious," Mom said. "I think either way would have been all right, though," she added. "Surely John Mark knows the rest of your family would see these flowers, but just to be sure, I'll ask your father to speak with him. It isn't that we're trying to keep a secret from Luke or Addy; it's just that your father feels we need to respect John Mark's feelings about deciding when this becomes public knowledge." Carrie nodded her understanding as her mom continued, "Actually I'm quite sure your father intended that we tell Luke and Addy tonight at supper since John Mark will be home tomorrow. And it is different with family than with the rest of our acquaintances. After all, John Mark will be coming here to visit and you'll be going to Hendersons' from time to time. They pretty much have to know."

"Thanks, Mom. I'll be glad if you speak to Dad and we can maybe clear this up," Carrie said.

Later that evening before her father ever got a chance to make the call to John Mark, the phone rang. Dad was in his office putting the final touches on his sermon. He picked up the phone only to hear John Mark at the other end of the line. Carrie had heard the phone ring and from her seat at the parlor quilt frame, even though she could only hear her father's side of the conversation, she waited, listening breathlessly as soon as she realized it was John Mark discussing these details with her father. She was glad no one else was nearby to hear. She felt her cheeks redden as she listened.

"Hello, John Mark," Dad said, pleasantly.

Feeling a little like an intruder, she rose quietly, but a bit reluctantly, and closed the parlor doors to give her father more privacy, even though he would never have known she was overhearing.

"Hello, Sir," John Mark replied politely. "I just got home here a little while ago and we ….uh, that is I…well, my parents and I… were wondering if Carrie might be able to come here for dinner after church tomorrow? I'd like to announce the arrangement with Carrie and I to my whole family if it's all right with all of you. Actually, Eileen and Tommy know, but I'd like to tell the rest of them."

"Well, John Mark, believe it or not, I was just about to call you and inquire a bit about your plans as far as telling this news! You see, I told Carrie she should keep the news to herself until you decided you wanted it to be shared with other people. However, after the flowers arrived today, Luke became quite curious and I felt it was time the rest of the Brooks family knows, with your consent, of course."

"I'm sorry, Pastor Brooks. I guess I never thought that all your family wouldn't know," John Mark replied, sounding rather surprised. "Thank you for respecting my feelings, but I'm sort of surprised that Luke and Addy don't know yet. It's definitely all right with me if Carrie tells anyone she chooses."

"Ok," Dad assented.

"I look at this courtship this way, Pastor…. it's a time to prove my love to Carrie. I would never think of it as a test or trial of any sort--at least not on my part. My feelings for your daughter are sure and fixed. I can honestly say that. With all the prayer and fasting and the confirmation of my parents and you and Mrs. Brooks; well, that's just the way I feel about it."

Dad listened as John Mark continued.

"If for some reason Carrie would choose to call off the courtship, I would have to respect that, though I must admit I'd be very sorry," John Mark added, honestly. "But I never will; I'm sure of my feelings," he finished with emotion in his voice. "So actually, I was more concerned that you and Carrie were willing to have it known than the other way around."

"I understand, John Mark, and I commend your attitude. It shows real spiritual maturity. It's a good Christ-like quality to put others before yourself. This is the kind of character traits Mrs. Brooks and I appreciate in you and it's one of the many reasons we were glad to give our blessing to this courtship."

"Thank you, sir," John Mark replied. "May Carrie come for dinner, then?" he asked, returning to the original purpose for his call.

"Well, why don't you ask her yourself? Wait just a moment while I get her," Dad suggested. He rose from his chair and stepped to the office door. As soon as he caught his daughter's eye through the glass parlor doors, he held up the phone, motioning for her to come to the office. When she took the receiver, he smiled at her and nodded as he passed out of the office, closing the door behind him.

Interrupted Plans

Sunday arrived with its usual last-minute preparations at the Brooks household. Carrie had been awake long before the rest of the family. Not being able to sleep a moment past six, she had already made some breakfast for the others and tidied her room. The promise of this day was just too exciting for her to sleep any longer. Even though she had chosen her dress the night before as always, somehow she still looked at it analyzing its every fold and detail. Was it right? Would she look nice in it? And most importantly, would John Mark like it? It seemed all of life had taken on a new dimension. Now every mundane and once routine activity was weighed on a new scale!

Carrie finally sat down in her familiar window seat as she stared at the dress that hung on the closet door. She gave herself a little lecture, reminding herself that courtship wasn't a time of dressing up or of saying and doing all the right things just to impress someone. John Mark was interested in having dinner with her today because he was interested in her, not her taste in fashions. It was a chance to get to know John Mark's family better and to begin to experience the way he related to her as more than just a friend.

Sometimes it seemed to Carrie that for her and John Mark a courtship was almost unnecessary—after all they each knew the other's families well and had had many opportunities for getting to know one another in all their growing up years. They had always been members of the same church; they had even worked together at Blooming Hills. But the one thing Carrie failed to realize was that John Mark Henderson viewed this courtship as a time to win her heart. Although neither did he realize it would be no chore to do so, for the John Mark she had known and grown up with had already won her heart! He hoped to lift the bonds of friendship that had always seemed to exist between them to a new level of love and affection. The kind and generous gestures he would make in the coming months would do just that. Many years from now, they would each remember the time when they courted and fell in love. All the happy times spent together talking and planning were times no couple should miss. And today was only the first of such times. How excited Carrie was!

In some ways, for Carrie Brooks, this Sunday was really no different than any other, going to church and visiting with friends. Yet the recent events had changed everything! Still she wondered what it would be like once she stepped into the church building this particular morning to meet John Mark face to face with this courtship now under way. When she finally arrived, she took a deep breath, a sigh of relief. The Hendersons weren't here yet. She had hoped it would work out this way, for now she had time to touch up her hair and gain her composure.

As she stood alone in the ladies' coatroom, she combed and adjusted her wind-blown hair. "I wonder what I should do?" she thought aloud with a note of panic in her voice. "Should I stand around the foyer? Should I go on to Sunday school? How will it be to see John Mark for the first time since this new arrangement?"

Even the greeters weren't here yet and so there was no one to stand and chat with in the foyer. Carrie decided it wouldn't do for John Mark and his family to find her standing idly in the foyer as if she was waiting for them. So she finally decided to do what she always did every other Sunday morning, help her parents wherever she was needed and then go to Miss Winfield's Sunday School room and quietly wait for the class to begin. So, she did just that. There were no last minute duties this morning allowing Carrie the opportunity to go directly to her class. She made her way to the basement room, flipped the light on, and sat in her usual chair. None of the other girls had arrived yet, providing her a few moments alone to think and pray.

Luke passed by the classroom door and saw her. He stopped long enough to pop his head in and say, "I thought Prince

Charming would arrive early this morning, but I see he's not here yet. Do you suppose he had trouble with his gallant white horse?" He sped off, chuckling to himself, satisfied to have gotten an annoyed look from his sister. In all actuality, Luke had been very happy for Carrie when Dad and Mom broke the news to him last night. Luke and John Mark were good friends and Luke found the arrangement satisfactory to say the least, a good friend for a brother-in-law! What more could he have asked for?

Carrie thought over the events of last evening as she sat, quietly waiting for Sunday school to begin. She remembered how Luke had looked so shocked at first! In typical boyish fashion, he had never suspected a thing and the whole idea of his sister being courted was something to get used to! Addy too was excited, and even though she didn't understand much of what was going on she knew she loved John Mark who had always been so nice and attentive to her.

As Carrie sat waiting, she remembered how Luke had come to her later that evening after the family meeting broke up and finding themselves alone in the living room, he had given her a big congratulatory hug. His voice had seemed to almost crack as he had said, "I'll miss you around here when you leave. But I know you'll be happy with John Mark. I know he'll be good to you. I'm glad that if you do have to leave us that it's for a great guy like John Mark." Carrie knew that her brother meant that he cared deeply for her and even though he could be a big tease, he did love her.

Then she remembered the phone call—talking to John Mark for the first time since he had declared his feelings! How exciting it had been! She would never forget his voice. He sounded so mature and strong. In fact, she realized, for all the many years she had known him, she had never before spoken to him over the phone! Each conversation and every little detail was now so alive and meaningful. Life had certainly taken a glorious turn! "How had he worded it?" she thought, remembering, "Carrie, would you do me the honor of joining me for Sunday dinner with my family tomorrow after church?" Yes, that was it! Simple, ordinary, everyday words, yet with John Mark speaking them, they had come to mean so much.

How thankful she was that there had been no dating, for now every little detail of this courtship with this wonderful man was a thrilling event, standing on its own in her memory, never to be clouded or blurred, or compared with memories of someone else.

"Yes, I'd love to come over for dinner," she had replied.

"Good, I'll see you at church, then. I'm looking forward to spending the day with you," he had added.

"Oh! And thank you for the flowers," she had remembered to say. "I just adore them. They're beautiful!"

"I'm glad you like them," was his reply. "I'll see you tomorrow."

"Tomorrow. Good-bye."

"Good-bye!"

Click. The phone call was over just that soon, yet Carrie could feel the volumes of unspoken words still crossing the miles between the two of them long after she had hung up the phone.

"Ahhh!" she sighed to herself. In her daydreaming she had failed to hear the footsteps above her as the other families began arriving for church. Soon Miss Winfield arrived, Bible and study helps in hand, her usual cheerful manner surrounding her as a halo.

She and Carrie chatted while the other girls arrived. A few minutes later, John Mark passed by the Sunday school room. He seemed to pause a moment as he deliberately looked into the room until Carrie noticed him. The other young ladies and Miss Winfield were talking and didn't even see him or the looks he and Carrie exchanged. As their eyes met, he smiled directly at Carrie and she smiled back unconscious of anyone else in the room.

It seemed he stared at her for some seconds when in reality it was only a moment, but he was smiling all the while. Finally he seemed to remember himself and raised his arm, glanced at his watch and pointed to the face with a knowing grin, as if to say, "Excuse me, but if I don't go, I'll be late for class!" Carrie gave him a shy little half-concealed wave as he turned to leave. As he turned to head down the hall, he still gazed in her direction as if unwilling to depart from her presence.

In a moment, Eileen entered the room, looking flustered as she hurried to her usual seat by Carrie. She slipped into her chair just as the bell rang signaling the beginning of the Sunday school hour. Carrie looked at the breathless Eileen who had only time to whisper a quick greeting. But when Eileen's eyes met Carrie's, they were alive with a questioning exuberance. Carrie knew her best friend had been informed of the courtship because Eileen's expression spelled pure delight as she spontaneously grabbed Carrie's hand under the table and gave it an excited squeeze. Carrie smiled back—a smile that Eileen recognized in her best friend. All these years, it was the smile that had meant, "Yes, I know! We share a secret!"

When Sunday school was over, there was no time for Eileen to ask questions for Miss Winfield's presentation ran late. When they were dismissed, they each headed swiftly for the door in order to make it to the sanctuary on time.

John Mark had waited for Carrie just outside the Sunday school room. "Will you sit with me for church?" he asked with a polite smile when he met her in the hall.

"Yes, I'd like that," she answered, softly, turning to look at Eileen to assess her reaction. Eileen smiled broadly and winked at her best friend, as she followed several steps behind the happy couple.

Carrie felt she was walking on air as John Mark led her to a seat near the rows that the young people always occupied. He went right on confidently past their staring, curious friends who were now sizing up the situation with muffled whispers. He politely waited at the edge of the pew, allowing Carrie to be seated first while their friends looked on. He didn't seem to be trying to keep any of this a secret. He seemed to be glad that everyone was noticing that he was with Carrie Brooks.

"Well, this hasn't been uncomfortable or awkward after all," Carrie thought as she sat next to John Mark and listened to the last few notes of the piano music before the service. John Mark was so sweet and polite. He made her feel at ease. Soon the church service began and after a prayer, the chorister arose and announced an opening hymn, gesturing for the congregation to stand. Again, John Mark politely waited for Carrie to stand and he then rose and opened their hymn book to the proper page. She was keenly aware of his strong, gentle presence as they shared the hymn book, each holding one cover. It was as if they were holding hands, yet he never touched her! There was no need for a touch; it was enough just to be standing there with him, joining him in praise. What a beautiful, deep singing voice he had! She had never known that before!

After church, Carrie and John Mark rode to the Henderson

farm in his pickup truck. Joe and Katie were home for dinner as well as Alice and Steve. Eileen had found a chance to pull her friend to the side before dinner as the women worked in the big farmhouse kitchen. "Carrie, I'm so excited! You and John Mark courting!" Bubbly, exuberant Eileen could barely contain her excitement. "Tell me it's really true!" she whispered through a smile that lit her entire face.

"It's really true!" Carrie whispered back her assurance. Eileen squeezed her friend's hands mercilessly and talked on with fervor, "Mom and Daddy and John Mark told me and Tommy last night! I just cried for joy! They made me and Tommy promise not to tell. John Mark wants to tell the others at dinner! Oh, this is so exciting! It's so romantic!" Carrie just smiled at her friend's eager countenance, while inside, she quaked anew with wondering what it would be like to be presented this way in front of John Mark's entire family.

Mrs. Henderson called for Eileen to help mash the potatoes and Carrie asked if there was anything she might help with as well. She was given the job of pouring water in all the glasses. She counted it a blessing that she could be alone in the quiet dining room away from the warmth of the kitchen and all the chattering ladies for a few moments. It was a brief respite in which Carrie took a deep breath and tried to rid herself of the excited, nervous feelings now vying for control at the thought of John Mark's announcement.

Her hands trembled a bit as she carefully poured ice water into the ten glasses on the glisteningly set table. Soon John Mark entered the room and walked over to where Carrie was busily tending to her assignment. He politely, yet tenderly touched her arm, "Carrie, I'd like to tell the rest of my family about our plans at dinner time, with your permission."

Carrie's heart melted at the sound of his strong, tender voice asking her permission so kindly and gallantly, ever the gentleman. She noticed he smelled of a pleasant, manly cologne that was very attractive. "Certainly," she managed to say; already knowing what he meant by 'the rest of my family' for Eileen had informed her that the two oldest sisters and their husbands didn't yet know about the courtship. Carrie suddenly realized that Alice and Katie and their husbands must have been thinking she was Eileen's guest for the day and didn't yet suspect a thing!

"Are you sure you don't feel it's too soon? I mean, we haven't had time to talk alone or anything yet, Carrie," was his courteous question as his eyes searched hers.

Carrie looked back, not knowing quite what to say. She was sure she wanted to shout the wonderful news to everyone, but she tried to contain her emotions discreetly. Or could he possibly mean he wasn't sure of the arrangement himself? Was he having second thoughts and thinking it was too soon? Carrie's knees felt weak as she searched his face for an explanation. He sensed her questions and hurriedly continued, "I…I don't want to embarrass you or publicize something you're not ready to have known. That's what I meant. Do you understand?" he asked sensitively. "It's just that my older sisters don't yet know we've even made these few plans and they're going to begin wondering," he said with a twinkle in his eye. He paused a moment and said, "For instance, did you notice the way all our friends watched us at church today?" He was smiling his familiar sideways grin now, obviously enjoying the memory of the row of puzzled looks in the young people's section during the morning service.

"Yes," Carrie replied, smiling a bit now, relieved at his explanation. "I'm not unwilling for any of this to be known," she said. "It's fine with me," she added sincerely.

But the dinner plans were to be changed at Henderson's that day for just as Carrie finished speaking, she heard the door slam and someone talking loudly in the kitchen. She looked at John Mark in surprise and he looked back with concern as Eileen's alarmed voice called out, "Carrie!" She quickly put down the water pitcher and headed toward the kitchen, with John Mark close behind.

Luke had arrived and was headed for the dining room to find his sister. "Carrie!" he cried. "Mom cut her hand pretty badly and Dad's off to the Blue Creek hospital with her. He told me to come get you! Addy's in the car. I didn't want to take time to get her out of the car seat. She's upset! I can't make her quit crying! We're headed over there now!"

"I'll get your coat!" was John Mark's offer. Carrie felt her knees go weak and she was almost dizzy with fright. "What happened?" she implored Luke to explain. "Mom was trying to cut up some frozen meat to fix for dinner and the knife slipped and she cut her left hand," Luke said breathlessly.

The rest of the men, who had been outside, had followed Luke in to the kitchen. The entire Henderson family now stood in the kitchen offering Luke their concerns and entreating him to let them know of his mother's condition as soon as possible. In seconds John Mark appeared with Carrie's coat and held it for her as she quickly slipped it on. He whisked her out to the car where Luke had already returned to tend to a terrified Addy who waited in the back seat.

"Let me drive, Luke," John Mark said, very decidedly. He quickly opened the back door for Carrie and jumped into the driver's seat. Luke didn't argue, but just hurriedly got in the passenger's side as Carrie cuddled Addy in the back seat. Carrie's soft voice could be heard soothing the little girl between sobs. Before long she had been convinced to quiet down and now only cried softly.

John Mark steadily steered the group toward Blue Creek, remaining calm under the obvious pressure of the situation. Luke turned and finished explaining the events to his older sister in hushed tones as soon as Addy had quieted down. "Mom forgot to get out the meat that she had planned to fix for dinner. It was some steaks and she was trying to chip them apart with a sharp knife so Dad could grill them when the knife slipped. It really frightened Addy," Luke added. "I'm concerned," he said and then turned to John Mark. "I'm thinking it'll require several stitches at least from the way it looked." Luke tried to state the seriousness of the injury without upsetting Addy all over again. "They should be in the emergency room when we get there," Luke said.

"I'm hurrying," John Mark assured him, "but we want to get there safely ourselves; no sense in two accidents."

"Right!" Luke agreed.

As they reached the outskirts of Blue Creek, John Mark slowed the vehicle down but expertly maneuvered in and out of the traffic and stoplights. "I think we'll take a little short cut right here," he said with determination as he suddenly pulled onto a rarely used side street. "I found this route one day when I was headed to Farmer's Market with a load of fruit and the traffic was really bad. It goes right past the hospital." Carrie and Luke knew that the hospital was in the same general vicinity as the Farmer's Market grounds. Sure enough, John Mark was right and in a moment they were nearing the hospital parking area. As he pulled up to the emergency room entrance he instructed the Brooks, "You three go on in; I'll park the car and meet you."

Once inside it was no time at all until they found their mother and father for when they stopped at the nurse's station to inquire of Mom's whereabouts, they were pleased to see Amanda Melvin working at the desk. Her sweet countenance was a calming presence. Immediately recognizing their concern she steered them to where Mr. and Mrs. Brooks waited, comforting and assuring them all the way. "I knew you'd be here soon and I know you're concerned. When there's a deep cut, there's a lot of bleeding and that tends to alarm people. But the doctor is putting some stitches in and your mom is doing fine."

"We missed you at church today, but I'm so glad you're here!" Carrie said to Amanda as she squeezed her hand. "I feel better already!"

"That's good," Amanda said. "That's what we nurses are for, but I have to admit I miss you all when I have to work and can't make it to church," Just then they reached the door to Mom's room and Amanda gently knocked and peeked in. She announced to the doctor that Mrs. Brooks' children were here.

"Send them in," he consented.

Luke instinctively reached down and picked Addy up as they walked into the room, as if to shield her from a possible shock. The doctor was just finishing the stitches as they entered. Carrie gave her father a big hug and let the tears flow from her eyes, tears she had been holding back for Addy's sake.

"We're thanking the Lord that Mom's going to be fine." Dad said, reassuringly. Carrie looked to her mother who was stroking Addy's soft curls as the little girl now relaxed, seeing that her mother was all right.

"I'm fine," Mom smiled. "It hurts a little, but it will heal up and be just like new, the doctor tells me."

Luke watched with interest as the doctor bandaged a portion of his mother's hand. "Looks like you'll need our help for a while, Mom!" Luke said. "But I'm so glad to see you're all right."

The Brooks family thanked the doctor for his kind attention. Before he left the room, he told them, "Let's have Mrs. Brooks lay back and rest a bit before we release her. I just want to make sure she's not feeling light-headed or dizzy before sending her home. Maybe a half hour or forty-five minutes will be enough. The nurse can check your blood pressure, then you can be released."

"Fine. And thank you, Doctor," Dad added.

When they were alone in the room, Dad led the family in praying for Mom, thanking God that the injury had only been minor. When he finished, he motioned to the only chair in the room and said, "I'll sit here with Mom. Why don't you three go relax in the waiting room, or you can just head on home if you want. Mom's going to be fine."

Suddenly Carrie realized that John Mark must be alone in the waiting room, wondering where everyone was! "I guess we better go out there. John Mark drove us and he's probably out there wondering what's happening." Carrie kissed her mother's cheek and said, "See you in just a while." Addy asked to stay with Daddy and she climbed up on his lap and looked as if she could take a nap after the whole ordeal.

When Luke and Carrie reached the waiting room, John Mark was there with his head bowed low and his elbows on his knees. He looked up as they entered the room. He immediately stood up and walked toward Carrie. "How's she doing?" He asked with genuine concern, as he grasped Carrie's hands.

"She's going to be fine," Luke smiled. "It wasn't as serious as we thought. I guess it looked worse than it was. She's received several stitches and will need our help for a few days, but it's nothing really serious."

"Well, praise the Lord for that," John Mark replied.

"She's resting for awhile until the nurse releases her," Carrie explained.

"And Addy?" John Mark inquired, seeing that the little girl was not with them.

"Oh, she wanted to stay there with Dad," Luke answered.

"Are you all right, Carrie?" John Mark asked with deep concern, "You're trembling," he remarked as he looked down at the hands he held in his.

"I'm just kind of shaky yet, I guess," Carrie replied weakly.

"Let's go sit in the cafeteria while we wait," John Mark suggested. "I think you ought to get a little something to eat; after all, you missed dinner. When was the last time you ate anything?"

"This morning before church, I guess," Carrie admitted, remembering that she had only had a glass of orange juice before church. She had been too excited about the events of the day to feel like eating breakfast. "I do feel hungry, now that you mention it."

"I thought so," John Mark smiled.

Just then Amanda came into the waiting room. "I just saw your Dad," she said to Carrie and Luke. "He said your mom is probably going to go home soon. Addy was asleep. I guess it was a lot for a little girl to experience. I took your Dad and Addy some juice and a couple of sandwiches."

"Thank you, Amanda," Luke said politely. "I'm just going on my lunch break," Amanda said, "Would you like to join me and wait in the cafeteria instead of here?" she asked her three friends.

"We were just headed there ourselves," John Mark replied.

"That'll be nice, Amanda," Carrie added.

"I better call home first," John Mark said, "I'm sure they're all waiting to hear. You three go on and I'll meet you in just a few minutes."

"All right," they all agreed.

Soon John Mark was back at the cafeteria and joined them in line. "Why don't you go sit down and I'll bring whatever you want," he said to Carrie.

"Thank you," she said. "Just some juice and a chicken salad sandwich is all I need," she said, opening her purse to offer John Mark some money for the food.

"No, no," he said, putting his hand on hers. "I'll get it. After all, I did promise you lunch today," he said teasingly. "You go sit down and relax."

Carrie smiled at him gratefully and took a seat at a table in the far corner away from the other diners. When she finally sat down she realized how tired and hungry she really had been. Her legs felt weak and she was glad the ordeal was drawing to a close.

When the others arrived at the table, John Mark set his tray down and served Carrie while Luke and Amanda sat across the table. When everyone was situated, John Mark looked at Luke and said, "I'll ask the blessing."

"Thanks," Luke replied sincerely to his friend, "I think I'm still a little shaky myself," he confessed. John Mark and the others bowed their heads as he thanked God for the food and Mrs.

Brooks' soon return home.

Carrie was again reminded of his kindness and character. He had been like a tower of strength this afternoon. He had level-headedly taken over during the whole situation, sensing everyone's anxiety and politely laying aside his own plans. It had been obvious as he drove the car for the shaken Luke, parking so they could get into the hospital as fast as possible. Then he had remembered to call home and explain the details to his own concerned family who had been left with an interrupted Sunday afternoon. Now he was serving Carrie so she could relax.

Carrie glanced at his tray and realized how hungry John Mark must have been for he had ordered a large hamburger, a baked potato, and a piece of cake. Carrie laughed to herself, knowing that young men Luke and John Mark's age always had hearty appetites. Even amidst all the nervous upset of the last few hours, Luke's tray indicated the same as he heartily enjoyed some French fries and a hamburger, topped off with a chocolate shake.

"How have you been doing lately, Amanda?" John Mark asked.

"Oh, I'm doing well," she replied. Her eyes shone brightly as she spoke. Carrie sensed a certain excitement in her voice and she searched her friend's face for a clue to its source.

"Your work is going well here?" Luke asked.

"Oh, yes, I just love my nursing job," she smiled. "But I won't be working here much longer."

"Oh?" Carrie said. "What's up? Are you moving on to another hospital?"

"Well, no, not around here anyway," Amanda said slowly, with a curious smile.

"Tell us," Carrie implored. "You sound excited about something."

"Well, I am. I'm going to be doing mission work in the northern parts of Canada. I'll be working at a hospital with the mission group that Miss Winfield and Trent worked with."

"Great!" John Mark remarked enthusiastically. "When does your assignment begin?"

"Well, we are supposed to arrive at the mission by September."

"We?" Luke said nonchalantly. "Who's we? Are you going to be on a team of missionaries? I hope so for your sake, 'cause that's a long way from home," he reminded her.

Amanda smiled and looked down at the cake she was finishing. "Homer's going too," she said softly.

A short silence followed, then John Mark spoke, "Homer's going? That's nice. What's he going to be doing up there?" he asked.

"He's been asked to teach music at the native mission school. The position doesn't really require a formal teaching degree so he's able to do it with the schooling he's already had. He'll be done with his courses at Collier next week, you know." Amanda added.

"I hadn't heard from him for quite awhile," John Mark said, "Then yesterday when I got in, Mom said I had a call from him, but when I tried to return it, I got no answer. I'm not sure why he didn't call my place. Maybe he did but we missed each other somehow. I'd sure like to talk to him and catch up on everything."

Amanda was still smiling as she looked down at her plate. When she finally looked up at John Mark she said, "I see Homer hasn't told you yet."

"Told me what?" John Mark asked between bites.

"Well, I guess it's ok to tell you all. He said I might as well let anyone know that I chose."

"Let us know what?" Carrie asked. "What's going on?" she repeated.

"Well, back at Christmas when Homer came home from Collier on break, he visited our family and he and Trent really began to talk seriously about missions. Homer was quite interested in this particular area of the north and Trent supplied him with a lot of information. It became pretty obvious to Homer that he ought to pursue the one particular assignment when Trent found out about an opening for a teacher of music at the native mission school."

"Wow, I guess this was meant to be," Luke agreed.

"He's got all the qualifications and giftings they were looking for," Amanda went on. Then she paused a bit, "But.... seeing Trent about mission work was not the reason he came over in the first place. He wanted to speak to my parents about...well, us...me and him, I mean," she added, now looking up at her three friends hoping they would understand what she meant and share her joy.

Luke and Carrie stared back in amazement, smiling at the happy news. John Mark smiling as well, said, "I'm not a bit surprised. I thought I could see this coming all along!"

Everyone laughed as Amanda went on to finish recounting

the events. "We began corresponding when Homer went back to school the next week. We each decided to continue to seek the Lord about what we were feeling and wait for His leading. And then here's the exciting part! Homer called one evening in early March and said he had received a packet of information from the mission concerning his position. Enclosed in the papers was a notice that the mission nurse had just notified them of her intent to leave her position in August of this year. So they were desperately searching for a replacement and wanted all friends of the ministry to help spread the news and locate a new nurse. Homer suggested I apply, feeling this may be part of our answer. So I did and within one week, they had called back and interviewed me, offering me the position that starts the same time Homer's does—the first week of September!"

"Wow!" Carrie exclaimed. "It really was an answer to prayer. I'm so happy for both of you, Amanda!"

"Well, that's not all," Amanda continued. "Along with the nursing position comes free housing in a private cabin—another answer to prayer, because Homer's teaching position pays a bit more, so only dorm housing was included for him. Now he can work all summer and save our money. We won't need to pay for a house, so it'll be that much easier. We plan to be married August 22. We'll be taking a long wedding trip to Canada, arriving in time to unpack and settle in just in time for school."

"It sounds like a wonderful arrangement," John Mark said, "I'm really happy for you guys too."

"And to think, Carrie, all this may have never come about if you and your mom hadn't stopped that day so long ago at our garage sale when we first moved here. You're responsible for us getting introduced to the church and the home school group! I remember being sad when we moved here—having to leave my old friends and all—now I see how God worked everything out and I'm so glad He did!"

Carrie just smiled at her friend, thankful too that everything had worked the way it had and she had gained such a good friend in Amanda.

"I sure hope I didn't spoil things by telling you," Amanda asked, looking directly at John Mark. "Maybe you would have rather heard it from your old friend, Homer?"

"I'm sure it's ok," he replied. "But I suppose that is why he tried to call me."

"You two will make such a wonderful couple," Carrie commented.

"Thank you," Amanda replied. "We're intending to make a formal announcement next week at First Church, then at our church next."

At this John Mark looked at Carrie and she instinctively read his thoughts. She smiled as she nodded to him and he cleared his throat and addressed Amanda. "Well, Amanda, you'll be surprised to know that you're not the only one with exciting news." He looked at Carrie and smiled.

"What do you mean?" Amanda asked with mounting curiosity.

"Well," he began slowly, "There's another courtship going on among our old circle of friends."

"There is?" she asked eagerly. "Do tell me! Who is it?"

John Mark's face bore his typical sideways grin as he shyly answered Amanda's probing question. "It's Carrie Brooks and John Mark Henderson," he said quietly, but with a note of excitement.

"Oh! Really?" Amanda shrieked with delight. "I wondered why you were with Luke and Carrie today! Now, I understand! I couldn't be happier! This is wonderful news!" She grasped Carrie's hand and said, "Congratulations! Congratulations!"

After a few moments of happy talk among the three, Luke leaned back in his chair and folded his arms. "I can't believe this," he said, "All my friends, married off! It's absolutely strange!" he joked. "What am I going to do? I won't have anybody to hang around with at all!" Everyone laughed at Luke.

"Someday it'll be you announcing this to us," Amanda reminded him.

"No way!" Luke retorted, "Not me! I'm going to go to school and study agriculture, then when I'm done with that I want to do a little traveling; see the world, you know. Then I'll probably do a little mission work, then…"

"Then you'll be so old there won't be a single girl left your age!" Carrie interrupted. Everyone enjoyed the joke; even Luke who took their teasing good-naturedly, insisting all the while that he'd never be anybody's husband.

Soon Dad came in to the cafeteria, leading Addy by the hand.

He smiled as he hurried up to their table. "Your mother has been released and we're going to head home now."

"Oh, good," Carrie said.

"We'll be right along, Dad," Luke told him. "We'll be right there after we drop John Mark off."

"Ok, see you at home," Dad replied. "Addy will go with us," he informed them and he and the little girl were off.

Amanda said good-bye to the other three as they finished the last of their food and rose to leave. "Let's get together soon," Carrie said to her old friend as they strode down the hall to the emergency room desk. "It's been too long since we were able to spend any real time together." Amanda agreed as she walked with them the rest of the way down the hall toward the doors.

"I can drive again," John Mark offered and went to pull the car up to the entrance.

It was a calmer ride back than it had been a few hours earlier, Carrie noticed. The conversation was centered on pleasant things like Amanda and Homer and summer soon to come. Everyone was more relaxed now and thankful to be leaving the hospital without complications.

"I'm really sorry to have caused you to miss your family's Sunday dinner," Carrie said to John Mark as they neared Blooming Hills.

"Oh, that's alright. You didn't cause me to miss it--I chose to go with you. I wouldn't have had it any other way," he said and glanced at Carrie with a loving smile.

When John Mark pulled the car up the Blooming Hills drive just minutes later, it wasn't long until Mr. and Mrs. Henderson and Eileen came out of the house to meet them. John Mark and Luke got out of the car and Luke slid behind the wheel. Mr. and Mrs. Henderson were filled with questions. While Mr. Henderson talked with the two boys, Eileen and Mrs. Henderson stood near the passenger side where Carrie was still seated.

"How's your mother doing?" Esther Henderson queried as she leaned over to speak to Carrie.

"She's fine now, thank you. She had several stitches and will need help for a while, but we're thankful it wasn't worse."

Esther pressed Carrie's hand into hers and said, "You tell her if there's anything I can do to help, just anything at all, please let me know."

"Thank you, I will," Carrie replied.

"We certainly did miss you at dinner today," Esther whispered to Carrie. "We'll have to plan a family dinner again real soon!" Eileen echoed her mother's sentiment as well.

Mrs. Henderson smiled knowingly at Carrie and for the first time, Carrie thought she caught a glimpse of John Mark's shy smile in his mother's face. It was as if Mrs. Henderson had expressed many more thoughts than what she spoke. Thoughts like, "Welcome to the Henderson family, Carrie Brooks; I'm glad my son chose you," and so on. It was the same subtle way that John Mark had of speaking with his eyes and his expressions. It reminded Carrie of the unspoken words she had been so sure she had heard from John Mark many times over the years before he could court her—those words that kept her praying about their future.

As Luke started the car, Mr. and Mrs. Henderson and Eileen waved good-bye as they walked back to the house.

Now it was John Mark's turn to lean in to Carrie's window for a few words, "Luke," he began, "I'd really like to drive your sister home if you don't mind. If that's ok with you, Carrie," he quickly added.

"I'd like that, John Mark. But are you sure? It looks like we got you home just in time for you to turn around and head back to Bixley," Carrie said, glancing first at her watch, then to John Mark.

"Well, that's ok, there's still time for me to get back. I was glad to be able to be with the two of you and drive you both in there. How about it, Luke?" John Mark said returning to his request to drive Carrie home. "I really feel responsible to take her home since I would have anyway after dinner today—besides it'll give us a little time to talk," he finished as he opened the door for Carrie.

"No, problem," Luke replied. "Hey, thanks for everything man," he said to his friend as he pulled the car around and out of the drive.

John Mark and Carrie arrived at the Brooks' farm not long after Luke. After going in to check on Mrs. Brooks and finding her comfortably seated in the front room, John Mark excused himself, explaining that he had to get back to Bixley. Carrie walked outside with him into the approaching evening.

"I sure hope your mom will get along all right with the stitches and all; I'll be praying for her," John Mark said sincerely.

"I'll tell her that. Thanks for everything, John Mark," she replied. "I guess it's a good thing we didn't have church scheduled for this evening," she added.

"I guess so," John Mark agreed. "I'll call you," he said, then quickly added, "…if that's ok?"

"Yes, please do," Carrie beamed.

"Come to think of it, we never got to tell the rest of my family the news," John Mark remembered, "Is it ok with you if I just give them a call sometime this week—they'll find out from someone else if I don't," he added thoughtfully. "After all, we told Amanda and I suppose the news could get around now. I'd like them to hear it from me."

"I agree. It's fine with me," Carrie assured him.

As John Mark left, Carrie waved and stood watching until his pickup was out of sight.

A Trip to the English Hills

The next few weeks were busy ones for Carrie. She found herself picking up even more of the household chores with her mother's hand injured. Now, with strawberry season only days away, it was also time to go back to work at Blooming Hills to help Eileen. Carrie happily anticipated a weekly call or letter from John Mark, for he too was busy at his farm and she saw him only on Sundays.

One Thursday afternoon Eileen looked at Carrie as they neared the end of the work day at the bakery and said, "Well, I think it's time for a little holiday for a few of us around here. We've been working awfully hard, wouldn't you say, Carrie?"

"It has been hectic, getting ready for strawberry season," Carrie agreed, "But I guess it's always that way on a farm in the spring."

"You're right," Eileen said, "But on Saturday that's all going to change!" Eileen's eyes twinkled as if she held a secret. "I've got a little trip planned for us," she smiled.

"What do you mean?" Carrie asked, leaning against the counter.

"Well, we've worked so hard lately, all of us I mean. Luke's been here everyday after school helping Joe and Daddy and you and I've been really digging in to get everything set for another season. So I thought it would be great if all of us—you and Luke and Joe and Katie, maybe even Steve and Alice, could do something fun together. It might be our last chance before the strawberries are on and all the graduation open houses start."

"Great idea, Eileen. What have you got planned?" Carrie asked eagerly.

"I thought we'd pack a real big lunch with all the trimmings and then head out in the morning and go to John Mark's farm for the day. After all, you've never been there have you?"

"No," Carrie said slowly with a tone of excited bewilderment. "I've wanted to go, but so far I haven't been able to. He's mentioned it several times."

"Well, then I guess it's about time!" Eileen announced. "Mom found some end tables at a garage sale the other day and she bought them for John Mark. It's a good excuse to take them over there. It's absolutely pitiful the way that house of his is so bare. But I'm sure you'll change all that! It needs a woman's touch."

"The idea of going sounds great, Eileen. But are you sure John Mark wants us to come? I mean, maybe he's not wanting any company," Carrie cautioned.

"Nonsense!" Eileen retorted. "I've already called him and he was glad I thought of it. He said any home-cooked meal will be welcome and he is anxious for you to see the farm!"

"Well, ok, then! I'll ask Mom and Dad and make sure nothing else is going on," Carrie said exuberantly, "It sounds like fun!"

"It will be," Eileen assured her, "We'll spend all afternoon tomorrow making up the food. We'll have a grand time! I'll tell Steve and Alice and Joe and Katie; you tell Luke. We can all carpool from here on Saturday morning."

So it was all decided and the trip planned. When Carrie arrived home that day, Dad informed her that John Mark had called requesting that Carrie and Luke come for the get together. Carrie was only sorry she had missed his call and the opportunity to talk awhile.

Friday in the Blooming Hills Bakery kitchen was spent in preparing enough fried chicken for eight hungry friends. Also included in the menu was potato salad, baked beans, homemade bread, and several pies, including cherry, John Mark's personal favorite. Eileen slyly set Carrie to making that one with the thought that John Mark would be impressed by her baking abilities.

When Saturday finally came, Carrie awoke early. The idea of seeing John Mark's farm for the first time was so exciting that she found it impossible to sleep beyond six a.m. She arose and read some scriptures as she sat at her window seat in the early dawn. Then she carefully chose an outfit to wear. She hoped there would be an opportunity to walk around and see John Mark's entire farm. There would probably even be some games, knowing how the Henderson family enjoyed outdoor games. Horseshoes, croquet, even badminton, were among their favorites.

When Luke and Carrie were finally ready to leave, Mom took Carrie aside and whispered to her gently, "Be careful how you react when you see John Mark's farm," was her motherly advice. "The house may be sort of rough and unpolished from what I hear. Don't let him see your disappointment if it looks pretty uncomfortable. After all, a woman's touch can make a great difference in a place. Remember what this house looked like before we moved in?"

"I sure do!" Carrie replied. "I'll try to be very courteous," she assured her mother.

"I'm sure it's very important to him that you're pleased with the place," Mom added. Carrie nodded her agreement.

"Have a good day," Mom reminded as her daughter packed the last few items in the car.

"Drive safely, Luke," Dad called as they headed out.

When Luke and Carrie reached Blooming Hills, Steve and Alice were already there. Joe had driven one of the farm trucks up to the bakery kitchen door where Eileen, obviously enjoying the occasion, bustled in and out packing coolers with salads and pies. Mrs. Henderson was tucking some old blankets around the two attractive end tables that were to ride the long distance to Bixley. Joe was loading horseshoes and croquet sets in as well.

Luke hopped out of the car and helped the men while Carrie headed in to assist Eileen. Alice was in the kitchen too and gave Carrie a big hug as she entered. "I feel like I haven't seen you forever!" she exclaimed. Something in Alice's hug seemed to say, "I'm glad you'll be my sister-in-law."

Before long the group had paired up in different vehicles and started off. Joe and Katie led the way in the farm truck, followed by Steve and Alice while Eileen, Luke and Carrie were in the last car. The three had a fine time visiting on the long drive. Eileen and Luke, both veterans of the drive to Bixley, pointed out familiar landmarks along the way.

About forty-five minutes later as they neared Bixley, Carrie noticed that the scenery became decidedly hillier. It was very beautiful; the hills dressed in the greens of spring were like shimmering emeralds in the late-morning sun. As Carrie looked out her window, she soon saw a little sign that read, "BIXLEY--3 MILES." Her heart fluttered excitedly when she saw it. She watched the rolling hills where clean little farms were nestled cozily, and wondered if soon one of them would be John Mark's. But she relaxed a bit as the houses grew closer together and Bixley, what little there was of it, appeared, for Eileen soon supplied the information that answered Carrie's unasked questions. "John Mark's farm is on the other side of Bixley," she offered.

"It's a little ways yet." Luke agreed.

Bixley was gone in a flash since the main street consisted of only a grocery, post office, feed mill, and hardware. A little church and cemetery was situated at the outskirts of town and seemed to bring Bixley to an end. As they drove on through the countryside, the road curved first this way and then that. With each turn, Carrie thought the hills grew lovelier. This was obviously fruit country as fields of berries and slopes of fruit trees and grape arbors dressed in their spring finery covered the countryside.

"This area is called English Hills," Eileen said dreamily. "Isn't it lovely?" she asked.

"It certainly is," Carrie said softly as she admired the scenery.

"Oh! Don't forget to turn here!" Eileen cautioned as Luke came up to a nearly hidden road veering off to the left.

"Oh, thanks. I remember now," Luke said.

Carrie noticed the road sign, "ENGLISH HILLS ROAD", a name she recognized as part of John Mark's address that had appeared on the many notes and letters she had been receiving from him. She watched now with growing excitement as her eyes searched the countryside for landmarks she had heard Eileen and the others mention from time to time--landmarks that she had etched in the memory of her heart since John Mark had moved away.

"When I see the little church, I'll know it's just around the next corner," she told herself. She felt a range of emotions as they rode on, the road dipping and twisting. At each turn of a curve her heart leapt with anticipation, yet her expectancy sometimes bordered on fear, as she wondered what the farm would really look like and how she would feel about it. Suddenly around the next curve, a pretty little church came into view and Carrie recognized it instantly from Eileen's poignant description so long ago the day after they had moved John Mark to his new home.

As Luke drove past, Carrie read the sign while Eileen reminded her that John Mark's place was just up the road from here. "English Hills Christian Church"…Carrie's heart was warmed as she thought of John Mark attending there on those rare Sundays when he hadn't been able to make it home. And here was the pretty stone bridge that Eileen had so loved! Carrie recognized it as the backdrop of her friend's senior pictures. It was beautiful! A lazy creek wound past the church and under the road.

Luke slowed the car as they crossed the narrow bridge. Colorful woodland flowers dotted the banks and spread into the woodsy places along the creek. Carrie thought this must be one of the most beautiful places she'd ever seen! She was filled with joy and anticipation, impressed with the gorgeous scenery. Her mind was filled with dreamy thoughts when she heard Eileen say, "We're here! This is it!"

Luke turned into John Mark's drive as Carrie peered somewhat anxiously out the window, trying not to appear too curious. Somehow an old familiar feeling seemed to envelop her as she saw the farm for the first time. All her apprehension melted into joy as she looked at the farmhouse. It was the same comfortable, at-home feeling she had experienced when her parents had taken her and Luke to Blossom Lane for the first time!

The slightly sad condition of the house escaped Carrie's notice as she looked dreamily at the faded red of the barns and saw the remnants of old flower gardens dotting the yard, just waiting for a woman to care for them once again. Tears welled up in Carrie's eyes when she suddenly noticed the little, white-flowered bushes circling the front porch, welcoming her in her favorite May way! She suddenly realized these were the bushes Luke had helped John Mark plant long ago. Surely he had done this just for her!

John Mark stepped out onto the porch just as Luke pulled the car to a stop. His eyes searched to find Carrie. He smiled proudly when he saw her and headed toward the car. Eileen bounded out of the back seat long before Carrie had even gathered up her purse and other belongings. Eileen greeted her brother enthusiastically and announced, "We're here!" as she gave him a loving, sisterly hug. She immediately made her way to the truck and began giving orders about where to put the coolers and so on. Eileen was the organizer of this event and everyone gladly followed her directions.

By now, John Mark had reached the car and opened the door for Carrie. "Welcome!" he greeted her with his eyes sparkling. For a moment they were alone as all the others were busying themselves with unpacking coolers, games, and furniture. He held out his hand and politely helped her out of the car. She recognized the significance of the moment as she saw in his eyes an eager searching and she was reminded of her mother's parting words, "I'm sure it's very important to him that you are pleased with the place."

She realized she must communicate her approval and delight to him somehow. "Oh, John Mark," was all she could say for a moment, as her voice caught in her throat. "It's so beautiful!" she said in a whisper, gazing at the surroundings.

He still held her hand in his as he replied, "I'm glad you think so."

"I do," she said softly, a radiant smile lighting her face. Now she looked directly into his eyes and said, "John Mark, the flowers around the front porch—they're my favorites!"

"I know, I remember," he said in his even, pleasant voice. "I planted them for you because you once told me you'd never really feel at home anywhere without them."

He gazed at her, awaiting her reply.

"Thank you," she said, tears of joy welling up in her eyes as she remembered their conversation so long ago on graduation night.

Their private world was soon disturbed though, with the banging of the back porch screen door as Eileen directed Luke and Joe, who were carrying loads of food into John Mark's kitchen. "I'm making everyone feel right at home, big brother!" Eileen said as she swept by the dreamy-eyed couple a few seconds later. "I'm just going to take your kitchen right over!" she said, hurrying toward the truck where the last of the items were being unloaded.

Now Steve and Alice walked toward John Mark and Carrie. "Hi, John Mark," Alice said, giving her brother a hug. Steve reached out and shook hands with his brother-in-law. "How are you, John Mark?" he smiled.

"Great, Steve! Glad you both could come over today," John Mark said.

"Well, we're glad we could join the party today too," Steve smiled.

"I think I better go in and help Eileen," Alice said, beginning to excuse herself from the group.

"We're right behind you," John Mark replied.

"That's all right," Alice began, "I know my way around. You probably want to show Carrie around the farm a bit," she said as she and Steve started toward the house.

"I do want to show you the rest of the place," John Mark said to Carrie after everyone else was out of earshot. "But I really had hoped we could take a long, slow walk around the farm after dinner, if that's ok. We've got so much to talk about," John Mark said hopefully.

"Sure; that sounds so nice," Carrie happily agreed, "I probably ought to see if I can help Eileen with dinner right now anyway."

"Oh, it looks like she's got it all under control," John Mark grinned as he headed Carrie toward the house. They both knew Eileen was more than capable of handling any dinner all by herself.

"But we can start by seeing the kitchen, I guess!" he said and led her to the rear of the house. "I hope you're not disappointed in this place," John Mark warned her a bit apologetically as they approached the back door. "It's still in pretty simple shape in some rooms," he added.

"I'm sure I won't be disappointed, " Carrie stated honestly, for she was already so in love with the home's exterior that she was sure nothing could spoil her delight. And she was to be proven right, even though she was about to find out that John Mark's words were a true assessment of its condition. As they rounded the side of the house, Carrie heard the others happily chattering inside.

An old pump was standing at the edge of a porch foundation that ran along the back of the house. A little narrow sidewalk went straight out from the back door, disappearing into the yard where a tall pole stood with a dinner bell at its top. A few feet beyond the bell was the clothesline and several yards beyond the clothesline, the strawberry fields began.

At a quick glance, Carrie could see many cozy, interesting places in the backyard, a shade tree here and there, a fenced-in area which was the remnant of an old vegetable garden, and a little stone milk house building.

John Mark opened the screen door, escorting Carrie into the back porch. "Carrie, I hope you don't mind, coming in the back way; the kitchen's here," he said. "I guess you could call this the back porch slash laundry room," he joked. "At least it's the laundry room for now. I hope someday I can make a better room out of it—a real utility room, I mean."

"It's nice just like this," Carrie replied sincerely, for the big sunny windows on all sides of the room welcomed the spring sun in a most cheerful way.

John Mark stepped up one step and led Carrie into the big farmhouse kitchen where Eileen had taken over as promised and was hurrying to get dinner prepared. Alice and Katie were helping their sister and John Mark's tiny kitchen table was already laden with food.

"Where do you keep the silverware, John Mark?" Eileen asked as they stepped in the door.

"Uh, over in that top drawer, I guess," he smiled rather sheepishly, as his sister started toward the drawer he had pointed out.

"You guess?" Eileen asked, opening the drawer. "Oh!" she said with mild shock as she examined the contents of the drawer, a motley assortment of mismatched eating utensils. "I guess it's a good thing I thought to bring extras," she mumbled.

"Well, this is the kitchen," John Mark said to Carrie with a note of apology in his voice.

"I see. It's quite pleasant," she smiled. As she sized up its condition, she was tempted to sympathize with Eileen concerning the fact that it needed a woman's touch. Its one redeeming factor was its spaciousness.

"Oh, by the way, you're almost out of dish soap," Eileen said to John Mark in a motherly tone as she held up a nearly empty bottle from under the sink.

"Thanks," he said blankly, dish soap being the least of his current concerns.

Alice flashed a smile at Carrie from across the room as she worked putting the plates and glasses out on the counter. Carrie discerned Alice's look since she understood the different personalities of the Henderson girls. Alice would never have pointed out anything like the empty bottle of soap or the disorganization of John Mark's kitchen in front of a visitor, especially his bride-to-be, like Eileen had just done.

"Can I help you do anything here?" Carrie quickly asked the others to try to draw attention away from Eileen's comments.

"Oh, no!" Eileen answered. "We're all set here. Go see the rest of the house," she said with a wave of her hand. "The sooner you can do something about it, the better!" Her tart reply caused Carrie's attempt at rescuing John Mark to backfire.

Now Katie looked at Carrie with the same knowing smile, for Eileen was the most kind-hearted girl in the world, but was known for her straightforward remarks. John Mark looked a bit embarrassed, but Alice came to his rescue in her tactful, sweet manner, smoothing Eileen's comment away as she added, "Thank you, Carrie, but we're doing fine here. Do go see the rest of John Mark's house; he's really done wonders with it already. It's such a delightful place."

Before Eileen could comment again, John Mark led Carrie to the dining room, his pride a bit restored by Alice's kind observations.

"The dining room," he said quietly as he introduced Carrie to a rather plain but large room, devoid of furniture, save some rickety looking old dining chairs parked against the south wall.

"It's a very...big...room," Carrie said, assessing it and searching for features to compliment. She was truly glad to see that the rooms were spacious and in good repair. It was just that they lacked that homey feeling a woman would strive to create. "A few curtains and some furniture here and there would make a great difference," Carrie observed silently as she eyed the yellowed pull shades on the windows. "Maybe a picture or two and some throw rugs," she thought. She was not disappointed in the house at all; in fact she liked it, but she had to admit to herself once again that Eileen was right—it needed a woman's touch.

On they went, John Mark leading her from room to room, introducing her to the house. They found Joe and Luke were sprawled on the living room floor visiting with Steve who sat in the only chair, an old rocker that Carrie recognized as having been part of John Mark's furniture that was loaded on the truck the day he moved from Blooming Hills. The two new end tables were quite nice but looked rather lonely next to the single chair.

While John Mark walked Carrie through the rooms, somewhere during the tour she suddenly realized that this would be her home and began making a private assessment of the projects she would have to look forward to--a lot of curtain sewing and used furniture shopping—maybe a little papering and painting. Her heart leapt at the realization that she was seeing her home for the first time! This house she had always thought of as John Mark's place was going to be their first home!

The more she got used to the thought, the more her mental list of projects grew. She began to view the house like an artist would view an empty canvas, her excitement mounting with the discovery of each new room.

Soon, dinner was served buffet style with everyone taking a plate and finding any available chair. Luke and Joe had to sit on lawn chairs but everyone else found a more permanent-type chair to drag to the dining room where they sat in a circle and enjoyed the girls' fine cooking, balancing their plates on their laps. Admitting to being tired of his own cooking, John Mark seemed to enjoy the dinner more than anyone else. Everyone laughed as he went for his second heaping plateful complete with a generous slice of cherry pie.

With the first bite of pie, he exclaimed enthusiastically, "I don't know if cherry pie ever tasted so good!"

"Carrie made it," Eileen was quick to announce, obviously seizing the opportunity to share this little fact. The others agreed with John Mark's observation and Carrie blushed as she looked down at her plate and kept eating.

"Is that so?" John Mark said between bites. "It's really good!" he repeated. Carrie felt so proud to have met with his approval in the matter of his favorite pie, glad she done something to help make this day memorable. Knowing all eyes were on her, she hesitated to look up, but she was able to manage a shy smile.

After dinner the men retired to the yard. Luke, John Mark, and Joe relaxed under the sprawling shade trees by the drive while Steve walked around the yard a bit.

Carrie helped the other ladies clear away the meal and do the dishes. They carefully rationed out the remaining dish soap. While Eileen washed the dishes, Carrie dried them and put them away. Katie and Alice visited at the little kitchen table.

Carrie was secretly enjoying her task. Being unfamiliar with John Mark's kitchen and having to search the drawers and cupboards to get everything put away, gave her an opportunity to learn more about him. The first thing she discovered was that he was a typical man—there seemed to be no rhyme or reason to his arrangement of dishes. Many of the cupboards were next to bare while others were overcrowded. He appeared to have most of the kitchenware he owned crowded randomly into one small cupboard nearest the sink. Everything was mismatched and the kitchen seemed to be seriously short of dishtowels—he owned two to be exact!

When the first towel was too wet to use anymore, Carrie returned it to the towel bar from where she had originally taken it and began to hunt for clean, dry ones. Noticing her dilemma as she opened first one drawer, then another; Katie asked, "What's wrong, Carrie?"

"Oh, I can't find any more dry dishtowels," she replied. Then the search was on. All the girls were hunting for dishtowels! Finally a shriek of victory went up from Eileen, who located one clean, but worn towel haphazardly folded and resting in a bowl in the cupboard where John Mark kept his rather generous supply of crackers, bread, peanut butter and jelly.

"I don't believe it," Alice joked and shook her head. "In a bowl of all places!" They all laughed and giggled at John Mark's lack of kitchen order.

"Really!" Eileen said, rather annoyed. "I know Mama sent more than two dishtowels with him when he moved—I remember packing them! We certainly had this kitchen in better order than this when we moved him in!"

"Well, there are probably plenty more towels here if we could only find them!" Katie smiled. "Maybe we should look in all the unlikely places, like the refrigerator!"

All the girls were still giggling over the incident when John Mark's voice was heard at the door to the back room. "What's so funny?" he grinned as he leaned against the door frame.

"Oh, nothing," Alice replied as they all still smiled.

"What do you need?" Eileen asked. "Surely you're not hungry again already?"

"Not for at least another hour," he joked as he patted his stomach. All the girls laughed again. "Actually," he began in his typically shy manner, "I was just going to see if you were done so Carrie and I could take a walk around the farm." He glanced quickly at Carrie as if to get her consent.

"Oh sure, go on and take a walk. We're almost done here," Eileen said.

"It's our turn to help anyway," Alice announced as she and Katie rose from the table. Alice took the towel from Carrie and began helping with the last of the dishes.

"Are you sure?" Carrie asked.

"Yes. Go have a nice walk and take your time!" Katie assured her.

"Well, all right," Carrie said, smiling. John Mark looked pleased as he escorted her out the door.

The two walked slowly around the parts of the farm closest to the house, Carrie listening closely to John Mark's explanations of the grounds. He told her of his plans for this barn and that field, proudly pointing out the different improvements he'd already made. She listened with real interest, falling deeper in love with the farm with each step.

After they had seen the barns and the livestock, they crossed the driveway to the backyard and walked north along the strawberry field. Laughter and the occasional clanging of a horseshoe could be heard as the men competed hotly for a championship round. The girls were now outside as well, sitting in John Mark's dining room chairs which they had placed under a shade tree. Eileen could be heard among the others as she cheered Luke on. John Mark glanced at Carrie and smiled as they walked on in silence until at the north end of the yard they came to a double row of fruit trees running almost two-thirds the length of the lawn.

"These trees are for our own use," John Mark said proudly. "They are some of the finest varieties of apples, peaches, and cherries that I know of." He turned to the east end of the trees and they walked a short way to where the aisle of trees began.

John Mark led Carrie down through the grassy center of the double row of stately trees, most of which were almost done blooming. Their lovely blossoms shed a sweet and heavy perfume into the air, carpeting the grass beneath their gnarled old limbs, "How beautiful!" Carrie breathed.

"Do you like them?" John Mark asked, "They're for you to use," he repeated. "You'll be able to get all kinds of fruit for the kitchen here." He paused for a moment. "Every kind of baking apple you could want, peaches, pears, even cherries...for pie," he added with a shy smile. Carrie blushed at his obvious praise in reference to her baking.

"I can't get over their beauty," Carrie commented again as they walked on. The trees were bordered on the north and west with a fence where the strawberry fields began. When they reached the end of the orchard aisle, Carrie noticed a quaint, little, old stile over the west fence. "Oh, how interesting!" she said enthusiastically. "This must have been here for a long time," she deduced as she stepped up on the first step. She turned around and sat down atop the fence on the center step. "I love it!" she smiled with delight. "Look at the view from here!" she marveled, pointing down the center of the rows of trees.

John Mark looked proud and pleased as he leaned contentedly against the fence, close to Carrie and looked across the fields of berries. "There's more orchards—large ones—beyond the berry field. It's almost easier to get to them from the other road." he said, pointing to the west. As Carrie turned and looked she could see the tops of many trees in the distance. She took a deep breath as she drank in the serene beauty of the place and they were both silent for some time.

Finally John Mark spoke. "Carrie," he began, "I'm glad we're finally getting a chance to talk," he said as he stared into her eyes. "There's so much I've wanted to say…for so long." She smiled back as he continued to speak. "I'm not sure what all your father has told you about the conversation he and I had," he began, "but I spent a long time in serious prayer before approaching your parents."

"Yes, I know," Carrie acknowledged softly. "I really appreciate that, John Mark," she said sincerely.

He nodded. "I can't remember a time when I wasn't attracted to you," he began after a moment, "but I knew I couldn't tell you or give you much indication of my feelings until I was able to make a proposal of courtship." He searched her eyes and she nodded her understanding. "Carrie, you don't know how many times over the years I wanted to say, 'Carrie, please wait for me.' I was so afraid someone else would capture your heart first." Her eyes became misty as she remembered the many times she had thought she sensed John Mark's interest and affection.

He went on speaking, "But I knew I shouldn't allow myself to dwell on thoughts of marrying you as young as we were. I knew I should be pursuing God's will for my life and trusting Him to add all things to me in His own time. During our senior year I really dedicated myself to prayer. I was feeling such a pull toward missions and some of the places Trent and I were seriously looking at were not fit to take a wife." Carrie understood what he meant having seen the pictures from missionaries' travels many times.

"So I asked God to make it very clear to me what to do." John Mark recounted. "I don't think Dad and Mom even realized how seriously I was considering missions, because then Dad came to me with the proposal of this farm right before graduation. I took that as an indication from God that I was to wait a bit more. I felt I should come here and farm for a while." Carrie gazed at John Mark, listening intently to his every word. As he related the details of events leading up to his proposal, she found herself falling more and more in love with this gentle, but strong and dedicated man.

"I knew being alone here would give me the perfect opportunity to pray and think and listen to God. And, that's just what it did." He laughed a little at remembering the experience. "Can you imagine what it was like coming over here and living all alone after being a part of the Blooming Hills hustle and bustle?" Carrie smiled and nodded, knowing how close the Henderson family was and how busy their farm could get. "Finally I realized God did have a place for me in missions and that place was as a financial contributor. Trent and I talked and he assured me it's vital that there be dedicated people on the home front backing the missionaries in the field with money to continue their work."

"It reminds me of the Bible account of Aaron and Hur holding up Moses' arms during the battle so the Israelites would keep winning," Carrie offered.

"I remember that account," John Mark smiled. "I guess I'm called to be like Aaron and Hur for missionaries. But I need you to help me."

Now his voice became earnest as his eyes seemed to implore Carrie to catch the vision he so clearly saw. "This farm is a good, productive investment; I could see that almost right away—but it would be so much easier to have a help meet in this effort." He looked entreatingly at Carrie who was nodding her agreement. "I can't do all I need to do to run this farm to its potential all by myself. I mean, I have visions of living off the land as much as possible with our own cows for milk and chickens for meat and eggs. Surely there's all the fruit here a family could ever use and space for a garden. All that will save money for the Lord's work. And Carrie, you are the perfect Proverbs 31 woman in my eyes," he said lovingly. "You know, 'the heart of her husband safely trusts in her and he shall have no need of spoil,'" he quoted. "I want to obey some other advice from Proverbs too; it says to 'honor the Lord with all your possessions and with the first fruits of all your increase.' I want to use this farm to honor God by supporting the sending of His word around the world."

"It's a fine plan, John Mark," Carrie said admiringly. "There's a part of my heart that is drawn to missions too but I never felt exactly called to any particular assignment. Your vision is wonderful. I can't think of a better way to spend my life," she said sincerely.

A long silence followed, for neither one felt the need to speak. John Mark gazed across the fields and seemed to be studying the land. After a while he looked again at Carrie and said, "I told your father..." he paused and cleared his throat rather nervously, "that if we have another good season on the farm, I'd like to marry you then." He looked into the distant hills and went on, "Carrie, I've got enough money saved up that I probably could support us now, but if we wait until harvest there'll really be plenty, enough to send some away to missions for the first time. It will give me a chance to be true to the vision right from the start. Do you agree?"

"Yes, I do," Carrie replied, assuring him of her support.

John Mark reached out and took her hands in his. "Then.... Carrie May Brooks...will you do me the honor of allowing me to court you with a wedding in mind?" he asked in his characteristically even and deliberate way.

Carrie smiled as her voice caught in her throat, "Yes, John Mark," she replied with shining eyes. "Now shall I tell you what the Lord spoke to me?" she asked. John Mark looked at her eagerly, encouraging her to express the thoughts in her heart.

"Please do," he replied.

"In the few days after my parents first told me of your proposal, I spent some time praying too. I asked the Lord to confirm His will to me because I knew what my will was...." she said, blushing. She continued to relate the events of those days to him, allowing him to share the significance of the intimate moments she had spent with God concerning their relationship. She finished by telling him the verse that she had been given from the Psalms confirming her desires.

For a long while they continued there at the fence talking at length about their future, their hopes and dreams. Finally they realized they had been there at the end of the orchard a very long time when they noticed Joe and Luke pulling up the horseshoe stakes at the other end of the yard. "I guess we better start back," Carrie suggested.

"I guess so," John Mark replied reluctantly, helping her down from her seat on the fence. "I probably won't be home as much after this week," he said as they slowly walked back, hand in hand. "The berries will soon be ready and so now the real work begins!"

"I realize," Carrie said. "I'll be praying for you—and thinking about you."

"Thank you," John Mark replied, with a squeeze of her hand. "I'll do the same. I'll call you as much as possible and see you on Sundays." Carrie nodded. Her heart was so full of joy that she found it hard to speak. So they walked on in silence down the aisle of trees white with blossoms. Just as they reached the east end of the orchard corridor, a sudden gust of wind sent a shower of the last of the white petals circling about them.

John Mark smiled with enjoyment as he noticed Carrie's delight at the happenstance. "Like a shower of rice on a bride and groom," she thought to herself. It was to be a cherished memory of a most romantic day!

A Wedding, A Watch, and a Proposal

John Mark was right. Within the next few weeks, the work began. The ripe, red berries lay like rubies in the fields and hordes of people descended on Blooming Hills with baskets in hand. Of course, the same was true of John Mark's farm over in Bixley. The first Sunday after strawberry season was in full swing, Carrie thought John Mark looked extra tired when he arrived at church. "Are you working too hard?" Carrie asked him.

"No, I'm alright," he said pleasantly, "It's just a busy time. I got in late last night. I guess I am a little tired."

"Well, if you're too tired to come over for dinner, I'll understand," Carrie said kindly, hoping he would choose to come to the Brooks' after all.

"No!" he assured her. "I wouldn't miss it. I get so tired of my own cooking! Besides, I wouldn't pass up the opportunity to spend the afternoon with you," he smiled.

After church services were over, John Mark drove Carrie to Blossom Lane in his pickup. "We'll have to stop by Blooming Hills on our way to your house, if that's ok," he said as they left the church. Carrie wondered what he could possibly mean.

"Sure," she agreed.

"I've got a little present for you and your family," he said with a twinkle in his eye.

Moments later John Mark pulled the truck into the Blooming

Hills drive. He circled up to the main barn and parked the truck. He hopped out of the driver's seat and said, "This'll take just a minute!" He unlocked the barn door and slid it to the side. Carrie could see several boxes of the most beautiful strawberries she had ever seen and John Mark was loading them onto the truck. "For us?" Carrie asked excitedly as she leaned out of the passenger side window.

"Uh huh," he replied, stooping to pick up another crate. "I picked them last night."

"No wonder you're tired!" Carrie said. "John Mark, you shouldn't have!"

"Oh, it's ok." He said as he finished with the last box and closed the barn door. "The one neighbor down the road has a couple of teenage boys; they helped me." Jumping back into the truck, he added, "I wanted to do it. I thought your folks would appreciate it. I know your mom's got a few rows in her garden, but I thought she'd appreciate extras. I remember last year you got some from Blooming Hills because there weren't enough of yours. Now you won't have to do that," he smiled. "I unloaded them here this morning so they wouldn't have to sit in the back of my truck in the sun during church."

"Thank you so much!" Carrie replied sincerely. "John Mark you are too generous." As she looked at the heaping boxes of fruit, she exclaimed, "There's more here than our family will ever use!"

"I know," he replied matter-of-factly. She wondered what he meant by that but said nothing. Soon he continued, "I thought... maybe...well, you might like to put some up for...us...you and me," he suggested shyly.

"Oh," she replied, almost embarrassed not to have realized his intentions. "Of course, I should be thinking of canning and freezing for John Mark and I," she realized. "Especially if we're going to try to save money!" She remembered the day he had quoted the verse from Proverbs 31 to her, "the heart of her husband safely trusts in her and he shall have no need of spoil." Her cheeks began to color as she realized how far ahead of her John Mark had been in the area of economy!

As they rode on in silence, she suddenly realized for the first time that he probably meant to set a wedding date for sometime before next year's crop! "Yes, this will be my only chance then to prepare food ahead of time for us if that's the case!" Soon she spoke as if there had been no silence and John Mark had been hearing her thoughts all along. "How do you prefer your strawberries, canned or frozen?" she asked seriously.

John Mark's face lit up with the familiar sideways grin as he turned and said, "I prefer them in pie!" Carrie laughed with him about his statement and they rode on in silence until they reached Blossom Lane.

After dinner that day, the men retired to the living room while Mom and Carrie cleared the table and did the dishes. In the privacy of the kitchen, Carrie told her mother how John Mark had hinted at his love of strawberry pie and how he had worked late last evening picking the berries for them. "His neighbors' boys helped him, but I know he had worked hard all day and was probably really tired by then," Carrie said sympathetically.

"I guess that stands to reason," her mother agreed.

"Mom, would it be ok if I made up a pie for him to take home tonight in appreciation for the berries? He doesn't get much home cooking. I discovered that when I saw how ill-equipped his kitchen was. He barely has any large bowls. That tells me he's not mixing anything up!" The two women laughed knowingly.

"Sure, Carrie. It's a good idea to make a pie," Mom agreed. "I think we've got some pie shells in the freezer."

"It won't take long at all and they'll never miss us," Carrie said as she leaned around the doorway and pointed to the living room where all three men had dozed off in the comfortable chairs. Even Addy was napping with her Daddy in his chair.

Mom smiled at the sight and said, "I'll get the berries hulled." She set to work washing and hulling enough berries for a pie while Carrie put a pie shell in the oven and stirred up a sweet, red glaze for the fruit. When the glaze was finished cooking, she set it in the freezer to chill quickly and whipped some cream for a topping. Soon the shell was done and she turned off the oven and set the shell on the counter to cool.

"I'll put it together for him right before he's ready to leave," she said. "That will give the filling time to really get chilled," Carrie said to her mother. They wiped the counters and decided to tiptoe out to relax on the porch swing, leaving the tired men to their naps.

Not long later, the women's visiting was interrupted as they heard the porch door open. A sleepy looking John Mark appeared and stepped out onto the porch. "I'm sorry," he said politely. "I guess I was more tired than I thought."

"That's no problem," Carrie said. "I thought you looked really exhausted this morning."

"You're not the only one," Mom chuckled as she gestured toward the living room, "You were in good company!" she said as she rose and walked to the door. "I'm glad you feel comfortable here with our family," she smiled and patted John Mark on the shoulder.

"Thank you, Ma'am, I do," he said as she disappeared inside.

John Mark smiled at Carrie and slowly walked over and sat down next to her on the porch swing. He just sat in silence for a moment. "I guess I haven't been much company today," he said apologetically.

"It's ok," Carrie offered again.

"I'll make it up to you," he said, "We'll spend some more time together when I get rested up. Strawberry season can be the worst, I always thought," he added. "You're never ready for it after the long winter and there's always so much demand to keep up with."

"I know," Carrie agreed. "You forget, I work at Blooming Hills!" she teased.

"Oh, yeah," he grinned.

"But don't apologize," she added. "I'm glad for any little time we can spend together."

He smiled as he relaxed a bit and stretched his long legs out, pushing his feet against the porch rail and rocking the swing gently. "If the strawberry crop is any indication, we're off to a good start this year, Carrie," he said.

"I'm glad. I've been praying a lot for you and the farm." Remembering the story of the old watch prompted Carrie to keep praying diligently.

"Thanks," he said, as he turned to her and smiled.

After a short visit, John Mark announced, "Carrie, I sure hate to go, but I think I better be heading back. Since we don't have church tonight, I can get the chores done now and maybe get to bed a little early. I wouldn't think of going yet, but with the hour's drive, I guess I better. And.... tomorrow's another day of work," he sighed, although contentedly.

"I suppose you're right," Carrie conceded, "But can you wait just a few minutes?" she asked. "I've got a surprise for you now!" she said.

"Ok," he grinned as she stepped in the door.

"Be right back," she smiled through the screen as she headed in the house. In a few minutes, Carrie stepped to the door and said, "John Mark, would you come here please?" He rose from his seat on the porch swing and followed her through the house to the kitchen where a delectable looking strawberry pie awaited him.

"For you to take with you," she beamed.

"Wow! Thanks, Carrie! This looks so good!"

"Mom and I made it while you guys slept," she explained. "It's from the berries you brought—which by the way, we appreciate very much; thanks again," she added.

"Thank you," he said.

Carrie put the pie in a little cooler with an ice pack placed carefully in the bottom. "This should keep it cool on your way home," she said as she shut the lid.

"Mmm!" he said, "I can't wait to get home and have a midnight snack!" John Mark went to the living room and thanked Mr. and Mrs. Brooks for the meal and said goodbye to the rest of the family. Together he and Carrie walked out to the truck.

"Drive carefully," Carrie reminded him as he set the pie gently on the front seat.

"I will," he said. "Thanks again for the pie. I'll be praying for you," he said as gazed into her eyes for a moment.

"See you next week," she smiled, and he was off.

She watched from the front porch as his truck rolled off into the distance and disappeared into the sinking sun.

So, on went the busy summer with Carrie working for Eileen at Blooming Hills, John Mark working diligently at the farm, and both of them praying for a bountiful year with the crops. With each successive fruit crop, John Mark presented Carrie with the best of the fields' and orchards' offerings that she promptly canned, froze, or made into jams and jellies to be saved for use in their new home. The Brooks family benefited as well from John Mark's generosity and prosperity for there was always plenty for Mom to put up for them as well.

Eileen had offered to let Carrie store her frozen items in the big bakery freezer until she and John Mark could find a used freezer to buy. Carrie gladly took Eileen's offer while looking forward to the day when she would be able to place the items in storage at her own new home.

All summer Carrie diligently watched the classified ads in the Blue Creek paper for a used freezer that she and John Mark could buy. Finally near the end of the summer someone advertised one that upon inspection proved to be a bargain and Carrie wisely lost no time purchasing it. John Mark picked it up in his truck one weekend and took it to Bixley, and placed it on the back porch. Seeing all of Carrie's diligence in canning the fruits he supplied her with, he surprised her by building a large set of shelves in the basement at the farm. Things were really shaping up at John Mark's farm as the hot summer season wore on.

As August approached, Carrie looked forward to Homer and Amanda's wedding. She and John Mark had been asked to be part of the wedding party, an event that Carrie happily anticipated. Summer was nearly over when the time for the ceremony finally arrived. The week of the wedding was warm, but pleasant.

All week long Eileen and Carrie worked diligently to finish Homer and Amanda's cake, devoting every spare moment to the task. It was a large confection and many hours had to be devoted to crafting the frosting decorations. Eileen was glad Katie was able to cover for her at the Farmer's Market today. Early in the afternoon the two girls delivered the cake to First Church while Mrs. Henderson watched the bakery for a while.

As they drove up to the church, Carrie noticed that the parking lot was full of cars. "Wow! Eileen, it looks like there's plenty of people already here!"

"Yes. Amanda said they'd be here several hours before rehearsal to decorate."

"Oh, good!" Carrie said. "We'll get a preview of the festivities."

Readily agreeing with Carrie's sentiments, Eileen pulled the van up to the door of the church kitchen. A lady from the First Church fellowship committee met them. She welcomed them in and showed them where the cake was to be set for the wedding.

As Carrie passed by the back of the sanctuary carrying one of the layers of the cake, she spotted Amanda directing some girls about how the pew decorations were to be done. Upon seeing that Carrie and Eileen had arrived, Amanda soon made her way to the fellowship hall. "Oh, the cake is just beautiful!" she exclaimed, showing her obvious delight at their workmanship.

By now Eileen had joined them, carrying the last layer to the beautifully adorned table where the cake was to be served. "How are you doing, Amanda?" Eileen asked as she carefully placed the last layer of cake on the table.

"Oh, I'm fine, just a little jittery though," she admitted. "Will you be here in time for rehearsal?" Amanda inquired nervously.

"Oh, yes!" Carrie answered. "Of course; we wouldn't think of being late!" she assured her friend.

"John Mark told me he's coming as soon as he can get away today," Eileen added.

"We want to get started by six-fifteen sharp so we'll have plenty of time for the dinner afterward," Amanda reminded Carrie.

"Fine, don't worry we'll be here," Carrie answered.

"I'll be back well before the wedding tomorrow to set the cake up for you," Eileen said. "I don't want to do it just now. There's too much chance of it getting knocked over by then. It'll be safer just like it is here, on the table in the boxes with the layers and pillars unassembled."

"That's fine and thank you for all your hard work. It's just like I wanted it to be," Amanda said, admiring the cakes. She gave Eileen and Carrie a quick hug of appreciation.

"Is your dress all set for tomorrow?" she asked Carrie.

"Yes, Amanda. I love it. I can't wait to wear it," Carrie replied exuberantly. The soft green color that Amanda had chosen for the wedding complimented Carrie's eyes and hair and was a lovely addition to her summer wardrobe. The girls had found dresses that they all liked at a bridal shop in Blue Creek.

"Well, if you'll excuse me, I've got a lot to do yet. I'll see you later," Amanda explained and hurried back to the decorating.

Luke had just come back from Farmer's Market by the time the girls reached Blooming Hills. As Carrie and Eileen got out of the car, another familiar vehicle was just pulling up the drive. It was the red pickup. John Mark was done with another day's hard work. He smiled and waved as he saw Carrie. Just then Luke came out of the main barn with his weekly check in hand. Knowing Carrie and

John Mark would probably want to talk a bit, he looked at Eileen and said, "Looks like I've got a few minutes. Can I get a tall, cold iced tea to go?"

"Sure!" she said with a chuckle as she opened the door to the bakery and Luke followed her inside.

As soon as he parked the truck, John Mark walked over to see Carrie. "Hi," he said as he strode up to meet her.

"Hi," she replied sweetly.

"How was your week?" he asked with a big smile.

"Really good!" she replied.

"I'll be over to pick you up for the rehearsal about a quarter to six if that's ok," he said.

"That's fine," she said, and glanced at her watch. "Oh, my! I didn't realize it's almost three thirty now!" she exclaimed. "I guess I better get Luke and hurry home or we'll never be ready in time."

"Ok," John Mark smiled. "I'm looking forward to being with you this evening. Maybe we'll get a chance to talk a while," he added quickly, reaching out to clasp her hand.

Carrie thought John Mark's smile looked especially bright today for some reason. He seemed to be in a very happy frame of mind—almost as though he knew some important or exciting news. Carrie wanted so much to ask him what had caused this spark of enthusiasm, but she decided to wait until this evening, hoping that there would be time to talk at length. Maybe his enthusiasm was due to Homer's wedding affording him the closest thing to a vacation that a farmer ever got in the summer, Carrie supposed. She knew he probably had secured the Thompson brothers to do this evening's chores and most likely tomorrow's also. They were good neighbors and very dependable at watching things over at the farm in Bixley when necessary.

"I'll see you in a few hours then?" he said as he squeezed her hand.

"I'll be ready," she smiled. At that John Mark turned back toward the house and Carrie opened the door of the bakery, motioning for Luke to hurry. He seemed to be enjoying a piece of pie as well as an iced tea. He had apparently said something quite entertaining since both Eileen and Mrs. Henderson were consumed with laughter as Luke scooped up his last bite of pie and waved them a goodbye, grabbling his iced tea on his way out.

Eileen managed a wave between giggles and Luke arrived at the door still grinning from the scene.

"We've got to hurry up, Luke," Carrie informed him. "It's getting late and we've got to get ready for rehearsal."

"Yeah, you're right. Let's get going," he said, and they hurried home.

When John Mark neared Blossom Lane, Carrie was just putting the last pins in her hair. She could see his pickup truck from her bay window as he pulled in the drive. She finished quickly and hurried downstairs to join the rest of the family. Her father had met John Mark at the door. They were talking as Carrie came down the stairs. John Mark's gaze turned toward her as soon as she was in view. When Pastor Brooks saw his daughter, he remarked, "I was just telling John Mark that Mrs. Brooks isn't quite ready yet, so why don't you two go on ahead of us. We'll be along in a few minutes."

"Ok, Dad," Carrie said, smiling as she descended the last few stair steps. With Dad helping to perform the ceremony and Luke and Carrie in the wedding party, all the Brooks' family had been invited to the rehearsal. Carrie knew it would be a fun evening with many friends present for the occasion.

John Mark offered Carrie his arm and together they walked to the door. He politely opened it for her as they stepped out onto the porch. "See you at the church, Pastor," he said to Carrie's father as he escorted her to the truck.

When they reached the truck, John Mark opened Carrie's door and helped her step up into the seat. "I'm sorry you have to ride in an old truck," he said with an apologetic smile. "I hope someday I'll get a car."

"I don't mind a bit," Carrie replied sincerely, for she was just so thrilled to be with him that it wouldn't have mattered if his only transportation had been a hay wagon! This was one of the few times so far in their courtship when they had had occasion to ride somewhere together and spend a few minutes alone visiting.

Carrie's parents genuinely trusted John Mark and had come to appreciate his sincerity and behavior since he had asked for permission to court their daughter. He had always kept Carrie's and the Brooks' best interests foremost, politely considering her family and never attempting to push the limits of any guidelines her parents set. Mom and Dad had come to trust this young man in a new and deeper way than ever before. They had always thought of him as an exemplary young Christian man, but now they had come to fully appreciate his many deep character qualities firsthand in the time they had spent with him the last few months.

"Well," John Mark began after he started the truck and pointed it down the drive, "It's just too bad I don't have a more comfortable vehicle for someone who's looking so nice," he said with a bit of his old shyness. "You do look very nice this evening, Carrie," he said again, emphasizing his compliment. Before anyone spoke again, Carrie heard the loving compliment over and over in her mind, "You do look very nice this evening, Carrie."

"He always makes me feel so special," she thought. "I remember one other time when he said the same thing and how it made me feel," she recalled. Her mind wandered back to that evening of the FCH Spring Banquet so long ago when he had said the same thing to her. She looked down at her dress and realized she was wearing the same dress tonight that she had worn that special evening! "He must like this dress on me," she thought and determined then and there to use the pattern for her wedding dress.

John Mark looked over at her and they exchanged smiles. No one spoke, but Carrie felt her heart skip a beat at the loving look in his eyes. Finally he broke the silence. "It's going to be a great evening, Carrie," he began. "I've looked forward to it all week."

"Me too," Carrie admitted, her cheeks rosy with color. She knew what he meant. While they had been spending a lot of time on the phone or with family over the past few months, there hadn't been a lot of opportunities for them to visit alone or be out as a couple among friends.

"I'm anxious to see old Homer," John Mark smiled. "It's been a week or so since I talked to him. He called me to give me some details on getting fitted for the tuxes and stuff and he was so nervous already then that he was nearly a basket case!"

"Really?" Carrie exclaimed. "Homer nervous? I can hardly imagine it!"

"I know, but he couldn't remember half the stuff he was trying to tell me!" he laughed. Carrie laughed and shook her head disbelievingly at the thought.

It was only minutes before they arrived at First Church and

as far as each of them was concerned, the ride was altogether too short. There never seemed to be enough time for all they'd like to say to each other. They longed for time together, knowing that someday it would be theirs.

The rehearsal went so well that it only lasted until seven, giving plenty of time for a leisurely dinner. Everyone left the church in a long caravan headed for Schenkel's restaurant in Blue Creek. Carrie was again grateful to have the opportunity to be alone with John Mark on the drive to the restaurant.

The quiet dinner was very relaxing and enjoyable. John Mark and Carrie were seated with the Brooks family and some others from the wedding party at a circular table nicely arrayed with a white tablecloth and candles. Everyone enjoyed pleasant conversation while they were served a delicious meal in the elegant surroundings. Carrie could rarely remember dining out at such a fine restaurant as Schenkel's. "This dinner must have cost the Martinsons a small fortune," she thought. With John Mark at her side, it was an evening to remember. He was so pleasant and easy to talk to. He seemed to be growing more at ease with the Brooks family each time they were together. Carrie noticed how well they all got along. Luke and John Mark were like brothers and Addy adored John Mark because he always took time to talk to her "as if I was all grown up," the little girl had once observed.

Carrie enjoyed seeing all the old gang of friends together once again. There was Homer and Amanda, Luke and John Mark, even Timothy Cox, for he too was to be an usher for the wedding.

When the dinner was over John Mark drove Carrie back to Blossom Lane and the Brooks family was close behind. Upon arriving at the farm, John Mark parked the truck and came around to open the door for Carrie. Politely he offered her his hand, helping her out of the truck. "It's a beautiful evening," John Mark said, looking up at the millions of stars in the late August sky.

"It is!" Carrie replied, genuinely. The entire week had been warm, but it had cooled just a bit today and the evening was not as sultry as the previous ones had been. The gentle breeze was welcome refreshment from the hot August days and carried the scent of new mown hay from some nearby field.

Carrie unfolded the lace shawl that was draped over her arm and seeing her do so, John Mark politely helped her place it around her shoulders. "It's just a bit cooler now that the sun's gone down," she commented as they started up the walk. Just then the headlights of the Brooks family vehicle pulled into the driveway. Within a moment Mom and Dad were getting out. Luke climbed out of the back seat but stooped back into the car to pick up a sleeping Addy and carry her to bed.

As Mom and Dad reached the sidewalk where John Mark and Carrie stood, Mom told them, "I guess this was a big evening for a little girl." Everyone chuckled as Luke carried his sister in the house.

Pastor Brooks placed his hand on John Mark's shoulder. "Why don't you stay awhile and visit, if you like? It's a nice evening and since you don't have the long drive to Bixley I thought you and Carrie might enjoy the chance to talk," he winked at them.

"Thank you, sir," John Mark replied and turning to Carrie he asked, "Would you mind if I stayed a while?"

"No, I'd like that. It would be very nice," she agreed as they all walked up to the pretty old porch.

"You two could visit in the parlor, but tonight it's just as pleasant out here," Dad suggested.

"Thanks, Daddy," Carrie said. "Maybe we will sit on the porch, if that's ok with you, John Mark," she quickly added.

"Fine by me," he said.

Dad opened the door and he and Mom stepped inside. John Mark and Carrie strolled slowly around the curve of the porch to where the swing hung by the front door. John Mark motioned for Carrie to be seated, and then joined her on the swing. Mom had gone to the parlor and switched on one of the old-fashioned hurricane lamps near the parlor window. Its gentle light cast a romantic glow through the lacey curtains and onto the porch. Carrie smiled to herself knowing her mother had probably done that on purpose to add a sweet, homey touch to their visit. She vowed to thank her later.

As they sat in silence, John Mark turned to Carrie and gave her one of his special smiles. Then he looked away again at the night sky and said, "Wasn't it great how happy Homer and Amanda looked tonight?"

"Yes it was," Carrie replied. She thought about how beautiful tomorrow's ceremony was going to be as she remembered the touching song Homer had sung to his bride as she walked down the aisle. The groomsmen were all standing at the front of the church as the bridesmaids filed down to meet them one by one. Carrie recalled the way John Mark had looked at her as she had walked down the aisle! The thought! She was almost lost in the memory as she gazed up dreamily at the stars.

"I wonder what time it is—maybe I better be going. I surely don't want to wear out my welcome," John Mark said after a while, breaking the silence.

"Oh, you couldn't ever do that," Carrie assured him as she pulled Great Grandma Haywood's watch from the pocket of her dress. "It's nine-thirty," she said as her eyes strained in the dim light to look at the delicate watch face.

"Thank you," he replied. "Say, I've noticed you wearing that watch before." Then he added, "Is it an antique?"

"Yes, actually it is," Carrie began. "Have I never told you about it?" She moved to unclasp it from its chain so John Mark might look at it when suddenly the chain broke letting the watch fall into her lap. "Oh, no!" she exclaimed in disappointment. "That chain has been loose for awhile now. I need to either replace it or quit wearing it, I guess," she said sadly and handed the watch to John Mark to inspect.

"It's very nice," he remarked as he ran his finger over the gold carving on its case. "How did you come to own it?" he inquired.

"Well, it's quite a story actually," Carrie started. "It belonged to my Great Grandmother Haywood, my mother's grandmother."

"Oh, really?" John Mark said as he attempted to re-attach the chain.

"It seems that one certain autumn long ago when Great Grandma was a young girl she was being courted by a man named Josiah Haywood." Carrie looked shyly at John Mark. "He was a farmer," she supplied with a knowing smile that John Mark promptly returned.

"Well, it seems that Josiah had asked Great Grandma to marry him," Carrie said. Her face began to color a bit as she remembered the significance of the story. She was glad that in the near darkness John Mark probably hadn't noticed that she was blushing.

She wondered if he would recognize the similarity to their situation. As she resumed the story, she spoke slowly and John Mark could hear a hint of emotion in her voice as she re-told the touching account. "But her father, my great, great grandpa, wouldn't let them get married until Mr. Haywood could bring in some good profitable crops and prove he had a little nest egg built up." She stopped and looked at John Mark in an attempt to assess his reaction but he was still looking down at the watch, inspecting its every detail while he listened to the story.

"So after Josiah got all the crops in that year, he went to town and put money in the bank and bought this watch for her because it had not only been a good year, but a very good year," she emphasized. "He promptly went to call at Great Grandma's house and gave her father the report of his finances, asking permission to present her with this gift and marry her."

John Mark was still listening as he turned the watch over in his strong, work-calloused hands. As he continued to work with the chain, trying to re-attach it, he asked, "So, what happened then?"

"Well," Carrie began, "I guess her father thought he must have been quite successful to have afforded such a gift, and he agreed to let them marry. They were married soon after," Carrie said softly. "Mom inherited the watch and now she lets me wear it for special occasions. Someday it will be mine to keep," she added.

John Mark's face was alight with the old familiar smile; he laughed softly and shook his head. "Is something funny?" Carrie asked, her sentimental voice changing to a questioning tone.

"No," he replied, thoughtfully, "I was just thinking how some things don't change, even in several generations." He looked intently at her with a deep, contented gaze. "It's a very moving story," he said, now more seriously. "It reminds me of some other people I know. And speaking of special occasions…" he began. "I couldn't help wishing it was our wedding today," he said quietly. "Carrie, when I drove in from Bixley today, I went into Blue Creek and stopped at the hardware to speak with your Dad before I came to Blooming Hills. I gave him an update on the farm and got his opinion on a few things," he paused. "I asked his permission to talk to you about setting a date for our wedding. That is…" he hastily added, "…if you're ready. I mean… if you still agree to marry me." He seemed to fumble for the right words to express himself.

"Still agree?" Carrie asked in surprise. "Did you ever think I didn't want to marry you?" she queried.

"I don't know. I guess not," John Mark conceded, "At least, I hoped not. I told your father that I considered this courtship as a time to prove my love to you. I never thought of it as dating or a test or trial or whatever. I've been committed to making you my wife from the start." He stopped to gather his thoughts before finishing. "I was just allowing time for the farm to get one more good season; like your great grandfather… and for you to be sure you were ready to marry me," he added.

Carrie searched John Mark's face through the near darkness as she waited for him to go on, "And now, that brings me to another point." With this he paused again and then continued to speak, trying to carefully express what was in his heart. "I was just totaling some numbers from the crops to date yesterday, and well, let's just say the farm's output has already exceeded last year and the apples and grapes haven't even ripened yet." Carrie smiled at the thought of answered prayer. "Like Josiah Haywood's crops, I guess," John Mark said proudly. He looked more confident now as he reached out and gently placed the watch in the palm of Carrie's hand. He closed her fingers around the heirloom, lovingly circling her delicate fingers with his strong hand.

"Your father said I should ask you about a date whenever I wanted. I think the farm has proven itself and there's nothing standing in the way of our setting a wedding date now if you agree," John Mark said, looking down at their hands that together clasped the watch.

"I very much agree and I'm happy to set a date for our wedding, John Mark," she emphasized his name in a near whisper, although she felt as if her heart were shouting the words with joy.

John Mark smiled widely and sat silently for a few moments, rocking the swing slowly back and forth with his foot. Then he turned to Carrie and reached for her other hand and held it in his. "Come to think of it," he said, "there's something I've never said to you." He paused a moment and looked directly into her eyes, "Carrie…I love you. Will you marry me?"

Carrie felt as if she would nearly burst with happiness at this declaration. She had longed to hear the sound of John Mark's voice speaking the words she knew were true, yet she had waited so long to hear. And now it was happening! The moment had come; the words of the man she would spend her life with danced softly on the evening air. She felt as if time were standing still. The memory of this moment would live forever in her thoughts. "How wonderful he is; how romantic this experience of courtship has been!" she thought. But even amidst the overwhelming emotion of the moment, she finally found her voice and replied, "Yes! Yes, John Mark, I will marry you! I love you too."

They sat quietly for some time gently swinging in the old swing, its rhythmic creaking joining in with the night sounds of crickets, the silence between them being conversation enough.

"I guess I better be going," John Mark said after a while. "It's a big day tomorrow," he reminded her.

"I guess you're right," Carrie reluctantly agreed.

"Will you think about a date?" he asked.

"I will," Carrie assured him.

"We'll talk again tomorrow," he said as he rose to leave. He held out his arm and escorted her to the front door. "I'll see you tomorrow," he told her and stepped down from the porch. Carrie waved at him through the darkness as he walked across the lawn. As she slipped inside the screen door, she leaned dreamily against the door frame and watched the lights of his truck finally disappear down the road.

Wedding Days

Homer and Amanda's wedding had been "absolutely dreamy" in Eileen's words. Carrie floated through the day as if she were on a cloud, as if it were her own wedding day. Knowing she and John Mark were to be married soon, she was happily memorizing all the details of every romantic moment, mentally filing them for the task of planning their own special day.

At the end of the afternoon, Carrie and John Mark, Eileen, Luke, and a host of friends and family prayed together in a large circle in the First Church parking lot as Homer and Amanda—the happy couple—prepared to leave for Canada. Everyone cheered and showered them with birdseed as they drove away in Homer's car now decorated with tin cans, streamers, and signs by a group of fun-loving friends.

Such a beautiful day it had been. Eileen caught up with Carrie as the crowd was dispersing. John Mark, Trent, and Luke were talking with some other guys in the parking lot so the girls had a few moments alone before leaving. Eileen linked arms with her old friend and sighed dreamily, "Did you ever experience anything like it—the wedding, I mean? I've never seen such beautiful flowers all in one place!"

"I know," Carrie sincerely agreed.

"And the church! How the sun streamed through those stained glass windows! Did you notice how a ray of sunlight seemed to shine down on them just as Steve pronounced them man and wife? It was as if God's blessing was pouring down to earth just for them!" Eileen exclaimed romantically. "I certainly hope the photographer was able to capture that!"

Carrie smiled at Eileen's vivid assessment of the ceremony. "But everyone said that the flowers were just from the gardens of a few friends," Carrie reminded Eileen.

"Oh, but the way they were arranged!" Eileen gushed dramatically. "Oh, and Carrie, didn't you just want to melt inside when Amanda came down the aisle to Homer's beautiful solo?"

"I admit I shed a tear or two there," Carrie replied as both of them smiled at the memory.

"Oh, Carrie," Eileen exclaimed as they walked through the pretty First Church gardens, "I just love weddings!"

Carrie smiled at her enthusiastic friend as they sat down on a nearby bench. "I hope someday I'll get married and have a beautiful wedding!" Eileen said, gazing wistfully at the clouds. "And it'll be a day just like this—sunny, pleasant, full of flowers and blue skies," she described poetically. "And the groom...I can almost see him," she said, closing her eyes and lowering her voice to a near whisper. "He'll be incredibly handsome and wear a dashing suit and sing to me as I walk down the aisle in my gorgeous gown, a long train of filmy lace stretching out yards behind me!" Her voice trailed off and she turned back to look at Carrie who was smiling at her friend.

Carrie now replied in a practical tone, "Of course we all want to have beautiful occasions in life. But, Eileen, let's face it; on some people's wedding days it rains or snows and well...life just isn't always perfect." Eileen still looked dreamily out over the flowers in the little garden area as Carrie went on. "Let me give you some loving advice," Carrie said sincerely. "Don't waste precious time daydreaming too much," she counseled gently. "I had a tendency to do that at one point in my life. Then God showed me that my thoughts needed to be focused on Him instead of building dream castles. It's alright to hope for a nice life, but I found that when I turned my life completely over to God, He added all things to me, just as the scripture verse says."

Eileen looked at her friend with a rather puzzled look. "I mean if you pray and seek God, you'll be in a position to hear Him when He speaks to you," Carrie explained. "If God's plan for you includes marriage, then that's wonderful! Seek God and He will reveal to you and your folks when and if the time is right. But if you spend all your time dreaming and you don't seek God, you may build such an ideal image of the perfect man, that you'll miss God's choice for you when he does come along. Because, after all, no one's perfect."

"I think I see what you mean, Carrie," Eileen replied reflectively. "You're always so wise," she commented.

"Well, I don't know about that!" Carrie laughed.

"But come on now; tell me the truth," Eileen begged, "Didn't you dream of the perfect wedding day—and the perfect groom?" she teased.

"Well, yes, I have to admit I did. But I also will tell you that I became very convicted of what I just told you—that I should seek God first with my whole heart and allow Him to plan my future. I struggled with that for a long time but it seemed like almost as soon as I really decided to trust God with my future, the future was here!" Carrie smiled at the thought. "Really, Eileen, that's just the way it was. I'm not trying to say if you seek God that the very next day you'll find yourself in a courtship. God may have very different plans for you. But regardless, we all should seek the Lord and His will above all things."

Eileen sat silently pondering Carrie's words until they both saw Luke and John Mark heading toward them. "Speaking of the future and the perfect man for someone—here he comes now," Eileen teased. "So I guess our little talk is over. But thank you for the advice. I'll will try to seek the Lord more diligently," she promised sincerely as the boys neared the bench where they sat.

"Everyone's leaving, " John Mark announced as he approached, "Are you about ready to head for home?" he asked Carrie.

"Yes, it's been a wonderful, but long day," she admitted.

"I agree," Eileen said, standing to her feet. "I need to find Mom and Dad. They're probably ready to head home too. See you later… and thanks," she said to Carrie and walked back toward the church where a few families still stood visiting.

"I'm going to help put chairs and tables away," Luke told Carrie. "Trent's bringing me home. Mom and Dad left a few minutes ago and said for you to ride home with Mr. Henderson here," he said with a wink as he slapped John Mark on the shoulder, following Eileen back toward the fellowship hall.

As they stood alone in the churchyard, John Mark said to Carrie, "Are you too tired for a visit later—say toward evening?"

"Never!" she replied.

"Good. I thought I'd take you home and then I'll go back to Blooming Hills, catch a nap, and come back to your house later on and we can talk—maybe take a walk before sunset."

"Sounds nice," Carrie agreed as John Mark held out his arm to escort her to his truck.

A few minutes later they arrived at Blossom Lane. After seeing her into the house and excusing himself until later in the afternoon, John Mark left. Carrie decided to try to take a nap, but she found it difficult to sleep. She tossed and turned on her bed as she thought about possible wedding dates that John Mark was sure to want to discuss. She finally got up, deciding her time would be better spent making a fresh batch of brownies to serve for John Mark's visit this evening.

A short time later as she set the pan of brownies out in the back room to cool, from the window she saw the familiar red truck pull into the drive. She watched John Mark's tall frame sauntering up the walk. She opened the back door to greet him.

"Hi," he said tenderly.

"Hi, John Mark, did you find some time to rest this afternoon?" she asked as he reached the porch steps.

"I did get a bit of a nap," he said, "but I found it hard to sleep; so I read my Bible a while and decided to come on over. I hope I'm not too early," he added.

"No, not at all. I know what you mean about the nap," Carrie admitted. "I guess I wasn't as tired as I thought I was either, so I got up and made brownies. I thought we could have a snack later."

"Sounds good," John Mark agreed heartily.

They talked a while, leaning against the back porch rail. Then John Mark asked, "Shall we take a little walk before the sun goes down?"

"That's a nice idea," Carrie agreed as she looked up at the sky. The sun was lowering on the horizon as the day swiftly waned. It was a beautiful, peaceful time of evening to enjoy a leisurely walk around the farm. "Let's tell my parents where we're going," Carrie suggested. The two walked into the living room where Mom and Dad sat relaxing.

"Hi, John Mart!" Addy squealed, leaving her toys behind and running up to him.

"Hi, honey," he said. He reached into the pocket of his jeans and pulled out a handful of peppermints.

"Thank you," she said sweetly as she accepted the gift.

"Pastor Brooks, Mrs. Brooks," John Mark said, politely, "Carrie and I would like to take a short walk before sunset, if you don't mind. We wanted to let you know where we were going."

"Sure, go right ahead," Dad said, folding up the paper he'd been reading.

"Maybe we'll have some popcorn and sandwiches when you get back," Mom suggested.

"Hey, didn't I smell something baking out in the kitchen too?" Dad asked.

"Yes, I made some brownies for later," Carrie smiled.

"Hope there's some left for you when you get back, John Mark," Luke teased from the couch where he had been relaxing amidst several books he'd been reading.

"There better be!" John Mark teased back as they turned to leave.

"Let me get a shawl," Carrie said to him as she opened the door to the hall closet.

In a few minutes they were outside, strolling slowly along the pasture lane. Blossom Lane was such a beautiful place in the late summer.

"It was really hot last week with some of the farm work," John Mark commented.

"It is nicer now, isn't it?" Carrie said as she stopped and leaned against the pasture fence. "There's a hint of fall in the air today though," she said, pulling the shawl around her shoulders. The evening was becoming cooler as the sun sunk lower and lower.

"There sure is a hint of fall," John Mark agreed. "To everything there is a season…" he said, smiling. They looked out over the fields at Blossom, the milk cow who now plodded instinctively toward the barn. "That's an especially meaningful verse for a farmer," John Mark pondered thoughtfully. "I'm glad we're getting a chance to talk some today. I'm going to head home right after church tomorrow. So I won't be able to spend any time with you tomorrow afternoon." Carrie looked slightly disappointed. "I'm sorry, believe me, but I've been gone long enough considering we're in the middle of the peach harvest right now. I've got Abel and Cyrus doing my chores and looking after things and I think it's best if I get back a little earlier than usual."

"I understand," Carrie replied sympathetically.

Carrie knew that John Mark was thankful to have the Thompson brothers, his closest neighbors to depend on to do chores when he had to be away. The two elderly bachelor brothers had befriended him the first season he bought the farm. The last living siblings in their family of eight, Abel and Cyrus lived alone on their family farm and were glad to lend a helping hand. But Carrie also knew that John Mark was careful not to take advantage of their generosity and understandably felt the need to return home before too late on Sunday.

"You know that verse I just mentioned...'to everything there is a season,'?"

"Yes," she replied.

"Well, there's another part of that section of scripture too. 'There is a time for marrying and giving in marriage,'" he quoted decisively.

Carrie looked straight ahead at John Mark as he spoke. She felt her heart leap at the mention of the subject.

"Carrie, you know what we discussed last night?"

"Yes, I remember," she replied, lowering her eyes.

"Well, I know it isn't much time, but have you prayed about it or thought about it at all?" he asked.

"Yes, I have," she said, with a note of excitement in her voice.

He kept looking at her but didn't speak. Finally he asked, "Well, what do you think?"

"Well," Carrie began, "you know May has always been my favorite month. I think the weather's so pretty and maybe Homer and Amanda could be back by then too..." Carrie announced enthusiastically. But when she stopped to look up at John Mark, she saw the look of disappointment on his face. He was very considerately trying to hide it, but having known him for some time, she instantly detected the hint of sadness in his eyes.

"You want to wait that long?" he questioned gently.

Her heart melted as she realized she had been inconsiderate, pushing her plans ahead of his. After all he had worked so hard to fix the house up and to make the farm run on a profit basis and now she was asking him to wait several more months just to fulfill her "dream castles!" She felt a bit of conviction as she remembered her own advice to Eileen earlier that day. She put herself in John Mark's place alone way over in Bixley for another long winter and then replied sincerely, "But, then, if you have another suggestion, I'm open to it. I'm certainly ready whenever you think it's the best time."

A look of joy returned to his eyes, and he said, "Thank you, Carrie." He was silent a moment as if what he was about to say next deserved careful thought. "I was really hoping it wouldn't be too soon for you if we considered December," he began. "By then I can have all the outdoor work and the book work from the crops done and maybe even get a few more things done around the house. "I really was dreading spending another long winter over there…alone. And winter really is the best time for a farmer to take a little time off." Carrie nodded, for she well knew the rigors of summer and fall with the Hendersons' large orchard operation. "I understand what you mean about May and the nice weather and all, but I'm afraid it would be really difficult at that time of year," John Mark explained. "We couldn't take any time off for a little wedding trip or anything right in the middle of preparation for strawberry season," he added.

"You're right," Carrie said genuinely. "I wasn't being very practical."

"I hope you're not disappointed," John Mark said tenderly.

"I'm not disappointed at all!" she said, smiling up into his eyes. "Looking forward to being with you could never be disappointing."

"We could always celebrate our anniversary in May," he offered with a twinkle in his eyes. "After all that time of year always reminds me of something very special," he said.

"Oh, what's that?" Carrie asked.

"Well, a long time ago I remember one particular Sunday in May when I watched you and Eileen walking around the church-yard after service. We were pretty young then, but that was the day when I first felt in my heart that someday I'd marry you. I've been praying for you ever since. Those white flowers you love so much were in bloom and you had your arms full of them," he smiled, remembering. "You looked so pretty," he added quietly. Carrie's eyes misted with happy tears. "I'll always remember the way you looked that day; and next year when those flowers bloom around our front porch, I won't have to pray anymore about that—you'll be my wife," he said with a note of emotion in his voice.

An Unbroken Chain

Long-awaited December finally arrived, though more slowly than Carrie and John Mark would have preferred. Eileen was the only one who had appeared shocked when learning of the December wedding date. "How on earth do you expect us to get everything ready in time?" she had protested excitedly, as if she was solely responsible for every detail. "Why! That's only three months away! What about the reception, what about the flowers? It's right after harvest!" she reminded them. "Don't you want a beautiful spring wedding?" she had pleaded.

After she saw that John Mark and Carrie were resolved to hold to their plans, she began to redirect her excited thoughts to the details of a reception and anything else Carrie would allow her to help with. She plunged into the planning as if the wedding was her own. John Mark and Carrie assured her that they really were only interested in a simple ceremony and that she shouldn't exhaust herself with endless planning. However, the energetic and well-meaning Eileen soon convinced them that this was not just an everyday occasion, but it was their special day. Finally they were persuaded to allow Eileen to fuss a bit over the preparations and details. "After all," Eileen said, "This is not just any wedding. This is the wedding of my brother and my best friend!"

Carrie helped Eileen plan a nice reception to be held at Blooming Hills Banquet rooms. Next Eileen began designing ideas for a lovely cake. Carrie spent most of her free time making curtains for the farm house, sewing new clothes to start married life with, or accompanying Mom and various of the Henderson ladies on trips to Bixley. The women spent endless hours scrubbing and painting, papering and furnishing the rooms of John Mark's house as he finished them one by one with whatever repairs were needed.

Finally the week of the wedding was upon the two families. Carrie had spent much of the last few days working on the details of her wedding dress while John Mark had been finishing the final work on the house. Early in the afternoon on Tuesday, he called the Brooks' farm and Carrie answered. "Hello!" he said with loving excitement, upon recognizing her voice.

"Hi, John Mark," she answered, her smile sounding in her tone.

"Believe it or not, I actually think I'm done with everything around here!" he announced proudly. "So, I was wondering if Luke would have time to help load up some of your things so I can move them in over here.... that is if you have anything packed up and ready to go. I could get Tommy to help if he can't do it."

"No, don't bother Tommy, I'm sure Luke's going to be here and that could be arranged," Carrie said sweetly.

"Well, I figure it's the best day to do it," John Mark said. "Because I thought I'd spend the night at home...uh, that is at Blooming Hills...on Thursday, so I wouldn't have to rush around for the rehearsal on Friday."

"Good idea," Carrie agreed.

"I'll bring the truck over in a few hours if that's not too soon," he suggested.

"That'll be fine," Carrie assured him.

"Sweetheart..." he said after a pause.

"Yes?" she answered, nearly swept off her feet at this term of endearment with which he had just gently addressed her for the first time.

"I hope we can find a few minutes alone sometime before Friday...to talk a little. I've missed you so. It feels like I haven't really spent any time with you for days," he said, referring to the fact that they had both been working diligently, whether it was on details for the upcoming wedding or doing work on their house.

"Why don't you plan on eating supper with us this evening when you get here?" Carrie suggested.

"That's really sounds good," he said, "But actually I was wondering if maybe we...just the two of us, that is... could eat at the

Italian restaurant in Maplecrest. I know your family will only have you there at home for a few more days but do you think they'd let me borrow you for the evening?"

"I think they would," Carrie said, "And that really sounds nice. I've been bent over my sewing for hours and it might be good to get out and think of something else for awhile," she determined. "I'll say something to Mom and Dad."

"Well, Carrie, let me say something to your father when I get there to pick up your stuff. Then if for some reason they'd rather we didn't go, I'll plan on staying for supper with your family, ok?"

"Ok, that's probably a good plan," she agreed. She was thankful for John Mark's chivalrous behavior. He had always gone the extra mile to behave as a gentleman where Carrie and her family were concerned.

"Have whatever you want me to bring over here to Bixley ready and Luke and I can load it up before supper."

"I will," she promised.

"Carrie…" he said slowly, "I'm really looking forward to seeing you this afternoon, whether we go out to eat or just visit at your place," he said with the familiar loving tone he seemed to lately reserve for the only the most special things he wished to communicate to her.

"Me too," she said softly.

Carrie put the final details of handwork on her wedding dress after she hung up the phone from John Mark's call. Hearing his voice gave new vigor to her sewing and she thought of him and the wedding with every tiny stitch.

She breathed a sigh of relief and delight at her accomplishment a short time later when she carefully hung the dress on her closet door. She tried it on with her mother's excited assistance and together they stood admiring the dress in front of the long mirror in Carrie's room. "It's very beautiful!" Mom said, her eyes glistening. "John Mark will be so pleased," she smiled at her daughter.

"Oh, do you really think so, Mom?" Carrie asked hopefully as she ran her hands over the delicate fabric, smoothing the soft gathers of the skirt. True to her idea, she had fashioned her wedding dress from the same pattern that her spring banquet dress had been made from so long ago. A few fancier embellishments and special details had turned it into an exquisite wedding gown. "Do you really think he'll like it?" she implored.

"I know he will," her mother replied. "He adores you. Dad and I can tell how much he loves you by the way he speaks to you and how he looks at you," she told Carrie happily. "We're both so pleased for you and how God has worked everything out."

The two women were silent a moment as Carrie stared into the mirror. "Mom," she said seriously, "thank you for the standards you set. Thank you…you and Daddy both for training me to pray for God's will and to wait for a courtship and not settle for the world's way of romance."

"That's quite all right, dear," Mom replied. "Actually don't thank us. Thank God for revealing His plans to us." She finished her statement by giving Carrie a loving hug.

"Mom, let's get the watch and pin it on the dress to see what it's going to look like," Carrie suggested with a hint of anticipation in her voice.

"I think we better wait 'til Saturday morning," Mom advised. Carrie gave her mother a questioning look. "This dress fabric is so fine, let's not put the pin in and out more than necessary. It may weigh on the material and cause a tear."

"I guess you're right, Mom," Carrie agreed as she touched the delicate voile and netting at the neckline of the dress. She put the pretty, old-fashioned dress back on its hanger and gently adjusted it to hang just perfectly. She zipped the garment bag shut to protect the dress until Saturday. She then set about getting ready for John Mark to arrive. Carrie searched her closet for just the right dress for this evening. She knew John Mark especially liked the one she had worn to the banquet so long ago, but since it was the same pattern as the wedding dress and the fabric was too lightweight for this weather, she decided a different choice would be better. Knowing that he meant this to be a rather special evening she pondered the choices of wardrobe for a long while. "I don't want to be too fancy if for some reason Mom and Dad would rather we stayed here for supper. Yet I want to really look special," she reasoned. "But I'm pretty sure the restaurant is very elegant and formal," she reminded herself.

Suddenly her eyes fell on one dress she had not worn much, a dress she had recently finished sewing for winter. It was plain, dark gray velveteen with princess lines from the bodice to the hem. Even though the dress was quite simple in fabric and pattern, Carrie had dressed up its high-necked, button-down front with decorative metal buttons. She had constructed the dark colored dress with the idea of wearing her white lace shawl with it. It was a perfect contrast to show off the intricately patterned lace wrap. "This one's perfect!" she realized as she lifted the hanger from the back of the closet. "I can dress it up with the shawl if we go to the restaurant or wear it plain if we stay here!" She chose her black, lace-up dress boots to wear with it, satisfied that the outfit was complete and very appropriate for the occasion.

When John Mark pulled in the drive a short time later, she saw him from her bay window. Dad and Luke were out in the yard and seeing John Mark approach her father, Carrie decided not to head downstairs just yet. She knew he would be asking permission to take her to dinner in town. So she busied herself packing a few more of her things in a box that Mom had brought up for her, getting them ready to go to Bixley.

The last item she packed was the Double Wedding Ring quilt that she and her mother had pieced for her hope chest. She folded it carefully and tucked it into her cedar chest that would be going to Bixley tonight. As she folded it she thought of all it represented—the years of pretty dresses and special occasions, the evenings spent with Mom bent over the quilting frame sharing their hopes and dreams. She remembered the evening it had sat in the parlor corner, the object of her concerned gaze—the same evening she had learned that someone had asked for her hand in marriage. She remembered her nervous feelings as she had waited for her father to reveal the identity of the man who was declaring his love for her. How suddenly her whole life had changed with Dad's few words, "John Mark Henderson has asked for your hand in marriage." The memory of that evening still sent tremors of thrilling excitement through her whole being every time she thought about it.

As she looked around her room, she noticed it was beginning to seem rather empty. Her chair had been carried downstairs earlier and some of her clothes were gone from the closet and drawers. Many of her knickknacks, books, and pictures were packed away as well with only a few items left here and there. Bittersweet feelings washed over her as she looked around. This pretty room she had loved so much was all her own for only a few more days. But then she remembered that she had enjoyed it for several years and the Lord had graciously blessed her with a 'hope and a future' just as the scriptures promised, a bright and exciting future in a home of her own!

When she finally heard Dad and Luke and John Mark come in, she made her way downstairs. John Mark greeted her politely as she entered the room, but with a look of adoration that he didn't try to hide.

"We thought we'd load your things on the truck right now. It'll be easier than doing it later since it gets dark so early," Dad said to her. She felt a bit of disappointment at her father's words, for he must not have wanted them to go to dinner tonight for some reason after all. Otherwise he wouldn't be suggesting loading the things now. He wouldn't expect them to drive around Maplecrest with her furniture in the back of John Mark's truck.

"May we go up and get whatever boxes you've got ready now so you and John Mark can have the whole evening to visit? He'd like to take you to Maplecrest for dinner," Dad said with a wink.

At this, Carrie's happy smile returned and her father went on, "I suggested to John Mark that you two take our van. You don't want to drive around with a load of boxes and furniture."

"Thanks, Daddy," Carrie said sweetly as the three made their way up the stairs.

After everything was carefully loaded, John Mark tucked a protective tarp over the items and backed his truck into one of the barns. He pulled the Brooks' family van up to the drive and stepped inside the kitchen to escort Carrie to the car. "We'll be back early, sir," John Mark said to Pastor Brooks. "I expect that we'll not be much later than nine," he said conscientiously, glancing at his watch.

"We'll get the rest of Carrie's things over to Bixley on another truck load sometime this week," Dad thought to assure John Mark.

"Thank you, sir," he replied, "But I'll try to come over again for another load; I don't want you to have to make the trip."

"That's fine, John Mark, its no problem. You two have enough to do in the next few days. Let us take care of some details for you. Now you two take your time tonight. Eat a leisurely dinner and enjoy yourselves. And don't worry about the time. We trust you," Dad assured him. "We wouldn't have agreed to let you marry our daughter if we didn't," he winked. "The rest of this week will be pretty hectic for you two," he wisely reminded them.

"Thank you," John Mark replied with a smile.

"Have a nice time," Mom said as she helped Carrie adjust the lace shawl around her shoulders. John Mark held her coat, helping her slip it on just before leaving.

"Bye Mom, Dad," Carrie said and they were off into the chilly evening.

———————

Carrie could only remember being at this particular restaurant once before and it had been so long ago that she couldn't recall much about it. When she and John Mark stepped inside the door, she was delighted with the nice atmosphere.

"Dad brought us all here last year for Mom's birthday," John Mark whispered as the hostess approached. "I thought right then that someday I'd like to bring you here."

"Good evening," the hostess greeted them pleasantly.

"Good evening," they echoed.

"We'd like a table for two, please," John Mark requested. "Do you have a booth—somewhat private?" he asked. Carrie smiled to herself at John Mark's request.

"Just a moment, I'll check," the lady offered. Carrie could see her consulting with the head waiter. Soon she was back and said with a smile, "Right this way, please." She led Carrie and John Mark to a secluded corner table in a little booth. There were only a few other diners in the large room, but none were sitting close to the far corner, offering the two a bit of privacy. Overall the room was dimly lit, but a friendly, glowing fire crackled warmly from a stone fireplace on one end of the room, sending gentle light dancing across the tables.

The hostess left two menus as she lit the little candle at the center of the table. "The waitress will be with you in a few minutes. Can I get you anything else?" she asked politely.

John Mark looked at Carrie who said, "No, thank you," to the hostess.

"This place is very nice," Carrie remarked in an awed tone of voice.

"I thought you'd like it," he beamed. "Now, order anything you want," he instructed as he opened his menu. "I'm pretty sure I want their lasagna—that's what I had last time and it was really good."

"Oh, I wouldn't know what to order," Carrie confessed. "It all sounds so delicious. But I'm afraid I couldn't eat a large portion of anything—I'm so excited! I've never been to such a fine restaurant more than a few times in my whole life! Most of the time we've gone to the buffet restaurants in Blue Creek, or the eating places at Farmer's Market," she said with a smile. John Mark just smiled and continued to look at the menu, glad he had thought of treating her to a very elegant evening.

"I'm kind of excited too," he admitted, smiling his familiar sideways smile. "But not about the restaurant. I'm glad to be spending time with you. However, I still think I can eat," he added mischievously. "So I'm going to order the lasagna with a salad and they always bring all the French bread you can eat," he said as he folded the menu and placed it on the table. "Now what would you like?" he asked.

"Oh, I still don't know," Carrie said, studying the menu. "Maybe a small order of spaghetti," she finally decided. Then considering the difficulty of eating spaghetti delicately, she reconsidered her decision. "Maybe I'll get lasagna too, if you say it's really good."

"Whatever you like," John Mark assured her.

Soon the waitress came and took their orders. While they waited for their food, they found time to talk. "When I take your things back to the house tonight; I'll just set the boxes in the living room," John Mark was saying. "You can unpack them later. Is that all right?"

"Sure, that's fine with me. Are you sure those boxes won't be in your way?" Carrie asked thoughtfully.

"No," John Mark laughed. "You know how bare that house has been for so long. I like the way it's filling up now. The changes you've made are great. It's finally starting to feel like a real home," he said.

"I'm just sorry I won't be able to make it over there to help you put all the stuff away," Carrie apologized. "It seems like you're having to do a lot of the work. But this week is so busy; I just don't know how I could manage. Maybe Thursday..."

"No, don't even worry about it," John Mark interrupted. "Just keeping Eileen calmed down is a job in itself!" They both laughed at the thought of the energetic Eileen who was absolutely absorbed in the wedding plans and loving every minute of it.

"It's best if you see to the details of the wedding and I'll do the moving. You've got enough to do. I'm not much help planning weddings anyway so this gives me something to keep busy with while I wait," he smiled.

"Well, I just sometimes think I ought to be over there getting everything set up and home-like for us," Carrie lamented.

"There'll be plenty of time for that," he assured her. "Carrie...it'll really feel like home when you're there to stay," he said, looking at her with the nicest smile she had ever remembered seeing from him.

"Thank you," she said.

"Only four days," he winked from across the table. "Only four days and you'll be my wife!" he repeated emphatically. "Sometimes I can hardly believe it! I'm so thankful to God for bringing us together. I can't imagine life without you," he said to her.

The happy conversation continued even after the delicious food was served. Carrie was still too excited to really have an appetite but she politely ate as much of her dinner as she could. When they were finished the waitress came to take their dessert orders.

"Nothing for me, thank you," Carrie answered honestly.

"Are you sure?" John Mark asked her.

"Oh, I'm already too full. I really can't order dessert, but you go ahead," she urged him.

"They have a delicious cheesecake here," John Mark said, trying to convince her.

"Maybe I'll just eat a few bites of yours if you don't mind sharing," she finally conceded.

"Ok," he said. "I'll have a slice of cheesecake, please," he told the waitress.

John Mark really seemed to be enjoying his food tonight and this romantic evening at a fine restaurant hadn't hurt his appetite at all, Carrie observed. Then she remembered that he hadn't been home to Blooming Hills for at least a week and had probably once again fallen victim to his own cooking! After he took the last bite of cheesecake he pushed the dessert plate aside and said, "Carrie, do you make cheesecake?"

"Yes, I have occasionally, but I dare say it's not as good as this one was," she replied.

"Good, I'm glad to hear you make it and I'll bet it's even better than this," he said with a satisfied air. "Of course, I do know you make cherry pie," he teased. Carrie laughed at his expression, remembering with satisfaction how he had enjoyed the pie she had made to take to the farm last spring. With his next words, his tone changed to a more serious one but still with a shy yet mysterious smile he said, "Carrie, there's something I've always wanted to give you." Carrie looked across the table, waiting for him to explain. Instead of speaking he reached into the inner pocket of his jacket and drew out a piece of folded paper that Carrie instantly recognized as one of the weekly bulletins from church. Holding it out across the table, he smiled a loving smile that still conveyed a bit of teasing suspense.

Carrie gently reached for the bulletin. "What's this?" she asked curiously.

"Well, do you remember one Sunday morning a long time ago when me and Kirk Davis were greeters?" Carrie instantly smiled, remembering the day John Mark was referring to. How could she forget? The situation that had transpired that day was one of the first times she had noticed John Mark's polite thoughtfulness. She nodded her head in answer.

"Well, apparently we were both a bit taken by your charms," he grinned. "I remember wanting to be the one to give you the bulletin but I could see you were embarrassed."

As Carrie looked down at the paper in her hands she felt some sentimental tears well up in her eyes. She thought of the crippling shyness that she had struggled with for so many years and remembered how John Mark's thoughtfulness that day had rescued her.

"Maybe you think this is kind of dumb," John Mark said, rather awkwardly, referring to the bulletin.

"No, not at all," Carrie replied in a soft voice. "The way you behaved during that little incident that day made me realize you were someone very special. I remember it well," she assured him.

For a long, silent moment she held the bulletin in her hand, gazing at it. John Mark reached out and touched her hand, suggesting, "Well, why don't you open it and read it?"

Carrie looked up at him somewhat questioningly but obeying his directive she slowly opened the paper. John Mark watched her face as she began to read. Slowly a smile pulled at the corners of her mouth while a few tears that had made their way to her eyes moments ago slipped to her cheeks.

It took Carrie a few moments to read what John Mark had circled on the letters of the sentences in the bulletin. A flood of memories washed over her as she realized once and for all that the note she had found so many years ago must truly have been from John Mark Henderson. Remembering the excitement she had felt that night when that first note had slipped from the pages of her Spanish book, she now searched this paper with equal anticipation. As she began to read the message, she pondered how to ask him about the old note. Did he realize she had seen it? He must! But... maybe not! Should she even mention it? With a heart full of love and happy memories and their wedding only days away, she decided to share the many questions that now raced through her mind. Stopping her reading midstream, she looked up and spoke slowly.

"John Mark, there's something I've always wanted to ask you," she began.

"What's that?" he said with a hint of surprise in his voice.

"A long time ago, I found a note that looked a lot like this one," she looked up at him now. Still looking a bit confused, he listened as she explained. While she recounted the story of the other note, explaining to him that she was never completely sure of the identity of the author, his expression changed to one of understanding mixed with a little embarrassment.

"I guess I have some explaining to do," he smiled shyly. "I did write that note and to tell you the truth, I had forgotten it until you mentioned it just now," he added. " Me and the rest of us kids used to leave notes like this around the house just for fun," he grinned. "It was kind of childish maybe, but when Mom would put the bulletin or other announcements on the refrigerator, we kids got into the habit of sending coded messages to each other this way. I don't know who first started it, Katie, maybe. Just a Henderson family game, I guess," he laughed. "I sure never thought you'd find that one note," he said as he rolled his eyes and breathed a deep sigh.

John Mark's expression reminded Carrie of a little boy who had been caught at some sort of mischief. Smiling at him, she spoke again, "When I first read it, I was confused... maybe a little disappointed," she started. He looked at her with concern, wondering what she meant, as she continued to explain. "I couldn't imagine the John Mark I knew sitting and doodling during the Holcomb's seminar and not paying attention."

"I didn't," he confessed sincerely. "I was taking notes while they spoke. I wrote that other note up in my room one night—I think it was the night of the seminar, come to think of it—the same night they handed those notes out-- a Friday night." Carrie listened intently, smiling all the while at John Mark's explanation. "It's all coming back now," he went on with a faraway look. "I think when Eileen and I came home from Friday classes that day, she handed her note immediately to Mom. Mine must have been stuffed in my backpack. Mom probably took Eileen's and read it. That's why mine got left in my book," John Mark was now smiling at the memory as he went on.

"I remember doing some homework later in the evening up in my room and circling that little thought on that paper. I must have stuffed it back in my Spanish book before I went to bed and then forgot about it," he continued to explain. "I used to spend time at that desk doing my homework and praying. Carrie, you don't realize this, but from the way Blooming Hills sits on that little bit of high ground, I could almost see Maplecrest from my bedroom window. In the evening I could see the lights of town in the distance. I used to imagine one of the lights I was seeing was from your house on the west end of town and I'd pray for you."

Carrie's eyes misted afresh at the sound of John Mark's tender voice, revealing some long held secrets to her. He seemed to suddenly lose a bit of his old shyness as he spoke these words to her, a long held declaration of the love in his heart toward her.

"That night as I sat there, I was doing some homework and thinking about the way I had already begun to feel about you. I guess some stuff they taught that day was probably fresh in my mind too," he confided. "You know, things like keeping the meditations of your heart acceptable before the Lord. I was tossing a lot of things around in my heart and mind at that point in my life. As I've told you before, I knew I didn't dare tell you how much I liked you when we were so young. I really didn't want to dishonor the Lord by running ahead of His plans. I had to lay down my will and let things work out."

"I understand," Carrie assured him.

"I never meant for you to find that note. I'm sorry if it was some kind of hindrance to you," he sincerely apologized.

"It's ok. I forgive you," Carrie smiled. "It did kind of keep me wondering all those years, but just like you, I had to come to a time when I decided to lay my will down to really seek God's plans. I'm just glad I finally found out the whole story behind that note," Carrie said with a smile. "I'd hate to think my future husband would sit doodling during church!" she added light-heartedly. John Mark grinned, appreciative of her understanding manner.

Looking back to the bulletin in her hand, Carrie, slowly began to read the message once again.

"What does it say, Carrie?"

"John Mark Henderson loves Carrie May Brooks.... and wants to marry her," she began repeating with obvious joy the words she had already deciphered.

"And...?" he coached.

Carrie began to decode the last few lines that had more circled letters. "H-E-R-E-S....here's..." Carrie spelled, "a-l-i-t-t-l-e-g-i..." Carrie stumbled over the words for a few moments. "f-t," she finished as she worked to separate the words.

"Here's a little gift," John Mark quoted, helping her. As she looked up, she noticed he was holding a small box. His eyes danced with delight and the warm glow of candlelight flickered in the little booth. Carrie looked at John Mark with a surprised expression. She had been totally unaware that he would give her a gift! Such a complete surprise this was. She hadn't even considered anything like this since she knew they were intent on saving money and had even decided to forego wedding rings. "For a long time I wanted to give you a courtship gift, but I wanted it to be something very special. A ring just didn't seem quite right. Rings are so common. You're more special and I thought you deserved something unique." He paused to assess her reaction so far and she seemed genuinely flattered at his words. Sensing this, he continued to speak. "When we decided not to have wedding rings, I was pretty sure you weren't interested in an engagement ring either. I felt this was something more personal and has a lot of meaning. I hope you'll agree."

She took the little package with trembling hands as she untied the tiny ribbon that encircled it. The tissue paper fell open to reveal a skillfully constructed box of gleaming wood. She stared at the box as she ran her fingers over the smooth surface. "Go ahead, open it," John Mark urged her.

She lifted the lid and to her surprise she found that the inside of the box was lined with a soft, green, velvet and Great Grandma Haywood's watch was lying there fitted with a beautiful new chain. "Oh, John Mark!" she gasped. Her eyes filled with tears as she gently lifted the watch from its place and looked at the glistening new chain. It was obviously of high quality and matched the watch perfectly. "I…I don't know what to say!" she whispered. "I love it! And I love you!" she finally said. Seeing her tears, he offered her his handkerchief and she dabbed it to the corners of her eyes as she gazed down at the thoughtful gift.

"I'm glad you like it," he said. " I got it from your mom and took it to the jeweler's and had the chain replaced for you. Meanwhile I made the case for it."

"You made it?" she asked with surprise and admiration. "It's beautiful!" She lovingly ran her hands once again over the fine wood.

"It's cherry wood that I took from an old tree I had to cut down at the farm when we first bought the property. I couldn't bear to burn it so I saved some of the good sections for woodworking," John Mark explained. Carrie's sentiments were touched anew with the significance of the details surrounding this meaningful gift.

"So Mom and Dad knew about this all along?" Carrie asked through her tears, remembering her mother's reluctance to get the watch out this afternoon.

"Yes," he smiled. "We couldn't have you wearing the watch on our wedding day with a broken chain, could we?" he asked.

"No, I don't suppose so!" she agreed.

"You were intending to wear it on our wedding day, weren't you?" he asked hopefully. "After all, I think it's such a perfect symbol of our courtship and everything that's happened."

"I wouldn't think of leaving it out of our wedding," she smiled, "In fact, just this afternoon I finished my dress and suggested to Mom that we pin the watch on it to see how it looked. I understand her reaction now. While she didn't tell me an untruth, she was pretty slyly making up excuses why we shouldn't pin it on the dress just yet!" Carrie told him with a smile.

She looked thoughtfully at the watch as John Mark went on. "It's interesting how the story of that watch is so like our own," he said. "Something from the lives of two people so long ago is still important to us this many years later." He paused a moment and took her hands in his and looked at her, speaking seriously. "Carrie, that's how I want our life together to be—like an unbroken chain. I want us to live in such a way that our lives influence future generations—for righteousness."

"I do too," she agreed softly.

"Together we can leave a legacy of faith and dedication to God for our grandchildren," he said, his eyes shining with hope.

The days before the wedding were filled with preparation but on Thursday afternoon, Carrie actually found herself with a bit of free time. Her dress was done, many of her belongings had already been moved and rehearsal was not until tomorrow night. Mom wisely suggested Carrie use the time for a well-deserved nap while she still could.

When Carrie lay down on her bed, she found it hard to sleep. As she rested there with her eyes open, the memories of her teen years flooded her mind at the sight of various belongings still left in her room. There on the desk was the old rock that she and Eileen had found the day of the home school picnic at the Peterson farm on Birch Lake. She had brought it home and used it for a paperweight all these years, remembering Mr. and Mrs. Peterson and the memorable day with friends each time she saw it.

Pictures of friends and family lined her bulletin board. Even the wallpaper and curtains stirred memories of all the work the family had done when they purchased this lovely old house! She lay a long time, remembering the many years leading up to this happy time. Then her eyes fell on her wedding dress, hanging in the garment bag on her closet door and she happily drifted off to sleep for a while with dreams of her future dancing in her mind.

Amidst all the busyness of the week, Saturday finally arrived. The Maplewood Christian Fellowship church building was beautifully decorated at the hands of Eileen, Carrie, her mother, and all the women of the Henderson family. By noon the church was abuzz with activity. Large numbers of friends and family packed the sanctuary to overflowing for the joyous event.

Downstairs in the girls' familiar old Sunday school room, Carrie and her bridesmaids dressed and readied for the ceremony. Miss Winfield popped in a few minutes before one o'clock to give Carrie some encouraging words and a loving hug. Carrie thanked her for the many years of encouragement and Christ-like example the older lady had given. Carrie's sincere words were a blessing to Miss Winfield and a confirmation to the calling she had fulfilled in her later years. The dear, gentle-spirited lady was warmed with a deep satisfaction in her heart as she wished Carrie well and left to find her seat in the sanctuary.

A few minutes later, Carrie and the bridesmaids filed upstairs much as she remembered they had for Alice's wedding not long ago. But the feeling in Carrie's heart the day of Alice's wedding was nothing like what she felt today. She was nervous, yet excited, full of joy, and happily smiling amidst her jitters, with the knowledge that this special day was hers and John Mark's alone!

Before the ceremony everything seemed to happen so fast, yet she felt as if it all drew to a slow motion when she stepped into the aisle on her father's arm and began making her way down to meet John Mark. He gazed at her lovingly, completely enamored with the sight of her in her delicate wedding gown and wearing the watch with the new gold chain. His eyes never left her—she was the only one in the world at that moment as far as he was concerned. Even the sea of people filling the sanctuary faded from his view. She too saw no one but him. There he was standing, waiting for her, ready to pledge his love to her forever.

When she reached the front, her father kissed her cheek, released her arm to John Mark and continued the service with Pastor Stanford assisting.

Even though there were many musical selections, a touching sermon, and a communion service for the bride and groom, Carrie thought it seemed like only minutes until she heard her father say the words, "I now pronounce you man and wife. You may kiss the bride!"

John Mark turned to her and brushed her cheek with a quick, but loving kiss and whispered something to her through the veil that softly draped the side of her face. Muffled, quiet laughter rippled through the crowd. Carrie felt herself blushing and then heard her father's strong voice declare, "I am pleased to present to you Mr. and Mrs. John Mark Henderson!" The music began to play as John Mark offered her his arm, escorting her down the aisle. She leaned on his strong arm as they walked to the rear of the church. Carrie smiled amidst her nervousness while the crowd of people was only a blur. It felt to Carrie like everything had happened so fast, yet it seemed to be all in slow motion.

The entire day had been beautiful and sentimental, just exactly the way Carrie and John Mark wanted. So many people congratulated the happy pair and exclaimed about the sincerity of the touching ceremony. The reception was a joyous celebration of family and friends that Eileen seemed to be enjoying immensely—and rightly so, for she had worked so diligently to help present her brother and best friend with a real event to remember and she had succeeded.

When Carrie and John Mark readied to leave at the close of the day, a large group of family and friends bid them farewell amidst a shower of rice and teary-eyed wishes. Eileen caught Carrie's bouquet as she tossed it through the crisp winter air from the step of John Mark's truck. Everyone present clapped at the blushing Eileen who nearly fell backwards into the crowd as she reached for the flowers that flew right above her head. Luke caught her, steadying her with his sturdy arms just in time to keep her from an awkward tumble. Laughing, she turned to him and quickly whispered, "Thanks, Luke! You saved me from a real embarrassing scene! I'll be forever grateful you were there for me!"

Neither John Mark nor Carrie had revealed the secret of their honeymoon destination to anyone. Everyone assumed they were leaving for a drive to the southern states to escape the cold and enjoy a warmer climate for a few weeks. Tommy had tried diligently to get John Mark to share the secret with him to no avail.

As they rode along the early evening twilit country roads to the place where they had planned to spend their honeymoon, the sun was making quite a grand show of its departure on the cold December horizon. "The sunset is beautiful this evening but it sure was a cold, December day, wasn't it?" John Mark said.

"Yes! It was," Carrie agreed.

"Are you sorry we didn't wait to have our wedding in May like you'd always dreamed—it would have probably been nicer weather, at least."

"No, I'm not sorry," Carrie smiled as she slid over in the seat to sit close beside John Mark. She lay her head on his shoulder as they drove, now nearing the English Hills. "I'm not sorry at all," she repeated. "But you promised we'd celebrate in May as well, remember?" she said, looking up into his eyes.

"I do," he replied. "It'll be our half-year anniversary by then and we'll be sure to celebrate," he said with a wink as he put his arm around her shoulder.

It was dark by the time they pulled into the drive of their farm and Carrie remembered how she had felt when she first came here in May with the bridal veil bushes in full bloom. It had a been a sense that she was 'home' and now that same feeling covered her once again even in the chill of winter with the bushes around the porch covered in a different coat of white.

John Mark pulled the truck off the driveway right up into their front yard and stopped at the steps. "Why, John Mark! What are you doing?" Carrie asked with a surprised look.

"I'm going to carry my bride over the threshold, of course! Wait here!" he said as he jumped out of the truck and ran up on the porch to unlock the door. He reached inside and switched on a light that Carrie recognized from the truck as her old bedside lamp from her dressing table. It glowed warmly, softly welcoming her through the window of her new home. He came back out, opened the door and helped her out of the truck. Her feet had barely touched the ground when he swept her up in his arms and carried her into the house, the snow that had fallen since he had left the farm crunching beneath his every step. He set her gently on her feet in the center of their living room and drew her close to him in a warm embrace. "Remember what I whispered to you during the ceremony when your father said, 'You may kiss the bride,'?" She smiled and nodded in answer. "I didn't want our first real kiss to be in front of all those people today," he said shyly, as he looked at her for a long moment, "Welcome home, my love," he said and kissed his bride.

––––––––––––––

It was an unusually cool evening for the month of May. Carrie Henderson had decided to make a large pot of soup in the morning. She had been letting it gently simmer all day, its inviting odors filling the farmhouse. The anniversary cake she had made earlier in the day, waited on a table in the back room. She was putting the finishing touches on a green salad when the oven timer went off, alerting her that the dinner rolls were done. She opened the oven door and peered in at the pans of crusty, golden buns looking like amber bubbles, their beckoning aroma wafting through the cheery kitchen.

She removed the pans from the oven and set them on the

counter to cool. She rubbed a generous portion of butter over the tops and let its golden sweetness drip down over their sides.

Carrie's eyes quickly surveyed the kitchen, checking to be sure all the last-minute preparations for supper were done. She examined the dining room table that was obviously set with much love and care. A pretty embroidered cloth she had made years ago adorned the table. The ruby glass dishes, a wedding gift from her grandmother, sparkled as she lit two candles in the center of the table. Soon she was satisfied that no detail had been overlooked. The meal was simple, the way they had agreed it should be—the way their life was, the way they were in their hearts....

Carrie stepped onto the back porch and untied her apron, hanging it on a peg. She smoothed her yellow dress, one of John Mark's favorites and walked out to the back yard. The late spring sun was sinking low on the horizon, nearly behind the hills of the peach orchard at the far west border of their land.

She pulled the beautiful old watch from the pocket of her dress—the watch that had come to represent so much in their courtship and marriage. "Just the time I told him I'd ring the bell for supper," she thought as she snapped the watch closed. Reaching up, she pulled the strong, new rope on the old dinner bell several times.

Moments later John Mark appeared from around the corner of one of the barns. He smiled and waved as he saw her there. As he walked toward her she silently thanked God for this strong, but gentle man that she had grown to love so much. The last six months had been a wonderful time of starting their life together and today was a celebration.

"Time to celebrate our anniversary!" she called as he neared the house.

Knowing they had decided long ago to celebrate their anniversary in May, he smiled and stepped up his pace as he neared the sidewalk where she stood.

When he reached her, he put his arms around her and kissed her. "You've never looked lovelier, Carrie," he whispered sincerely. Still in his embrace, she rested her head on his chest as they stood for a moment and gazed across their land. "God has really blessed us," he said as they turned and strolled to their house with their hearts full of dreams and the fields of May that lay behind them green with the abundant promise of another year's harvest.

Printed in the United States
115403LV00001B/1-75/P